Men,
Amplified

Literotica Edited By
MICHAEL HUXLEY

A STARbooks Press Publication

Published and printed in the United States
FLF/STARbooks Press
P.O. Box 711612
Herndon, VA 20171

The exquisite photograph on the front and back cover of this edition was reproduced by kind permission granted by Za Hazzanani. Ms. Hazzanani can be reached at her studio in London by telephone at 011-44-207-581-9448, by fax at 011-44-207-581-4445 or email at _eliigeba@citiboxcenter.com_.

Many thanks to graphic artist, John Nail for his enthusiastic collaboration on the design of _Men, Amplified's_ extraordinary cover. He may be reached at _tojonail@earthlink.net_.

Text design and layout by Michael Huxley.

"Indulge Yourself" © 1997 by Barry Alexander, reprinted with permission from _Indulge Magazine_ #20; "Geezers" © 2001 by Simon Sheppard, reprinted with permission from _Hotter Than Hell and Other Stories_ (Alyson Publications); "Johnny Was" © 2002 by Greg Wharton, reprinted with permission from _Velvet Mafia.com & Roughed Up_ (Alyson Publications 2003); "Man Overboard" © 2001 by Ian Phillips, reprinted with permission from _See Dick Deconstruct_ (AttaGirl Press); "Snowbound" © 2002 by Ken Anderson, reprinted with permission from Suspect Thoughts Press.

Library of Congress Card Catalogue No. Pending
ISBN No. 1-891855-36-0

Acknowledgments:

This book is dedicated to Paul J. Willis for both his friendship and unflagging professional support, which have enabled me to take an amplified step forward in this wonderfully incestuous genre of literature.

I would like to extend special thanks to Greg Herren, Blake Harper, Jonathan Asche, John Butler, Jay Johnson, Mike Powers, Peggy Savani, Jeffrey Jones and anyone else whom I might have made crazy during the protracted genesis of this book—most especially my darling "Marquis de Love," Paul.

CONTENTS

Men,
Amplified

MAN OVERBOARD!
Ian Philips

go ahead …you've got eyes …take a look …a long, hard look… here… lemme come closer… you want it, don'tcha… un huh… you're drooling…

hey, faggot, who told you to move… you can suck my **man** tool when I say suck it…

poor sonofabitch… gotta get your lips around my ten inches of salami, huh, cocksucker… won't my **man** meat taste good… look at it… think you can swallow this fucker… ever seen so many veins popping from a cock… yeah, my dick's in a fucking rage…wants to push your pussy lips open…plow your tight **man** hole…then blow its wad deep inside you…

you'd like that, huh, faggot… go ahead…touch yourself… yeah, show me you're **man** enough… you're gonna have to get a helluva lot harder than that… nice…nice… oh, yeah, now that's a boner… good faggot…

now get over there and get Johnny up… no…no hands… be creative… you big-city faggots are supposed to be creative… stop looking at me, dumbfuck, and use that pretty mouth of yours… that's it… go for the **man** titties… yeah, suck 'em… umm…nice… Johnny's got big, hard **man** tits, huh… go ahead, chew on his nipple… harder… hear him moaning… Johnny likes you…

okay, untie his gag… yeah, use your hands…but I want you to pull it out with your tongue… awww…look at my little pussy boys kissing… yeah…lick his face like the dog you are… Johnny, you like the puppy I brought home to play with you… yeah, Johnny likes the puppy…

hey…faggot…that's enough kissing… get down there and chew on Johnny's jock… Johnny, spread your legs… more… as wide as the ropes'll let you… awww…that hurt, boy… Daddy's ropes biting into your skin… good… yeah…that's it… sniff that basket, puppy… shove your nose into his big bulging **man** basket… yeah, smell his **man** funk… get a good whiff of all that dried splooge and piss… that's right…that's my boy's lucky jock… I've never let him wash it…till now…

stop grinning, faggot, and start licking it clean… get it wet… suck it… ummm…taste him yet… pretty bitter piss, huh… get a dried chunk of his thick spunk…ummm… now get his dick out and lemme see how a big-city faggot sucks cock… yeah, that's it…bite into it… nice… pull it out and let my boy's balls flop out… no, you're not done yet… I said I wanna see you suck his dick…so suck his dick, cocksucker… you'll bite his shaved balls when I say so… next time I won't kick your ass so lightly… I'll just mash your lame-ass nuts under my boot…

now get that dick out and suck it… that's it…tug at the **man** pouch… good puppy…keep tugging…I see one fat dickhead… that's it… bingo…pull it out… now swallow it… I wanna see puppy chow down on Johnny's **man** meat… all of it…what the fuck kinda cocksucking is that… his dickhead ain't no lollipop… hey…that's enough of that kissy stuff… and save all that licking for this dick cuz you're gonna want it wet when I shove it in you, faggot…

Christ, just swallow the **man** fucker… what the fuck's wrong with you… you give head like a virgin on her honeymoon… don't tell me I got the only faggot from the big city who can't deep throat… you better say goodbye to that gag-reflex now, dumbfuck…cuz it'll be long gone after you get a workover from THIS jawbreaker… yeah, it's gonna shove your tonsils out your ass if you don't take my boy's dick down to his balls…NOW!

ah, did I scare the little girl… poor baby… poor little cocksucker… not sure what the mean old neighbor **man**'s gonna do if she don't suck the jizz outta his boy's cock… well, shit, Johnny, look at that… we got a sword swallower after all… feels good huh, Johnny… yeah, take that **man** shaft, faggot… good, Johnny…stick it in him… harder, boy …real hard… **man** hard… make your Daddy proud… I wanna see that fat dickhead of yours trying to push through his cheeks…

you… faggot… better keep trying to swallow that mouthful… you stop, even to breathe, while I'm untying Johnny and I'm throwing you out that door…you hear… you can walk back to the city naked for all I fucking care… ah, Johnny boy, someone give you a rope burn… good boy… you like it when your Daddy twists your little boy titties, don't you… hurts **man** good, huh… yeah… makes you want choke that sick faggot with your big boy dick… yeah…that's it, son… show him who's running this fuck… yeah, the big-city cocksucker thinks he's sucking your boy cock…but he ain't… naw…cuz Daddy's boy is **man** fucking his face… yeah, **man** fuck his faggot face, boy… show him who's the **man**…

better watch out, cocksucker…Johnny's bucking hard… he's gonna fill your mouth with a few quarts of his **man** cream…and I don't have to tell you who his **man** cream belongs to, do I, faggot… good… now get Johnny's big **man** boy cock outta your mouth… yeah…that's right…leave his stiffie out to dry… cold, huh, baby… you want something warm inside you, huh… well, I've got it, boy…and if you're good, you'll get some too…

so what are you waiting for, faggot…crawl over here… pull off your jock… did I say you could stand up… pull it off already… now get over here…lemme see you tug at your own **man** balls… go ahead… yeah…that's it…tug 'em…pull at your **man** nuts… yeah… now get rougher… yeah, you can pinch your **man** tits too…but I wanna see that other hand down there jugglin' some **man** huevos... nice... oh, yeah...real nice... now let's see you do that with some king-sized **man** eggs...

yeah, that's right...THESE king-size **man** eggs... crawl over here, faggot... sit up... yeah, you like it when I slap you in the face with 'em... hell, I could knock you out with 'em... you're gonna have to use both hands, boy... ah, yeah... shit that feels good... now put 'em in your mouth... suck that huge **man** sac...yeah... ever sucked on **man** nuts this big... oh, yeah...suck those **man** nuts...stuff 'em both in your **man** mouth... do it... you better get used to **man** choking if you're gonna take this **man** rammer...and you are, faggot...you are... oh, yeah...that's right...suck those big **man** balls... oh, yeah...**man** suck 'em...

hey, Johnny...you come before I tell you to and I'm sending you to your room without a fucking... stop **man** playing with yourself and get over here... suck some **man** ass, boy... no, you've gotta earn the right to eat out this **man** hole... first, I wanna see you eat the faggot's **man** cunt... that's it... I want it real **man** wet before I plug it with my **man** fuckpole... how's that feel, **man** puppy...**man** good, huh... why don'tcha show your Master how **man** grateful you are to have Johnny **man** eating you...

that's right...**man** lick your Master's **man** balls... lap 'em up with your whole **man** tongue...lap 'em up...good **man** puppy... ah, yeah...lap 'em up with that big fat **man** tongue...yeah...

hey, Johnny... JOHNNY... you still tongue-fucking the faggot's **man** twat...or d'you fall asleep down there... let Daddy see you **man** cram that pretty **man** face of yours further up his hairy little **man** crack...now...before I make you... further, boy... tug his **man** balls too...twist 'em... that's it... ah, yeah... get **man** puppy so confused he **man** bites... that's it **man** puppy...**man** bite that big **man** dick... harder... harder, you dumbfuck...it's all **man** gristle...it can take it...**man** bite it...gnaw on that big hard **man** bone... yeah... oh, yeah... sweet Jesus, yes... yes... **man** bite me... shit, that hurts so **man** good... ah... good **man** puppy... now you're ready...to suck it...

man swallow it...all of it...now... **man** swallow this **man** pole... un huh...that's it...down to the thick, black **man** bush... nice... get that **man** nose in there...get a **man** whiff of some heavy-duty **man** musk... yeah, un huh...nothing smells as **man** good as a real **man**'s crotch-funk... oh, yeah...

now...lick my **man** piss slit... yeah, shove your **man** tongue in the little **man** hole...get that wet **man** tongue right up under my **man** dickhead... oh... ohhh... oh, yeah, **man**...right there... yeah...right there on my **man** joy button... lick it...yeah... oh, yeah ... **man** jab it...you heard me... **man** jab that big **man** joy button with your **man** tongue... oh, God, yes...

now...**man** suck down all my **man** meat... yeah...**man** suck that big **man** dick... yeah...**man** suck it... yeah...**man** suck that big **man** dick... you like **man** sucking that big **man** cock, huh... yeah, you like it, **man** cocksucker...

3

yeah...**man** suck it... yeah...**man** suck that **man** meat... oh yeah...go, **man** cocksucker...go...

oh...oh, yeah...I'm gonna **man** fuck your **man** mouth... gonna **man** fuck your **man** mouth, faggot... **man** fuck it with my **man** fuckpole... oh, yeah...umm... **man** fuck your wet, hot **man** mouth...umm...yeah... fuck, **man**, yeah... oh, yeah...I'm gonna **man** fuck your **man** hole, faggot...yeah... I'm gonna shove my ten-inch **man** dick up your **man** ass...yeah... ten fucking **man** inches...fuck yeah, **man**... I'm gonna **man** plug your **man** pussy, faggot...**man** plug it with my ten-inch **man** hose...yeah...

now lemme see that little **man** ass of yours... yeah, lemme see your **man** boy twat...yeah... hey... whoa... slow down, **man** cocksucker...I'm gonna bust my **man** nuts... I'm saving my **man** buckets of **man** milk for your little pink **man** pussy... yeah, you'd like me to **man** whack your **man** face some more with that big **man** fuckstick...but it's going up your **man** ass, faggot...all ten **man** inches...

Johnny, you done yet... then get over here and get that fat **man** tongue of yours up Daddy's sweaty **man** ass... wait...faggot... **man** thank Johnny for getting your **man** hole ready for his Daddy's **man** donkey dong... well...**man** kiss him, dickhead...it's just your own **man** shit... suck it off his **man** tongue... awww...what a cute little **man** couple of **man**-shit-eating queers...

now get over here and **man** suck my **man** butt, boy... yeah, **man** lick my **man** crack... yeah...get my **man** thick **man** ass hairs **man** wet... yeah, **man** chew on 'em, boy... that's it, boy...**man** bite Daddy's **man** butt... **man** rub your pretty **man** face in Daddy's **man** crack... **man** kiss my **man** hole... oh, yeah, boy...tease that hot **man** hole...**man** tease it with your **man** tongue...just like when you used to clit-flick your girlfriends in high school...ahh... now, **man** shove it, boy... good, boy... ah, shit, boy...you're getting **man** good at **man** eating Dad out... good boy... **man** fuck Daddy with your **man** tongue while he **man** fucks the faggot's **man** hole... yeah... good boy...

now, faggot, get up on the **man** bed... shove that little faggot **man** ass of yours up in the air... poor faggot...your **man** butt cheeks are so cold...lemme get you **man** warmed up... yeah, you like it when your Master **man** whacks 'em... what d'you say...harder... you want Sir to **man** spank your **man** ass **man** harder... okay then...

now that they're **man** warm...**man** spread those pink **man** cheeks, faggot... don't make me **man** pull 'em apart for you... nice... oh yeah...that's real **man** nice... fuck...your **man** pussy's t-i-i-i-ght, faggot... shit...don't tell me I got me a **man** piece of virgin **man** ass... just got my **man** thumb...not even two **man** fingers up there... I've got myself a big-city faggot with a cherry **man** ass... oh, faggot, you are so **man** mine... better bite **man** hard into that **man** pillow, you poor sonofa**man**bitch...cuz here comes the **man** rammer that's gonna **man** pop your cherry **man** ass...

oh, yeah...**man** suck that meaty **man** knob in... unnh... unnh... just try and **man** push me out, faggot ...unnh... unnh... UNNH... oh, Christ, yes...it's in, Johnny... Daddy's gonna **man** pop the faggot's **man** cherry... unnh... unnh... oh, suh-weet...oh, faggot, I am so gonna **man** tear you up tonight... you ain't felt no **man** pain yet... unnh... unnnnh... unnnnh... unnnnh... ahhh...that's it... tighten your **man** ass around that **man** long, **man** hard **man** shitpoker... you **man** crying yet, faggot... go ahead...scream your **man** heart out...

man scream, faggot...lemme hear you beg for it... **man** beg for it, you **man** pussy **man** bitch...you know you **man** want it... you **man** want Sir to **man** give it to you **man** long...and **man** hard... real **man** hard... real... real... real **man** hard...yeah... **man** take it, faggot...take it... c'mon, you sick **man** fuck...**man** take that **man** big **man** dick... yeah, take that, **man** pussy boy...and that... and that... and that... ah, shit, **man**...my **man** nuts are gonna **man** burst... get ready, faggot...cuz I'm gonna **man** pump you **man** full of my **man** hot...**man** white...**man** thick...**man** juice... yeah...**man**... pump...you...**man**...full...**man**...fucker... whee ooo... I'm...gonna...**man**...shoot...my...**man**...sperm...yeah... whee ooo... yeah... unh... fuck...yeah...**man**... till...it... whee ooo... **man**...gushes... out...your... fucking... whee ooo... **man**...pussy...**man**...lips... unnh... whee ooo... yeah... whee ooo... yeah... whee ooo... OH, **MAN** YEEAAAHHHH!!!!!...whee ooo, whee ooo, whee ooo, whee ooo, whee ooo, whee ooo...

((((□))))

He jolted awake. The sirens were several blocks up the street now. He blinked. Shit. He'd fallen asleep before the final scene of *Verbiage à Trois 2*. He looked down. Blinked again. Fuck. His dick had shrunken and fallen asleep on his thigh. It looked glazed from the lube. The TV hissed. The screen swarmed with gray dots. A red 3:43 jumped out and back and out again from the shadows. Fuck. Fuck. Fuck.

He flicked off the TV and rolled onto his belly. He punched down the pillows and dug his fingers under the blankets and yanked, pulling and kicking until he'd wedged himself between the strata of sheets and comforters. Squinting his eyes, he reached his hand toward the light and twisted it off. He rolled over. His crotch slimed the sheets. Fuck. He rolled back, away from the cold, sticky spot.

For the next few minutes, seconds, he staggered outside the black room of sleep, all the while stringing a few words into one sentence, one thought. *I'll shower my **man** body in the **man** morning.* He repeated it, maybe out loud, maybe not. And, with that, he found the door open and stumbled in.

5

INTRODUCTION
Michael Huxley

ZAP!!!
WHERE THE ~~BOYS~~ MEN ARE!

Fact: The volume you are currently reading is the first anthology in STARbooks' twenty-year history to include the word 'man' or 'men' in its title. Fact: *Men, Amplified*'s first inclusion, Ian Philips' outrageous parody, "Man Overboard!" utilizes the word 'man' 244 times. Fact: "Man Overboard!" is 2,533 words long. Now, I purport a math acumen no greater than a rocket scientist's chimpanzee, but I reckon *that there* accounts for almost 10% of Mr. Philips' entire parody.

But why on earth does it appear *before the intro*? In placing it so, am I attempting to prove some nonsensical theory that it's never too soon to begin making up for lost time, or am I simply unable to resist the temptation to flaunt publishing convention?

The answer would be yes—and yes, but there are other, far more valid reasons at play.

I believe it's safe to say that every editor of an anthology, genre notwithstanding, chooses their first piece with careful deliberation, consciously selecting a strong inclusion that will set a tone for the entire collection and grab the reader's attention. In my humble opinion "Man Overboard!" does both, not in aces but in **man(s)**. Written specifically for this anthology long before Ian Philips had ever heard of yours truly, let alone the guidelines for this collection, "Man Overboard!" first appeared in Philips' phenomenal single-author collection of short prose *See Dick Deconstruct* (AttaGirl Press, 2001). Encouraging the reader to *not* ponder the logic of that sentence too terribly long, please allow me to move right ahead.

Men, Amplified's call for submission was intentionally generic, an unsullied coloring book of information. Honest-to-a-fault lazybone that I tend to be, I essentially concocted an evocative title and specified what I was *not* looking for, hoping that the submitters would define the volume's theme *for me*.

Well, it worked:

<u>Needed by STARbooks Press:</u> **Men, Amplified**

Okay boys. You can run along and play now…

This book will be about men who love men. About men who define the word 'love' for themselves, as best suits *who they are*…

No, I am not seeking stories about virgins, but I *am* seeking stories that explore the psychology of adult male sexuality…

We have all learned by now, glorious men of experience that we have become, that exquisitely constructed sexual depiction should warrant inclusion within a *great story*, that it not be gratuitous…

And blah, blah, blah…

About halfway into receiving the happy barrage of submissions that I eventually did, while reading Mr. Philips' *See Dick Deconstruct*, within which I happened upon "Man Overboard," I knew instantly that if I could acquire permission to reprint the story in my collection, it would appear before any intro I composed—a task I never fail to defer until the eleventh hour—because doing so would make it *that much easier to write*! For what could better define a theme than exquisitely constructed parody that reduces to rubble that which a theme intends to exploit?

IF the notion that men are somehow "amplified" by participation in homo-coital inclination, IF sex acts between men are indicative of a ritualistic redoubling of male sexuality, then WHY did I receive such a disproportionate number of manuscripts in which themes of domination and/or submission prevail *when none were solicited*? Are we, the still-oppressed, achieving a desired level of compensation in continuing to define what constitutes a man by that which he can dominate or subjugate himself to?

I suspect Mr. Philips would be more than willing to address these concerns, as his foul-mouthed "protagonist" in the aptly titled "Man Overboard!" stands as a perfect case-in-point. I.P.'s hero dominates two men, one of whom is referred to as "his *boy*" (my italics), who is bound and gagged at the beginning of the piece. The other participant, condescendingly referred to as a "big-city faggot," is a plaything brought in for fun and games. Are we to presume that the SM couple are small-town rednecks, that Southern Comfort bumpkins are more "manly," more "grassroots?" Hailing from Kentucky myself, I can only hope so!

From however small a hellhole our conquering hero has emerged, he *does* wield a ten-inch cock like a weapon of mass destruction—an inspired length considering that the numbers constituting Philips' mythic 244 uses of the word 'man,' when added up, equal 10. But such is the unconscious nature of creative genius, no?

At any rate, our bad-ass Ampman is quick to dish out the "hey faggot(s)" and "my pussy boys" with their "pussy lips" and "shaved balls" and "**man** cunt(s)" or "**man** twat(s)," eventually (and vociferously) demanding that his "daddy's boy fuck" the plaything's "faggot face" in order to show him "who's the **man**..." I mean, here we have a hierarchical triumvirate of *Men, Amplified* invented, set in motion, and effectively parodied in less than 3,000 words—an achievement unparalleled since the Father, Son and Holy Ghost were crammed down our cocksucking throats lo these many centuries ago!

Challenging and expanding Philips' premise are three other inclusions that non-satirically reflect the sub-textural theme of domination ebbing and flowing throughout *Men, Amplified*. The most vicious example would have to be S. M. Jeffrey's "Athletic Performance" in which amplification is achieved, not through the application of electrical current used to subjugate innocent rape victims—ZAP!!!—but through unapologetic indulgence in algolagnic criminal activity for recreation and, *getting away with it*, looking forward to the next time. Oh, the revelry!

Diametrically opposed is Christopher Pierce's rather amazing "White-hot Smoky Night", a cerebral in-flight borne on wings of smoke into the erotic underpinnings of an obsequious submissive's worldview, the complex intimacy of which reveals an almost embarrassing amplification of sincerity.

From somewhere in the middle of mayhem emerges Carlo, the mad Argentine, *el* furious *Chef* who storms about Don Luis de la Cosa's novella, "Bigger than Life" like some outraged and sadistic Santa/Falstaff, inflicting his gourmet domination with a heart to the loyal deemed worthy, and without to those who dare to challenge his birth-righteous and patrician "generosity." In examining the master/slave dichotomy from both perspectives, in basting his "beast" with the sumptuous herb paste of verve and certainty, Señor de la Cosa amplifies the very definition of family in order to accommodate characters who *are* "bigger than life itself," who, if purchased for what they're worth and sold for what they *think* they're worth would a wealthy investor make.

Apropos of something I'll undoubtedly figure out later, I remember a little bird (presumably the same one that deflowered the Blessed Virgin) telling me that: "Homosexuals are more oftentimes than not their own worst enemy in swallowing—hook, line and sinker—the 'lifestyles' that have been imposed upon them by the Christian-Judaic patriarchy, that limit their potential for actualization, and which they oh-so-*sheepishly* embrace as their liberation. Seemingly content to remain 'boys' who caricaturize heterosexist prototypes, banding together in ghettos where they mistake feeling safe for being free, striving for tolerance rather than acceptance, homosexuals poise themselves for easy transference, en masse, to the slaughter yards."

So tipped off in advance, my similarly jaded boyfriend and I moved to Sarasota, Florida (where *untold* adventure lay in wait), well aware why former slaves and their subsequent generations of male progeny have traditionally taken such umbrage at being referred to as "boy" by the powers that be, favoring the much-ballyhooed update, "Sir." But what does all this garble have to do with the thematic foundation of *Men, Amplified*—the anthology? Having read between the **man(s)** in "Man Overboard", please feel free to skip the rest of this intro, launch into the book, and find out for yourself.

Read Jim McDonough's "The Other Half of Me" which gently tackles that most vilified of subject matters dared to be examined in male homoerotic literature: complacent, vanilla monogamy, or Simon Sheppard's touching "Geezers", in which an *elderly*, non-monogamous couple prove that "old dogs" learning "new tricks" (in this case, not settling for a decades-long tolerance imposed by their family members), for seat confirmation on the *Men, Amplified* chariot of fire.

Speaking of Mr. Sheppard, I received an email from him not long ago in which Smart Simon Sez: "...Lately I'm thinking that queers who love one another are probably more challenging to the status quo than queers who flog each other." Now, keeping that in mind, check out Mark Wildyr's heroic "Mythas" or Mel Smith's magnificent and torturous allegory, "The Spell of Georval" and *tell* me that true love between men cannot epitomize the very definition of amplification.

Check out the radical political agenda glossed over in Jesse Monteagudo's deceptively whimsical "One Out Of Ten Is Magic", or the quirky, crime-stopping fetishist in "The Power" by Blaise Bulot, or the way Peter Rice steers the old genie-in-a-bottle yarn to its unexpected and mind-amplifying conclusion in "Another Way"—all of which present characters imbued with magical powers—**ZAP!!!**

It is the humbling forces of nature—the poetic Mexican surf in Henry Iblis's "Sergio Swimming" and the blinding blizzard in Ken Anderson's "Snowbound" that amplify the men involved, thus enabling them to emerge—from *drifting*—greater than they previously were.

Hedonic butchness, plain and simple, more than adequately amplifies Leo Cardini's mythical "Mineshaft Men" and Thom Nickels sheds light on not one, or two, or three, but *four* generations of gay men in "Elijah For Real"—the double entendre, Elijah *Cometh*, clearly understood by the likes of Eugene

O'Neill's *Iceman*, or anyone else for that matter who has fallen from grace (with the Holy See) into prophetic amplification.

M. Christian's Subadar Mahia should have no problem clinching a *nomination* for Most Amplified Character in this anthology. He's cool; he's understated—a porn-lit Solomon, in fact. But I seriously doubt that he'll *win* because, like certain U.S. presidential aspirants, Mahia's shrewd intelligence and compassion, his being so privy to The Truth, will render him less-than-credible with your average academy voter.

Contrary to GLBT political correctness, Jerome Szymczak demonstrates that retreating *back into the closet* can indeed produce amplifying results, but the real man, amplified in "The Same Words" is Szymczak himself for having so elegantly assembled the very same words that constitute this marvelous travelogue of prose.

Of the *many* submissions I received that contained the sentence "Aegospotami and Antietam were witty apothegms compared to the savaging I suffered within those first six inches of my ravaged ass," Rick Jackson's "Working Things Out" is the only one I included. *Amplified* enough for you?

Oh, but there's more.

Significantly, "Man Overboard" proved but one man's dream in the end, the virgin having been deflowered, successfully overpowered.

"To sleep: perchance to dream: ay there's the rub…"

Wait, Michael! That's the next *anthology.*

Sorry about that.

And so, as Mr. Philips' *slightly* amplified dreamer rolls back and away from the universal "cold sticky spot" on his sheet, back once again through the open door of sleep while promising himself to "shower my **man** body in the **man** morning," an unidentified poet, donning his strange collar of non-exchange, once again ponders the dream-sequential significance of Tammy Wynette's wise recommendation:

> "And if you love him,
> Oh, be proud of him,
> 'Cause after all he's *just a man*."

(My italics.)

YOUR ATTENTION PLEASE:

THE CHARIOT OF FIRE WILL SOON BE DEPARTING.

Like Vladimir and Estragon, we are all "(Amplified by) Anticipation". Anticipation is what keeps us living. Thank you, Jamie Joy, for that astute, postscriptive reminder and further defining the theme of this collection, but… needing to wait for Godot no longer, compliments of Horehound Stillpoint's having cometh in the nick of time, there is no point whatsoever in *my* going on about it any further.

AND THE NOMINEES ARE…
ZAP!!!

INDULGE YOURSELF
Barry Alexander

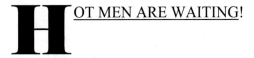

H OT MEN ARE WAITING!

Blond men and dark men and bald men...
HOT MEN ARE WAITING!
Cops and cowboys and construction workers...
HOT MEN ARE WAITING!
Hungry men sprawled across rumpled beds, waiting to be filled!
HOT MEN ARE WAITING!
Macho studs bristling with leather and attitude, waiting to be worshipped!
HOT MEN ARE WAITING!
In bedrooms and boardrooms, in backrooms and alleys...
HOT MEN ARE WAITING!
On white sheets and golden sands...

HOT MEN ARE WAITING!

...naked body dark against the white sheets. Moonlight spilled between the curtains and washed over the taut planes of his body. I felt brazen standing there with my swollen cock standing tall against my belly. I wanted him so much. I slipped into his arms, achingly aware of the hardening mass of his genitals, pressed hot...

GWM, B/Br iso
GBM 25-30
VA, B/D, TT,
Gr A/P, Fr A/P

Barry Alexander

1-800-HOT-MEN
HUGE DICKS! ORGIES! LEATHER!
EXPLORE YOUR FANTASIES!

➢ Local Dating
➢ One on One
➢ Private Backrooms

CALL NOW! LIVE! 24 HRS.A DAY!

…leather jacket, gaped open, exposing a tangled mat of dark, sweet-smelling hair on his chest. A tiny silver dagger speared through his left nipple, and I got hard just thinking about rubbing my tongue over it. I longed to bury my nose in the thick chest hair and suck those big nipples. I wanted to follow the trail of hair down to the tight leather pants, bulging with my master's flesh, but I knew better than to touch him without permission. My cock strained against my jeans, soaking the worn denim with my eagerness. He nodded permission and I knelt at his feet. My mouth inches away from that enticing bulge.

"Boots, first," he snarled, pushing my shaven head down…

LIVE THE FANTASY!

…shaved close and dusted with gold. His slender body was pierced and hung with jewels that shone against his dusky skin. A shimmering pouch cupped his genitals. The Sultan laughed when he saw my interest. He reached out and unhooked the pouch. His cock swung free, was bigger than I had anticipated. A single ruby dangled from the tip like a drop of blood. Even his pubes were dusted with gold. The Sultan stroked his shaft. The man gritted his teeth, but did not move. His cock rose in jerks and starts until it stabbed the air. "Once he was a warrior," the Sultan leered. "Now he is my toy. Take him, if you like. He is yours."

Blood surged through my cock and my heart pounded. I…

Honey, don't forget we're having dinner with the Johnson's.

…cool water dripping off his golden skin, beading on his naked flesh, trickling between his pecs, rippling over the sharp ridges of his stomach. His cock arched full and heavy, a cascade of flesh over swaying balls. I couldn't take my eyes…

14

…slid under my hair and cupped the back of my neck. Slowly, he drew me down in the hot sand until our lips touched. He crushed me to him, probing every inch of my mouth with his hot tongue. Slowly, deliciously, his lips moved up my throat. His mouth swooped down on mine, devouring me, taking control and possessing…

1-800-MAN-SEX

…afraid to hurt him with my strength. His lips parted and he let me in, sucking hungrily at my tongue like a man starved for the taste and touch of another man. He groaned and clung to me as I savaged his mouth. The hard ridge of his cock pressed against my belly. I yanked his shirt free and slid my hands up his sculptured back. We ground our pelvises…

ALL THE RIGHT PLACES

...gilded the warrior's massive body like the statue of some ancient god cast in bronze. Sweat glistened in the tangle of red hair spreading across his broad chest and tapering down the ripple of stomach muscles to curl around his large, soft cock and swollen balls. I stripped silently, locking my eyes with his. I crawled across the tangle of furs and straddled his body. His cock stirred beneath me, rising to throb between my legs. I could feel his blood pulsing as I leaned close.

I brushed the thick fiery mane of hair aside. His head arched back, offering the taunt column of his throat as I bared my teeth and...

TULSA-MARK
26, 6'1", 165, dark hair, green
eyes Interested in cooking, good
food, good music, and good
friends. Maybe more? Let's talk.

...ripped his shirt open, buttons bouncing on the floor and plopping into the pool. I stared in awe at the dense coils of moist brown fur covering his chest and belly and disappearing beneath his belt. He looked like a big brown bear. Unable to resist, I ran both hands through his luxuriant pelt and leaned in to nuzzle him, sliding my tongue over the silky strands and tugging them with my teeth. I lapped a circle around the big nipples buried within all that fur, flattening the hair into a dark sunburst. They popped into hard points, begging for attention.

I wanted to spend a long time getting to know his body, savor the taste of fresh sweat in the dark-tufted hollows under his arms, the silky smooth texture of the skin between the rounds of his ass, the warm musky smell rising from his balls as my tongue traced the corded ridges of his stomach, hear his soft gasps as...

John, haven't you got that dryer fixed yet?

UNLEASH YOUR MIND!

...wet with his precum, and I wiped it in the black thicket covering my chest. I grabbed him by the back of the neck and pulled his face close.

Eagerly, he went to work, licking his own juices off my sweat-dampened hair. As I explored the firm muscles of his back and shoulders, his lips found the point of my left nipple and sucked it in. He bit it lightly and flicked his tongue over the rubbery peak. His lips trailed the narrow path of hair leading to my heavy bush, licking and kissing my flesh along the way. He dropped to his knees, hypnotized by my turgid inches of cock, swaying in the...

...skin slid smoothly back, exposing the deep red glans and gathering in soft ripples behind the crown. I darted my tongue inside the glistening slit, tasting him for the first time. Gently, I stretched the skin until it shrouded the head. Slipping beneath the silky overhang, my tongue swirled over the sensitive rim. I wondered what it would feel like to have that delicate membrane sliding over one's cockhead. Then I had a wild idea. I stood up, pushed my cock against his—nose to nose—and eased the skin forward until it hooded my cock. I shivered at the exquisite sensation. He put his arms around my shoulders and held me in place. It was wonderful, our two cocks throbbing together, heartbeat against heartbeat, sheathed in the same living skin. I had a hard time holding...

...throbbed in its eagerness to be touched. I teased the sparse blond hairs, touching them with the tip of my tongue and driving him wild. I washed the sides of the crevice with my warm tongue. His hole expanded, begging to be filled with my hard cock. I traced the wrinkled circle, laving it with moisture. His legs spread open even farther, and he rocked back against me. I stopped, catching my breath and huffing warm puffs of air against the glistening pink bud as his legs quivered.

"Oh God, please don't stop," he pleaded. "No one's ever done this to me before."

I didn't make him wait. He gasped when he felt the thickness of my

Barry Alexander

tongue deep inside him, my beard stubble rasping against the inner walls of his cleft. His cheeks tightened for a second, then he bloomed open, exposing the blood-pink interior. My lips pressed tightly against his anal ring, my tongue plunging…

<u>WORKING STIFFS</u>

Who says work can't be fun?
These men LOVE cumming to work
and handling all the heavy equipment on the night shift, 'cause
it's never dull when these horny, blue-collar studs are hard at work!
Why not stroke along while watching these up-and-cumming working stiffs mix
a little work with a LOT of steamy pleasure!
Features Rod Peters * Harry Butz * Sir Hugo Ballsmore *
Guy Rammer * Jack Offhere * Dick Moore
XXX   #9272 $39.95

…struggling to free my hands and control the unbearable sensations. But he held my hands locked at my hips, teasing me with huffs of warm breath over my hypersensitive dick and tiny flicks of his tongue—a taste here, a nip there— driving me insane with desire.

My hips bucked upwards in an effort to force my turgid cock into his mouth, but he just laughed at me. "Now you know what it feels like," he gloated.

I hadn't realized he was so strong and squirmed helplessly against his exquisite torment, but I wouldn't ask him for it; I just *wouldn't*, although I felt like crying from frustration. My cock poked futilely at the empty air, aching for contact, but still I refused to beg. His head hovered over me, his hot mouth inches away. The tip of his tongue poked between his lips, a drop of saliva suspended above my dick, a millimeter from contact. He caught it on his thumb. I shivered in anticipation, eager to be touched. Then the bastard rubbed it over his own cock.

"Suck me." I groaned. "Please, I need it so bad. Suck me."

"Why didn't you say so?"

Within seconds, his mouth had engulfed the condom he'd rolled down my aching dick. I still wanted to throttle him, but soon forgot everything but the pleasure my cock in his hot, slick mouth was giving me. His tongue flickered over the head of my cock, pushing the latex into my cum slit. With a growl, I drove my hips forward, slamming my cock down his throat. His lips pressed tightly against my groin as his tongue slithered and stroked the…

18

1-800-STUDLY:
WANT IT HARD? WANT IT DEEP? CALL NOW!

…know what you need. I pushed his legs apart and lay between them. His cock rose like a sword freshly drawn from a fire—red and glowing and stabbing the air. The broad helmet, dripping pre-cum, was covered with a long foreskin. His balls were swollen, pulled up tightly against the base of his cock. I took them gently in my hand and bent to savor their heady fragrance and the way they slid so reluctantly in their silken pouch. His cock throbbed in my hand as I carefully slid his foreskin back and exposed the ruby head.

I could almost taste the honey that oozed from his slit. His stomach muscles clenched when I leaned closer and breathed on the glistening cockhead. I swirled my tongue across the silken skin. He moaned, arching his back as I dipped my tongue in the gaping slit and lapped the abundant fluid. His balls shifted under my hand, attempting to rise against my grip. I opened wide and swallowed his cock, loving the slippery heat and bulk of it. It glided over my tongue, thumped against my palate and coasted right down…

CONSTRUCTION WORKER

My name is Rick—6'6", 275,
blond/blue, uncut. I'm into leather,
role-playing, B/D—anything kinky.
Lkg 4 well-hung top, 35-40 to fuck
me hard!

…over this desk and prepare to get fucked."

With one sweep of his massive arm, he cleared his desk, knocking the blueprints to the floor. Pushing my face down against its mahogany surface and holding it there, he yanked my hard-on backwards between my spread legs, ran his finger up my fat cum tube, gathered the abundant lubricant oozing from my cockhead and slicked it over and into my throbbing target. I shuddered with anticipation and parted my legs even farther.

He dropped his huge cock between my greasy cheeks and bumped its crown against my hole several times before seriously driving his hips forward. My throbbing bud gradually adjusting to his massive girth, it seemed to take forever as, inch by inch, the full length of his immense cock filled me, until at last I felt his wiry pubes scouring my ass cheeks. He then began repeatedly pulling back and driving forward—the length of his stroke increasing with each repetition. He rode me long and hard, rocking my body, and my mind with the exquisite force of his thrusting. I clutched at the desk to keep my sweaty body from sliding across the slick surface, as my raging hard-on thumped against its wooden edge with every smack of his balls against my voracious ass.

"Like that?"

"Yeah, *ram* that big dick in me."

He lunged viciously, slamming the entire length…

Honey, did you remember to mail the house insurance payment?

…weighed his furry balls in my hand. Hungrily I drew in more of the thick veiny shaft. I sucked harder, my head dipping lower each time. I struggled to take it all. He was bigger than anyone I had ever had, but I wanted all of him.

Finally, I plunged all the way down, my throat packed with hot manmeat at last. My lips mashed against his groin—my mustache tangling in his pubes—while I breathed in his scent, hot and musky and totally male. It was wonderful! But it wasn't enough. There was another part of me that was aching to be filled.

"I want you inside me," I slurred, rolling the condom over his hard, red cock. "I want every *inch* of you inside me."

He looked into my eyes and smiled. I thrust upwards to meet his descending cock. I gasped as it breached me, as it stretched me to the limit, as he slowly filled me with his gargantuan capacity for passion, which succeeded in bringing us closer than we had ever been before. He rode me slowly, his long hair tickling my chest, as he rocked back and forth, gliding effortlessly in and out of me. My cock, continuously drooling precum, plowed through the silky hair on his chest with every thrust, lubricating the tender underside of my ecstasy as we rocked and moaned in total...

Honey, it's almost time to go. You've GOT to get ready!

SKIN ZINE 2: HOT OFF THE PRESS

Stars: * "Milkbone" Huxley & "Frenchlips" Marquis *
These guys are HARD at work every day, getting it on and getting OFF
on bringing your hottest fantasies to life!
Humpy marketing and sales reps!
Butch ex-cons in shipping and receiving who fuck like dogs!
Way-horny editors! Sex-crazed Writers! Cum shots galore!
It's a dirty job, but... SOMEONE'S gotta do it!
#069... Rated XXX...120 minutes... only $59.95!

MARRIED

30 Y.O. MAN, eager to explore my true desires. Looking for discreet companion, 25-40, to show me the way. Prefer hairy, but will respond to all. Leave number and I'll call you. Promise.

...rode me down. His balls slapped against my ass as he pounded me.

"Oh *yeah*... give me *more*."

My inflamed cock rutted against the tangled sheets as his rhythm rocked

Barry Alexander

my body. I could feel the juice swelling my balls as I got closer to shooting my load.

"Is this... the way you want it?" he gasped, his breath hot and moist against my back.

"Yes!" I shouted. "Don't *stop*, man. Give me all you got!"

He launched into a fucking frenzy, his pelvis slamming my butt with increasing fury. I didn't know how much longer I could last.

"Hot," he moaned. "You're so fuckin' *hot*. I've gotta get *deeper*, get *more* of that sweet butt."

In a frenzy of carnal abandon, I hiked my ass as high as his relentless pounding would permit, pulling my knees upward to give him that extra inch because God knows I wanted him buried as deep as possible when he...

John, what are you DOING down there?

UNCHAIN YOUR DESIRES!
1-800-CUM-NOW

...trickled down his smooth chest, the drops glistening in the moonlight. I strained to reach them, lifting my torso off the pillow. My lips caught one as it trembled on his skin. I licked my way upwards and sucked in one of his nipples. I traced the pebbly ring and lashed the hard nub with my tongue. His hips undulated, driving that huge cock into every hungry corner of my bowels. His balls slapped against my ass. Face strained and sweating, he fought to hold off his orgasm. I clamped down, milking his dick with my guts, determined to make him cum. His hips went into overdrive, pistoning his cock in and out. He locked his hands on my hips and bucked wildly against me. He howled and shook and suddenly let go. I felt the hot surges of cum inflating the reservoir tip of his condom. His muscles strained and his back arched as he filled me with masculine heat. My balls tightened, sending needles of pleasure up my spine and shooting through my cock. I couldn't hold back and blasted my load all over his body. White-hot steamers of cum ran down his chest and puddled in the tangled sheets. He collapsed against me, crushing me with his weight as the final spasms racked our bodies. I didn't ever want to move. I had never felt so close to any man in my...

Honey? Honey? Are you all right? Why are you BREATHING so hard?

22

!INDULGE YOURSELF!

HOT MEN ARE WAITING!
Bikers and lumberjacks and drill sergeants...

HOT MEN ARE WAITING!
Bodybuilders and punks and porn stars...

HOT MEN ARE WAITING!
Bears and bottoms, tops and queens...

HOT MEN ARE WAITING!
Tattooed and pierced, shaved or stubbled...

HOT MEN ARE WAITING!
Shy men in glasses, waiting to be noticed...

HOT MEN ARE WAITING!
In bars and pickups and right next door...

HOT MEN ARE WAITING!

!INDULGE YOURSELF!

THE GREAT MAN
Dale Chase

I knew all about Martin Sullivan. Mixed with my admiration of his literary prowess was a measure of caution, for he had a reputation for devouring people, mostly male. When I was asked by a well-known publisher to write Sullivan's biography, I readily accepted but told myself I wouldn't, under any circumstance, allow him to fuck me.

I learned he'd been impressed with my credentials. Two best-selling biographies of literary men—one the outgrowth of my master's thesis—had led Martin Sullivan to me. He'd apparently read both books and approved. At least that was what my agent said.

The danger, I knew, lay in Sullivan's ruthless charm. Age had managed to enhance rather than diminish his good looks, giving him a slightly rugged appearance on top of an already formidable masculinity. I was attracted to him before we ever met—his novels so incredibly male yet emotionally wrenching, turbulent in a way I couldn't resist. I knew going in that I'd want him and that he'd consider me a given, thus my vow of resistance. I was his biographer, after all, a professional.

It was not to be a brief relationship. Hours would be spent interviewing people who knew him, then hours with him, days of questions and answers, endless discourse. I thought of this as I settled into a chair in his study that first day, watching him pace the room like a lion contemplating a run at some antelope.

"I don't want to start at the beginning," he told me before I turned on the tape recorder. "The early years are a bore and you probably already know the details—son of, schools, trivial facts."

I said nothing, let him dictate the rules, but already his energy was overtaking me. He had a musky presence, handsome in a blood-red turtleneck sweater and charcoal slacks. His gray hair was thick, curly, his body solid, yet trim. When he turned his back to me I traced broad shoulders and a back that funneled down to narrow hips, firm ass. And I knew he knew I was taking note.

"Let's begin with Roy," he said, turning to face me like he'd thrown down a challenge.

"Roy?"

"Aha, you don't know as much as you thought you would."

"Apparently not."

"Because I've never spoken of him. I've let the public and the media wallow in supposition and I've taken great delight in just how far down the wrong path it's possible for the hordes to travel."

"So who was Roy?"

Sullivan poured himself a drink before he answered. When I declined, he chuckled. "I see, keep a clear head. I prefer not."

He stood at the fireplace, thought for a few seconds, then began. "Roy was the first boy I fucked." He paused, looking for a reaction from me, and receiving none, he continued. "I went to boys' schools, as you know, and there was lots of fooling around, but I was in college before I actually did any real fucking. Roy was my roommate in more ways than one. Beautiful, blond Midwesterner… clearly out of his element. I had him the first night and kept on all year. It turned out he was experienced; farm boys often are, you know. Tell me, Mr. Collins, are you gay?"

I had turned on the tape when he started in about Roy and let it run. "Yes, I am," I said.

"I thought so. Your previous work is too insightful into the homosexual psyche to be otherwise. Are you in a relationship?"

"No."

He raised a brow. "No partner? Lover? Fuck buddy?"

"This is supposed to be about you."

"Ah, yes, but I think I have a right to know my biographer."

"We're going to be spending a lot of time together," I said. "You'll get to know me as we go along."

"Yes, I suppose I will."

And so began an experience that was to result in a well-received book and a good dose of the Sullivan turbulence. Of course my no-sex resolve collapsed after just two weeks. I traded all my professional ethics for the fucking of a lifetime and will probably wonder for years if it was worth it.

A week into the project, I was jerking off to thoughts of Martin Sullivan. His recollections were so heavily laced with sexual escapades that I'd invariably have a hard-on and he knew it. When I'd excuse myself to use the bathroom, he'd offer a knowing smile or a comment like "take your time." He knew what I was doing. And then, on that fateful day, he followed me in.

I didn't turn when I heard the door open and when I stopped pumping my dick, he came up behind me and said, "Don't stop on my account." And he lowered my pants and began to squeeze my butt cheeks, getting his thumbs down inside my crack. Instead of picking up the pace, I slowed down, wanting it to last. I was going to get fucked by the great man and I wanted it to be an event, the famous cock up my humble ass, to hell with professional ethics. He fingered me awhile, looked over my shoulder at my dripping prong, then withdrawing, got a condom on, got out the lube. When he ran a gob into my hole I let out a moan and he kept his finger in there, prodding. "More than ready," he murmured, then pulled out his finger and stuck in his prick.

I'd had no idea how big he was. His reputation was for conquest, not endowment, but I quickly learned he was equal on both fronts. It felt like a fire hose going up my rectum and I squirmed with a mix of pleasure and pain while he offered encouragement. "Nothing like a big dick, is there? Cockhead up in your bowels?" He began to thrust—a slow, easy stroke that utilized every inch of his big thing—pulling out all the way sometimes, then easing back in. With every thrust I let out a gasp or moan and a couple times a swear word or two. "This is what I did to Roy that first year," he told me as he began to settle into a smooth, rocking rhythm. I'd let go of my dick with his entry and, still hard, it flailed blindly while I received him. "I never get enough," Sullivan said. "You young things with your tight little asses. And you never get enough dick up there, do you, hmmm? Do you?"

"No," I managed because he seemed to require a reply.

"Tell me how much you want it. Tell me. I want to hear it."

I let out a long groan because he was picking up speed, pounding me, and it hurt, but it also felt like I was going to come unaided, balls tight, cock poised to fire. "Fuck me," was all I could say because I was shooting my load by then, pulsing semen onto the floor. Sullivan kept pumping his cock into me until he grunted and went over himself. I grabbed my dick, squeezing out the last drops of jism while that fire hose exploded in my gut.

He wasn't quick. He kept pounding, growling like the animal he was and I loved every second. When he finally stopped, he wrapped his arms around me and held on, sweaty forehead pressed against my shoulder. He ground his hips, the spent cock still formidable, and we experienced a gradual descent. Only when he softened did he slide out and even then he reached under my shirt and tweaked my nipples, then worked his way down to my limp dick. "Let's not work any more today," he said. "There are so many other things to do." He turned me around and kissed me and I knew right then I was lost. As I sucked his tongue, my dick stirred and I started climbing the front of him. "I think we need to get to a bed," he offered.

Atop a royal blue comforter, he stripped away our clothes and only then did I get a good look at the man. I was truly impressed. On his knees, he reared back while I lay inert below and I looked from formidable, furry thighs to the big cock hanging between them, fat balls underneath. A fine pelt ran up his stomach and spread across his well-defined chest. If I had to describe the ideal mature body, it would be Martin Sullivan's.

As he looked me over, his dick began to rise and when it was about halfway along, he slid down, pushed my legs back, and got his face in my ass, his tongue on my rim. He licked and played and periodically stopped to narrate. "What a sweet little hole you have, Mr. Collins." He stuck in a finger, worked it around. "Nice and tight but I think by the time we get this book written, it'll be loosened up quite a bit."

He pulled on a condom at that point, slathered on the lube, then guided his stiff prick into me again. "This time…" he said as he buried himself to the root, "…will be unhurried. I'm going to fuck you until you come at least twice, until you're so spent you can't walk. You'll sleep then and when you wake, we'll work awhile. Then fuck awhile. Oh, yes, this is going to be a wonderful relationship."

He pumped steadily, sweat glistening beneath his fur, and everything else disappeared, time included. His staying power was remarkable, cock like a piece of hot iron, thighs taut, balls slapping. It didn't take long for me to grab my cock and shoot another load and Sullivan cheered every spurt, then pulled out, gathered up the come, and smeared it down his shaft. "Fuck you with your own juice," he said, and I could see he loved the idea, that he wanted to get everything in everywhere. He fucked a while longer, then turned me over and rode me from behind.

I don't think I'd ever felt more like a piece of meat, nor enjoyed it so much. Reeling from the sex-high, I imagined us in some forest, a big furry creature fucking the small animal who'd happened upon his path. We were Dick and Ass, nothing more. He had me until deep in the night when we finally slept. My last thought before drifting off was that we hadn't returned to work.

"You might as well move in for the duration," Sullivan said the next morning as he prepared to mount me. He'd awakened me by sucking my cock and now had me on all fours, greasing me with a finger.

"That's probably not a good idea," I said and he prodded my prostate, which made my breath catch. "Of course it's not," he said, "but it will be so much more expedient in the long run. Keep me satisfied and I'll tell you everything."

He entered me without waiting for a reply and as he pumped that big cock I thought about the publisher who was paying for my time. It was wrong, what I was doing, but I was powerless to stop myself. I vowed then and there to capture that very feeling in the book, the overwhelmingness of the man. "We'll have a long session after breakfast," he said, maintaining a steady thrust. "On the book, I mean."

From that point on, the challenge became to balance the sex with the work. Not exactly a chore but still requiring a concentrated effort. Retaining at least some professional standing while being taken to ecstatic heights wasn't easy but proved worthwhile in the long run.

The trouble, I soon found, was that Sullivan's recollections remained relentlessly sexual. Every time I tried to guide him back to what he termed the "boring" facts of his life, he would veer off into yet another sexual encounter. These were difficult to resist since no two were alike. Fucking, yes, but when related by a prose master, each became its own singular play with Martin

Sullivan the star. The tapes were becoming a collection of verbal porn that I knew was not what the publisher wanted.

The reward, however, in addition to an enviable sex life, was that I captured the man's energy. How could I not? It engulfed me, permeated my very being. Never mind his cock in my ass; he himself was inside me and holding fast. Halfway through the project I began to dread its end, to consider the unsettling fact that there had to *be* an end. Not easy to view from the sexual wallow.

Getting my narrative down was managed in those periods when Sullivan worked on his latest novel. He'd put in three or four hours, usually mid-day, and it was during those respites that I'd record the man himself. And then, after we'd been together two months, after we'd filled nearly a hundred tapes, I realized my overview was slipping, that I was falling in love with Martin Sullivan. I could hear it in my voice, in the choice of things I wrote about him.

"What's wrong?" he asked one evening. He'd fucked me for over an hour and I hadn't come, hadn't even gotten hard. He fondled my limp dick and, when I said nothing, added, "Concern of some sort?"

I got out of bed, stormed to the bathroom, and closed the door. "You stupid shit," I said to the mirror, knowing I would be eaten alive and not in the way I'd have liked. There was no outcome to what was going on; nothing would endure once the book was done. It was borrowed time, the account steadily depleting. I returned to bed but didn't get in. Sitting on the edge, I tried to avoid him, but from the periphery he worked his cock with a slow caressing stroke that made me long to get it inside me and fuck, literally, everything else.

"Tell me," he said finally.

"You don't want to hear it."

"So now you speak for me?"

I sighed. "I know you and it makes me wish I didn't."

"Ah, a conundrum."

He was so sure of himself, almost cold. All that heat he generated, yet he still remained the predator. "Have you ever been in love?" I asked.

He laughed. "Oh, God, is that it? You've taken the leap and, mid-flight, are having second thoughts?"

"Can you blame me?"

"I prefer to spend my emotions on the page. If you love me, so be it. It doesn't have to play like a tragedy."

A shiver ran through me. I had never felt so alone. I wanted him to sit up, put his arms around me, tell me how much he cared, but knew he wouldn't. He let go of his cock, rolled onto his side, but said nothing. "You didn't answer me," I said.

"Sorry. What was the question?"

"Have you ever been in love?"

"If I haven't does it render me a lesser man?"

29

"This was such a mistake," I told him, my voice shaking.

"Which? The biography or the fucking?"

"I promised myself I wouldn't go to bed with you."

"Did you?" His tone was mock indulgence and also the last straw. I shot out of bed, looking for my clothes. "They're in the living room," he said. "If I recall."

Still naked, he followed me, watched me dress. "Surely you're not going to let feelings put asunder all we've accomplished."

I tied my shoes and tried not to look at him but he was larger than life, once again intruding into my peripheral vision as he stroked his cock. "Don't be foolish," he coaxed, his voice softening, taking on a compromising, almost endearing tone. I paused, my resolve pierced. The possibility of a connection, however remote, took hold. I slumped, hands over my face.

He came to me then. "The one thing I've learned with my years," he said, "is to not try and define things."

I looked up at him and he raised a hand to my cheek. My heart filled. I was overcome with joy and when he guided his prick to my lips, I took it willingly.

After that there was a certain indulgence on his part, enjoyable so long as I didn't let myself acknowledge that was all it was. He became almost gentle between bouts of insatiable sex. He appeased my emotions just enough to circumvent my caution. As a result, I fell deeper-still in love. He became my world. I forgot anything had existed before him and contemplated nothing after. Months passed, we fell into habits, a pair of sorts. Not quite a couple but far from biographer and subject.

Some days we didn't even work on the book. When it was warm we'd swim nude, fuck poolside, then lie glistening with sweat until we slid back into the water and started again.

We never went out. He did, but would leave me behind and I tried not to let my jealousy show. He'd arrive home from an event—a reading or a party— and fall on me, fucking me rabidly as if time spent away had sent him into a panic. Later he'd tell me about his evening. I'd note details to use in the book but I was beginning to see that the biggest part of him, the part with me, could never reach the page. I tried not to dwell on this, kept to my work, my life with him. And then one day while he worked in his study, I sat at my desk and stared at the book's final page. I wanted to cry.

"Why so quiet?" Sullivan asked over dinner. We normally ate well, but I couldn't manage a thing at that moment besides wine, and plenty of it. I didn't answer him, just refilled my glass.

"Better have some of the fish with that," he counseled. "Otherwise you're not going to be much company."

I fled. "What is it?" he called out but didn't immediately follow. He let me drink myself into a near stupor, then wandered onto the patio where I lay on a chaise, the view starting to swirl. He sighed heavily, sat nearby. "One more should do it," he said. "You'll either pass out or throw up."

"Company," I slurred.

"Pardon?"

"I'm not going to be much *company*."

"Oh, dear God. Is that it? You've seized upon a simple remark and infused it with meaning, never mind how offhand it may have been?"

"That's all I am to you." The tears had begun. I hated them but couldn't stop. "Now the book's done and where does that leave me?"

"Ah, the plot thickens, so to speak. First of all, congratulations on the accomplishment. No one has ever managed to get me onto the page before. I commend you. As for where this leaves you, that's up to you. You're welcome to stay on."

This was and was not what I wanted to hear—an invitation rather than a declaration. I said nothing.

"Come on, let's get you to bed."

I thought then he might say it. He undressed me, turned down the covers, put me beneath them, then began to rub my chest as a mother would her ailing child. I watched him through my drunken haze, tried to find what I needed. His finger found a nipple, rubbed gently until it became a hard little nub. He seemed so quiet, almost contented as his hand slid down my stomach and into my pubes, inched toward my soft cock. He palmed me, looking into my eyes all the while, and I knew there was something there but no matter how much I wanted him to frame the emotional tie in words, it would remain a physical one. He confirmed this when he pulled aside the covers, lowered his head, and took me into his mouth.

I still can't believe he made me come. I was beyond ready to pass out, but my dick remained sober and filled under his ministrations. When I came I lost consciousness.

The next morning I awakened to a monumental hangover and Sullivan's dick entering my ass. "Lie still," he commanded when I protested. He was mercifully gentle but still he fucked me thoroughly and when he neared his climax his thrusts set my stomach on a path of no return. Seconds after he came, I ran to the bathroom and threw up.

It was an awful day; I was hung over on two levels, the emotional ultimately outdistancing the physical. As my head cleared, I recalled the night before, the invitation. I could stay on. It was up to me.

I kept my distance from Sullivan and he was gracious enough not to press. I sat with my completed draft, thumbing the pages. He was in those pages. As my fingers ran the edges, I thought, *how appropriate. Ink and paper, lifeless until someone begins to read.*

I called the publisher and told him the first draft was completed. He was elated. "When can I see it?"

"It needs some polish," I told him, suddenly glad I had a reason to stay on. Staying on: would it ever be palatable?

I no longer conducted interviews with Martin Sullivan. The tape recorder was put away, the hours of him relating his exploits concluded. I tinkered with the manuscript and tried to ignore the hollow in me. When I drank I said things I shouldn't and Sullivan accepted both protestations of love and angry rebukes for his failure to reciprocate. Another month passed. The publisher pressed me to deliver the book. I resisted.

Sullivan caught me one day in his study, pages stacked before me, an empty box to one side, a vodka bottle the other. He chuckled. "Second thoughts?" he asked.

"I can't do it."

"What, send it off? Is there a problem?"

He hadn't asked to read it which unsettled me on two levels: one, that he had faith that I'd do him justice, and two, that he was so arrogant he didn't care what was said about him, even by me.

"I don't know," I finally said, reaching for bottle. He took it from me. "You'll make yourself sick," he said. "Come with me."

He led me out into the warm fall afternoon, undressed me, then himself, and eased us into the pool. And there he wrapped his arms around me from behind and lay on the steps with me against him. His cock stiffened but he didn't do anything beyond parking it against my butt. Relief spread through me. If he'd fucked me, I would have crumbled.

"There's one more chapter," he said after awhile and my breath caught because I thought he was going to concede at last, concoct the two of us into a perfect ending.

"When I was 25," he began, "David Jennings came into my life. He left it the same year. He was a dancer; we met at a club in New York and became inseparable. You asked me if I'd ever been in love. The answer is yes. A series of infatuations in my early 20s and then David. He was beautiful in every way imaginable: lithe, angular, boyish. Golden, tawny, catlike... Graceful, long fingered, long dicked... We fucked constantly, everywhere." He paused, then spoke the next words as if they tasted badly. "We... made love."

"This should be in the book," I said.

"No. The goddamned world doesn't need every drop of my blood and besides, it's not who I am."

"So what happened?"

"Some months later a new dancer joined the company, Johnny Hodges. Not unlike me, he was a man to David's boy. I knew the first time I saw them together, that David was lost to me. There is nothing to compare a moment like that, exchanging pleasantries with the man who is fucking your lover and taking him from you. David and I weren't living together so there wasn't much subterfuge involved. Having trusted him, I learned a great lesson."

My first thought was *that's it*? A breakup? Like he should be exempt from the pain of life? Anger seized me. I wanted to scream but held everything in check, became solicitous even, because I still wanted him to love me. "That must have been rough," I soothed.

"No, I learned the lesson that love is not for me and life has proven it out. I don't waste energy on matters of the heart. I channel it elsewhere and am perfectly happy in that regard." He stirred beneath me, pushed up a bit. End of story, time to fuck.

I pulled away, swam to the middle of the pool where I lingered for a bit, then paddled to the side. Sullivan watched me. I thought about his cock under the water, what he would do with it. He liked me to sit on it while he lay on the steps. He waited, arms out to the side, floating there.

I thought of all the times I'd fallen in love and been hurt. About the times I'd done the hurting to someone else. Like love was some sandy bog you had to keep wading into and struggling out of because maybe, just once, it wouldn't prove all muck and mire. Love had never lasted for me either but at least I hadn't written it off. Just the opposite. Each new experience was laced with possibility, even if it ultimately proved a disappointment on some level. Martin Sullivan, for all his genius, couldn't see this simple foundation. On paper he was a master, his imagination soared, but in reality, here in the pool, he was no more than a hard dick awaiting service. I swam to him, climbed on facing him, and let him fuck me.

It set me free, knowing it was the last time, and I thought about him up inside me, doing what he allowed himself. We were even at last, in some way I couldn't define. I would send off the manuscript, leave out his "last chapter" because he was right, it wasn't him. But I still didn't see it as he did. While he considered the affair with David Jennings a turning point, a justification for the wall he'd built around his heart, I saw a man who had simply abandoned hope prematurely, who let pain take him over and the fear of it rob him of life. In walling off his pain, he hadn't so much protected his heart as left it to thicken and dry like any ill-used muscle. No, the public need not see this. The man on the tapes was who he would remain, the man who led with his prick. I reminded myself that I'd known the danger going in, and how right my first instincts had been. When Sullivan came I watched the familiar grimace and no longer searched for more.

THE POWER
Blaise Bulot

Caterpillars. I believe that's when I first realized that I possessed the power—caterpillars.

I was kneeling down, weeding my garden when I noticed a large green caterpillar slowly but determinedly inching its way up an iris leaf. My first impulse was to squash it, but I resisted and bent closer to the creature to watch its progress. Sensing my presence, it crawled a bit more rapidly. I don't know why, but in my mind I "ordered" the caterpillar to reverse direction. It did; it turned and began crawling back down the leaf!

At the time I recall not being the least bit surprised. *Coincidence. Just a coincidence….* I concentrated my will and "ordered" the insect to change direction again. And it did! Thinking, *now, this could be more than a coincidence*, I tried again—and it worked. My third, fourth, fifth, and sixth tries proved no less successful; I had the hapless caterpillar marching back and forth at my will. I spotted another caterpillar and repeated my experiment with the same result. This was no coincidence

Realizing that caterpillars are fairly low on the food chain, I wondered if my newfound power would work on "higher" creatures. Now, I love dogs, but don't have one of my own, so how to test my theory? With Boston's leash law in effect, every available dog had a not-always friendly owner attached to the end of its lead. Remembering that in the park their owners oftentimes ignored the law and let their dogs run free, I decided to put my gardening on hold and take a little stroll.

At the park, several dogs were clearly enjoying this illegal liberty, much too busy frisking about and sniffing every tree, shrub, lamp post, and each other's butts to pay any attention to me—until, that is, I focused mentally and ordered them one at a time to quit sniffing and come to me. And come they did, every time, without fail! A couple of the owners, voicing their astonishment, remarked that their pets never approached strangers as theirs had me, before releasing their canines.

After my success with dogs, I decided to advance a notch or two up the evolutionary scale and focus my attention on their owners. Spotting a particularly adorable Beagle (my favorite breed of dog), I could not help but notice that there was something pretty adorable on the other end of its leash—an extremely pretty young man. And friendly too, it turned out—all smiles and small talk about his dog. *An excellent candidate*, I decided. Bending over to pat the dog's head, I ordered Pretty Boy to goose me. And so he did, with a better aim than I'd anticipated, deep between my butt cheeks!

Later the same day I spotted an outstandingly butch stud with a chick hanging onto him, approaching in my direction, walking with that *macho*-male, *macho*-male, *macho*-male swagger as if he had way too much of a good thing sandwiched between his loins. His tank top scarcely concealed a wonderful torso molded with muscle, and fell just short of his jeans, revealing a whorl of hair on his hard belly, which I could only assume got thicker and thicker as it descended and fanned out around his... ah, you know what. *Man*, did he fill out those jeans! Enveloped in distressed denim from his lean waist down—from behind, with his tight bubble-butt-to-die-for to front, with his fully-packed 'n' promising bulge of a basket—the guy, in those jeans, was a real button buster.

Thinking, *Damn girls get all the best stuff,* I willed him to flash me his best smile, wet his full lips with the tip of his tongue, and rub the fly of his jeans in a most provocative way. These gestures did not escape the attention of his girlfriend, and as I sauntered beyond them and turned around I saw her screaming "Faggot!" into his face. *No need to worry,* I told myself. *When he gets her home and slides his hard meat into her pussy, she'll scream a different tune.*

Okay, so far so good. What should I try next?

I admit it: I'm an ass man. I love male asses. And, of course, if you love asses, you gotta love black ass, no? *Yeah... hung on narrow hips—a big tight ass, jutting out firm and flawless and fine... The cloven cheeks hard and smooth, silky and hairless, but with an Afro sheen deep down in the crack...? Oh yeah....* But not to stereotype; hey, white guys have great asses too. I've seen some beauts. Real *pearly* gates. Makes you want to ease right in and....

Ahem!

It wasn't too many days after all this occurred when I was walking along the street early one morning and happened upon a workman, Italian I think, patching the masonry on a door stoop. He obviously didn't have on any underwear because when he squatted down on his heels his pants rode down his wonderful, pale and gleaming, lightly hairy ass, exposing at least four or five inches of crack filled with denser, curly black hair. Well, no way could I pass *that* up so, glancing around to make sure nobody was around, I cast my spell, squatted down behind him, and lowered his pants further until his cock 'n' balls dropped down. Naturally he didn't resist. He *couldn't* resist. I then placed my right hand in his furry ass cleavage and, dropping a thick glob of saliva into it, began fingering his tight and creamy asshole, all pursed like a pouting little mouth, while running my left hand between his hairy legs and cupping his heavy balls. Quickly noting that someone was coming along the sidewalk toward us, I quit, stood up, and walked away, leaving him there with his sweet ass—and his tongue—hanging out. Too much fun!

Quite frankly I don't know how The Power works. Does anybody else have it or do I alone possess it? Just imagine the ability to make *anybody* do *anything* you want! No doubt others might use The Power to make the Brinks guards hand over the cash, or the dashing car salesman to just *give* them the Porsche, but I suppose I'm a simple-minded soul, because all I'm interested in is sex. Lots of it. With a lot of guys. Nobody twice. I know that's about as casual as casual sex gets, but back to The Power. I don't think it's a form of hypnosis—the first explanation that comes to mind—but more a case of taking over other people's will by projecting my own. In addition, I've discovered that I'm able to "disconnect" their will, leaving it intact to "watch" helplessly as I take over their bodies, all their motions, and make them do things that they would never think of doing themselves.

Let me tell you about one episode that illustrates this ability. I'm a park cruiser. I like to have sex out-of-doors, in public places, preferably while being watched by strange eyes, but the park is very dangerous for exhibitionists like me. Many a poor faerie has been robbed, beaten, or even killed in the park. I use to carry a gun, but it became such a hassle. Every time a police cruiser would come through with its searchlight I'd have to hide the gun in the bushes and come back later and try and find it, so I switched to Mace. But now, armed with The Power, I certainly don't need Mace or anything else.

One dark night I was flitting through the bushes, stalking prey. I'd passed over a couple of very presentable hunks, confident (because The Power has enabled me to become very very particular) that I could find something superior. I didn't see the black guy standing beside the tree until he spoke to me. He was fine. *Extremely* fine. He backed away from the path, wordlessly encouraging me to follow, but my antennae were picking something up—bad vibrations. He was too friendly, asked me if I had any rush, then asked what time it was. My vibe proved correct. When I said I didn't have a watch, he pulled a knife and an *I'm-going-to-cut-you-good-if-you-don't-give-me-everything-you-have* smirk spread across his face. Boy, was *he* ever picking on the wrong chicken! I left his will intact but took command of his body—and oh, what a beautiful body it was.

First I made him undress me: my sandals, my shirt, my pants. As I don't wear any underwear when I cruise—it only slows things down—his removing those three articles of clothing left me butt naked. His eyes having become a window through which I could clearly see what was going on in his mind, he stared at my cock as if it were a poisonous viper. I made him take it in his hand where, in his imposed, caressing grasp, it grew hard in a matter of seconds. Sure it felt good, but the fun was just beginning.

I willed him to release me and then got down to the business of stripping him. Off came the $200 sneakers; off came the plush, white socks. I tossed them into the River Charles—splash, splash. Next, I pulled his black T-shirt up and over his head—off into the river. I then yanked his pants down his amazing legs and off over his feet. I checked the pockets and kept his money—the robber effectively robbed, his eyes registering more than a little alarm as he watched his pants follow the shirt into the river.

I knelt in front of him, took the waistband of his sparkly-white, Calvin Klein briefs into my fingers, and slowly, very slowly, peeled them down his hips. His kinky pubic hair was thick and crisp. His muscled arms, which had fallen limply to his sides, made a feeble little jerk, as if to offer resistance, but fell back immediately. Pulling them ever so slowly down, I held my breath as his schlong flopped out and over the waistband of his briefs. Freed at last, it grew and stiffened the moment it hit the warm night air. Hey, I wasn't doing that!

His cock matched the rest of his body; it was magnificent, black black black, long, thick, and uncut. To the touch—and you can bet I touched it—it was super-warm, smooth and silky as velvet. But, remember, I'm an ass man so, after gently kissing his cock's soft foreskin, I grabbed hold of his hips and spun him around. Jackpot! The perfect ass, *my my my*: I wanted to jump right into it. I spread his buns and plunged my face into his crack as far as I could. It was moist and warm and funky. Breathing in his wonderful scent, I lapped the firm, perfectly-shaped buns, lapped his sweaty crack, starting at the top, at the bottom of his tapered back, then down… down… down… past his sphincter, deeper and deeper to his crotch. I spread his legs and pushed my face into his crotch. I lapped the hairs on his scrotum, tongued his balls, took them in my mouth, and sucked them like the most luscious of fruits.

The guy was so beautiful I felt compelled to drink him in, in his entirety, with my eyes. I stood, backed up a bit and just stared at him standing there in the moonlight, naked as a Nubian god, lusting for every inch of him. But wait a minute, not *quite* naked it seemed. He still wore his Walkman radio! Ha, what had he been listening to before he spoke to me, I wonder? "Midnight Mozart for Muggers" on WCRB? I don't *think* so…

Ooops, I'd forgotten; I was so fascinated by his ebony prick I forgot all about the briefs, still lying on the ground where I had dropped them. I picked them up, wiped my face with them, took a deep sniff, and tossed them into the river. The pants had sunk quickly, but the white briefs floated on the water's surface, floated slowly away into the night like a swan. I pressed my hot body against his and pulled the headphone set out of his cute little ears. I tossed it into the river with a splash, his eyes appearing particularly distressed by that.

Now he was *naked* naked, as nude as I. I wrapped my arms around him and gripped his buns. I kissed him on his forehead, then on his eyelids with their marvelous, long and curved lashes, then on the tip of his broad nose. I ground my pubes into his, my erection rigid against his belly and his hot cock pressed against mine. I kissed him on his moist, full lips, pushed my tongue into his mouth, but just for a delicious moment. I kissed his throat, ran my adventuresome tongue down his neck to his collarbone and chest. I kissed his nipples, nibbled them, sucked them.

Down my tongue slithered—his belly, his navel, and below. His bush tickled my face. My tongue journeyed along the thick, hard shaft of his cock, revisited his balls and crotch, descended to between his muscular legs, the inside of his thighs. My tongue lavished his knees, his shins, both ankles, the insteps of his feet. I nibbled at his toes, pushing my tongue between all ten of them.

I spun him around and began at his heels, progressing up his bulging calves and hamstrings, up to the crease where his buns jutted so dramatically out. Practically drooling, I lapped every luscious inch of them both, loving their smooth texture with my lips and lucky tongue. I bent him over, spread his firm cheeks, and plunged my face into his wonderfully aromatic crack. Oh, Nirvana, my favorite place! I extended my tongue and began deep-licking, dragging my wet tongue from his crotch to the small of his back, over and over again. His bunghole was pursed tight like a small, pouty mouth. I tickled its hairy rim with the tip of my tongue—around the whirl in eighty licks—and he unfurled like some kind of dark flower. Jammin' my tongue in as far as it would go…

After pigging out on just about the best soul food ever, I decided it was time for him to circle *my* globe and willed him to take his time, just the way I like it. He was very thorough. Exploding in thick, white increments, I couldn't help but wonder which is more humiliating for a straight guy: a mouth full of cock or a face full of ass…?

When I release my prey they "wake up" as if from a dream, remembering very little, if anything, of what has happened to them. It's always fun to watch their reaction when this happens—finding themselves stark naked in a public place for instance, my having hidden their clothes always adding immeasurably to the fun.

But my robber friend deserved better, I felt—an extra-special grand finale. Quickly pulling my clothes on, I then paraded him along the busy paths. In no time at all he'd attracted a growing group of… how shall I describe them? Obvious *admirers.* When I got him to his knees, pants began to drop. Cocks were out and pulsing and hands proceeded to get busy; I stepped back to enjoy the show. In no time flat the biggest cock in the crowd speared up his asshole, not very gently, I might add, and began pumping in and out like a piston gone haywire while the runner-up, no mean tool by any stretch, rudely rammed his throat. Two stiff and veiny pricks, one in each of his hands, appeared out of nowhere.

Just because I'm a nice guy, I allowed a naked youth to crawl beneath him and take that ebony treasure into his eager, chocolate-deprived mouth. Let's see, have I forgotten anything? Oh yes, his tits. Seeing to it that the guy fucking began pinching the mugger's nipples *hard* with his sharp fingernails, I settled back amongst the bushes, practically squealing with delight at the hot little orgy going on before my eyes.

After a whole lot of panting and moaning and the slap slap of cocks being catered to in any number of ways, the dude he was blowing suddenly withdrew and blasted his sticky-white faerie sperm all over robber-man's face, just as the guys he was jerking began spurting off in his hands. The perfect time to "wake" him up, I thought. And so I did.

Oh my God—the look on his face…!

THE OTHER HALF OF ME
Jim McDonough

I groaned as the alarm buzzed. I wasn't ready to get up. I was never ready to get up.

I nudged my boyfriend, Paul, who was sleeping soundly to my left. The man was able to sleep though just about anything. I nudged him again and got no response.

"Paul, *Paul*... Wake up. You'll be late for work again."

I then crawled on top of the sleeping hunk with whom I'd shared my bed, my thoughts, my hopes, and my dreams for the past four years.

"Wake up. You're going to be late."

Paul groaned and rubbed his eyes.

"Huh?"

"It's time to get up," I repeated. "Don't blame me if you're late for work again."

I reached under the blankets and tickled him. Paul squirmed like a fish flopping on dry land.

"Okay, okay. I'm up. I'm up."

He pushed me off him and I pulled the covers back over me as he headed off to the bathroom. Paul paused at the bathroom door. He turned and flashed me the smile that made me fall in love with him over and over again.

Paul looked so damn good standing naked at the bathroom door. Just looking at him—with his broad shoulders, his beefy pecs covered in a swirl of dark hair and his flat stomach just a few crunches short of being a total washboard—was giving me more than a few ideas.

"What time is your shift at the store?" he asked, scratching his balls, totally unaware just how much he was getting to me.

"I go in at ten," I said.

"Bastard," he replied.

I rolled over, feeling a bit frustrated. I pulled the covers over my head and grabbed Paul's pillow, pulling it close to me. I lay there for a few minutes while listening to the sound of the water running in the shower and Paul's off-key singing echoing off the tile bathroom walls.

When it became apparent that I wouldn't be able to get a couple more hours of sleep, I hopped out of bed, figuring that I could get a few things done around the house before having to go play the helpful salesclerk at Crate & Barrel.

I padded into the bathroom to take a leak and brush my teeth. Paul was still singing—one of the many things I loved about him.

"Justin, what are you doing out of bed?" he asked over the sound of the water. I briefly thought about shucking my jockeys and joining him, but I knew if I did, one thing would lead to another, and I'd get blamed for making him late for work again.

"I'm going to take a shower and do a few things before I go to work. We need groceries and I can stop by the cleaners and pick up your shirts."

Paul turned off the water, got out of the shower and grabbed a towel. He stepped closer to me, smiling as he approached.

"Well, it's all yours then," he said.

Paul stood in front of me, still damp from the shower. He rubbed the bright yellow towel through this thick wavy hair and then wrapped it around his middle.

I turned and smiled. Paul stepped closer and gave me a look. There he stood, smelling all fresh and clean, whereas I was filled with nothing but dirty thoughts.

He grabbed his toothbrush and squeezed a big dollop of toothpaste. Sometimes I could just lose myself, watching Paul doing the simplest things. I particularly loved the faces he made in the mirror while brushing his teeth: scrunching up his face and squinting his eyes while foaming at the mouth.

I chuckled quietly to myself.

"What?" asked Paul. The bright red toothbrush was sticking out of his mouth.

"Nothing," I said.

Paul shook his head and rolled his eyes at me. Sometimes I wondered if he really knew just how much I loved being with him.

"Aren't you going to take a shower?" he asked.

I shrugged. Paul stepped closer. He wiped his mouth with his forearm.

"You know, I could go in a little late," he said.

"I know," I said, gulping.

I looked quickly at Paul and then averted my glance.

"You could go in late, too," he said. "Or maybe not at all."

"Yeah, I *could*," I said, knowing that wasn't going to happen. We had played this game before.

A few seconds passed.

"You going to shower, or what?" asked Paul.

"Or what," I said smugly, feeling myself smirk.

Paul dropped the towel and it puddled on the floor around his ankles. He flashed me that smile again and I immediately tented my shorts.

It was a mad dash back to bed. We collapsed in a heap on our old down comforter in a fit of giggles. Paul pulled me close and his lips brushed my cheek.

He pulled back slightly and grinned. "You need to shave," he said.

"You need to shut up and kiss me," I shot back.

Paul pressed his lips to mine and locked his arms around me, pulling me tightly to his slightly damp body. He tasted of peppermint and smelled of Ivory soap. I ran my fingers through his damp hair and kissed him deeper.

We rolled around the bed several times until I was finally able to pin Paul's shoulders to the mattress while repositioning myself on top of him.

We both tried to catch our breath. I sat on top of Paul, just staring into his brown eyes, occasionally catching a glimpse of myself reflected in his pupils. I was smiling. Lately I was always smiling. In a million years I could never have imagined myself so happy. And Paul was the one most responsible.

We had met at a party, introduced by mutual friends who thought we'd be perfect for each other. Had I known I was being set up, I would have stayed home—and suspect Paul would have done the same. He was shy and awkward at first, and I'm sure he sensed my resistance to being set up, but before the end of the evening we were off in a corner totally unaware of the party around us.

The first clumsy date led to the second, the second to a third. Friendship led to familiarity, familiarity to comfort and comfort to closeness, and finally to love.

"You know, I still have to get to work," said Paul.

"So, then… you're just looking for a quickie?" I asked. I rolled off Paul and lay next to him, wrapping my arm around him and snuggling close.

Paul reached over, stuck his hands in my shorts, pulled them down around my butt and then finally off before depositing them on the floor. He laughed and I kissed him again. Paul pulled me close and kissed me harder. As he hugged me tight, I thought just how comfortable my naked body felt pressed against his.

I noticed Paul watching the alarm clock. I hoped he really wasn't concerned about the time. More often than not, I was the one to instigate our morning romps—he being the "responsible" one. He was the one with the well-paying job that covered the mortgage and most of the bills. I, on the other hand, jumped from retail job to retail job and took a couple of evening classes, hoping I'd be able to figure out what I wanted to do with the rest of my life besides lying in Paul's embrace.

Paul didn't seem to mind that he carried most of the weight when it came to the finances. His friends had told me that he seemed much more at ease since we'd moved in together. Even with that knowledge I sometimes felt guilty about not doing my fair share.

Oh yes, he was a catch, as all my friends constantly reminded me. For one, he was classically handsome with his dark wavy hair and deep brown eyes. Even with the demands of his job he made a point of getting to the gym on the nights I was in class. He didn't have to work too hard to stay in shape either. He played soccer in high school and college and still did occasionally with his friends on weekends.

While Paul kissed me, I ran my fingers across his back and broad shoulders, playing with the drops of water that he hadn't toweled off. I wished that we could spend the entire morning together in bed. It was so rare that we got to do that, given our crazy schedules.

Each kiss left me wanting more, but I knew Paul was pressed for time. I would have to work fast. I began to kiss the nape of his neck and worked my way lower and lower.

When I kissed Paul's shoulder, he closed his eyes and let out a deep breath. I flicked my tongue across his nipples and then continued my way down to his taut belly.

I teased and taunted Paul with my tongue until I knew he couldn't take anymore. When I finally took him into my mouth he sighed. I could feel his entire body relax as his cock got harder.

"Oh, Justin. Don't stop."

I kept on and it wasn't long before Paul was gasping for breath on the verge of coming.

When I knew he was really close, I let up on sucking his dick, took him in my hand and, with a few slight jerks, Paul shot his load all over his belly, groaning "Oh, *fuck…*"

Paul gasped for air a few more times. I sat there and stared at him, happy to know I'd be sending him off to work with a smile on his face.

"What are you grinning about?" he asked.

"Oh, nothing," I said.

Paul repositioned himself on the bed and leaned up against the headboard.

"Your turn," he said.

"You're really going to be late," I reminded.

"Well, I can't leave you like *that*," he said.

I looked down at my erection and chuckled. I could have taken care of the problem myself while Paul cleaned up, but I generally let Paul get his way.

"If you lose your job, don't go blaming me," I said.

"I can get another job."

I rolled my eyes at that comment. Paul loved his job. He was probably the only person I knew who truly enjoyed going to work.

Paul scooted down the bed and positioned himself between my legs. I closed my eyes, lay back down with my head on the pillows and sort of drifted off as Paul went down on me.

As always, there was something about sex with somebody who truly knows me that I really enjoyed. I'd done my share of tricking before meeting Paul but it always left me cold. I'd even made a few failed attempts at relationships, but never found anything close to what I had with Paul. It was like the man could read my mind or sense my every feeling. He knew exactly what I liked, what made me feel so good. I often wondered if he thought the same of me. Perhaps I'll ask him someday.

"Oh shit, that feels great. Don't stop," I groaned.

I opened my eyes and glanced at Paul. He looked up at me and grinned. Our eyes locked. I watched as Paul licked his lips slightly and the corners of his mouth turned up.

"You like that, don't you?" he asked.

He knew I did. Before I could protest one more time, Paul worked his way even lower and I began to squirm.

"Oh stop. I'm getting close," I said.

Paul ignored my pleas and continued to work his magic. I tensed up and thought I was going to lose it. I sucked in a deep breath and tried to relax, not quite ready to come just yet.

I found myself looking around our bedroom, trying to distract myself so it would last. I never told Paul, but I loved it when we got a little carried away in the morning, which more often than not led to his having to rush to work. I loved the idea of Paul sitting at his desk thinking about us together, the same way I tended to get lost in thought while at work.

I focused on a pair of Paul's well-faded jeans that were rolled in a ball at the foot of the bed. He'd dropped them there right before crawling into bed with me the night before. He never put anything in the hamper, the slob. Next to the jeans were a pair of his bright white boxer shorts and a pair of tube socks.

Next, I focused on a photograph of Paul and me that was sitting on top of the dresser, taken while we were on vacation in Palm Springs the year before he asked me to move in with him. Paul was standing behind me, his arms wrapped around my middle with his head nestled on my shoulder. We were both sunburned, but smiling. Years later, I was just as happy, if not more so, than the afternoon that photo was taken.

I got to the point where I was no longer able to hold my orgasm at bay. Paul was making me crazy. I let out a soft groan and felt the familiar wet gush dash across my belly.

Paul gently kissed my shoulder. He then scooted up the bed and lay next to me. He kissed me softly one more time.

We lay there for a few minutes in silence. Paul glanced over at the alarm clock which was ticking away the minutes.

"I'm going to be *so* late," he said.

"I told you."

Paul hopped out of bed and made a dash for the bathroom.

"Just tell them you got stuck in traffic," I said, turning on the radio and fiddling with the dial, trying to catch the traffic report.

"That's what I always tell them," he said. "I guess I should come up with a new excuse."

"You could tell them the truth," I said.

Paul laughed. Although we are both very much "out," I somehow couldn't imagine him telling his boss he was late because he'd been screwing around with his boyfriend.

"Better save me some hot water," I said.

Paul stopped at the bathroom door. He turned and flashed me that smile once again.

"Well, you coming or not?"

THE GENITALS OF GOD
Horehound Stillpoint

I was a noncocksucking wordsmith for a tender while
neither breast-smacking slammer nor ass-venting performer
an unfucking anti-fucked artiste for oh! many moons
i had mythical aspirations
writing poetry that read like… poetry
on a high horse, with wings and shit
in a cool blue sky gliding on puffy clouds
even falling to earth was an iambic piece of work
i was on a soap box to scrub this tongue, cleanse those ears
       wash yesterday's seed from my throat
i was on a mission to turn down the temperatures of hell

a young lady with a voice as clear as god
told me to get back to the cock and balls of the matter
we need to hear what your asshole's been up to (or vice versa)
we need jism, johnsons, and jerkin' chickens
god wants ya to talk about your dick
scar tissue and all
god needs ya to put your peccadilloes on parade
you are god's genitalia
for every guy who thinks cock and balls are ugly
not for airing out in public
       to be shared with the fewest number of people possible
       in the darkest places on earth
the american bedroom—actually an accessory to the closet—
god needs a faggot to wax poetic
about every inch of flesh stretching out
to expound bold as brass about precious nuggets
profound loads: unh hunh
to enlarge upon each peek-a-boo bulge
screwball hair and prickly nerve: woo-hooo

the world's in a jam and all i can think is
       cock and balls to the rescue
we got war and we know it
we're playing with fire

Horehound Stillpoint

the backroom's already full of smoke
we're going to hell and whistling dixie
we got milk dribbling out of our asses
oil spilling out of our pores
it's not much to brag about; it sure ain't poetry
it's all confused together, as it pisses and shoots
oozes and squirts
the root, the stem, the ground and the dew
my cross, my heart, the issue of my issues
my captain, my ride, the singer and the song,
the only muscle i've ever whipped into perfect shape
cock and balls, not to coin a phrase or anything but
pull it out and give it to me
you have no idea how much i need it
i need it like bush and cheney need war
            to define me, to bolster ego, to buttress courage
i wish we could all just blow each other
why can't we all just blow each other

send me to iraq
i won't blow 'em away, i'll just blow 'em
teach the fine points of fellating stiff young military forces
show them the holiest of wars
is not being fought in heaven
is not being fought down here on earth
the war is in our skins, behind our blood, beneath the bone
in the infinite field of cock and balls
and clits and ovaries just as much
(though that is someone else's poetry)
you can hardly believe how much i need my sex
i need it like osama needs scripture
i need it like saddam hussein needs an enemy
            to distinguish me, to deliver me, to justify everything
i need it like madonna needs exposure
i need it like zz top needs beards
i need it like bowie needs style
it's my thing and i'm not letting go
i need it like mozart needed notes
give me something to hang onto
get me out of my own little pool of consciousness
i'm so sick of this particular pool of consciousness
the same old well of repetitive stupidity and humiliation
only talent i've ever had is for accidental public humiliation

thank heaven i'm not a performer
who demands audience participation
if i were a guy who demanded audience participation
i would tell ya: now is an excellent time to get hard
we know we're going to war, so get hard
everything is beautifully fucked up, it's a miracle, we still get hard
armageddon's been around the corner since i was born...
getting hard yet baby?
the next generation is being born with logos on their foreheads
          you know that's getting somebody hard
this whole country is big and dumb and full of backed up cum
          and yes it makes me hard
our bodies are drowning in poisons
it's copasetic so long as we are hard
we can't even imagine a revolution without getting hard
truth's piss, sincerity's spit, honesty's dumped for a third rate fart joke
don't you wish i had one now but i don't, so fuck it, let's get hard

put your hands wherever you want
put your hands all over yourselves
push your tits up
pull your tits out
work that saliva on those nipples
smother me with your breast honey
mother me with your milk duds
i need your chiseled this and floppy that
suffocate me with your memories of go go goodness
i need everybody in the room to love me and i'm not kidding
it's the only thing that can make this world supportable
i need your underwear above all
i need to see your underwear
your bulges make life bearable
gimme anything you got to give
it's no joke how much i need your underwear
cock and balls in full cotton candy glory
that's my lifesaver, my life jacket, my raft in turbulent waters
this individual pool of consciousness is definitely going down

talk talk i am nothing but talk
i would never stick my hand inside my own pants
not in this room full of brains
i might accidentally humiliate myself
i would never unzip my zipper and pull it out

49

Horehound Stillpoint

it'd be so much more fun if you did it
you can be my ticket to ride on those hot rails to hell
be my ac/dc transformer plugging us in
to the electric fucking cirque du cock and balls
we can still get out of this shit by getting into it
the aladdin cranial overlord, master of darkness and danger
not exactly s&m, just good old rock 'n' roll
with a beautiful david, some powerful apollo
another wickedly angelic michael
in a slippery moonlit moment on the road of excess
i rode my bike, but if you can fit us in
you can take me home
                use all the horsepower you got
use your vehicle, use your path, use me, use ideas
use every muscle, bone, and emotion available
use your tongue, use spit, use lips, use words
talk to me, for fuck's sake
talk to me with everything you've got

it's not a matter of having actual cock and balls goddammit
cause girls have been better at this lately than the guys
the new tranny boys, jesus christ
                they got more cock n balls than you can spit at
                throughout a week of barhopping in the castro
i don't know maybe i was a woman in my last 100 lifetimes
maybe i'm moving in that direction for the next 100
cause you all have so much of what i want
so much of what i want to believe is in me
women have everything, everything i want
except for the old school cocks and balls of which
                i cannot get enough
i could die a happy man if i could just find
                an infinite field of cock and balls
and i'm not talking about blow buddies
nor the power exchange nor the back rooms
                of the powerhouse and my place
we enter those places piecemeal
we enter those places fronting and representing
we enter those places for power and control
for getting over, for getting off
for getting back to the graces of animal darkness
i could waft such a sigh in my fluttering hanky
if i were just a tad less butch

*

my intended is a field of cock and balls full of laughter
lengthy one-liners, low-slung jokes
amazingly plump packages
jackinnaboxes that jump out of their skin
in ticklish moments, with momentous veins
a whole field of cock and balls
        wrapped inside the most sensational speedos
wet and warm, hugging and practically transparent
the softest skimpiest briefs
warm and comfortable, with the cutest stains
        and practically transparent
jockstraps on top of jockstraps on top of jockstraps
damp, stretched out, and naturally practically transparent
the jockstrap is holy…
the jockstrap is one hundred percent nothing if not holy
alan ginsberg forgot that one in his footnote to 'howl'
at least patti smith doesn't quote him as saying that in her 'spell'
i can't be bothered reading alan ginsberg's footnotes
those old beat poets never did shit for me

there is not one cool bone in my body
my nerves are on fire one hundred percent of the time
i've got no heart of darkness and no idea what i'm doing
i wear my queerness on my sleeve
i'm afraid of everyone and everything
everything is a really big deal to me
i don't know nothing about nothing
except the pleasures of cock and balls
thus pleasure plus dullness = sin
sin plus dullness = addiction, cha cha cha
if i have to bring us down, i will bring us down
        to the cock and balls of the matter
namely—don't get excited; it is just a metaphor—
sometimes i really do feel like the genitals of god
squeezing me, hard
pumping me, whipping me into a frenzy
tickling me past the point of mercy
fingering me to the height of exhaustion
forcing me to shoot my shot when i don't know what's what
shaking me dry
and hanging me out for a giggle
then every so often, feeling so warm and safe

Horehound Stillpoint

loved and taken care of
i burst with joy, smearing my kiss across the body of the universe
        and loving… just loving it
well how else can god play with himself but through us
if i slide, at least i will slide down the shaft of what i know
if i lie or overstate my case, don't be surprised
i am full of cock and balls

here's how full of shit i am: i'm really an ass man
i'd rather eat sticky buns than anything in the world
how's that for a footnote
forget everything i said and get your ass over here
i'm hungry
i'm hard
i'm sick of heart
i'm 50 years old and almost human
i'm busting out of my jeans
i am the genitals of god (and it's not a metaphor)
i'm not that easy to live with
i'm a holy terror in the sack… but in a nice way
i'm clean and fluffy and utterly, miraculously, void

i'm self absorbed to the point of parody
i'm self absorbed to the point of enlightenment
what i am is nothing that can be described
and nothing else is worth talking about
i'm constantly focused on the fig leaf in the garden of Eden
        that which covers the truth
        safeguards nothing, and misleads in the extreme
        war poverty disease and plague
        filling the universe of my dreams
        i practically never wake up
i'm wondering if we'll ever stop chasing our tails into the grave
i'm worried about the future because i know i'll be there
i'm not even a footnote in history
i'm worth saving anyhow
i'm a bottom who crossed over and became a top
i'm a woman more than content to pass as a man
i'm not hard, i'm not even soft
nor liquid slippery nor cloud-light nor thought subtle
I'm simpler and purer than that
I'm yesterday's poetry on a tranny boy's refrigerator
I'm happy as a clam for a day and a half

I'm wondering how much of this will leak out
      on the moment of my death
will it seem like the bluest joke in the world:
well, i'll be! god used me to cum in his eye
laughing so fucking hard, tears wash away the sting
as a hallelujah chorus dribbles into the slow, black, night

FOOTNOTE TO AN EX

so an ex-boyfriend calls, getting all angry about our stalled vacation
he starts shouting at me, accusingly
"where is your freedom?"
"when do you get to see god?"
i don't want to argue so i don't say
i see nothing but god wherever i look
not just sky and clouds, brooks and oceans, trees and grassy fields
not just opera and jackson pollack is god
the damned are god, cramps are god
cellphones are not the antichrist
manmade viruses are not manmade and synthetics are not unnatural
not just rock is god
but sidewalks, cracks in the sidewalk, crack
crack pipes are god, needles are god, hookers are god, johns are god
vice squads are god, uniforms are god, donuts are god, fat is god
rich bastards are god, stinky cigars are god
black and white stretch suv's are god
wrinkles are god, saggy tits are god
dirty cheap brown rugs are god
harmless medicine is god, valencia is god
how i learned to snap! is god
the matrix is god, the ring is god, the sword is god, guns are god
bullets are god, blood is god, pain is god, loss is god, denial is god
email is god, trashy chat rooms are god
      fatgaycocks.com is god
      my sex addiction is god
      otherwise it wouldn't be addictive
nothing nowhere is not in its essence god
but how do you say this to an ex, except in a desert
under stars, miles from cynicism
in the period of the new moon
where time can unwind and make space
for a whiff and a puff of the divine

FOOTNOTE FOR THE Y

you there, with the flesh and the thing and the stuff
when god commands: cock and balls to the rescue!
do not think this means anyone but you
only you can save that ass by tearing it apart
eat everything that sits on your face
take what you want and to hell with resting
my only regret is that i have but one life with which to fuck up
my only regret is that after a million million million lives
i still hardly ever remember
it's always the same
man or woman, rotten or pure, corrupted or lilywhite
queenly king or surfboy punk
royal slut or hellacious diva
only you can save this mouth by coming down a throat
there's only you and no one else
only you to unwrap this package
only you to send it back, back to big bang wholeness
only you to tickle and tease the child
            from under sheets of shame and pressure
only you to keep me burning with hope
don't just seize the day
seize my cock and balls
take them hold them own them
i give it all to you, only you
i dedicate all my comings and goings to you
ejaculations to you!
fall-on-my-knees to you!
all my little deaths to you!
goddamn, good lord, you don't mind keeping me waiting
a trillion trillion years until i can rest
i am holding on and still
i am holding on to you
on my cock and balls i thus swear

ISHTA DEVATAA
Ron Jackson

I swore my sandals left the floor of the elevator as it lurched downward. Not that I'm a cursing man, but even the better four-star hotels in Mumbai were prone to mishap, I thought in a flush of panic. I white-knuckled the rail and issued a sigh and a silent prayer: Please please *please* just grant me the grace to hang on until my flight tomorrow, back to the States.

Another half-floor drop—I could barely hold on. Careening between, awash in, and edging away from tears for the past three days, I had left that glaring-sun morning, with virtually everything I owned packed in two suitcases, including the "Dear Ron" letter that had arrived on my birthday. My world was disintegrating under my feet and I longed for someone with whom I could unburden my heart's secrets—yet my shame kept me from asking a soul alive for advice or succor.

Two years earlier, Sriji had instructed me to save money to spend six months with him in India. I was working at a low-paying job, struggling to save the money when I met, fell in love, and moved in with Jerry, who bravely supported my efforts, knowing I'd eventually have to leave him and travel halfway around the world to fulfill my spiritual obligation.

When I left for India, I knew I couldn't expect Jerry to remain abstinent, as I expected of myself, but felt secure in our bond of love. For four months there, I meditated and studied and practiced yoga, worked in the gardens and lost fifteen pounds.

Jerry's long letters, filled with detailed, amorous descriptions, inflamed and embarrassed me. On the nights after I'd received his letters, I awoke to find myself grappling with my steel-hard manhood, my blood boiling, on the verge of losing control. But I managed to catch myself in time, squeezing around the base of my bloated erection and churning balls in order to retain the precious semen, a retention we were taught was fundamental to advancing in meditation. It was true, I think—I could feel the energy going straight to *sahasrara*, at the crown of my head, as I struggled with my engorged sex, willing the monster to wilt. I dared not respond to Jerry in kind and tell him how I longed so deeply for the hot touch of his hirsute flesh, his tongue swimming in my mouth, his fat love-stick buried deep in my ass. So I returned very sweet, polite letters, avoiding the topic of sex entirely. I could barely control my own lust, let alone manage his.

So perhaps I shouldn't have been surprised when Jerry's birthday card arrived, informing me that not only had he fallen in love with another man, but that the guy had moved in with him. I certainly didn't expect Jerry not to have sex with anyone, but to leave me half a world away without a home to return to was beyond comprehension. My heart broke and rebroke a thousand times that day, yet I dared not approach Sriji, who was in silence that month, or the orange-clad swamis, or any of the other senior students for comfort; to the miniscule extent that the ashram acknowledged sexual awareness, it was flat-out hetero.

Inconsolable with despair, I decided to return home two months early. I left the ashram quickly the next day, choking on the stupid heart stuck in my throat, and as I watched the sacred, squalid countryside pass safely away on the other side of the taxi's windows, held on for the sweaty, bumpy taxi ride, one-hundred interminable kilometers to the airport hotel.

Still in shock, I dropped my bags inside my eighth-story room. It struck me that I had no plan of action other than to board a plane in twenty-four hours. Had I eaten since the letter arrived? A drowning wave of emptiness threatened to catch up with me, but I fought it off. A good meal and a cold bottle of Singha beer seemed the most sensible way to get through the evening. In the loo I splashed off the first layer of grit on my weathered skin, eyes avoiding the mirror, and headed downstairs.

I stepped into the ancient, rickety elevator and pressed the lobby button. The chamber jerked and rattled on its cables as it dropped rapidly two floors at a time—typical Indian mechanical efficiency—and I considered the bumbling irony of dying there.

The elevator doors banged open at the second floor and, rather than risk the final drop, I launched myself out before the machine could swallow me again. I felt the breath knocked out of my chest and the flash of my head-banging impact into another person before I actually saw him. We collided so hard that we rolled over each other several times before coming to a full stop in a pile on the red-patterned carpeting, him atop me. Galaxies swirled in a jazzy axis around his head before his face came into focus.

He was a handsome middle-aged Indian businessman with deep-set black eyes and a pronounced temple. His trimmed beard outlined a short, squarish jaw and ran up into a thick head of hair—jet-black with flecks of gray throughout. His skin looked the texture of poured milk chocolate layered with fine dark chocolate jimmies. His lips made me want to cry, I wanted so badly to kiss them. He looked intensely into my eyes, piercing my soul like a laser cutting through glass.

Darshan means, "to have the spiritual vision of," and I was experiencing the *darshan* of this stranger, just as he was apparently viewing me. I was truly *seeing* him, and immediately sensed that he knew me from the inside—knew my sadness, my desire, my journey—perhaps better than I knew myself. A rush of feelings flooded my throat and threatened to choke me.

I gasped at the realization that this was the first time in four months anyone had held me. A wail of immense proportions of pain, larger than my throat and lungs and heart, borne from the pit of my soul, began as a low-pitched spattering of rain and quickly mounted into a monsoon of raw emotion—tears washing my eyes completely. Although barely aware I was causing a small commotion among several guests emerging from their rooms, I heard the man's voice, speaking to them in a velvet Marathi dialect, as he gathered me from the floor like a pile of wet laundry.

With one arm wound tightly around my waist, he guided me down the hall. I had little or no idea what was transpiring, but felt as if I'd fallen from my boundless grief into the warm succor of a dream, into the solace of my handsome friend's body next to mine.

In Hinduism, *Ishta Devataa* refers to one's chosen deity—not unlike the patron saint concept—but it also means one's personal savior. If a person in dire need approaches another and requests refuge in him, the *Ishta Devataa* cannot refuse to offer his care and consolation.

We entered a room and I stumbled forward into its darkness. I knew better than to enter a stranger's room, but I could scarcely bring myself to care for my own physical welfare. I collapsed face-forward onto the bed, where I allowed my hot tears to scald the cool, cotton sheets. Silently my host locked the door, removed both our sandals, lit incense and candles, and adjusted the A/C. He then stepped into the bathroom and ran some water before quickly reappearing. He then gently moved onto the bed next to me and applied a cool, damp towel to my neck and temples.

His silence consoled me as my dramatic cascade of shame turned tide. As slowly as the moon changes phases, my breathing became regular, at which time he gently turned me on my side to face him. Tissues appeared in my hand and I blew my nose, unexpectedly breathing in the tangy musk of *khus* oil. Gradually my blinking eyes cleared, and only then did the gravity of love I was requested to bear become apparent in his adoring, onyx eyes. Probing them deeply, I searched for the reason behind his kindness and found it when I heard his voice, speaking within my mind:

You are my tender child and deserve the deepest love.

I knew there was no need to explain my sorrow or situation, no need to speak at all.

We lay facing one another on the flat expanse of dun- and beige-colored sheets. For the first time I noticed his powder-blue, button-down Oxford, the tuft of chest hair the clean, white t-shirt worn beneath it could not completely conceal, his neatly pressed khakis, worn without a belt. It was hard to tell from my horizontal perspective, but he seemed of average height and weight, certainly better fed than most.

We held each other's tender gaze. Chamois-soft hands stroked my cheek, his right thumb, with its neatly trimmed nail, positioned just below my left eye. Imagining that I could graph the whorls of his thumbprint onto my skin, I meticulously studied his face in an attempt to absorb each and every cell simultaneously. Perhaps he was searching for an imperfection, some flaw that would excuse me from releasing the full dominion of my heart, but he gazed into my eyes with such passionate sweetness that my confidence was restored a hundredfold.

My groin stirred from the telepathic "wake up!" messages to my neglected sex. A fist of fear clenched its knuckles in my chest. I hesitated to allow myself to be fully sexual with this stranger—surely he would break my already fractured heart all over again, just as it began to creak open.

In answer, he placed his left hand on my heart and I felt a dusting of trust sweep over me. I inhaled and absorbed its new strength. We pressed together gently, not yet embracing, though I could feel the heat of his hardness glowing through our pants.

With the subtlest dip of his eyes, he indicated that we undress. With eyes still locked, we somehow managed to remove our clothes lying side by side. His skin proved a soft expanse of dark terrain, over which was planted a uniformly short crop of black hair, except between his prominent, purplish nipples, where the hair whorled out thickly. Though well toned, his body was not particularly muscular, and I resisted the temptation to drop my eyes as his white cotton shorts fell away. Once naked and holding hands, my eyes once again filled with tears. He paused in patience, stroking my temples and hair, instilling me with courage, until my weeping ceased.

At last, delicately holding my head as if handling a precious antiquity, he drew my lips to his—his sweet-tasting breath enlarging my lungs and chest and mind. He brushed his lips lightly yet repeatedly against mine and held my gaze steady as I prepared myself for whatever might happen.

After several minutes of kissing in silence, save for the increasing intensity of our breathing, his eyes took on a determined demeanor. I signaled my readiness to continue. With a rainwater-soft touch, yet not at all tentative, he gradually enveloped me loosely in his arms. He kissed and pressed and kneaded my willing body with his magical touch. His wet sex brushed and bobbed around my navel, and mine responded in kind along and against and in between his and my hairy bellies. He planted small kisses with his lips and thick beard all over my face and neck while massaging my back—pulling us deeper together, his wet, smooth snake slid halfway between my slender thighs like a reptile slithering up to its prey, until his glans hovered deliciously near my crack.

He rolled me on top and pleasure rippled through me as full body contact intermingled our chest hair and beards, his straight-standing *lingam* becoming my hanging-peg. The erotic lubrication of his wetness and our sweat spread between our bodies, further inflaming my passion.

A playful grin crept over his bearded face. He pushed me up and off his chest and blew a miraculous stream of marigold-scented breath across my chest. My nipples ached and my head arched back in delight. I'd been oozing too and noticed a small, hazy puddle in his hairy navel.

His palms hovered over my nips, emanating heat that seemed to singe my chest hair and irradiate my skin. He then placed his thumbs on my lips and rubbed them lightly before slipping them together into my mouth. Coating them with thick saliva, I gurgle-sucked them onto the back of my tongue as if they were my dinner, tasting as they did, of *khus*, curry, and my own musky perspiration,

He withdrew his thumbs from my mouth and, relocating them to my nipples, replaced them with his tongue—his look of delight turned teasing. He kissed and fluttered and wetted the hair surrounding our mouths before entering softly, then he would dance his tongue outside my mouth again, then dart back in, probing a little deeper each time.

His hard maleness remained positioned between my legs. Although dripping steadily, he did not thrust it at all. Instead, he began to orbit my nipples with the balls of his thumbs. Not just in circles, it seemed, but a peculiar coiling pattern that spiraled, in three and one half revolutions, from the outer rim of my sensitive aureoles to the hardened nubs, before spiraling centrifugally out, in the opposite direction, employing the same number of orbits, before starting over. He utilized a very slight but constant pressure that caused my tongue to loll from my moaning mouth like a panting dog's, which proved convenient for him to rewet his thumbs as needed. For perhaps half an hour or more, he attended to my chest—occasionally licking my tongue—until my nipples jutted proudly pink and hard. My cock dribbled a steady overflow of precum into his belly button that soon ran up to his sternum and off his sides.

His ability to stay rigid, as yet unthrust and untouched between my legs, amazed and tantalized me. The hot proximity of his glans tickled my ass hairs, and I pined to be filled with him. As he worked my chest, my sphincter clenched and unclenched with involuntary anticipation of swallowing his purple-headed rod, yet he remained impassive, refusing to move his torso even a centimeter toward my gratification. While circling his thumbs on my engorged nipples, his hands held my chest in place. Even more compelling, his hypnotic eyes, pouring passion into mine, completely arrested my ability to straddle him, as my breath came in short gasps.

After agitating my nipples near to bursting, he slowed and then discontinued the circling pattern and rested his thumbs on my pulsing buds. He was changing the pace for some reason, and wordlessly, yet in consternation, I searched his eyes, which had narrowed somewhat, for a reason why. Had I done something wrong? Didn't he want to fuck me? Hard? What needed to change?

I slowly understood that he was waiting for me to gain control of my emotions, that I was too eager, too needy, too ready to surrender to him, that he needed me to be completely present with him when he entered me. I was anticipating his moves and trying too hard to please him—just as I tried to please everyone, physically as well as emotionally and spiritually. It was time to recognize the truth: I'd allowed far too many people to take power over me.

Now was the time to grow up and become a man, rather than remain a greedy kid set loose in a candy shop.

I willed myself to quiet my hole, but it wasn't easy. My butt had long had a mind of its own, and for a few minutes continued to lurch toward his hardness. Moving into meditation, I slowed my breathing and allowed my cheeks to relax. My friend smiled encouragingly and blew cool air over my body. When I eventually relaxed without clenching at all, he beamed approvingly, his pearly teeth a stark contrast with his dark lips and beard. Once again I lost myself in his compassionate, raven gaze as he pulled me closer and mischief entered his eyes.

He placed his hands on the back of my thighs and grazed the hair with his fingertips, making it stand on end. He then began stroking the flesh beneath with the flat of his palms as, very gently yet firmly, without moving my torso from against his, he opened my legs so that they straddled his hips. Cool air instantly caressed the very damp skin all along my crotch and inner thighs, where the hard, burning length of his cock remained arched against my hairy crack.

He allowed my legs to stretch and become accustomed to this new position while gliding his hands all over them—down my calves to my ankles, up to the small of my back, then gently cupping my tight, muscular mounds. He took a deep breath, reminding me to breathe with him, and our hearts pulsed in unison.

I reveled in the most peculiar and wonderful sexual sensations. His marvelous, long and slender sex, locked hard between my upper thighs—for hours it seemed—now began to *vibrate*. Not that he was moving his pelvis in the least, but… his cock began tickling my butt hairs, began wiggling slightly, as if animatronic. Very gradually, a millimeter at a time, the mushroom head increasingly stirred and moved in most amazing ways, first side to side before it then, fantastically, began scribing wet circles around the perimeter.

I gasped as he maneuvered his cock with the utmost dexterity, his look telling me to maintain our simultaneous breathing and refrain from the impulse to grab at him. It felt as if a large, plum-headed finger were stimulating my ass, wriggling and twisting and burrowing inward.

Gently raising my legs until I was nearly kneeling astride him—my nipples still poking his—my rectum throbbed and salivated with desire. The control he maintained over his manhood was so deliberately exerted that he was able to wave it back and forth across the surface of my ass-gutter like a velvet windshield wiper, *without moving his body*. When, after several minutes of gentle nuzzling, caressing, and teasing, I felt the tip of his erection burrowing up and down my crack, I realized that I had literally run into a tantric snake charmer of the highest possible caliber!

The entire time his joystick danced over my backside, he lovingly smiled at me—his lips perhaps an inch from mine—while breathing his pleasure into me and monitoring my inner state. I'd never spent so much time staring directly at someone, and became aware that I'd entered a state of meditation where nothing existed beyond our lovemaking. The rawness of the hunger in my ass completely dissolved and I felt sublimely at peace. We could lay meshed together forever and I would not have noticed the hours and days and years passing.

Breathing deeply, I felt his manhead tapping at the entrance of my deepest desire. His eyes widened, indicating that the time had come. Several drops of his nectar fell directly into my already drizzled opening before his glans, as if of its own accord, lodged into my portal. In response to his removing his hands from my backside and intertwining them with my trembling fingers, I surrendered not only my sphincter muscles, but my *self* to his entry.

The head slid effortlessly just inside my asslips, then held steady, lodged there for several minutes, while his soft beard and lips brushed mine. I nearly cried with joy, but his loving look told me that the best was yet to come, so I checked my tide of emotions as his juicing glans throbbed ever-so-slightly deeper inside me. He did not push with his pelvis but made his cock twinge in a way that sent gentle waves of pleasure up my spine.

His tongue probed into my mouth and I let it dance there, gently sucking. When he withdrew his tongue, I understood his silent cue. After taking in several extra-deep breaths together, I gently began applying the same suctioning action to my inner chamber as his cock eased into me like a reptile slipping into its underground lair. About halfway penetrated (by my best reckoning), he stopped advancing and began to throb his glans again, in mid-canal, shooting small ripples of delight that ricocheted throughout my entire being as I rested.

My flesh felt vastly opened, seemed merely a shell that encased an immense, blue sky, as if my Ishta Devataa could insert his entire body into mine and fill me entirely and yet still not fill me entirely. His tongue slithered over mine like a water serpent on a lily pad, then edged deeper into my mouth, where we engaged in oral mating rituals at the entrance of my throat.

He lowered his eyes almost imperceptibly and I resumed the slow suction of his manhood up my chute, his pisshole issuing warm increments of natural lubrication as it slid deep inside me. When the last inch of cock had entered my guts, I paused and he pulsed again, whereupon I heard a high-pitched hum in my head, like a hive full of buzzing of bees or a concert of violoncellos.

His cockhead vibrated, just a bit at first, but then I felt a much stronger undulation vibrate from that point down through the upper part of his shaft and move down its length, humming along my prostate on the way down to the base of his cock, which had yet to grind against my gaping anal ring. The sensation was unbelievable, like one of those heated, pulsing, vibrating chair backs— except this was living man-flesh, massaging the entire length of my lower rectal cavity!

He unclasped his fingers from mine and placed my hands on his mid-back, then his on my shoulder blades, kneading and gently adjusting my posture. He stopped vibrating his cock and we lay very still for a long while. I was expecting him to begin fucking in and out, but he thrust his tongue further toward the back of my throat instead, impaling my mouth heavily but leaving plenty of room for me to breathe. He slyly wiggled the tip of his tongue toward the very back of my palate, where I had to suppress a gag-induced giggle.

He subtly lowered his eyes again, directing me to continue where I'd left off. I couldn't imagine there was much left of his cock I hadn't taken in, but did as he desired and resumed the inner-ass suction of his meat, slowly inhaling the last inch, until at last I felt the hair from his nutsac bristle against, and then intermingle with, my butthair. His cock hadn't seemed abnormally long when resting between my thighs, but I was positive it had passed beneath my navel, well into the area behind my ribcage. I scarcely believed it physically possible to accommodate such extremes of a man's sexual penetration, from both ends no less, but I continued to breathe through any discomfort, and in no time felt myself floating on this great ship of a lover, gently rocking above him as waves of ecstasy passed through his body into mine.

My magical snake charmer began vibrating inside me again, but much more intensely than before. Passing his vibe down the length of his cock, from oozing tip to his furry balls, which lay heavily pressed against my crotch, and then back again, his entire sex organ pulsated in sync with our labored breathing. I had thought his cock rather slender—how else could I have managed to take it all?—but I suddenly felt it thicken at the base, pressing deliciously against my prostate. With our every pulsing intake of breath, the root of his magnificent organ stretched my asslips wider.

Although his torso remained motionless other than his deep rhythmic breathing, miraculously, the midsection of his joystick began throbbing and swelling with blood, eventually matching the circumference of the base. Feeling like a beer bottle had been rolled up my chute, I grew rapidly delirious with the bliss derived from his incredible, oscillating cock.

Once I'd grown accustomed to the new thickness, he resumed the throbbing expansion of his monster organ up the shaft to the corona. I almost passed out from the sheer volume and pressure ballooning within me. I was rapid-breathing almost to the point of hyperventilation, yet wouldn't have cared if my intestines or lungs or heart burst. My entire being had become a symbiotic extension of his body. I say "his" and "mine" only to approximate a differential between the actions of two separate human beings here, but at the time I felt no delineation between us whatsoever.

Yet there remained more to open up to, to let go of, to surrender to this man who had reached so far inside me—into places I thought I'd never allow anyone to touch ever again—as his luminous, black-shining eyes implored me to yield even further. Although firmly impaled on his massive cockstand, I felt his cock*head* move independently, stirring deep in the center of my guts, as if nudging at my very heart. Completely liberated from concern for this shell I thought of as "myself" or "this body," I could actually feel his masterful organ licking my heart like a lioness lapping her wounded cub. Although he betrayed no sign of an orgasm, I received the distinct sensation that his cocklips were exuding a healing salve, secreting a suprasexual saliva from his soul through his manhood that spread like liquid salvation around my heart.

His glans finally expanded and extended until it matched the rest of the pulsing, oversized phallus boring into my very core, which utterly filled and energized every tingling molecule of my being. His breathing slowed and I matched his inhalation and exhalation and, as it slowed, his entire tool deflated slowly, a quarter inch at a time, until it returned to its previous slender girth, yet still extended far into me. My inner chamber felt suddenly collapsed and abandoned, became a void that threatened to unbalance my newfound and extraordinary sense of fulfillment.

I looked at him in bewilderment, but before I could even blink in protest, he thickened again in huge, whooshing pulsations that took my breath away. With complete control, he held me thickly impaled for a moment before deflating again, much like a water balloon filling and emptying over and over again, during which glorious time I came to understand that he did not thrust his penis like an ordinary man, but rather, had attained such amazing self-control over his powerful fucktool, he could engorge and disgorge it with the same rapidity that most men work the old in-and-out routine. In either case, it was inconceivable that he could have entered any deeper into the nether regions of my vital organs, and so, adjusting to the unique rhythm of that mind-blowing, tantric masterfuck, I rode him, expanding and contracting my chute.

Just when I thought I'd become acclimated to that new action, I felt something different churning my insides. All at once he began twisting his bone like a corkscrew as it grew and thinned, first in one direction and then the opposite—yet his loins remained relatively stable, proving a solid root upon which his magic muscle rotated. Every nerve cell in my overstretched anus was spiraling with sensual delight and soon becoming insensible, my eyes rolled up like a madman's.

By then his talented tongue was tickling my back palate, but he unexpectedly withdrew it somewhat and, lifting my body slightly, drew me away from his torso. Although it was true that I'd reached a point where I doubted if I could endure the intensity of our extraordinary lovemaking, I couldn't bear to think of the exquisite sensations ending.

I hadn't attended at all to my own cock during the hours he'd been tunneling my bowels but, lifted away from him, I could see that I was not only still raging-hard, but leaking copiously, having completely slicked his chest hair flat with my ooze and sweat, the musky scent of which made my head spin as he lovingly but firmly pinched my nipples for quite some time.

Without warning, he stopped twisting inside of me, and resting his cock in a relatively deflated state, grabbed me behind the knees and rolled us both over, still firmly skewered, onto my back. I quivered and cried out in sweet surprise, in complete awe of his mastery over the art of love: always the perfect, unexpected move.

We held perfectly still and allowed our postures and breathing to readjust, his uninterrupted penetration of me, suddenly perceived from beneath him, evoking an entirely different panoply of erotic sensations, which revitalized a whole new region of my innards.

I felt my heartbeat and his pulsing member throb in unison, as if one organ. If his manhood were the least bit longer, would it stab, and then extricate my heart, skewered on his mushroom head? His eyes burned fiercely into mine with godly intensity, rupturing my emotional core. He had reached through endless pain and touched a golden star. I felt fleshless, as if I consisted entirely of fluid, had become a lake in a windless valley, beneath the most magnificent of mountains.

I hardly had to wait to discover what thrilling new contortions he would will his manmuscle to perform. His organ thickened at the base, pulsed, then the thick band of girth bubbled up its length, filling his glans to the size of a hardball. The distended cockhead then returned to normal size as the base reinflated and once again rolled up his prong. The feeling was unimaginably pleasurable. He'd removed his tongue from my mouth, so I could have articulated my joy, had I been able to find words to do so, but all I could do was babble in time with his repeated pulse-thrusts and drool like an infant.

I felt weak from the hours of lovemaking and found my eyeballs rolling upward again in search of rest. Sensing my fatigue, he slowed his pulses, grabbed my chest hair with both hands, encouraged me up, and slipped his legs into a cross-legged position beneath me. I then wrapped my legs around his lower back, and we locked into the classic Shiva–Shakti coital position. Although we were both sweat-soaked, he looked as if he could continue endlessly. With fatherly attention and a slightly determined air furrowing his eyebrows, he drew me in again, into a heavy kiss, his cardamom-flavored tongue playing over mine, then curling to the back of my throat.

As he resumed throbbing his masterful bone, pillared straight up into my burning bowels, my own organ, which had softened somewhat, reenergized all over again. The sweat dripping from our beards onto my meat, I resumed squeezing my channel around his root and, for the first time, we began to move our pelvises together. Actually, he didn't *move* so much as draw his heavy ballsac tightly up against my entrance while I sucked and milked his lingam with every remaining ounce of strength I possessed.

His potent desire enveloped my thoughts and subsumed my will into his. Each expanding throb shot up the length of his magnificent sex to its crown and bumped my heart, causing waves of love to permeate my body. These vibrations came faster and faster, rippled from the epicenter of my being, and completely washed away all my doubts and feelings of abandonment—my fear of being unloved and unlovable. Although my other senses were totally alive, I found myself unable to remain conscious of my outer surroundings, single-focused as I was upon my contact with his sublime body. I had been using my sphincter muscles to suck him but soon lost control of even that function.

His sex-throbs increased in force and tempo until I thought my inner organs had liquefied, when suddenly it all stopped—whereupon he ever-so-slowly began drawing his entire nutsac upward until it too was fully planted inside me. His already over-bloated manhood began humming, vibrating, further expanding up its entire length to maximum-plus density. When he exploded inside me, I released and imploded around him, as we merged in a brilliant blaze of white light collapsing toward a pinpoint.

The image of a diminutive consort impaled upon an impossibly massive Shiva godhead floated in my mind, and I mentally performed abhishek—the ritual bathing of the Deva—allowing the blood of my punctured heart to wash over his lingam as an offering, my last karma in this lifetime. My nipples were red chrysanthemums on the puja tray; my eyes were the flames of the Self, my chosen deity; my hair was the rice symbolic of fertility; my reddened lips became fragrant kumkum powder; my unconditional love was the brilliant, gold, dakshina offering.

I awoke in *shavasana,* corpse pose, in my own hotel bed, soaked with midday-heat sweat, fully clothed. I checked the clock: my flight was scheduled to leave in exactly four hours. I must have crashed straight off, I thought, and slept through the night and day.

I knew I'd had vivid, sexual dreams—my shorts were quite soaked through with a rather prominent, wet and sticky spot. But rather than chide myself, as per habit, for my lack of restraint, I shrugged it off, unperturbed.

My mind was tranquil as I climbed out of bed, peed, then drew a bath.

I called room service and ordered breakfast. I stripped, and felt unusually happy, just being naked. I fingered the erotic cream coating my shorts and pooled in my navel, contemplated it, then brought it to my tongue and tasted my pungent potency.

Vague images of some man came to mind. One of those impossibly handsome, bearded, Indian fellows downstairs in the lobby? Who knew…?

I looked at my bags, sitting unopened exactly where I'd dropped them. I opened one, retrieved my toiletries and a fresh outfit, then did some light stretching for several minutes until the bath was full.

Recalling the events that had precipitated my early departure from the ashram, I felt completely removed from the pain those events had caused me, much to my surprise. It was as if a distinct reality of something vital having been torn, horribly and violently, from deep within me had been wholly repaired with only the vaguest impression of sexual release—hazy, like cum floating in water.

I poured a drop of *khus* oil into the steaming bathwater and eased in. I regarded, for a moment, my naked body… my fat, hairy sex bobbing in the water like a floating island… then closed my eyes with satisfaction and let myself float pleasantly away, like an unmoored ballast. Soon I would be back on my feet, walking on the tarmac toward the plane, ready to fly.

WORKING THINGS OUT
Rick Jackson

Iprefer going to a serious gym in LA for my workouts. Most of the guys who go there are gay, so I have been known to meet a new "friend" from time to time, but it's not the sort of place with rental rooms for afternoon trysts and steam rooms spraying more cream than steam. I've nothing against cruiser clubs, mind you, but I don't go to them unless I want to find some quick, meaningless ass to wrap around my big dick. When I go to work out, I go to work out.

That's why the bastard put me in such an awkward position. I don't know how long he'd been using the rowing machine, as I'd only been at the Universals a couple minutes before I noticed him. He was hard to miss. His T-shirt was drenched with the sweat that stippled his entire body in gleaming droplets that made any sane man want to lick him clean. Everybody in the room was sweating, of course, but no one had what this guy did.

Every time he hauled himself forward, his loose-fitting shorts splayed so wide around his massive thighs that I couldn't help noticing his massive advantages. I've seen many a big dick before; I have one myself. More men than I can count have choked on my thick, double-digit inches, but I'd never seen anyone as thickly hung as the vision stroking across from me. The appendage wasn't human. From what I could see, it wasn't much over average length, but more like a can of beans in girth than anything you'd ever consider letting up your ass.

At first I only scoped out the show while resting between reps, but ever so gradually that freak of nature began to seriously prey on my mind. Every rowing stroke of his hard body sent that big-headed snake sneering out at me, teasing me, daring me to slap it down where it belonged. Even from twenty feet away, I knew his stubby shaft was far shorter than mine, but its head ballooned out like some gigantic sci-fi mushroom creature, threatening to take over my brain and ass and, if I weren't very careful, maybe even my heart.

All I could think about was how that monster would feel crammed up my butt—how it would hurt so good, how I would scream as it ripped my guts wide with spine-shattering ecstasy. The irony of this pesky line of thought, however, was… that I'm a confirmed top! I've been fucked maybe five times in my life, total, and each time I'd sworn never to do it again. Even Needledick Dawson— one of the guys who lived in my college dorm and was built like an anorexic tadpole—had managed to rough me up something fierce. So why was I even fantasizing about allowing the rower's revenge near my ass? Was I crazy? Masochistic? Did I have a death wish?

For the next forty-five minutes, I worked alternate muscle groups and did the usual number of sets and reps, but the one muscle that represented the cynosure of my undivided attention wasn't even mine. Consequently, my own dick wouldn't stay down. I wasn't wearing a jock, either. Unable to stand the pressure another second, I had to either leave, or face drawing a crowd, or....

Opting for the last of those options, I grabbed my towel and cruised over to the stud, whom I later learned was, despite appearances, not a Greek god but a UCLA systems administrator named Brad Jensen. He gave me a dimpled point of his chin and a gasping grunt by way of hello, so, placing my right foot up on a nearby bench in order to give him a gawk at my dangle, I whispered that if he was trying to crank up my testosterone flow, he was doing a fine job—that, even if he was just hanging loose, he should at least be aware that he was on display and that I, for one, liked what I saw.

The poor bastard blushed about nine shades of crimson, tossed his towel between his legs, and thanked me for the heads-up—so to speak. He then took a long (again, so to speak) look at my thaang and asked, "You live around here? I'm about done and sure could use a shower."

The gym had plenty of showers. We both knew why he was coming home with me—*for* me, and ultimately inside me. I was glad, naturally, that he'd opted to pop over for a visit; but even as we drove to my place and rode up in elevator, making small talk and exchanging glances along the way, I didn't know whether to quicken my guts in anticipation of a fantasy fulfilled or take the far more sensible course and run screaming into the night.

I offered Brad a beer. After about four swigs he was all over me, fumbling with my shirt and shorts, flinging my sneakers to the four corners as his tongue and lips and hands raped my body with the rough enthusiasm of a satyr desperate to do things right.

I reached low and found two handfuls of hard butt muscle, already grinding and clenching as though they were as starved for dick as I obviously was. When I pulled his hips hard against mine, that can-sized crank threatened mayhem as it molested my own thick dick and balls and belly, effectively mangling any reserve I might still have been affecting.

Brad's body was the dictionary definition of buff—a cobbled mass of writhing muscles, each flowing perfectly into the next like a Michelangelo marble, or more accurately, one of the sweaty, butch models he must have used to inspire all that hot, hard Renaissance passion. Despite having the body of *David*, Brad's face would have been more appropriate on a Velázquez peasant: tanned skin, raven-black hair hanging low over a strong brow, a single, thick eyebrow bristling above obsidian pools of infinite depth, his clean-shaven, blue-bearded cheeks and dimpled chin setting off a full, wide mouth created specifically for wrapping around a man's meat and holding on forever.

As our hips humped and my hands first savaged then worshiped his glutes, I filled my lungs with the harsh scent of his sweat and man-musk. I filled my eyes and mind with his soulful beauty. His beer-slicked lips, parted for pleasure, invited my tongue to visit, so I moved in and made a home for pleasure there. Suddenly I was naked and pulling his clothes off as well, and our hands were everywhere at once.

His body was almost a caricature of perfection, a seamless balance of vulnerability and masculine power. His skin was baby-soft, yet stretched across muscle definition that would inspire WWF contenders' wetdreams of envy. His eyes were hungry and impatient, and although they clearly communicated how much he needed to fuck, they also reflected a reverential awe of my body and a certain shyness at my rejoicing in the wonder of his.

When I slipped my tongue into his ear and pried his hard, hairless glutes wide and happy with my fingers, his body collapsed into cascading shudders of surrender. A gasp of pleasure escaped his lips, faintly at first, but with a growing recognition of how helpless one man can be in the arms of another.

I was careful at first not to go too fast, to polish his clenching glutes with my palms as my fingers danced deftly deeper into that gloriously hairless crack. The more the stud bucked and heaved however, the harder it got for me to keep away from his groping pucker of pink perfection. In the end, he managed to snare the tip of my finger. From that instant, impaling his guts on my hand seemingly became the man's main mission in life.

He threw himself brutally onto my fingers again and again until I surrendered and allowed a knuckle or two to pass up into his ass, where I played about and poked his prostate. But it wasn't until I heard him moan in soulful desperation, "Go ahead. Fuck me. Fuck me hard. I want you to bust that big bone's nut up my ass and make me bleed!" I recognized that we had a problem.

Naturally I'd been aware how hard a time the poor gorgeous bastard would have had handling my gargantuan inches of swollen shank if I tried to shove it up his ass (though I'd come to question that, seeing that I was feeling his silky insides with several of my fingers buried knuckle-deep up his rectum), but I wasn't worried about *his* hard time. Hell, under normal circumstances he could scream and chew the pillows all he wanted. I'd even drive his sorry ass to the emergency room afterwards if he liked.

No, what I'd been worried about all along was what condition *I* would be in after Brad had boned *my* practically-virgin hole to hell and back! I wasn't even sure anything human could *take* a dick that big around; all I knew was that I had to try—when all of a sudden I realized that the son-of-a-bitch didn't even *want* to fuck me. The clueless bastard wanted me to fuck *him*! Shit, with anyone else, I'd have turned anything but tail, but Brad was not just anyone, not just another piece of meat. In one of life's dirty little jokes, here was a guy with a dick so huge and a body so buff and a face so devastating that I wanted him to split my ass open and use me hard—and all the hapless, hulking shit wanted was a taste of the same prodigious number of dick-inches I'd slammed up half the asses in the state.

Stalling a bit more in hopes of coming up with a plan more in keeping with my goal than merely perfecting my foreplay, I pulled my lips and dick away from his, my fingers out of his ass, and wrapped both of my hands around his stubby R2-D2 of a dick. He bucked and pounded between my palms, his blue vein standing out and throbbing like a wandering road to ruin as a constant stream of pre-cummy rheum oozed from his monster's eye and dribbled down my hands. I reached a slick paw down to cup his hairless balls and found them tender and heavy with a load in bad need of being sprayed.

I couldn't begin to take that dick, but *had* to. When I told Brad I'd be happy to fuck him hard—after he had blown a load up my ass—he tried to talk sense into me, but it wasn't sense I *wanted* in me. Fortunately, the guy was young enough to be an eternal optimist and just so happened to have a stash of those mongo, triple-large, super-human, hero-sized rubbers in his gym bag. The bastard was so hard and huge, though, that it took both of us, plus his dick-honey to work one of the bad boys down his bone.

He still thought I was insane as I lay back and spread my legs, and I fucking *knew* I was as I hooked my heels behind Brad's neck and eased my hands around his waist. But I also knew I had no choice in the matter whatsoever. My eyes drifted upwards from the monster cock that was about to cleave me comatose, upwards across his cobbled abs, and past the massive, iron-tipped wet-glistening pecs, upwards past shoulders a Titan would envy and lips so luscious that Aphrodite would have abandoned her Adonis for a single taste of them, further upwards to deliver my soul into the dark keeping of those bottomless and magical eyes.

I waited. Brad looked down at my ass and then at his dick, after which he sunk his eyes back into mine and asked one last time if I was sure. I was sure twice over—sure to the very core of my being that his huge dick was somehow destined to be up my ass, and even more sure that I'd be very, very sorry in the end. I shifted my pucker against the huge head of his shank, loosened up in that pseudo-shitting mode designed to relax a man's sphincter, and hoped for the best.

Oh, Brad did his best all right. He pushed and shoved and hammered his way against my ass, but to no avail. He reached for my shoulders and pulled me down, fighting to force my shithole around his monster. The thing simply would not slide in. I might as well have been trying to fuck myself with a can of chili. He was thick and stubby and just too *con carne* to bring it home. I finally gave up, rolled the fucker onto his back, squatted about a yard off the bed, and dropped my twitching shithole down to its doom and destiny.

I'm not sure whether I passed out completely or just fell backwards between Brad's legs, but I suddenly found myself on my back with my ass in the air, getting packed with every last inch he had, up where it would do the most good. Who knows, I may even have felt his glossy black curly-cues grinding against my glutes for a moment before the billions of shattered nerve endings up my ass remembered who they were pissed at and came after me big time. If the other dicks I'd been dumb enough to allow up my ass had hurt me bad, Brad's was fucking killing me. Pasiphaë herself could not have taken that wide a stretch of wicked manmeat without splitting in two.

A thousand terrors ricocheted back and forth inside my guts like rockets run amok as the tender tissues of my ass were ripped and reamed and riven wide. True, I couldn't feel the pressure very far up, but Aegospotami and Antietam were witty apothegms compared to the savaging I suffered within those first six inches of my ravaged ass. I couldn't scream or breathe or even think. I spurred Brad's butt with my heels, instinctively seated him in my saddle, hung on tight, and hoped for eventual understanding.

To his credit Brad did try to be as gentle as he could while cleaving me like a carp fillet, but my sole salvation was the passing seconds and the wanton perversity wrought of my own pain. The red waves of searing rapture had no sooner swept across the parched landscape of my soul than my brain surrendered to a sweet and sublime fantasy that up was down and pain, pleasure. Brad's bone was just long enough to batter into the last baneful bastion resisting the inevitability of bliss. Holding my shoulders down with his hands as he rammed and slammed and bammed his brutal way against my prostate, as his huge cockhead and stocky shaft ripped me ever wider, as my eyes finally opened and locked into his, our bodies fused together as one and a vortex of violent, frenzied, abject rapture swept us cleanly away until time wove itself inside out and perished in confusion.

Seconds or years later, I surfaced back to life again to discover Brad humping hard over my body as if he were the village cur and I the visiting parson's shin. His bestial snorts and growls and grunts of anguish filled my ears almost as fully as his tongue. My hands reached down his massive, sweat-streaked back to assist my heels in holding me tighter onto the grinding, bucking, twisting tool buried up my butt. Within seconds I felt my unhanded inches detonate, spewing his recently-shaven chest and both our arms and faces with the biggest and best load of my life.

Secure in his arms, still impaled on his demonic dick like some ghastly parody of an auto-da-fé, I could not stop spewing sperm. Even when we were both awash in my slick, creamy seed, my balls continued to pump wad after wad after hot, tangy wad. I opened my mouth to catch some on the fly and accidentally licked Brad's smooth, stunning face as he rode me hard and fast across his own finish line. The seizing of breath and ancient howls of agonized rapture confirmed his good time so I bit down on his neck, as hard as some mating tom, and held him tighter still against my slick body. Locked fore and aft, we rocked in man's oldest rite of revelation until my fount of wisdom finally ceased to overflow and Brad ground and humped and spurted slowly to an end.

71

Rick Jackson

We held each other tight, slick and sweaty, both gasping for air, both hoping we weren't about to awaken from a dream. When at last we each began to believe in what we had just done, in what we had just discovered about life and love and each other, I reached between us and found that my big dick was still as thick and hard and mean as ever. I latexed myself in a flash, flipped Brad backwards onto our bed of sin, and shoved the best time of his life up through his ass and into legend.

The studly man-slut howled and carried on something fierce. I knew I was hurting him like hell, but entire libraries of Dante's *Inferno* couldn't have described what he'd just done to me—or how gloriously I had loved it in the end. Having just spewed enough sperm to reseed the cosmos, I was in no fucking hurry whatsoever and so continued humping his hole and making him scream and beg for me to do him harder and deeper and faster until even the cows had forgotten the way home. By the time I finally busted my second nut of the evening, the throb up my ass had begun to heal and it was time to begin our workout routine all over again.

GEEZERS
Simon Sheppard

"**B**ut honey, he's forty years younger than you are."

"Thirty. Not forty, thirty."

"Thirty, then."

"Not even. He's thirty-three years old."

"Okay, he's *twenty-nine* years younger. So when he gets to be your age…"

"I'll be ninety-one. I know, I already figured."

"*And* he's a goy."

"Shut up and order already. Here comes the waitress… Oh hello, dear. I'll have the mu shu pork."

"Pork?" Bert looked askance at Manny. "*Already* he's a bad influence."

On the way home from the earlybird special at the Mandarin Gardens, Manny thought about it. Him. Garrison Park IV. One evening at the supermarket, Park had struck up a conversation in the checkout line. Just the presence of a younger man in the semi-airless expanses of Delray Beach was a novelty. One who was good-looking and apparently intelligent and had no qualms about approaching a man of Manny's age… well, *he* was a blessing. A miracle, even.

In the beginning, Manny hadn't been sure what Park wanted. When the young man suggested they throw their groceries in their cars and go for a coffee together, Manny began to get an idea. A hope, at least. And then, over two decafs—Manny couldn't tolerate caffeine after mid-afternoon—Garrison Park IV made it all quite explicit.

"I like older men," he said.

Manny had almost choked on his cheese Danish.

"But *this* much older?" was all he could think of to say.

"You're a handsome fella," Park had said, and Manny's cock began to swell beneath the Formica tabletop. "Are you taken?"

Well, *that* was direct.

"I have a partner," Manny found himself saying, "but it's an open relationship." Which was, technically, true. After the first decade or so of their being together, Bert had started seeing other men, barely bothering to cover his tracks. And Manny, to his surprise, hadn't minded much. So each of them had been allowed his flings and fancies, both of them always eventually heading home to their apartment on Manhattan's Upper West Side. And so it endured, the two becoming ever closer and closer, notwithstanding where they chose to put their dicks. Maybe one thing that had always made it work was that, come hell, high water, or handsome hunks, they continued to have sex with each other. Sure, as time took its toll, what had been a youthful mutual passion matured into a tender regard that sometimes ended up in "maintenance sex." But even the maintenance sex was a token of their deep affection. And Bert still gave the best head in the world. As their bodies aged and thickened and gravity did its work, as the hair on their heads grew thinner and the hair elsewhere the opposite, Bert, to Manny's amazement, looked even more beautiful, not less.

When Bert had been young he'd been invited to the Schulmans' fiftieth anniversary party; Len Schulman had been a client of his father's law firm. Bert had played the piano while Manny sang. Then Schulman had made a toast: "To my wife Maxine, the most beautiful girl in the world." At the time, Manny had stared at the shrunken little old woman, all wrinkles, creases, and wispy gray hair, and thought that her husband was crazy or a liar. Or a crazy liar. But now, Manny realized one of love's weird truths—to him, Bert *was* the most beautiful man in the world, a man made handsome by his heart, his history, and all the time the two of them had spent together. What difference did it make if he had hair growing out of his ears?

When Bert took early retirement, they'd decided to move to Florida. February in New York was just too brutal for Bert's increasing frailties, and Manny could continue his freelance editing in sunnier climes. They settled on Delray Beach because that's where Bert's sister Roz lived. And because, as Bert had pointed out, it was where old middle-class Jews went to die. Somewhat surprisingly, though, retirement and warm weather had worked minor miracles, and Bert ended up feeling better than he had in years.

But Florida had put the final seal on their extramarital affairs. Even if one of the *alter kockers* in Delray had the imagination to sneak out on his wife for a quickie in a tearoom, he would never be able to remain standing upright for the blow job. So Bert and Manny had sex together, once or twice a week, and gave dinner parties for their neighbors—the married couples and the widows, the liberal ones and the PFLAG parents with kids in San Francisco or the Village— and became known as the town fags. The *old* town fags. Life, over the last couple of years, had turned into a soft, humid, predictable routine: the earlybird dinners; the Sunday brunches in the Florida room; the trips to Fort Lauderdale to see the latest gay play, with male nudity on stage if they were lucky. And then Garrison Park showed up with his cart full of Haagen Dazs and his perfect smile.

"Call me Chip," Garrison Park had said.
"So Chip, what brings you to Delray Beach?"
"My Dad died, and I came here from Milwaukee to straighten out his affairs."

Manny had wanted to ask what a man with a WASP name like "Garrison Park III" had been doing living in Delray Beach, but he didn't. Instead, he started wondering about what the young man's crotch would smell like, trying to hold up his end of the conversation all the while.

"So would you like to come over?" Chip asked. "Or would you prefer a warm-up on that coffee?"

Chip's father's house was in the older, quainter part of town, not one of the limitless, walled-in tracts of semi-detached houses surrounded by golf courses and wide, depopulated boulevards that broiled in the midday sun.

Park had gone into the kitchen to put away the ice cream, and when he returned he was shirtless, his torso a muscular vee. "Drink?" he asked.

"Scotch?" Manny said.

"Rocks?"

"Please."

And they sat there, making polite conversation, while Park leaned back in an armchair and ran his hand over his almost-perfect chest and belly.

"Am I succeeding in seducing you?" Chip asked.

"Have a look at me," Manny said, glancing down at his own crotch, the seersucker noticeably tented.

"I've been looking," Garrison Park said, and smiled. And then he slowly, deliberately slid his hand beneath the waistband of his shorts.

Manny's dick was so hard it ached. "Listen, I should call Bert. I don't want him to worry," he said.

"There's the phone."

And while Manny dialed the number and told Bert he'd be home, if not soon, at least eventually, Park began to strip. He stood, just a foot or two away from where Manny was talking to his partner, and slowly, slowly began to unzip his shorts and let them fall to his feet. His briefs were well-filled. He turned his back and peeled down his shorts, revealing a well-engineered tan line and one of the most beautiful butts Manny had seen in a long, long, long time. Chip bent over to retrieve his briefs: a line of brown hair, a perfect pink hole. When he stood up and turned around, his dick was hard. Uncut.

Manny had started to say goodbye to Bert, but his open mouth just gaped. "No, Bert, nothing's wrong," he said at last, when he could speak. "Love you. Bye."

So there he was, pretty as a porn star almost, a young man wearing nothing but white socks and a stiffy, a hard-on that was hard for *him*. It was all too perfect, too tempting, too much, too soon.

"Listen," said Manny at last, "don't take this the wrong way. It's not that I'm ungrateful... or uninterested. It's just that at my age, it's maybe unwise to make sudden moves. You never know what's gonna break."

"Manny," Chip said, stroking his dick gently, "I understand, I think. Don't worry about it. How about if I give you my phone number and you can think it over?"

"That'd be good," Manny said, not quite believing what he was doing.

Park traded his dick for a pencil.

"Here you go," he said, handing Manny a slip of paper. "Use it."

"I will."

"I know you will," said Garrison Park IV, and smiled.

"But Bert, a young man like that going for an old thing like me, it's... it's dysfunctional. Like he has a father complex or something."

"And you, Manny Doctor Freud Levine, I suppose *you're* the picture of mental health?" Bert smiled gently. They'd gotten home from the Mandarin Gardens and were cuddling on the sofa.

"So whaddya think?"

"I think you should go for it. He won't be here forever. *None* of us will be here forever, some sooner rather than later."

"But I don't want to hurt you and me, Bert, not for some boy."

"I thought you knew more about our love than that," Bert said.

Too busy burping up mu shu pork, Manny said nothing.

"Go on, honey. Give the boy a call."

The first time at Park's place was lovely, really. Chip unbuttoned Manny's shirt, stroking the mat of fluffy white hair, bending over to suck on a nipple while his hand rubbed the crotch of Manny's pants.

"Please kiss me," Manny said.

Chip's lips were on Manny's as he maneuvered down the older man's fly.

"No underwear?" Chip murmured.

"A nod to the old days."

"Nice dick."

"For an old guy?"

"For anyone." And Chip swooped down and took Manny's hard-on in his mouth. Not as good as Bert, maybe, but very, very good.

"Let's go to the bedroom," the young man said, his mouth off Manny's pulsing cock. And then they were in Chip's father's bed, tossing around, tearing at clothes, then finally naked together—Chip's youngish, smooth body, and Manny's older, hairier one, thick around the middle. Manny tried not to look down.

"Nice body," Park said.

Manny just sighed.

"No, really. I'm just so into guys your age. My friends think I'm crazy, but..."

Hell, I think you're crazy, Manny wanted to say, but he held off and started licking the boy's balls instead. Park spread his legs and Manny's tongue slid down between them. Now Manny knew: the boy's crotch smelled *good*. And his asshole opened up nicely at the touch of Manny's tongue.

"Oh, yeah, man," Garrison Park IV moaned, while Manny licked and slurped. Manny grabbed Chip's ankles and pushed his legs back, getting his tongue way up inside the boy's beautiful ass.

"Manny?"

"Mmm?"

"Why don't you just lie back and let me make you feel good?"

Chip unrolled a rubber on Manny's hard dick, a rueful reminder of what had happened since Manny was young. Then the boy slathered lube on the stiff dick, fingered some up his own ass, and straddled Manny's body. Bending over to kiss Manny's lips, he maneuvered the slippery cock up inside his ass, the shaft gliding in with a minimum of fuss.

"Oh my God," Manny gasped.

"What? Something wrong?"

"This is *sooo* good."

And then Chip sat upright and slid himself up and down on the older man's dick. As he rode the hard-on, he smiled.

Manny looked into the young man's face, a face so beautiful, not yet transformed by time. And he wanted him so much. But it was not just Chip Park there on his dick. It was also Bert. The young Bert, when they'd just met, not the older Bert, whom he hardly ever fucked any more. And it was also himself, Manny, a young Manny full of desires and fears and plans. Manny knew he would have to come or cry, one or the other, so he let the delicious tingling take control and asked "Are you ready?" and Chip reached down and jacked himself off and just at the split second Manny Levine came in his ass, Garrison Park IV shot a big load of semen all over the fluffy white hair of an old man's belly and chest.

"Nu?" Bert asked when Manny crept into the dark bedroom.

"Truth?"

"Truth," Bert said.

"It was wonderful."

"I'm so glad, *tatelah.* Now come to bed."

They slept, as they always slept, curled up like spoons in each other's arms. It was, they both thought, one of the best things about their life together, this closeness through the dark night.

And when they awoke they both had hard-ons, Manny's big and fat, Bert's bigger and fatter. Without a word, Bert slid down beneath the sheets and took Manny's cock in his mouth. Still the best. Always the best. His throat muscles milked at Manny's cockhead. Manny reached down and stroked his lover's beautiful, timeworn face.

"Oh, baby, I need you so much," he said.

Bert's mouth came away. "And I you," he said, voice muffled by the bedclothes.

"Fuck me?" Manny asked.

"Really?"

"Yeah."

"It's been so long. We got condoms somewhere?"

"Big boy, we're in our golden years," Manny said. "Let's live dangerously."

It wasn't so easy to get his legs over his head any more, but Manny managed it. And as Bert plowed into him, with surprising force and with the vigor of a, well, forty-year-old, Manny ran his hands over his lover's body, over the soft white hair that ran from cock all the way to shoulders, over the sags and folds of flesh, the gall bladder scar, the traces of the decades they'd spent in love.

"Fuck my ass," Manny said, "fuck it," precum dribbling from his slit. "Fuck it, fuck it."

And Bert's face began to redden, he pounded away, he groaned. "You ready, Manny?"

"Ready, Bert." And Manny reached down for his cock, still half-hard despite the plowing, and tugged at it till he felt his muscles tense.

"Come on, you old fuck," he blurted out. And then they both did; they came, Manny on his own belly, Bert up his lover's ass.

Muggy late summer faded into muggy early fall. It was almost time for the snowbirds to return. Chip and Manny had seen each other a dozen times, always at the Park house, always when Manny was sure Bert wouldn't mind.

"It's probably time for me to head back to Wisconsin soon. Rent out the house and go back to winter."

Manny didn't know what to say.

"Manny, I'd like to meet him," said Chip.

"Bert?"

"Bert."

"Well, his sister Roz is having an open house next week, but I'm not sure that bringing you along would be wise. She still refers to me as 'Bert's friend'." He made a wry face.

"Old dogs. New tricks."

"Yeah," said Manny, and bent to kiss the young man's brow. "Chip, don't take this the wrong way, but I'm not sure it would be such a good idea, your meeting Bert."

"But he sounds so wonderful. You really think he'd mind?"

"I'm sure he wouldn't. More than once he's said the same thing; that he'd like to meet you."

"So?"

"So for my sake. I can't explain. I don't know if I understand. I just feel so lucky...."

"Shh, shh. Don't cry. Don't cry, sweetie. Here, c'mere."

And he held Manny in his arms and stroked his face, wiped away the tears, until Manny had calmed down. Not as good as Bert. Good, but not as good as Bert.

"More brisket, Manny?

They were at Roz's house, having dinner with her and her taciturn husband Baruch. And things were tense.

Roz and Baruch were planning their fiftieth anniversary.

"Manny and I have been together nearly as long," Bert said to his sister. "Well, forty years."

"But it's not the same," Roz replied.

"Maybe not the same, but as good as," said Manny, trying to be conciliatory.

"Not the same," repeated Roz.

"Why?" Bert was livid. "Because we don't have kids?"

"No, because it's a different sort of commitment."

"Why?"

"It's not marriage, that's all," Baruch grumbled.

Bert was ready to go right for the throat. "What, because Manny and I have seen other men?" he snapped. Manny gasped. It was an unspoken thing, something never, ever to be mentioned in front of family. Bert went on, implacable. "At least neither of us have ever skulked around and cheated and lied, the way..." *Here it comes*, Manny thought, with a combination of dread and glee. Roz seemed near tears. "...the way Baruch did."

And there it was, out in the open. At last.

"Out. Get *out*," Baruch fumed.

As Manny and Bert were on their way out the door, Roz asked, "You sure you wouldn't like some brisket to take with...?"

"Just get them out of here, Roz," Baruch grumbled, shouting being too much effort.

So Bert and Manny left.

"Want to go for a walk on the beach?" Bert asked.

"Sounds nice."

As they drove through Delray, they passed the place the Parks had lived. Chip had been gone a year and some months. He and Manny still checked in by phone from time to time. The young man hadn't found anyone else. And no one had taken Chip's place in Manny's life.

"We can park here and walk," Bert said. "I fucking hate how they meter all the spaces at the beach."

"You sure are a troublemaker," Manny said and grinned.

"Yeah, ain't I?" Bert replied, grinning, too. "I'm a real bitch."

Manny looked at his lover. *The most beautiful man in the world,* he thought. *The most beautiful, courageous, man in the world.*

ATHLETIC PERFORMANCE
S. M. Jeffrey

Although the logistics might seem complicated, they are usually quite simple. Several times a year, our group kidnaps attractive, young, straight, college guys. We drug them, transport them about fifteen hundred miles, rape them *en masse*, and then send them back home. Interesting that never, in the many years we have been doing this, has one of our victims gone to law enforcement agencies and complained, no?

Last year, however, one program on the schedule was far more ambitious and certainly more complex. Our members decided it would be amusing to "dabble with" various National Football League players—those hulking paragons of heterosexuality, those super-straight Broncos and Cowboys and Steelers and Buccaneers and Raiders—a plan that was far more difficult to execute. For starters, we had to wait for the off-season. Next, we had to shadow our marks extensively, as there is no guarantee that a Packer will stay in Green Bay or a Saint in New Orleans during the off-season.

We unanimously decided to focus on younger men, guys drafted in the past few years, all unmarried. Our members have no desire to fuck some thirty-nine-year-old legend saddled with a bum knee, a spoiled trophy wife and six kids. No, we insisted upon targeting younger players with firm bubble butts and as few entanglements in their lives as possible, ensuring that their disappearance for a weekend would not raise undue alarm.

And so it happened that, for this special session, we "recruited" fifteen handsome NFL studs for an eight-hour fuckfest in a warehouse owned by one of our members on the West Coast. Working in teams, we nabbed them all on a Friday afternoon, every single one kidnapped under circumstances in which friends and families would not necessarily think twice about their loved one's two-day, unannounced absence. The plan was to transport them Friday and Saturday, fuck them Saturday night, and get them close to their homes before noon on Sunday. Without going into every minute detail, let it suffice to say that the plan worked: injected drugs, a ride in a closed van, a quick flight in a variety of private planes. Getting them to Los Angeles was easy; they remained unconscious the entire trip.

My captive was a Denver Bronco who owned a spacious condo in Lafayette, just north of Denver. We flew out of the JeffCo Airport (we certainly could not risk using DIA). When my strong-arm backup and I landed in the dark at a low-traffic airfield in Orange County, we loaded our prey into a van along with some other handlers' captives and drove to the warehouse, where several other vans were unloading "cargo" as well.

As usual, we conducted a one-on-one orientation with our abductees. I had the Bronco fullback, my closest friend, a tailback from the New York Giants. Much to our delight, there proved a connection between the two: both had played college ball together, but more about that later. Normally, orientation is fairly routine, since a 150-pound college diver or a 135-pound gymnast is rather easily subdued. But NFL players in their mid-to-late-20's are not so easily intimidated.

We attended to our charges separately. I stripped my guy naked and took the clippers to his pubic bush. Then I used lather and a razor to denude his crotch and ass crack completely. He was beginning to come around so I pulled the black cloth hood over my head to conceal my identity and quickly tied his hands behind his back. I then slipped a ball gag into his mouth and buckled it behind his head.

Little by little he regained consciousness. I helped him sit up on the cot, thoroughly amused by his look of disorientation and fear.

"You need to piss?"

He nodded his head vigorously so I blindfolded him, pulled him up from the cot and walked him out of the cubicle, down the hall to the latrine. There were seven or eight other proballers, all naked and bound as mine was, all being led by their individual escorts. I stood him in front of a urinal. When he was finished, I shoved him through the door and back to the cubicle. I forced him to sit on the cot again, removed my hood and sat on a short stool across from him.

"You probably noticed that I've shaved your crotch. We do that to make your cock and balls look bigger. That's a *good* thing, of course. Obviously you are naked and... as I can slug your nuts at any time, I... suggest you cooperate. Do you understand?"

He nodded that he did.

"*Excellent*, then! I am now going to attach some cuffs to your ankles. If you have any ideas about resisting me or kicking, be well advised to remember your testicular vulnerability. Your nuts effectively belong to me until I give them back to you. You got that?"

He did, offering no resistance when I applied the cuffs or attached them to the cot frame.

"Good man. So... I suppose you're wondering why you've been abducted, why you're naked, why your crotch was shaved, why you are bound and gagged and what's going to happen to you. Am I correct?"

He nodded vigorously.

"Then let's begin with what's going to happen, shall we? In a couple of hours, you and fourteen other fine examples of masculinity are going to suck cock and take it up your asses—repeatedly."

I allowed that to sink in as he sat there, stunned. After a moment, he roared a muffled negative behind his gag.

"Yep, after nabbing you in Lafayette, we brought you here, and in a little while will begin to administer a series of enemas that will ensure your status as a nice, clean fuck. When you were taking a leak, some of the other captives were there, as naked as you, doing the same thing. Undoubtedly you heard them. Well, what will happen to you is going to happen to them as well, so please don't get the idea that you're being... *picked* on. Actually, it is quite an honor to be one of the chosen. Surely you're aware how good-looking you are. Yes, that hunky body of yours, especially your ass, is pretty impressive on Invesco Field at Mile High—and even more so now that I've seen and touched you.

"At the risk of redundancy, I must remind you that it's much to your advantage to remember that nothing here is negotiable. You will suck cock and get fucked many times. What I need to know up front is whether you are a virgin—I mean, whether you have ever taken cock up your ass or in your mouth. Have you?"

He shook his head emphatically and verbalized a "Noooo!" behind the gag. I found his useless struggle to escape his bonds rather touching, so just watched, as a nice sheen broke out on his beautiful torso.

"I'm very pleased to hear that," I finally responded. "Our clients much prefer virgins. Of course, getting your ass plowed for the first few times *does* hurt in varying degrees, so if you like, I'd be... *happy* to break you in slowly before the festivities begin. Doing so would certainly help you understand what it feels like and take the edge off when the crowd arrives and you get gang-raped. Think about it. I'll remove the gag in a little while and we can talk it over, *hm?*"

He visibly shuddered.

"Now, here's the set-up: As I mentioned before, you are one of fifteen men we've kidnapped for this event. It will be conducted in a large warehouse where all of you will be restrained in various positions, each on a soft, padded platform. Our clients are paying a substantial fee, double the normal amount, for admission to this *particular* funfest, after which they will then be free to enjoy all of you as best they see fit—for hours. Oh, the revelry! It's one, huge orgy! Then, after we clear the clients out, we'll clean you up and get you back home back to Lafayette, simple as that."

He sat there motionless, his dick visibly shrinking.

"Naturally you will be drugged for your return, thus you will never know where you have been or who we are. You'll be back in *plenty* of time for whatever you might have planned for Monday. Are... we still on the same page here?"

He nodded.

I took the ball strap and grabbed his testicles. He yelped as I affixed the strap around his fine, loose scrotum and attached the wires to the TENS unit.

"*Now...*" I continued, "...as further regards your offering any resistance, allow me to demonstrate exactly how we ensure your cooperation—by electrifying your balls." I prepared to turn the unit on. "Like... *this*."

He screamed.

"I'm sure you get the picture. You cooperate or... we fry your balls, easy as pie! Here, allow me to demonstrate that again."

Another scream.

"All right, then. I can see that you understand. Now I'm going to remove the gag and we're going to talk civilly. We don't have much time because the enemas can take upwards of an hour. So, please don't waste my time by asking why we're *doing* this or... why we picked you *specifically*, or anything else that is superfluously non-negotiable. We don't expect you to enjoy being sodomized—in fact, our clients like it best when you struggle and resist. But my advice is simple: just go with it. In about eight hours it will all be over with and you'll be prepared to be sent home, albeit with a sore ass and an aching jaw!"

Chuckling a bit, I moved behind him and removed the gag. He exercised his jaw a little and sat there quietly.

"So, given that you can do nothing to stop what is going to happen to you, I will again present my offer to fuck you first, slowly and easily, with plenty of lubricant, before which I'll allow you to practice fellatio by sucking my cock. What do you say?"

He remained silent for several second. "This is fucking criminal!" he snapped all at once. "You motherfuckers are *sick*!"

"Correction, my friend: we are not motherfuckers. We are *man* fuckers, homosexuals. Because you breeders tend to think that we prey on weak and vulnerable heteros, we've decided to prey upon *you*. Give you an opportunity to experience a sort of self-fulfilling prophecy. Kinda neat, huh?"

He said nothing.

"Have I mentioned," I added, "that the other fourteen men who have been brought here for our little passion play are professional football players as well? It's NFL night!"

He remained silent but was clearly stunned.

"Oh, perhaps this would be a good time to inform you that we have no intention of revealing to your family or friends your sexual activities over the next several hours. And we *strongly* recommend that you keep things quiet yourself. I'm not sure your friends in the league, not to mention your fans, would understand how much cock you sucked and how much dick you took anally. The chances of you ever finding out who we are, let alone *where* we are... are slim to none," I added.

"Damned if I won't contact the police, you miserable freak!" he sneered.

"Well, let's not talk about that until later. At which time I'll give you several compelling reasons NOT to alert anyone in law enforcement. So, what's it going to be? Would you prefer losing your virginity by way of gang-rape or...

shall I feed you my nice big cock gently so you'll be prepared for the onslaught ahead?"

Upon receiving no reply, I lost my patience. Grabbing the TENS unit, I set it a hefty crank higher and turned it on. He howled and screamed and pleaded.

When I shut off the power, I slipped my hood on and removed my clothing. He had slumped back onto the cot, sobbing. "It was *extremely* rude of you to ignore my direct question, but I *assume* you get the point. I'm going to take your blindfold off now so you can take a good close look at the kind of dick you'll be dealing with."

I yanked off the blindfold and gave his eyes a moment to become accustomed to the light. Pulling him up into a sitting position, I stood with my penis mere inches from his face. I reset the electrical unit and began sending a slow trickle of current to his balls. "I'm going to get my dick hard while gradually increasing the electrical power and I'd *appreciate* your watching. The only way you'll be able to stop the misery in your scrotum is to take my cock into your mouth and start sucking. By the way, if you bite me, I'll turn the unit to full power at once and literally fry your nuts. After that, I will crush them with a mallet. You got that?"

He groaned. Yes, it was finally sinking in that I meant what I said.

"Of course, since you cannot avoid sucking my or any other cock presented to you this evening, there is very little point in holding out now. Believe me—if you don't become a tolerable cocksucker *pronto*, you will only succeed in getting yourself beaten up when the crowd shows. My advice," I added, increasing the surge a bit, "is to get on with it; take me into your mouth, and get a good lesson in cocksucking."

He was moaning as the power increased but apparently decided to accept my advice. He opened his mouth, leaned forward and took my rapidly swelling penis into his mouth.

"A wise decision... Now, listen carefully and I will teach you how to pleasure a man." I carefully instructed him, telling him how much to suck, when and how to use his tongue and how to ease a big dick further and further down his throat without choking. He did fairly well. Glancing at my watch and noting that we'd been at it for twenty minutes, I announced that his next lesson would be to simply allow me to fuck his face, which I did, shooting my load within a few minutes. It was a substantial load and he swallowed it without hesitation.

"All *right*," I sighed, wiping my cock with a towel and, having regained my composure, pulling on my clothes. "Now we must clean out your ass. You will be in the presence of your colleagues so don't turn modest on me. Enemas are a routine part of the man-to-man sex ritual these days and right now, for our purposes, you *are* homosexual."

"Never!" he spat.

"Look, pal; our clients are gay and you will be performing homosexual acts, so... just deal with it. It'll be over soon enough."

I shoved the gag into his mouth, reinstalled the blindfold, pulled him to his feet and led him to the room where my friend was just arriving with his New York tailback. We removed their blindfolds. When the former college teammates looked at one another, we thoroughly enjoyed the shock of recognition they both registered. We shoved them into the two-man stalls we used, bending both of them at the waist and securing their necks with straps to the stainless steel countertop. After securing their ankles in a widespread stance, we removed their gags. They were able to move their heads enough to look at each other and around much of the room, but couldn't straighten up. They could talk, scream, or plead for all we cared, just so long as their asses were properly cleansed.

"So," my partner asked, "your man suck your dick yet?"

"Yes," I answered, "and did a pretty decent job. He's followed instructions well *enough*, I suppose." I glanced at the Denver fullback, whose face was crimson. "How about your fellow?"

"Oh, he did excellently! I suspect he's sucked cock before!"

Now it was the New York athlete's turn to blush, cursing bitterly: "Yeah, with electricity shooting through my nuts—fuck *you*, asshole. Like I had a choice!"

My Bronco was just about to voice his agreement when we activated the units, zapping their balls again. After their shrieking subsided, my partner and I picked up a couple of flat mallets.

"When the fucking and sucking begins," I said, "just remember that you will be restrained and that we will utilize two primary methods of keeping you under control. The electrical current, of course, you have already experienced. But see these mallets? There will be one placed at each platform. If you become uncooperative in any way, or fail to pleasure a client the way he likes, we'll use the mallets. Like this, only harder..."

With that we hit the exposed testicles of the two athletes with moderate force and enjoyed the high-pitched screams that ensued.

The evening's host stepped into the stall and asked, "These are the players from Denver and New York, right?" Upon receiving confirmation, he handed us a couple of color photographs and left. The photographs were close-ups of the pair blowing my partner and me. We placed the photographs in front of our captives and allowed them to see their handsome mouths wrapped around our hard-ons. While they were looking at the photographs, we shoved Bardex nozzles into the athletes' sphincters and connected the hoses.

The enemas proceeded routinely except for the player's begging and whining, which my friend and I considered somewhat juvenile. Collecting their fecal discharge in buckets that we emptied into nearby toilets, we repeated the process four or five times. When the two were purged to our satisfaction, we left them alone for several minutes, adjourning to a nearby room where we used ear phones to listen to their conversation.

They compared notes on their kidnappings and predictably assured each other that they were not gay, using every homophobic epithet imaginable in swearing their revenge. No doubt the humiliated studs considered "gay football player" an oxymoron, and their vitriolic oaths proved a refreshing change of pace from the mouthings we typically heard from college lads.

When we returned to the stall, I wasted no time getting to the point. "All right, gentlemen," I said, "it's time to make up your minds about our offers to fuck you. You want to lose your virginity here and now or wait for the gang-bang?"

The two looked at each other. Neither could bring himself to agree to being fucked, yet it was obvious that both thought an initiation would be "helpful" before being sodomized by countless men over the next several hours.

Noting their crimson faces, I sweetened the pot. "Look, if you let me and my friend fuck you now, we'll use plenty of lubricant and make sure your asses are well-oiled when the action begins in the warehouse. Otherwise, we'll be happy to take you to your pallets right away, where the hordes will fuck you dry. It's totally your decision"

The Giant looked at the Bronco and asked, "What do you think?"

"Fuck, I don't know. Maybe…"

That was enough for me. I grabbed some lube and shot it into the Bronco's ass before handing the container to my friend. He repeated the process on his footballer and, both of us already quite aroused, we began deep-dicking the two athletes while listening to their pleas and protests and sobs. They quieted after about five minutes and simply submitted. We told them to use their sphincters to squeeze our cocks and they complied. In the end (perhaps a poor choice of words in this context), we blew our wads in their virgin asses, having thoroughly enjoyed ourselves.

"Well, what do you know," my friend announced, his cock still buried inside the panting Giant, "my guy has a hard-on!"

I reached down to feel my Bronco's cock and found his dick somewhat swollen but by no means fully hard. So I stroked it rapidly and *made* it hard, by God! Nodding to my friend, we continued stroking their cocks until both ultimately shot their loads. By now, the two athletes had abandoned any sense of personal modesty. Unlike their college counterparts, who at this stage typically beg to be allowed to shoot, our NFL pair remained stoic until they moaned involuntarily upon ejaculation.

We heard the buzzer and pulled our sticky cocks from the clean holes surrounding them. Using towels to wipe our dicks and their asses, as promised, we pumped more lube into them. We then released the neck restraints, pulled the pair to their feet, reinstalled the blindfolds and led them into the warehouse.

87

I pushed the Bronco onto his platform and assisted him onto its comfortably padded surface. In the center was a hole from which a bungee cord emerged. Instructing him to kneel over the hole, I attached a simple harness to his balls, covering the electrical pads that were connected to the TENS unit. Next, I slipped a small padlock into place, making sure that the bungee and harness could not be disconnected. I changed the nine-volt battery in the TENS unit and tested it, verifying that it would put out the required power—the Bronco's yelp confirming that it was working properly. I then placed the flat mallet on the platform and told the guy to relax for a few minutes.

All around us, similar arrangements were being made. For the first time, we could admire all fifteen of the fine and naked athletes. All were squeaky clean inside. All were wired. All were about to suck and get fucked. We handlers removed our hoods briefly, walked around the room, looking at the outstanding physiques. The platforms, about three feet high and arranged in three rows of five, were roomy and could easily accommodate several men at a time. The athletes my friend and I had prepped were placed side by side in the center row—such a happy reunion!

When the second buzzer sounded, we handlers returned to our individual charges and made sure their blindfolds were secure so that our wealthy clients' anonymity would be maintained.

The crowd began arriving. The first clients to do so walked around fully clothed to inspect the merchandise. More than pleased with what they saw, they withdrew to the locker room and secured their clothing before returning, wearing only socks, boots and big smiles, to begin their play. Those who arrived later, impressed by all the naked action already in progress, went directly to the lockers to undress.

In many respects, those who arrived first enjoyed the best action. After all, they heard the pleas and cries of our subjects who had refused their offer of an initiation fuck, and consequently were the first to deflower many of the athletes. On the other hand, those who arrived later enjoyed more compliant and willing subjects. Honestly, once a man has been fucked a few times, one more fucking doesn't seem to matter.

My Denver Bronco got off to a comparatively easy start. The first couple of guys simply wanted him on his belly for an extended fuck. They were pretty nice to him, complimenting him on his handsome body and tight hole. But they were followed by two really big men who were obviously a couple, determined to make the rounds as a team. They started off by getting the player on his knees and—once the Bronco had a large cock in his mouth—retied his wrists around the thighs of the man he was sucking. They motioned for me and I grabbed the camera. The second guy pulled the blindfold from the Bronco's eyes and I got several great shots of him with a mouthful of hard dick. They replaced the blindfold and the second man lifted the player by his hips and, making him stand, bent at the waist to insure his cock remained in the Bronco's mouth. This put a terrific strain on the player's balls because the bungee was nearly taut when the victim was kneeling. At that moment, with the Bronco's mouth impaled and his balls stretched painfully, the second man shoved his cock into the player's ass and the pair slammed him front and back mercilessly. Their sexy victim attempted to bend his knees but the man fucking his ass would not permit it. Clearly, the Bronco was miserable.

Much to our delight, it got worse for him. When the couple had finished, three huge guys climbed onto the platform and positioned the NFL player on his hands and knees. They called for the TENS unit, which I had temporarily disconnected, leaving the wires dangling from the Bronco's balls. They reconnected the unit and spent thirty minutes tormenting the young man, trying out all the different settings. The footballer screamed madly which pleased the threesome immensely. When they tired of that, they retied his hands behind his back and placed him on his back. One guy sat on the fullback's thighs; another squatted over his face and ordered the Bronco to lick his balls, while the third started stroking the player's super-fine cock. Once they succeeded in getting him hard, they called for the Condom Bowl to be replenished and, one at a time, sat on his dick and fucked themselves silly, never allowing the Bronco to shoot. Upon departure, they left him frustrated and covered with their semen.

Meanwhile, the New York Giant had the misfortune of being singled out by a couple of seasoned SM practitioners whose main interest was to determine if the NFL player could shoot a load while getting his testes shocked. With remarkable shrieking, the amplified young man proved that he could. Bored with that game, they called for a bench, which my friend supplied. Asking that the ball harness be removed, my comrade-in-crime accommodated them. One of the men then lay down on the bench and impaled the footballer with his cock. Once the man's erection was fully inserted, the footballer was shoved forward, his hands still secured behind his back, while the second man forced his erection into the same ass. Only the hip rotation of the man on top was necessary to torment the unfortunate Giant and bring both men to orgasm, the screams of the doubly impaled athlete delighting both men.

The event was proving a phenomenal success! The room was packed and the noise level quite high. I could hear whipping and spanking, endless pleas and cries, and the joyous exclamations of orgasm. Writhing, naked flesh glistened everywhere and the scent of sweat and semen and anal penetration was omnipresent. The odor of urine was not, however, because the ground rules prohibited water sports on the platforms, stipulating that the sex objects be lead to the shower area and introduced to the various pleasures of piss-play before being showered off and only then returned for continued performance on their platforms.

Inevitably, as the evening wore on, the fifteen athletes became accustomed to fucking and sucking and endured a wide variety of other torments inflicted by our clients. Well aware that the clock was ticking, we found ourselves ushering the satisfied clients into the showers, thanking them for their patronage and then out the door. What remained was to prepare the athletes for their journeys home.

For the two who were college teammates, my partner and I joined forces. We lugged the Bronco to the Giant's platform and got them into a lusty sixty-nine. Still blindfolded, both thought they were servicing another client with the added benefit that, for once, while each one sucked he was simultaneously *being* sucked. That was the point at which all fetters were released and we had the cameras ready. When my partner and I removed the blindfolds from the two players, we captured enough enthusiastic action to provide the insurance we wanted. Not until they had brought each other to orgasm did they realize that they had been paired. Both, I think, realized at that point that a great many photographs had been taken of them, none of them indicating anything other than acts of consensual, hard-core homosexual activity.

We led them to their cubicles and one-by-one, under the strict supervision of the hooded warders, they were allowed to use the commode and shower, after which they were drugged again and returned to the vicinity of their homes, each awaking to find in envelopes placed in their pockets, various copies of the compromising photographs. More copies arrived later by mail, postmarked in Canada, as further reminders that reporting their experiences or contacting law enforcement agencies would be inadvisable. None of course did.

I have to wonder, however… what, if anything at all—when the Broncos are next pitted against the Giants—will those two hotshots say to one another.

MYTHAS
Mark Wildyr

Mythas Devistan stirred uneasily as he recalled the first time his lean, muscled frame lay sprawled naked across this same bed, his hands and feet bound to the corner posts as he shivered in dread at what was about to happen.

Three moons past, he was the son of a prosperous peasant family that held itself aloof, turning its back on the druids in favor of a small, secretive Christian sect. Mythas' father, Baylon, excused him from the fields to the extent possible to be educated by his mother and the Christian father. Whether their ruin came about because of the spurned druids or other jealousies, Lord Cargyl's men came suddenly, dragging the family out into the cold light of dawn to demand ruinous taxes and outrageous penalties.

The bound, horrified Devistan men witnessed the rape of their women. Mythas' mother died quickly; his sister, with only eleven winters, lasted much, much longer. When they came for Mythas with his dark hair, smooth cheeks, and man's muscles, the captain beat them away, marking this prize too valuable to waste on the inflamed lust of common soldiers.

So Mythas watched in anguish as his father was beaten, burned, and castrated while stubbornly refusing to acknowledge his hoard of gold. Mythas understood. Acknowledging the wealth would have brought death as certainly as the denial. When Baylon finally died, the soldiers bore Mythas away to Castle Cargyl, leaving his beloved family as carrion for the crows.

Because he was a muscled youth of twenty winters unaccepting of his station, Mythas was confined. Daily, he was led out in chains to perform the low duties of the meanest servant in the castle until the Chancellor of the Lord's Purse learned Mythas could read and write and calculate. He was then moved to the second floor, where his clothing was less threadbare and the fetters fell away, to perform chores more worthy.

A fortnight prior, he had been figuring values for the Chancellor when the door was flung open to admit Lord Cargyl, himself. Mythas' liege was a man of more than thirty winters, fit and lightly bearded. He arrogantly demanded various accounts, pausing in his injunctions only when Mythas rose at the bidding of the Chancellor to deliver a scroll to his master. Mythas knew from the sudden silence that something significant had occurred. The Lord's hand on his arm stayed him. The scrutiny grew embarrassing.

"This is Mythas, Milord," the Chancellor offered reluctantly. "He's amazingly well-educated. Figures better than any I've had. Is quite valuable to me." The fat man gave such emphasis to the last that Mythas was surprised.

That evening, Lord Cargyl's guards came for him. Confused, Mythas allowed himself to be stripped and bathed. He resisted only when ordered into the Lord's bed, but was quickly overpowered. Lord Cargyl stood naked beside the bed. Ridges of muscle sheathed his chest and sides. His penis hung heavy at his groin. Mythas shivered at the look in those black, fathomless eyes.

"Please, Milord, there's been a mistake," Mythas tried to steady his voice.

Cargyl ignored him. "The gods made you especially for me, Mythas. You will be my favorite. Tell me you will love your Lord if he releases these bindings." Mythas shook his head. "Pity. But I shall enjoy you no less."

The night was a horror. Lord Cargyl mounted the boy and speared him roughly. The nobleman rutted vigorously before spilling his seed into Mythas. The pain was terrible, although it lessened with time. The youth thought it was over until the guards dragged him into a side room to cleanse himself, but they strapped him to the bed again, this time face up with blocks of wood holding his mouth open. The wait was agonizing before his master returned once more, dined, bathed, and freshly robed. Leaning over the boy, he smiled.

"Now I will avail myself of that pretty mouth." Cargyl mounted Mythas and drove his erection down the boy's immobilized throat. The man left his seed in Mythas' mouth, on his chest, in the soft pubic hair, on his leg, everywhere, until the youth was almost covered with dried, crusted semen. Mythas' jaws ached horribly from the wooden blocks. The guards made vulgar jests and laid filthy hands on him when they came to release him at first light, but none dared do more than touch.

And now on this night, the fourth time Mythas had been led to Cargyl's bedchamber, he had agreed to forego the restraints. In his own mind, he would not participate in his master's perversion; he would simply endure it.

Lord Cargyl approached the bed, naked and rampant. "How many women have you ploughed, Mythas? You were a virgin when I first took you, weren't you, boy?" The man's hand traced the curve of Mythas' back and buttocks. "Untouched. Untried. Unsullied. Beautiful. Long limbs. Good muscles," the man droned on. "The kind of skin women pray to the gods for. Dark, silky, pliant." He moved into Mythas' line of vision, his penis engorged. Cargyl rested it atop Mythas' arm where it beat against his skin rhythmically. "Where do you get your looks? I dare say some nobleman fostered your family. You are more beautiful than my wife. Those golden eyes… breathtaking!" A hand cupped his chin. "Natural red lips, no sign of a beard."

Pleased that this comely youth was learning to accept him, Cargyl stretched on the bed beside Mythas and pulled the boy's head to his groin. Reluctantly, Mythas opened his mouth, realizing that to refuse or to cause harm would be the death of him. He closed his eyes, trying without success to think of other things as he slipped his lips over the large cock. At least the nobleman was clean and a man, not some feminine male creatures like Mythas had seen.

Mythas took as much of the organ into his mouth as he could. When he choked and gagged, his liege ordered him to rise and suck his balls or lick his nipples. After what seemed hours, the boy learned to open his throat and relax his tongue so that he could accommodate most of the man's big cock. At last Cargyl lost patience, rolled over on top of the youth and fucked his mouth until he came. At the last moment, he drove himself completely to the hilt in his frenzy, and shot his seed straight down the boy's throat, almost strangling him.

As before, the man went to dine and refresh himself before returning to the bedchamber. Mythas waited, freshly scrubbed in water and scented oils. The man took in his nakedness, and smiled his pleasure. He moved between the boy's legs and grabbed his flaccid cock. Stroking Mythas' long, fat penis, he showed some impatience when the boy failed to respond. Realizing it was important, Mythas closed his eyes and tried to imagine Angelique, a girl he liked from his old village. He hardened marginally, bringing a cry from his lord. Mythas opened his eyes in surprise when an image of Dorork, a youth his own age, leapt to mind. He stiffened more.

"Aye, you're amply hung, young stud," Lord Cargyl growled in pleasure. "Now see how far you can spit!" He continued to work the boy with one hand, using the other to weigh the heavy balls, stroke the flat, work-hardened belly, tweak the dark brown aureoles crowned with pinkish nipples. As Mythas's body stiffened, the man cried: "Now! Spit your seed!"

Mythas gushed, releasing his seed for the first time in months. He might have been a virgin with both sexes, but occasionally, he gave himself release in the solitude of the forest. He spurted all the way to his chest, bringing a laugh of approval from the man. If Mythas thought Cargyl delivered him of his sperm simply for pleasure, he was mistaken.

The man mounted his belly and rubbed his hard cock in the youth's semen until it was slick and ready. He then lifted the boy's legs and pressed against his fundament. Mythas' strong hands ripped the covers on the bed as the mighty shaft penetrated him. The pain was terrible as Cargyl drove to the root of his cock on the first thrust. He smiled down at Mythas, seemingly pleased by the pain he caused. After a momentary pause, he proceeded to ram the boy mercilessly, never pausing, never caressing, never showing any concern other than for his own gratification. He howled aloud as he spewed his seed into the young channel. Then he paused, breathing heavily, still sheathed in Mythas' buttocks. "You may stay here. This shall be your room from now on."

With those words, Mythas knew that he was doomed to be his master's sex slave until he sickened or aged or became gross. Had his master shown any tenderness or consideration toward him, it might have been different, but although Mythas knew Cargyl was well pleased with him, the man never confirmed it. Nonetheless, the boy began to derive a modicum of reluctant pleasure when his liege penetrated his nether regions.

A noble visitor changed everything. Mythas was taken early one morning to a remote camp to await his Lord's return from a hunt. The boy's immediate thoughts of escape were dashed when a guard dogged his every step. The two nobles rode in at day's end in high spirits bearing stag and boar and pheasant. At dinner that evening, Mythas was placed at the left hand of Lord Cargyl. He ate placidly and listened with half an ear to the conversation between the two noblemen. Suddenly, his blood ran cold. After repeated refusals, Cargyl finally agreed that they would "share the boy".

Sent to clean and dress himself appropriately, Mythas determined to escape or die. The moment came when his guard turned away to relieve himself and exposed his neck to the youth's double-fisted blow. The soldier dropped. Unable to murder a helpless man, Mythas took the guard's weapons and boldly strode through the camp to the picket line. With little experience of horses, Mythas hoped only for a mount to bear him away before he was missed.

A sudden cry arose! The guard had recovered and was organizing pursuit. Mythas made a quick decision. He freed an animal and jabbed its haunches with the tip of the guard's knife. The charger bolted. Mythas melted into the dark forest and made haste to the north while the camp pursued a frightened, riderless animal.

Realizing it was not the cleverest thing to do, Mythas nonetheless headed home. What lay concealed in the hollow of a tree a mile from the cottage would make a great difference to his future. Less than an hour later, a distant baying froze his steps. Hounds. They had loosed the hunting dogs! He delayed the inevitable by wading through a stream, but slowly, inexorably, the canines grew closer. At dawn, the exhausted youth waded more water in a frantic effort to lose the dogs. Weakening rapidly, Mythas was forced to make a stand. From the baying he could tell there were no more than two or three dogs behind him. He doubled back to a spot where two boulders narrowed the path. He drew the guard's short sword from his belt and waited in hiding. The first dog had ceased howling, but its snuffling pant was clearly audible as it raced along the trail. Throwing himself into the pathway, Mythas brought the blade down on the beast's head.

The second dog was no more than fifty paces behind. With a savage snarl, the creature launched himself at the youth. Desperately freeing the blade from the slain beast's skull, Mythas managed to raise the point. The great mastiff impaled himself on the sword, knocking the blade from Mythas' grasp. Incredibly, the beast whirled, the blade buried in its thick neck. When it charged, the impact drove the blade deeper. The savage dog died quickly.

With his dirk at the ready, Mythas turned to face whatever came next, but only two dogs had been set upon him. Closer than was comfortable came a whistle from a handler. Refreshed by his victory, Mythas recovered his sword and raced up the trail. At the next stream, he hurriedly cleansed himself and his weapons and made for home.

The leather bags were safe where his father had hidden them, but Mythas was dismayed by their weight. Unable to resist a look at the cottage, he found a company of Cargyl's soldiers milling around the ruins, preparing to search the area for him. The boy's eyes swept the ground for the bones of his family, but someone, perhaps the Christian father, had buried his loved ones. Mythas turned his steps to the north… to the high mountains where Lord Cargyl's authority was tenuous at best.

He eluded his pursuers and climbed all night and most of the next day. He had cleared the foothills and reached the rugged mountains when the hounds came again. The dogs caught him by surprise this time, running silently until they were upon him. Warned by a growl, he turned as three feral beasts rushed across an expanse of cleared ground. He dealt with the first, but would have no chance with the other two. A yelp of pain caused him to twist around. One of the beasts was down with an arrow in its side. The third fell to another. Two soldiers raced across the clearing, swords drawn, shouts of fury on their lips.

His father had taught Mythas swordplay, but the youth had never drawn a blade in anger. Yet he met the first man with confidence. The second was suddenly thrown to the ground by a body launching itself from the rock above them. Disconcerted, Mythas' opponent dropped his guard and the boy ruthlessly cut him through the neck. Mythas turned to find a laughing blond giant clad in the sheepskins of the north people. The other soldier lay dead on the ground.

"We best go quickly," the giant said in a deep voice.

They labored up the steep slope of the mountainside in silence. Once, an arrow embedded itself in the thin soil beside Mythas' leg, but they rounded a turn and had no further sign of pursuit. Mythas was floundering like a beached cod in the thin mountain air before his savior broke stride. The big man—and Mythas now saw that he was a youth only slightly older and less than a hand-span taller than he—stationed him on the trail above and set traps for any pursuers.

"They'll not come up here, but in case they do, this will slow them." The blond youth turned suddenly. "I am Rogan."

"I am Mythas Devistan. I thank you for your help. I am weary so they might have presented a problem."

Rogan threw back his head and laughed. "Three dogs and two men would be a problem for most. Do you have the legs to go on?"

"Do I have the lungs is the real question. Lead away, highlander. I will struggle along in your wake."

The stranger took Mythas' two heavy bags, tossed them over his broad shoulders, and proceeded up the hill. Night had fallen before Rogan ushered his guest through the door of a sturdy stone cottage hidden in a small glen.

"'Twas my father's," Rogan explained. "But he has gone beyond, as have my mother and other kin. Feel free to share my solitude for a time. What have you in these bags you lug about so faithfully?"

"In truth, I do not know. There is gold of some amount. And a stone or two. My inheritance from my father, who was slain by Lord Cargyl's men. But whatever is here, my friend, half is yours except for a certain ring my father cautioned should never leave the family."

"Your inheritance is yours, Mythas, not mine to share. But I am curious. Let us see what is here."

There was indeed gold, four hefty pouches of foreign coins. And silver aplenty. Copper disks gleamed in the firelight as brightly as the noble ones. A bag of stones... rubies, emeralds, sapphires, and white glittering stones that doubtless were rare, priceless diamonds, drew their admiration. And finally, there was a ring, a gold signet bearing a great seal with Latin inscriptions.

"I do not understand," Mythas mused. "My father provided well, but he could never have amassed such riches from his farm. There is a mystery here."

"By the gods!" Rogan said, trickling a stream of precious stones through his big hands. "This is greater wealth than Lord Cargyl's... except for his land."

"This is not my father's doing, but someone else's. Such wealth is dangerous. What shall we do with it?"

"Bury it for the moment. It can do much good, but equal harm."

The two young men soon turned to more practical matters, laying in huge stores of fallen logs for the fireplaces and trapping and hunting meat for the larder. Winter was fast approaching. Preparations were no more than complete before the snows descended on the small glen. It was then that Mythas gave serious examination to his new friend.

Rogan stood a half a head taller than he with chest and shoulders broader and deeper than most men's. His body was well set up, and his features were pleasing... strong and manly. His head hair was blond, but the soft mat at his chest was brown, as was that at his groin. When they bathed, Rogan's manhood was revealed as massive. By the time they spoke of what had happened at Cargyl, their companionship was such that Mythas confessed all. The highlander accepted it without comment. Four nights later, Rogan stood at his bedside.

"Will you have me, Mythas Devistan?"

Wordlessly, the youth rose to his elbow and reached for the huge cock. When the monster began to grow, the bulbous end was all that Mythas' mouth could handle. It must have been enough, because Rogan soon let out a bellow and spewed a cupful of sperm. Mythas puzzled over how performing this act for his liege lord could be so vile, yet such a pleasure for his friend.

And so it was that they became lovers. Rogan took the role of man and gave his seed to the young lowlander. It required care and patience because he was so large, but eventually, they moved from oral copulation to anal. Mythas sat on Rogan's thighs one cold, blustery night and contemplated the huge organ he held in his hand. He leaned forward and coated the big tip with his saliva, moved forward, and sat down. He almost gave up because of the pain, but each time he did, another inch slipped into him, and he would pause to rest. Rogan watched with concern. At last, all of the rigid staff was contained in his channel, and when Rogan was convinced he was not injuring his lover, the big man rolled them over and proceeded to fuck with a joyful abandon. In time over the long winter months Mythas learned to take him without pain.

During other moments, Mythas taught his lover the rudiments of reading and writing and basic calculations. He pestered Rogan with questions about the mountains and drew a map with carbonblack on a sheepskin that encompassed the extent of Rogan's knowledge. Mythas knew the region's landmarks, its good folk, and deepest scoundrels without having seen or met a one.

Midway into the spring thaw, Rogan confessed a confidence. "I would not hurt you, Mythas. Our union has made this the most enjoyable winter I can recall. It passed too quickly, something I never thought I would say." The big youth paused. "While what we have is of great joy to me, there is a girl in the village named Guidrun. We have an understanding."

Mythas spoke through sudden pain. "You owe me no explanations, Rogan. You have given me comfort, and I have given you ease. I have no claim on you beyond a firm friendship. As long as I have that, I am wealthy."

"You have my love, Mythas, but it is different from the love she claims. Some girl from the village will make you a better companion than me. One with a proper hole where you can bury your rod for a change."

"Perhaps, but I think I am bent now, and must continue to grow in that direction."

Rogan made two trips into Belloden before Mythas accompanied him to the tiny village, a mean place without visible sign of affluence except for one slightly larger cottage adjoining a tavern. The dainty, doll-like Guidrun brightened Mythas' smile, but her brother stilled his heart and paralyzed his muscles.

Ronald Wydriff was taller, younger, and masculine, but otherwise a mirror to his sister's beauty. Mythas knew that Rogan had introductions, yet he stood staring like some dumb field creature. He roused himself and stepped forward, grasping Guidrun's dainty hand and touching it to his bowed forehead.

"Mistress Guidrun," Mythas lied in his friend's behalf, "all these dreary winter months I have heard of nothing but your radiant beauty from this clumsy ox. And sure enough, he had not the words to adequately describe it."

She gave a throaty laugh. "Yet he is eloquent in other ways." Her voice had origins in the gentry and the rudiments of an education. Here was the progeny of other exiles, he warranted.

Mythas next turned to her brother, a youth of his own age or a winter younger. His eyes searched the open, handsome face and found no guile in the sky-blue eyes. Golden locks fell across the boy's forehead. Mythas wanted to brush them aside. Instead, he spoke. "Master Ronald, I trust we shall become fast friends. At least that is my wish."

"And so it shall be." The man's voice coming through that beautifully bowed mouth startled him. The two grasped wrists in a firm shake. The flesh beneath Mythas' palm was firm and sinewy.

They spent the morning exploring the confines of the village and its small valley. At mid-day, Ronald left to work in his father's tavern. Mythas feigned thirst to accompany him, leaving Rogan and Guidrun in private.

The tavern was sparse with custom at this time of day, but those present eyed the stranger with frank suspicion. The innkeeper matched the frankness, but hid his suspicion. Ronald introduced his father, and Mythas endured a mild interrogation of his flight and all that went before it, making no mention of the services he had performed for Cargyl. The atmosphere grew slightly warmer. He was not the first fugitive from his Lordship's justice in these mountains.

The four young people developed in friendship and trust over the next few weeks. The time came when Mythas felt the need to know the territory personally rather than from a drawn map. He had expected Rogan to accompany him, but the big youth declined, saying that Ronald would be his guide. Mythas, of course, happily agreed. Ronald proved to be intelligent company, but toward sundown, Mythas had cause to wish the sturdy Rogan accompanied them when two sturdy youths somewhat older than they stepped onto the trail, blocking their way.

"The innkeeper's brat and the stranger," the larger of the two sneered. "What is your friend's name, Ronald?"

"Mythas. Mythas, this is Boras, and that's Henryn. Now let us pass."

"I don't like your looks, My-thus, or whatever your name is. I don't want you on my trail. Go back."

Mythas stayed Ronald with a hand on his arm and approached the other youth. "My name is Mythas, as you well know. I am new to these mountains and in search of friends. I trust I have found two new ones."

"Any friend of mine has to be worthy of it," Boras said with a harsh laugh.

"Do I prove my worthiness to you alone or both at the same time?"

"Just me," Boras said, tossing his knife to Henryn. Mythas gave his dirk to Ronald, who moved to Henryn's side.

The bigger boy rushed; Mythas danced nimbly aside. Boras whirled swiftly. Realizing he had to stay out of the reach of those burly arms, Mythas circled, as Baylon had taught him, lashing out with his fists. Most blows landed harmlessly on muscled forearms, but a few struck more vulnerable targets. Boras ignored his jabs and made little effort to defend himself, expending his energy in swift grasping charges.

Unaccustomed to the mountain air, Mythas felt himself weakening. He changed tactics, lunging suddenly at his opponent and tossing the boy over his hip. Boras struck the rocky ground hard. Injured, the bully struggled to his feet and lunged again. Mythas dropped to all fours; Boras flew over him, meeting a rocky ledge headlong. The youth turned over, but failed to regain his feet.

Mythas looked around and found Ronald sitting astride Henryn's chest, his dirk to the boy's throat. "He wanted to play," the fair youth said.

Mythas reached out a hand to his fallen opponent. "Have I earned your friendship?"

"You're a pushy bastard. Well, why not? Aye, I'll be proud to call you friend," the big youth answered, pulling himself to his feet. Their new companions lingered until almost nightfall.

Alone again, the two young men returned to the trail. Mythas, still excited by the recent conflict and exhilarated at turning adversaries into friends, feasted his eyes upon the broad back and slender hips of the youth in front of him. Ronald turned unexpectedly and caught him looking. They removed their shirts and washed away the day's grime in a cold, clear stream. Then they lowered their breeches and washed their private parts. His clothing safely restored, Ronald faced Mythas squarely.

"I know why you look at me," he said, leaving his friend at a loss for words. "I work in a tavern. My bottom's been pinched as much as any barmaid's."

Drawing on his shirt, Mythas studied the blue eyes. "And have you favored any of them?"

"Nay, I was waiting for you," Ronald said before turning up the trail. Flustered, Mythas followed along behind as they turned aside to a small bluff some distance away.

"This is a good place to rest," Ronald said, pointing through the gloom to a shallow cavity at the base of the rock. Mythas said nothing as he helped gather wood. Ronald built a large fire at the back of the hollow and a smaller one at its opening. They ate from their grub sacks in silence.

"What do you mean, you were 'waiting for me'?" Mythas ventured at length.

"I always knew someone was coming for me. I dreamed of a beautiful lady until your image came to me, right down to the golden eyes, curving nose, and dark hair. I confess to spilling my seed before your specter, but never with flesh and blood. When first I saw you, I knew my wait was almost at an end."

They cleared the fire's debris from the back of the hollow and spread their blankets. Luxuriating in the slow release of heat from the surrounding rocks, the two young men revealed themselves. Two naked male breasts met, one bronzed, the other fair, the muscles slightly more defined in one. Two hard, hairless bellies rubbed against one another. Two throbbing cocks kissed, one longer and thicker by only a little. Pubic hair as black as night matted against deep, red-blond. Two hungry mouths joined. Mythas entered Ronald's virgin channel as tenderly as his rampant staff would permit. He searched the boy's eyes for signs of distress, but found only love. He withdrew his cock entirely and savored sweet reentry. Ronald sighed. Mythas kept his strokes slow and languid, relishing his first act of intercourse in the role of a man

"Mythas," Roland whispered. "Your loving is wonderful, but fuck me now!"

The words unleashed him. He beat at Ronald savagely, drawing moans of joy. His long, hard cock ploughed the furrow, stroking Ronald's insides, beating his body, stretching his channel. Ronald's hand moved between them as he stroked himself. With a great cry, Mythas lunged against his lover and came. Ronald growled as he shot his seed against Mythas' belly. The storm abated slowly amid convulsions and contractions and groans of ecstasy.

"My love," Ronald whispered when they nestled together beneath the blankets. "It was worth the wait." The next morning, Mythas woke Ronald by taking him in his mouth and sucking the strong cock, riding the length up and down, fondling the solid, hairless balls, stroking the sensitive flesh on the inside of the thighs until he drew the sperm from the boy's excited body.

They spent a week exploring people and places by day and one another by night. Before they returned home, Mythas confessed his past. Ronald suffered with him through the ordeal with Lord Cargyl, and laughed over his affair with Rogan, after swearing never to use the information to Rogan's harm. As for Rogan himself, he took one look at the two youths when they entered his cottage and roared. "So it's like that, is it?"

Over the next two years, the four friends added to their number. Boras and Henryn became companions, bringing others. Mythas used a portion of his treasure to ease the greatest needs among the highlanders. With their own hands, the companions repaired cottages fallen into disrepair because of illness or infirmity. Mythas funded sheep, timber, iron ore, smelting, smithing, and a host of other ventures for individuals his friends deemed worthy, claiming one out of ten shares to be paid back to him for ten years. He found buyers for their trade, ensuring that the produce of their labors never found its way into Lord Cargyl's county. Soon the drain on his treasury ceased, and it began to grow. He shared revenues with members of the band, freeing many from the need to drudge for a living. Instead, they patrolled the villages, providing protection for the citizenry. Mythas contracted with the local ironmaster for weapons modeled upon his own short sword. He mounted his band on hardy mountain ponies. Playful swordsmanship and archery developed into disciplined training. Horseback charges became a part of that discipline.

Their first test came when Lord Cargyl's troops came to collect taxes from Ransweyden, a low-lying village at the edge of his territory. Mythas' band arranged itself in the forest above the village to watch. When the raping began, Rogan gave the command. Silently, the group descended, striking among the rutting soldiers before their presence was known. They spared few. Mythas had the pleasure of slaying the captain who had murdered his family.

"I am a fool! I made a mistake," Mythas said to his intimates that night in the cottage he and Ronald had built in the glen near Rogan's. "I should not have revealed myself."

"Were you so important to him?" Guidrun asked.

"Anyone who thwarts Cargyl's will is important to him," Ronald growled. "One of the men we spared confided that they were told to watch for you and bring you back in chains."

Mythas thought for a moment. "It does not really matter. Cargyl cannot permit any rising against his authority. This is the first time his soldiers have been attacked. The first time the populace has acted like anything but sheep to be shorn. He will have to react."

"You are right," Rogan boomed. "He will come."

So they set some lads to watch at the edge of the lowlands and sent others throughout the mountains to gather willing, able-bodied men, paying them like regular troops to train in a large valley west of the cottage. Five hundred lads and men responded. Forgers beat out weapons as fast as possible. Others went to buy more of the sturdy mountain horses. Archers made bows. Rogan was their commander, but all knew that Mythas was their leader.

A group of a dozen sat around the hearth in Mythas' cottage deep into the night. Suspicion of a Cargyl agent in their midst had arisen, not from outward sign, but from logic. Speculation centered around the innkeeper at Ransweyden who had not been touched during the raid on the town. Without proof, they decided to watch and wait.

"Cargyl should be coming soon," Rogan said, turning to other matters.

"He comes already," said a voice from the door. Lynam of Ransweyden joined their midst. "He moves into the foothills. He will be here tomorrow."

"Then we must finish our preparations," Ronald said.

"Beware," Boras warned. "This is the agent's spawn."

"Aye," Lynam admitted readily. "My father is a spy for Cargyl, and I his messenger. But hear me out."

"What did you tell him?" Mythas asked calmly.

"I went because no message would have roused his suspicions," Lynam explained. "I told him a force had been raised because he knew this from Ransweyden. I told him you were here, Mythas, because he would know from the survivors. I told him you would meet his forces in the meadow at Thundering Falls because that is a logical place, and one I've heard mentioned. But I told him that you'd been able to raise but two hundred men, if that. He comes with half a thousand."

"But we can match that number," Rogan said thoughtfully. "And our mountain ponies can run circles around their bigger lowland mounts. Aye, Lynam, you've given us an edge."

"Rogan," Mythas said thoughtfully. "You told me of a cavern behind the lower falls. How big is it?"

"It will hold a hundred men and their mounts."

"I want only half that number."

Ronald spoke. "There is only one way in and one way out, Mythas. If the cavern is known to but a single man, then all will die."

"And any who go with me must understand that risk."

"You need but forty eight more," Ronald declared. "I will ride with you." The problem was not getting volunteers, but cutting them down to the number required. Lynam, Boras, and Henryn were among the chosen.

That night, after they made love and were preparing to go, Mythas turned to his mate. "Whatever happens, Ronald, you have enriched my life beyond all expectation. I would ask you not to come, but that would be selfish."

"Aye, and a waste of good breath," Ronald replied. "You are my life, and I share in full measure what fate holds for you, Mythas."

Fifty cold and wet men and horses entered the cavern in the darkest hours of night. They pressed to the back of the huge cave, leaving two near the entrance to stand watch. Boras and Henryn obscured their hoof prints before joining their companions.

They had not been there long before voices at the pool below the falls revealed that Cargyl's scouts had come. His army arrived at early light to set up camp around the pool. They had traveled the night through, hoping to secure the upper reaches of the meadow before Rogan's forces could do so.

"Deny them!" Mythas hissed through clenched teeth. A commotion told him that Rogan had recognized the threat. "Now!" he prayed aloud, although the plan had been to wait until afternoon hours. But Cargyl's men would be tired from their long trek, and the time was right.

Thundering hooves drew Mythas to the falls. Through a curtain of water, he made out a captain reporting to Cargyl, who had set up his headquarters at the pool. Sudden orders stirred activity. Rogan was showing himself!

"Mount!" the youth called urgently to his men. Ronald approached with Mythas' horse. Moments later, they thundered through the cascading water and fell upon the surprised invaders. Cargyl had time to hiss "you!" before he died with Mythas' arrow in his breast.

A line of bowmen stepped from the forest to the east and loosed a rain of shafts upon the Cargyl men. Others stood atop the highest waterfall and let fly their arrows. Most of Cargyl's small army was laboring up the steep meadow where Rogan and his mounted men stood in full view, allowing the lowland horses to tire themselves. When the melee behind them became apparent, half the Cargyl force turned about. That was Rogan's signal to attack. The highlanders raced through the opposing troops striking mounted men from their saddles, sweeping foot soldiers before them.

It did not take long, and it was not without cost, but the victory was complete. Less than half the attackers ran for their lives to the south. Rogan permitted pursuit only for a short distance. Soon nearly five hundred jubilant men and boys milled about on the lea. Choruses of Mythas and Rogan and Hollow Falls, the locals' name for Thundering Falls, rose over the bloody meadow. Mythas and Rogan met and hugged in glee before counting their losses. Mythas' cohort had suffered most. Boras and Henryn and Lynam and twenty others lay dead or maimed. But Ronald, thank God, rode up, bloodied by other men's gore.

"Now, Mythas?" he asked simply.

"Now, Ronald. But change your clothing and take a lowland horse. There will be fresh mounts waiting at Ransweyden. For God's sake, remove any Cargyl colors, we do not need you hung as a horse thief!" Rogan and Mythas watched as the young warrior rode hard to the southwest bearing a missive Mythas had written the night before.

"Do not worry," Rogan growled. "He will be all right. I know you would ride with him, but that would not be wise."

The next few days were filled with fear for Mythas. Ronald's absence and exposure to harm preyed on his mind constantly. Then a new force from Castle Cargyl moved into the high country. A courier under flag brought news that Lady Cargyl wished counsel with Mythas.

He joined her beneath a silken pavilion and delivered the remains of Lord Cargyl. It quickly became clear that the good Lady was well rid of her husband, which freed her to raise her fourteen-year-old son in her own manner. In the span of a single afternoon, they laid aside thoughts of vengeance and arrived at a pact. Cargyl renounced its tenuous claim on the far north country in exchange for a secure border and half of the goods produced by the northmen to be channeled through its merchants and tradesmen.

Be clear on one thing, Mythas," the lady warned at the last. "Should any harm befall my son, I will wreak my wrath upon the head of the cause. And unlike my husband, I am warned of your cleverness."

"I do not murder children," Mythas said simply. "And there is a matter of which you should be aware. I have sent a courier to the High King advising that this was no rising against his authority, but rather a border dispute."

"Then let us set down our agreement and send him a copy, Milord."

He was startled at the title. "You do me too much honor, ma'am."

"Nay. I but recognize the truth."

Before the sun was low, the pact had been drawn to the satisfaction of both and signed. At her insistence, he sealed his name with the signet ring on his right hand. A copy was dispatched to the High King's court.

A tired, happy Ronald returned two days later. They met at the Wydriff Tavern in Belloden. Solemnly, the young man brought gifts and tidings from the High King who viewed the force in the highlands not as a threat but as an extension of his own power. The handsome courier's words practically emptied the casks of the tavern as people heard the news and joined the celebration

That night Mythas loaded an exhausted Ronald aboard his horse and led him home. He slipped the youth into bed fully clothed and allowed him to rest. In the small hours, Ronald roused Mythas with a hand on his chest.

"Will you help me bathe? I would be clean when I love you."

"Time enough. Rest for now."

"Nay. I want you more than ever before. I need you."

"In truth, I need you, as well," Mythas breathed.

Mythas heated water and bathed the tall, slim, manly body with great tenderness. When they returned to bed, he surprised his lover, drawing him atop his body and spreading his legs. Ronald fell through them, gasping. "Truly?"

Young Ronald achieved his first penetration from behind, preferring the feel of Mythas' firm buttocks against his sensitive groin. His efforts struck that deep, stroking sensation Mythas had long-since come to prize. Lost in the wonder of the experience, Ronald grew ever wilder, ever more urgent. At the end, he poured words of love in Mythas' ear as he poured his seed into a more intimate place. Then truly understanding the joy he gave to his mate, he withdrew and spread himself to be mounted. In moments came his familiar refrain: "Your loving is wonderful, Mythas. But will you fuck me now?"

Highland myths tell of a mighty province that rose in the far north country after the High King summoned the victor of the Battle of Hollow Falls to his seat in Loquium. The High King examined a certain signet ring, bade the youth kneel, and dubbed him not Mythas Devistan, but Malthus Denislaven, Lord of the North Highland, drawing a gasp from the assembled courtiers as they recognized the name of a fallen royal house from across the sea.

The province prospered under its new regent. Life continued to be hard because it was a high, harsh land, but perhaps not so drab as it had been before. Castle Denislaven rose on a promontory overlooking a cold fjord where ships docked to bear away goods produced by the sturdy highlanders. Its ruins can be seen today, although it is known by another name. In recent times, a sepulcher containing two tombs inscribed with noble escutcheons topped by modest coronets and crosses was excavated. The remains in each were male... a regal, Christian couple without issue, without progeny, perhaps the reason they passed into legend.

ONE OUT OF TEN IS MAGIC
Jesse Monteagudo

It was a hot day on Celia Cruz Boulevard when I got to Dad's house. He'd died in the middle of the night, or so my teacher, Dr. Gomez, informed me before Healing class the day following. Needless to say, I was a wreck. It took all the strength I had to secure a leave of absence from the school administrator and book an afternoon flight from Orlando to Miami.

"Hector, I'm so sorry about your dad," Dr. Gomez said as I departed the dorm. "Take as much time as you need. You're one of our best Healing students and we don't want to lose you."

"Thank, you, Sir. I should be back soon." But soon was not soon enough for my roommate, Paco, a swarthy muscle boy who shared my studies by day and fucked my ass by night. Not even waiting until after I left, Paco had already recruited a cute Filipino to take my place. Good riddance, I thought as I left, while holding back my tears.

On the plane to Miami, I thought about Dad and what he meant to me. *Papá* Gabriel was not my blood father, of course. Magic men don't have children of their own, for you see, whenever a Magic boy is born into a straight household—and one out of every ten boys born is Magic—a Magic man adopts him and raises him as his own. Oftentimes Magic men raise their sons with the help of a partner, but Dad didn't have a partner, at least not while I knew him. That didn't stop him from being the best dad around, however, at least as far as I was concerned.

"Some day, Hector, you'll meet a man who will love you as much as you love him," Dad had told me the last time I saw him. "You'll know when it happens, but that's all in the future. For now you have to study hard and work hard, in order to help others with your Healing. With Magic comes great responsibility."

Unlike straight men, who use their sexual energy to dominate women and make children, we who are Magic use ours to heal, subdue and channel the forces of the universe. Ours is a power so great that we only share sex with one another, with Magic males who alone are able to contain and harness and appreciate the tremendous sexual potency we possess. Naturally straights revere us, as we utilize our Magic to help them whenever needed. Thus we are encouraged to flourish in our own homes and our own schools and temples and places of Magic sex-play.

*

When the cab dropped me in front of Dad's house—suddenly *my* house—I knew I had work to do. Though Dad's body had already been cremated, I had to arrange his memorial, tally his debts and assets, and settle his considerable estate. Fortunately, Dad left me everything, but even so, I needed time to work out my grief, for the loss of a parent would be hard on any young Magic who's never known a greater love—Paco having been merely a diversion, as were the many other boys whom I've sex-played with growing up and at the College of Healing Arts.

ZAP!!!

As I was about to enter the house, a bolt of lightning rushed past me and hit the door. I turned around to find my old pal, Oscar, poised to throw me a second bolt. I'd first met Oscar when we were in school. We were boys going through puberty and having to deal with the Magic that attended it. Since those days I've graduated to the prestigious College of Healing Arts and Oscar has become a professional Jokester—one who uses his Magic to entertain, delight or annoy. And *annoy* is precisely what Oscar was doing to me at that very moment, but… I let it slide.

"Welcome back, Hector," said Oscar, shaking the bolt from his hand. "I'm really sorry about your dad. What can I do to help?"

"You can cut the jokes and help me with Dad's memorial," I said as we entered the house together. Oscar was my first sex-playmate in childhood, and I am still fond of his bleached blond hair, muscled body, beer-can cock and round thunder-buns. But we've gone our separate ways, Oscar and I (and besides, we're both bottoms).

"Here we are," I said, sighing as we glanced around the house, which looked the same as always. Everything was in its place, exactly the way Dad had always insisted. Everything was intact… except for Dad, who'd been reduced to an urnful of ashes sitting atop the dining room table.

That's when I broke down.

Like a brother, Oscar stayed with me during my two-week period of mourning. Each night he would lie down beside me, hold me in his beautiful arms, and make me believe that someone still loved me. Besides helping me with Dad's memorial, Oscar used his magic to make me laugh, succeeding more times than not. By the end of my two weeks, I was well on my way back to normalcy, and Oscar couldn't have been happier.

"Welcome back to the real world, Hector. We've missed you around here."

"Thanks for helping me, Oscar," I said. "I guess I did make a fool of myself…"

"Don't worry about it, *papi*! I know how those things are. When my dad's partner died, Dad was so wrecked he almost brought the house down with him! And let's face it: we Latinos tend to go overboard in that department, no?"

"Well, I'm much better now," I replied. "I just called Dr. Gomez and told him that I'll be taking a few more days off before diving back to school."

"I'm glad you're staying a bit longer, *chulo*. I'm playing at a party tomorrow and might need your help. You can let me saw you in half or something," he grinned. "And then, damn it, let's go out and have some fun! Hey, that reminds me: our old gang is getting together for a reunion rumble this afternoon. You feel like joining us?"

Now, a rumble is a skirmish between two gangs of Magics, though nothing like the fights between straight gangs. Instead of fists and knives, we use Magic to "knock each other out," or stun our opponents into submission, whatever comes first. Rumbles amongst Magics have become so popular that a fabulous park has been set aside for them, away from the eyes of narrow minds or modest souls, which is just as well, since rumbles are always fought in the nude.

"Wow," I replied. "I haven't been to a rumble in quite a while. Have they changed much?"

"Not really. It all the same in the end: you zap him before he zaps you."

"I guess I could handle that. Who are we fighting against?"

"A gang of Afros from the north side," he replied.

Since all of the "Anglos" departed Miami twenty years ago, the only groups left in town are Latinos, Afros, Haitians and Mikasukis. Though we all get along as a rule, Latinos live in the south side of town, Afros in the north, Haitians in the east and Mikasukis in the west. Though Magics do tend to live with their own ethnic group, this division has never been exclusive or ever stopped a Magic from crossing over the line to work, study, heal or sex-play with another group's Magic. Sometimes we even find love in the other sectors, as was the case with Oscar's dad, whose partner was Haitian.

"The last rumble I went to," Oscar continued, "was against a gang of Mikasukis. The Miku I challenged used his twelve-inch *pinga* to shoot rays at me. *Whew…* I'm surprised I lasted as long as I did!"

"I bet you enjoyed it afterwards," I said smugly, knowing Magics are notoriously horny, and that rumbles inevitably end with a sexual free for all. All that sex energy, you know!

"Yeah, the fucker made me suck his monster dick, right in front of his whole tribe! My jaw still hurts!"

"Poor Oscar!" I laughed.

107

"You wouldn't be laughing if it happened to you, *puto*. But if you're gonna do the rumble, you better start getting ready. I'll pick you up in an hour."

Assuring him I'd be ready, I saw Oscar out the door. The last time I'd rumbled, I recalled being spied upon by a bunch of numbskulls who thought that seeing a group of Magic guys fighting naked was the funniest thing ever. That is, until they were chased into a lake by a swarm of angry wasps, set upon them by both gangs of pissed-off, butt-naked Magics. That sure taught *them* a lesson, I thought, as I prepared for the rumble.

"So who's gonna be there?" I asked Oscar when he came to pick me up. We were both wearing the Latino uniform: bright red and blue tank tops, tight black compression shorts and black shoes. Each gang has its own uniform, although, as we strip naked to play, it doesn't really matter during the rumble itself.

"All the guys from school," he answered. "Pedro, Pablo, Chucho, Jacinto, José—all the guys you saw at your dad's memorial. It's gonna be a good rumble, dude; everybody's anxious to see you again before you go back to school."

"And what about the Afro team?"

"The usual crowd from the north side," he said. "You'll probably remember most of them. Their only newbie, this kid named Jacques, just moved here from out of town a few months ago."

"Where's he from?"

"New Orleans. His dad's a master of Creole Magic. Jacques came to Florida to attend school, though I'm not sure where. From what I heard he's quite a fighter. Since he's new and you're visiting, it's a safe bet you'll be matched against him."

"That's cool," I said, just as we reached Alex Penelas Park where we found a dozen Latinos and thirteen Afros waiting for us. Since with Oscar and me there were fourteen Latinos, one more Afro was needed to have a rumble. That's when Jacques showed up. He was wearing the standard Afro uniform: black shoes, a black and green tank top and black shorts that barely covered his tight, muscular body. As with many young Magics, the hair on Jacques's head and body was completely removed but for the wicked eyebrows that crowned his coal-black eyes and a mustache and goatee that framed his strong lips. Even more inviting to me was the bulge that pushed against the front of his shorts. I could have spent all day long gazing at Jacques if Oscar hadn't brought me back to earth.

"Guys, you know the rules. Pair off and use your Magic to take down your opponent. You are allowed to *subdue*, not injure him. Each man who succeeds in taking down his opponent wins a point for his group. After we're through we add up the points and the losers take the winners out for pizza. *Entiende?*"

"We know the rules, Oscar," said the captain of the Afro Gang, who'd already begun taking off his clothes. "You forgot to mention we have to get naked!" In no time we'd all torn off our clothes and were ready to rumble. Nudity has always been obligatory in a rumble, not just in order to distract your opponent but because, obviously, sex-based Magic, like sex itself, is far less restricted when practiced in the nude. Bottom line, however, is the fact that we Magics are blatant exhibitionists who are proud of our bodies and love showing them off—even those who don't spend the countless hours at the gym or the stadium that many of us do.

We immediately paired off: one-on-one, Afro vs. Latino. Like Oscar said, I was pitted against Jacques, whose beauty distracted me from the start. His body was slim and muscular, with broad shoulders, incredible arms and chest, abs to die for, and powerful legs. Above all else, Jacques had low-hanging balls and a cock that was long and thick and sheathed with a tight, dark foreskin—one of my strongest fetishes.

"Ready, Men?" shouted Oscar, standing opposite his own opponent. "All right then! Stand your ground, and... BEGIN!" Suddenly, flashes of light and bolts of energy zapped all around me, as fourteen Afros faced off fourteen young Latinos in a test of wits and Magic. I tried hard to concentrate, to work up a concentration of energy that would down Jacques, but he just stood there, smiling at me, driving me crazy.

"Hey, *papi chulo!* You like what you see?" Jacques taunted, grabbing his irresistible monster cock and shaking it in my direction. "I betcha don't see anything quite like *this* back at school!" Well, let it suffice to say that Jacques ruined my concentration. How could I think of working Magic in front of this virile stud's perfect face and dick and body? My legs got weak and my cock got hard just staring at him.

ZAP!!!

Suddenly, an unseen force struck me, dashing me to the ground. Before I knew it Jacques was on top of me, holding me down for the count with his strong hands. The guy knew how to fight, to be sure. And there I lay, no doubt the victim of Creole sex Magic. Fortunately, the soft grass had broken my fall.

"You admit defeat, right?" Jacques crowed, still holding me against the ground, the head of his cock—rapidly on its way to becoming fully erect—emerging from its foreskin, pressed against my stomach.

"I do."

"Then you should also know that I wanted you from the moment I saw you," Jacques confessed, leaning down to kiss me. The world disappeared as our lips touched, mustaches meshed and our tongues began to explore. Our arms wrapped around one another in a fevered embrace and our hard cocks throbbed side-by-side between our bellies.

"Oh, *baby*, suck my cock," swooned Jacques, looking into my eyes. "I want your beautiful Latin lips to taste my dick." I didn't have to be told twice. At once on my knees, I reached for the ripe object of my desire. My beautiful Creole lover moaned with approval as I grasped his thick prick in my hand, pushed the last of his foreskin back with my tongue, and took the thick shaft down my throat. Though Jacques' dick was plenty big enough to choke a newbie, I was a plenty good-enough cocksucker to take it in stride down to the pubes, licking his sensitive underside along the way.

"Fuck, man, don't *stop…*" Jacques purred as he pinched my nipples hard, which sent a bolt of sex-electricity shooting through my body that thrilled me to such an extent it was all I could do to keep from swallowing Jacques's entire body. At the same time, I played with my new boyfriend's low-hanging balls with one hand while stroking myself with the other.

"You're a good cocksucker, *papi*," Jacques slurred, changing positions. "But I want some of your hot Spanish cock, too!" Once we settled into classic 69 position, Jacques took my eight-inch *pinga* in his mouth, and proceeded to blow me as intensely as I was him. We were strong young men, each giving the other a type of pleasure only two males can share. All around us our teammates fought and fell, but we were far too busy creating our own sex Magic to take any notice.

While Jacques and I continued to pleasure one another, Jacques, utilizing his spit as lubricant, took hold of my round buns, spread my cheeks apart and thrust first one finger and then a second up my rectum until they reached my prostate. I gasped with pleasure as Jacques began to finger-fuck me deeply, massaging my tender gland and driving me out of my mind.

"Oh, *baby*, keep sucking my *cock*!" Jacques cried, looking up. "I'm gonna get your ass so hot and bothered that you're gonna *beg* me to fuck you!" As he spoke Jacques added a third finger to his assplay, driving me into a state of ecstasy I'd never before experienced. My body literally glowed as Jacques shoved his cock deep down my throat while finger-fucking me, and it wasn't long before he'd gotten me right where he wanted.

"You're driving me nuts," I whimpered. "I need more than your fingers, man; I need your *cock*." Jacques just smiled as I continued begging for mercy. "Oh, *fuck* me, Jacques. Now!"

"You *got* it!" said Jacques, zapping a lubricated condom into his hand from nowhere, adding, while slipping it over his dick, "Your hot little *culo* is gonna get a fuckin' it'll never forget!" Jacques tossed my muscular legs over his shoulders and thrust his ten inches inside me, making me scream with pain and pleasure. Though I'd taken it up the ass many times before, I was not fully prepared for either Jacques' prodigious size, or the ferocity of his thrusting as my young Afro lover plowed me expertly with one forceful lunge after another. I began stroking myself in an effort to keep pace with Jacques's intense fucking.

"*Fuck* me, Jacques, *fuck* me!" I begged, as time and space dissolved, and Jacques continued to do just that, as our lovemaking took us to a place beyond reality, into the primal aberration of man fucking man.

Jacques continued to breed me, working my nipples roughly, which only increased the ecstatic pleasure and sex Magic that coursed through my body. Before long, Jacques's relentless motion, his hands working my tits, and my blurry grip on my own restless cock took me past the point of no return.

"I'm coming, Jacques!" I yelled, as geysers of jism bolted from my cock onto my stomach. Almost immediately, Jacques withdrew his dick from my ass and, breaking the condom in the process, shot spurt after spurt of man-milk in every direction. "Shiiiiiit!" he cried, collapsing onto me. Our passion spent, Jacques and I just held one another before we found the energy to move. We embraced and kissed each other passionately, reluctant to ever let go.

"I never experienced anything like that with a man before, Jacques," I said, finally able to speak. "Is this Creole Magic at work?"

"No, *papi*," said Jacques, playfully tweaking my tit. "This is more than Magic." We kissed again and again and again.

"You guys sure put on a show!" yelled Oscar, who stood above us. We looked up and saw 26 naked guys staring at us, all covered in sweat and some dripping cum. As we sheepishly got to our feet, we were greeted with a bit of laughter, and then...a mighty round of applause. Though Jacques and I were black and brown respectively, our faces got pretty damned red from all the attention.

"That's the problem with rumbles," said Oscar. "Certain guys always wind up getting diverted and I say... three cheers for that!" Jacques grabbed my ass, just for good measure, giving us both the beginnings of instant replay hard-ons.

"Anyway," Oscar continued, "as it turned out, the rumble ended in a tie, so we're all gonna go out and treat each other to pizza. You guys up for it?" he said, looking at me. "Hector...? Is there something wrong?"

I looked up, suddenly overcome with sadness. "I was just thinking that... I'll be heading back to the College of Healing Arts next week, and... I won't be able to hang out with you guys, or... see Jacques."

Jacques laughed. "Well, don't worry, *papi*. I should have told you sooner, but it just so happens that I've been accepted at the Healing school, as a special student. I'm going to be working on the application of Creole Magic in healing. But I'll need an assistant—and a *roommate*," he added significantly, continuing to gently fondle my ass.

I blushed. "Well, I *will* be needing a roommate, now that Paco's found himself another boyfriend...."

Up until the day of that rumble I had no idea what it was like to be in love. Dad always said that I would find out, that I would know it when it happened. And at that moment, I knew.

Very shortly thereafter, Jacques enrolled at the College of Healing Arts, specialized in the unique healing aspects of Creole Magic, and did indeed become my roommate and partner. From that point on Jacques and I have lived, studied and worked together. But more important, we have loved one another, creating life and sex Magic with our cocks and balls and minds and hearts and assholes and tits and spirits and mouths and hands and... our souls.

No, I am happy to say, this is definitely not the end of our story.

THE GAME
Meander Weeks

"**B**egin…"
The Gambler leaned back in his chair, the brim of his hat canted down, keeping cold eyes hidden in a mask of shadow. In the darkness of the room, the ghostly glow from the overhead lantern, glinting off the shiny surface of the playing cards, sent thin, blue fingers of reflected light dancing through the shadows. Still, the Gambler maintained his unblinking gaze upon his opponent. The Gunslinger was no stranger to cards, that much was certain from the utter lack of expression on his face.

"Two." The Gunslinger stated. The Gambler watched as two of the Gunslinger's cards were set face down on the table, white edges glowing starkly as they were taken out of play.

Silently, the Gambler sent two cards sliding across the expanse of table, as—silently—two of his own cards were placed face down, another pair settled atop those he'd chosen to retain. Ignoring his cards, the Gambler folded his hands atop them, his cold eyes watching the Gunslinger rearranging his hand, only to pause and reshuffle them into a more pleasing order. When the Gunslinger looked up, the Gambler continued to stare, only the barest dip of his chin inviting his adversary to place a bet.

"Aren't you going to look at your cards?" The Gunslinger demanded.

The Gambler remained silent. Waiting…

The Gunslinger scowled, raised one hand to push his hat back, and dug at his scalp with his fingernails. Cursing under his breath, he jerked his hat back into place and attempted to ignore the lock of blond hair hanging in his eyes. He found the Gambler's silence infuriating, all the more so because of it's very smugness. Glancing at his cards, the Gunslinger's eyes narrowed—he knew better then to allow even a hint of a smile to grace his lips. A full house… Aces and tens… The chances of the Gambler being able to beat that hand after drawing two…? Slim. Self-assured, he sent his last two gold coins spinning into the center of the table.

"Well?" The Gunslinger demanded, confidant he had it beat. He *knew* he had it. There was no way the Gambler could have drawn what he needed. No way. Still, there was that snide suggestion of doubt hovering in the Gunslinger's mind. There *is* a chance, of course. There is always a chance. Leaning forward, he stared hard the Gambler, *willing* him to fold, to blink, to look the least bit disconcerted.

The Gambler smiled, the expression twisting the corners of his mouth into a near smirk—after an evening of revealing nothing, he knew it would throw the Gunslinger off. Slowly, calmly, his arm stretched out and nimble fingers dropped two gold coins atop those in the center of the table. The single word "Call" escaped his lips in a grating whisper, his hand dropping to rest alongside his cards as he watched the Gunslinger's face.

"Call?" the Gunslinger replied, staring at the gambler, disbelief more then evident on his features. The Gambler simply nodded, still wearing the barest hint of a smile. Lacing his fingers, he leaned back in his chair, the leather seat creaking in the hollow darkness of the room.

"Show me your cards."

For a moment, the Gunslinger looked uncertain; his lips pressed tightly as he stared down at the cards in his hand. He *had* to have it; there was simply no way the Gambler could beat his hand. Scowling, his gaze snapped back to the Gambler's face, whose smug expression did not go unnoticed. Nor did the fact that his opponent had yet to even peek at his cards. Still, the last of his gold lay on the table and his food and stable bills had yet to be paid. Frowning, he slapped his cards face up on the table.

"Full house. Aces and Tens." Smirking, the Gunslinger leaned back in his chair and, drawing a cheroot from his pocket, placed it between his lips. Striking a match off the tabletop, he continued to stare at the Gambler, his triumphant face illuminated by the flare from the match as he lit his smoke. Exhaling a cloud of smoke from the corner of his mouth, he snapped the match out, let it fall to the table, and said: "Well…?"

Across from him, the Gambler, his cold, pale eyes staring at the cards laid out on the table, did not so much as move. The Gunslinger felt a thrill run through him. He had the bastard; he *knew* it, but still… it was disturbing that the Gambler hadn't conceded the pot. No, it was *annoying*. Glancing down at the cards on the table, the Gunslinger narrowed his eyes, his anxiety escalating second by silent second. When at last the silence had grown unbearably loud, he slammed one hand on the table and, leaning forward in his chair, demanded of his opponent: "What are you waiting for? Turn the damn cards over."

Still relaxed back in his chair, the Gambler smiled, one hand moving to rest atop the facedown cards. He could feel the tension rolling off the Gunslinger. He could smell the man's sweat mingling with the bitter scent of the man's cheroot; he could *see* it, beading on his opponent's upper lip. Relishing every second that passed with malicious intensity, it was not until after The Gambler could discern the pulse ticking in the Gunslinger's neck that, chuckling, he leaned forward in his chair.

"If you lose, you have nothing left," The Gambler's stated plainly, his long fingers caressing the mysterious hand of cards lying face-down on the table, his voice lowered to a mellow thrum. After a pregnant pause, he tilted his chin down, the pale eyes seeming to glow in the hollow darkness as he caught the Gunslinger's eye. "How would you feel about an alternate bet?"

Alternate bet...? The Gunslinger frowned, his lips twisting into a scowl as he glanced from the Gambler's cards to the man's face. What the hell was he talking about? He had to realize he couldn't possibly win this hand.

"You can't change the bet now." The Gunslinger snarled. "My cards are on the table."

He watched as the Gambler nodded somberly, his fingers tracing a circle around the un-glimpsed hand of poker.

"And I've no idea what I'm holding," he answered with a smile.

"I'm going to win and you know it." The Gunslinger snarled. Chewing on the end of his cheroot, he exhaled another cloud of smoke into the air above the table. "You're trying to trick me."

"Not at all." The Gambler answered calmly. "If you win, you keep the pot. If I win, you *still* keep the pot, but... I keep *you*... for one night."

Rendered silent, the Gunslinger stared as time ground to a halt. When the Gambler leaned forward, he found himself leaning back, a look of consternation spreading across his face.

The Gunslinger snatched the cheroot from his lips. Having a fairly good idea of what the Gambler was implying, he was no stranger to the look in his opponent's eyes. Still, the coldness that resided within those pale orbs was not something that bespoke a pleasant night's affair. The Gambler was somehow trying to waylay him into relinquishing his hard-earned winnings. Looking down at his cards, the Gunslinger frowned and twisted the cheroot between his fingers before returning it to his lips. He couldn't afford to lose, that much was certain. Whatever underhanded game the Gambler was playing, he'd obviously outsmarted himself.

"Done." The Gunslinger smirked around the cheroot clutched between his teeth. "Turn over your cards."

"Patience, my friend," admonished the Gambler, flashing a predatory smile, his gaze remaining locked on the Gunslinger's face. "All things in due time." Flipping over the first card, he set it out in the center of the table.

"King of Hearts," the Gunslinger called.

The Gambler inclined his head, watching the Gunslinger rather than the cards. Again, nimble fingers turned another card, sliding it across the table to rest alongside the first.

"*Jack* of Hearts," the Gunslinger murmured. Tugging the cheroot from his lips, he scowled at the Gambler, his eyes narrowing in response to the smug look confronting him. "Turn the damned cards over."

The Gambler chuckled, his fingers rising to his brow in a mocking salute. "As you like." Flipping over the third card, he slid it to the center of the table, not so much as glancing down at his hand.

For a long moment, the Gunslinger stared incredulously at the three cards, his tongue darting out to moisten his lips. "Goddamned *Ten* of Hearts," he said. "Luck. Just dumb luck." Shifting in his chair, the Gunslinger scowled at his opponent and the cards on the table. "There's no way you have a royal flush."

The Gambler did not respond, his features remaining coldly flat as he watched the Gambler shifting nervously in his chair. Once his opponent had fallen silent he turned over the fourth card, sliding it to the center of the table alongside the others.

Silence.

The Gambler's eyes remained locked on the Gunslinger's face, one brow arching sharply. Across from him, the Gunslinger shifted in his chair; his right hand rose to mop the sweat beading on his brow. The Gambler observed the panic rising in his opponent's eyes, noticed his lips compressing into a thin, flat line. "Well?" he said, "tell me what you see."

"The Ace of Hearts." Almost convulsively, the Gunslinger jerked forward and stabbed the cheroot dead in the ashtray, the acrid tinge of burnt paper and tobacco immediately compelling him to sit back in his chair. For a long moment, he simply stared at the Gambler's exposed cards, his utter disbelief masked beneath the brim of his hat.

"Are you ready?"

The Gambler's voice echoed oddly, as if the words had reached the Gunslinger's ears from a great distance, or so he would have sworn. Shaking his head to clear it, he forced himself to look at the final unturned card on the table. Thinking that what was transpiring couldn't possibly be happening, he nodded curtly and returned his gaze to the Gambler's face. His eyes narrowed. The last card was flipped over and slid to the center of the table. Neither man looked down. The Gunslinger could have sworn he felt waves of satisfaction emanating from his opponent, could feel his own heart beating violently in his chest. His focus unwavering from those cold, pale eyes across the table, the Gunslinger watched as his opponent leaned back in his chair and calmly laced his fingers.

"Well?" The Gambler repeated, arching an eyebrow, his hands rising to place his interlocked knuckles gently against his lips. When his opponent finally looked down at the final card, the paling of his features told the Gambler all he needed to know.

"Queen of Hearts." The horrified Gunslinger whispered.

The Gambler calmly gathered his hat from where he'd placed it on the edge of the table. Returning it to his head, he smoothed nonexistent wrinkles from his coat before sliding the gold across the table toward the dumbfounded Gunslinger. Not once had he glanced at his cards, nor apparently had any intention of doing so. Instead, he drew back from the table and rolled smoothly to his feet, the heels of his boots thumping hollowly on the floor as he made his way toward the door.

Pausing at the door before exiting, the Gambler glanced back at the Gunslinger, a smirk distorting his impassive lips upon finding the man still staring in mute disbelief at the exposed cards. "I'll expect you at ten sharp, he said with authority. Room thirteen."

Somewhere in the distance, a clock chimed the hour. Ten O'clock. Standing in the hallway, the Gunslinger stared at the closed door confronting him. Room thirteen. He'd considered paying his bill and leaving town before the time to honor his debt came due, but pride had prevented him from doing so. Pride, however, deserted him the moment the clock finished chiming the tenth hour. The Gambler was in there; he knew that without having to knock. He could hear the crackle of fire burning in the hearth within. He'd have sworn he could hear the other man's breathing as well.

"Damn it..." he whispered to himself in a fury of self-recrimination, knowing that if he didn't knock soon, he'd turn on his heels and retreat: a welsher, a coward. Scowling, the Gunslinger pushed his hat to the back of his head, his hand racing to his brow in a nervous gesture. Dropping his hand, he curled his fingers into a tight fist. The rap of his knuckles sounded too loud to his own ears. Far too loud.

"Enter."

The Gambler's voice drifted into the hallway from behind the door. Hearing it, the Gunslinger paled; his hand dropped to the knob, but he simply stood there, unwilling or... unable to turn it, to nudge himself forward.

"You are already late," the Gambler's voice sounded from within, his tone holding a note of smugness or annoyance, perhaps both. Hearing it provided the impetus. Pushing the door open, the Gunslinger stepped into the room.

"Close the door." The Gambler's voice floated up from a large, wingback chair turned toward the fireplace. From where he stood at the door, only one black-clad leg and a long-fingered hand cupping a brandy snifter were visible to the Gunslinger. He closed the door behind him.

"Very good. Now, disrobe and come over here." The brandy snifter was raised aloft, the amber liquid in the glass shimmering in the firelight before it was carried out of sight.

The Gunslinger frowned and, squaring his shoulders, removed his hat and coat, which he hung on hooks next to the door. Boots, gun belt, pants, shirt and underclothing followed. Rather then leave them balled on the floor, the Gunslinger tossed them into a nearby chair before stepping away from the door. Two steps into the room, he paused, his hand raking the hair back off his face in a nervous gesture. Staring at the back of the Gambler's chair, he let his hand drop, his fingers brushing briefly along the semi-erection resting against the curve of his hip. He was no stranger to sex, but this situation was not one with which the Gunslinger was familiar. Drawing in a slow breath, he set his shoulders and stepped up to his adversary's chair.

The Gambler was fully dressed in black slacks, shiny, pointy-toed boots and a frilly white shirt that had to be French. His hair was down, free of the small leather clasp that had held it off his face during the game, but the thick cascade of ebony curls did nothing to soften the Gambler's features. If anything, they served to make his eyes all the more pale, hollow, and cold. The Gunslinger watched as the Gambler took a long sip of his brandy, the hand holding the snifter then lowering to rest on the arm of the chair. The Gambler hadn't looked at him… yet, his gaze remaining fixed on the flames dancing in the hearth. The Gunslinger swallowed, his Adam's apple bobbing as he took in the dandified form of the man seemingly ignoring him. Despite a momentary surge of annoyance, the Gunslinger felt his shaft lengthening, touched the welling bead of precum gathering in its tiny slit and brought it to his lips. The heat of the fire was intense, but he shivered nonetheless, and instinctively pressed his twitching fingers flat against his thighs.

The Gambler once again raised the brandy snifter, his gaze turning from the fire to the firelight playing on its amber contents, where it paused for a moment before crossing to the Gunslinger, whose pale eyes swept over the man's frame in a single, assessing glance.

"Very nice," he quietly leered. "Now, kneel." The Gambler raised the glass to his lips, taking another long sip of brandy. His lips twisting into a thin smile, he watched as the Gunslinger complied with his command. Leaning back in his chair, thinking how refreshing it was when a man took losing so graciously, the Gambler observed the Gunslinger in silence, noting that the man's posture, even on his knees, was proud—a fact that spoke in the Gunslinger's favor. "Very nice, indeed."

Leaning forward, the Gambler braced his arm against his black-clad thighs, his nimble fingers drumming against the snifter in his hand. He could literally smell the Gunslinger's arousal emanating from the sweat beading on the naked man's flesh. Smiling thinly, he took another swallow of brandy before pressing the glass into the Gunslinger's hand.

"Lean back until your shoulders touch the floor." The Gambler whispered. "Rest the brandy glass on the flat of your stomach with the mouth facing your erection." As the Gunslinger complied, the Gambler nudged his knees apart with the toe of his left boot. Leaning back in the chair, his lip remaining curled in a sardonic smile, he admired the subtle tightening of muscles forced into vivid definition by assuming such an awkward position. He could hear the Gunslinger's breathing increase to strained panting. When the

Gunslinger closed his eyes, the Gambler's smile turned triumphant; this was the moment he'd been waiting for.

"Open your eyes," He ordered. When the Gunslinger obeyed, the Gambler inclined his head. "Very good. Now, I want you to masturbate..." Pausing, his elbows braced on the arms of his chair, his long fingers lacing as he observed his prize, he then added, "...Into the glass."

The Gunslinger forced himself to suppress a low moan that rose in his throat at the Gambler's command, his gaze remaining locked on his companion's face. Exhaling a hissing breath, the tip of his tongue rounding his lips, he placed one hand on the brandy glass to hold it in place. *Men pay their debts*, he reminded himself, *as best they can*. Resisting the urge to close his eyes, his free hand smoothed down his torso, his fingers brushing a teasing caress over his nipples. Noting the glimmer of lust in the Gambler's eyes, he slowed the pace of his hand movement and allowed his fingers to trace random patterns in the sweat beading the tight musculature of his torso.

The Gunslinger spread his knees further apart and arched his spine as his fingers curled at last around the length of his turgid cock. Somewhat amazed that he was able to maintain an erection, much less derive any enjoyment from his predicament, he held the Gambler's lascivious gaze. His teeth clenched down on his lower lip as he slowly tightened his fist to the point of pain. Yanking the skin of his penis up, the Gunslinger brushed the rough pad of his thumb over the head of his cock, spreading glistening precum over his sensitive cockhead.

The Gambler licked his lips, his visual focus narrowing upon the Gunslinger's hand motion. He watched raptly as his companion's hand played along the length of glistening cock, noting the subtle play of the firelight over the distended muscles of the Gunslinger's forearm. Unlacing his hands, he eased to the edge of his chair and permitted his fingers to trace the quaking line of sinew straining in one of the Gunslinger's thighs. Nudging the Gunslinger's knees even further apart, he cupped the man's balls, kneading them with a firm grip that elicited a loud groan from the Gunslinger's lips.

"Shhhh," he admonished, releasing the Gunslinger's balls, "you're doing fine." The Gambler dropped to one knee alongside his companion's compromised form. Licking his lips, another predatory smile distorting his lips, the Gambler lowered his hand and, licking it first, pressed one finger into the kneeling man's anus.

The Gunslinger whispered, "Oh... *Christ*," and bucked his hips as the Gambler's finger probed deeply into his ass. His fingers tightening around the length of his throbbing cock, the Gunslinger tossed his head in an effort to free the longish bangs from his sweat-drenched brow. When the Gambler forced a second finger through the tight ring of muscle into the warm, caressing depths beyond, the Gunslinger's knees jerked involuntarily up off the floor. Panting, masturbating furiously, his entire body shuddering in an attempt to direct his orgasm into the glass, the Gunslinger howled wordlessly as his seed tore its way up through his bursting cock and spattered violently into the brandy snifter.

The Gambler's fingers slipped from the heat of the Gunslinger's sopping body.

"Drink it."

The Gambler's command just barely permeated the post-orgasmic fog clouding the Gunslinger's mind. Supporting his weight with his elbows, he once again met the Gambler's cold, pale stare.

"*Drink* it," the Gambler repeated with emphasis, his tone turned chill, his eyes narrowing as he rolled to his feet and scooted back into the high-backed chair. The Gunslinger closed his eyes, tightened his fingers around the brandy glass, and pushed himself up to his knees. Exhaling a ragged breath, he lowered his eyes and confronted the glass of brandy and semen resting on his thigh. *Drink it*, he thought, before reestablishing eye contact. The weight of the Gambler's stare—the rising anger it bore at his hesitance to drink—was palpable. *Yes, men pay their debts.*

Without so much as blinking, the Gunslinger raised the glass to his lips and swallowed the contents in a single gulp. Somewhere in the distance, a clock chimed the hour. Eleven O'clock. Had merely an hour passed? There were many yet to follow before dawn. Lowering the glass, maintaining eye contact, the Gunslinger's countenance remained unreadable.

"It's always so much nicer when one obeys without having to be told twice," the Gambler frowned, his hand reaching out to push the sweat-soaked bangs from the Gunslinger's brow. "Pity I'll only have this one night with you." Smirking, he drew his hand back, long fingers curling around the arm of his chair. "Stand up, please."

The Gunslinger obeyed, his pale eyes sweeping the length of the man's frame. Leaning back in his chair, the Gambler stretched one leg out, his hips rolling forward as he unfastened the ornate silver buckle which held his belt in place. He watched as the Gunslinger glanced at his groin, watched the man fight the urge to lick his lips and then fail. The Gambler smiled, for real, for the first real time that evening.

"Bend over my knee…" Drawing his belt free, the Gambler folded it in half, the buckle and opposite end held loosely in one hand. "…Like an errant child." The Gunslinger's incredulous eyes snapped up to the Gunslinger's face.

"What?"

"You heard me," the miscreant stated simply, staring beyond the rage the Gunslinger's eyes projected as he calmly ran the smooth leather loop along the length of the Gunslinger's thigh. Without warning, the belt snaked back and out, snapping a thin red welt along the curve of the Gunslinger's hip.

"You lost the bet, or… have you forgotten?"

The reminder prompted the Gunslinger to look away. Scowling, he stared at the flames dancing in the fireplace. He had lost the bet; he had lost the bet; he had lost the bet… Squaring his shoulders, he stepped up to the Gambler's chair and draped himself over black, velvet-clad thighs—the position alone, enough to bring a flush of humiliation to the Gunslinger's face.

"That's better," The Gambler murmured. Closing his eyes, the Gunslinger swallowed hard as the admittedly pleasant sensation of the Gambler's palm smoothed over the curve of his ass. Forcing himself to breathe naturally, he lowered his head, taking momentary shelter in the damp fall of his hair. Above him, the Gambler's voice hissed in the shadows shifting about the fire-lit room.

"There are times when even the strongest of men are forced to submit to forces beyond their control." The Gambler said. "Sometimes it takes… more strength to surrender then fight."

The Gunslinger's nostrils flared, his head snapping up as the belt landed across his ass in a vicious blow. Gasping, he sucked a sharp breath between his lips. He could feel the stinging heat radiating outward from the blow and his hips shifted against his will, the muscles twitching in anticipation of another blow, but it was not until the Gambler spread his legs farther apart that he let the belt drop again. The second blow landed alongside the first, the third and fourth tracing a steady path down the length of the Gunslinger's thighs. By the fifth blow, he found himself rising up on his toes, his ass pushed into the air as low grunts of pain escaped his lips, as he felt his cock beginning to stir, despite the degradation he suffered. The belt's finally being draped over his shoulders allowed him to ease back down against the Gambler's lap, being careful to adjust his crotch in such a way as to accommodate the erection pressed between black velvet and the flat of his stomach.

"That wasn't so bad now, was it?" The Gambler inquired smugly, his palm caressing the welts crisscrossing the Gunslinger's ass. "How many men have you fucked?"

The Gunslinger shook his head. The men he'd topped was not a topic open for conversation—No, most definitely not—though he made no effort to deny the truth of it. Instead, he pushed up again, pressing his ass against the hand that was consoling his seared flesh. It was the sound of the Gambler's pleased laughter that brought his head back up, that inspired his dark eyes to dart a glance over his shoulder to the man's face. He watched, unblinking, as the Gambler slipped a hand beneath his stomach, grabbed his cock, and cranked its hard length into the gap between his black-clad thighs. Closing his eyes, the Gunslinger bucked his hips forward to seat his cock fully between the Gambler's legs, the sensation of muscular thighs gripping his cock driving any additional thought of humiliation from his mind. When the Gambler's naked hand landed sharply on his ass, the groaning Gunslinger thrust his ass upward to meet the abusing palm before driving his erection forward into the sumptuous velvet grip of the Gambler's thighs.

The Gambler's eyes glittered in the firelight, his lips sculpted into a cruel smile as he continued to rain blows upon the Gunslinger's ass. The sight of the

Gunslinger draped over his lap, his ass red glowing with hand prints, his hips thrusting wildly into the black velvet crevasse, was almost too beautiful to bear. Restraining himself, the Gambler resumed the gentle smoothing of the Gunslinger's hips with his stinging palms. Without warning, he pressed two fingers into the Gunslinger's ass, his hand thrusting in time to the wildly bucking hips, his tapered fingers scissoring to loosen the tight muscle. Then, as if taking his cue from the Gunslinger's rapid breathing, he pulled his fingers free as abruptly as he had inserted them.

"Not yet," the Gambler hissed, suddenly yanking the Gunslinger's testicles down sharply to prevent the man from reaching orgasm. Abruptly, he pushed the Gunslinger from his lap and leapt to his feet in a single motion, where he loomed above the Gunslinger's prone form.

The Gambler unfastened his pants and withdrew his erection. He dropped to one knee between the panting Gunslinger's legs and, leaning over him, wrapped his overly elegant arm tightly around the battered man's waist.

"Not yet," the Gambler repeated.

Lugging the Gunslinger up to his knees, the Gambler nudged his debtor's legs apart as his free hand guided the head of his cock to the entrance of the Gunslinger's pre-relaxed sphincter muscle. The Gambler gritted his teeth and, tossing his head back, his lips parting to emit a guttural moan of untold pleasure, pressed into the tight orifice. Beneath him, the Gunslinger tensed; his back arched up; his fingers pressed white-knuckled against the floor as he lunged back against the cock thrusting into his body. Snarling, the Gambler released the Gunslinger's waist and curled his deft fingers around the length of the kneeling man's obvious sexual desire. While thrusting brutally, the Gambler's hand glided the penile skin up and down the throbbing length of the Gunslinger's erection with increasing rapidity.

Growing hoarse and hyperventilating, the Gunslinger rolled his head, an inarticulate bellow escaping his throat with every thrust of the Gambler's hips, pleasure's torment forcing him repeatedly backwards to strive for a deeper connection with the heathen laying claim to his body. With ecstatic ferocity the Gunslinger undulated beneath the Gambler. Unaware of licking the salty sweat from his lips, unaware of the Gambler jerking him off, unaware of anything but the exquisite passion rising from deep within his cock, the intense pressure that finally launched his first hot blast of seed upward against his chest and belly drew a feral cry from him.

Unable to support himself any longer, the Gunslinger collapsed on the floor, as the Gambler continued to brutally ravage his ass. Dripping with sweat and spattered with his own semen, the Gunslinger had been reduced to quiet whimpering—a sound the Gambler found provocative, which urged him onward until he finally tensed and, releasing a sharp bellow of his own into the shadowy room, deposited his seed into the Gunslinger's ass.

Having felt every wracking spurt of the Gambler's cock, the Gunslinger closed his eyes and focused on the act of breathing. The Gambler's withdrawal from his tortured rectum was signaled with little more than a grunt, but the Gunslinger lacked either the will or strength to notice anything but a sense of relief.

Behind him, the metallic sound of the Gambler's zipper being drawn up was followed by the hollow thumping of pointy-toed boots on the floor. The Gunslinger opened his eyes and took in what little view of the room surrounding him was afforded from his disadvantageous position before shutting them again. His every square inch was sore and aching; perhaps he'd momentarily slipped into unconsciousness, but all at once he felt himself being lifted from the floor and deposited upon a bed. He felt the Gambler's unforgettable hand once again smoothing the sweat-soaked hair away from his face. He felt coins being pressed into his palm.

The Gunslinger remained still for quite some time, only the numb curling of his fingers around the coins and his shallow breathing betraying signs of life. Without opening his eyes, he listened to the sound of withdrawing boot steps, to the sound of the door being opened and then closed.

The Gunslinger rolled onto his back, a self-satisfied smile ever so slowly tracing over his lips as he curled one arm between the pillow and the back of his head. The Gambler would not return to the room; he knew that without a doubt, but he also knew that the next saloon, the next lonely hotel room awaited any number of Gamblers less than a day's ride up the road. Fully grinning at that point, the Gunslinger snapped his fingers tight around the coins. He'd have to leave the room by noon, and then haul ass to make it by nightfall, but he was fairly certain that he'd find *the* Gambler there, waiting for him when he arrived, anxious to begin yet another round of The Game.

The Gunslinger extended his arm and, barking a laugh, deposited his fistful of gold upon the bedside table.

"Royal Flush, my ass."

MINESHAFT MEN
Leo Cardini

"**K**now why it's so fuckin' fat?" Butch, the beefy bartender, demanded of Fritz, arresting the attention of the dozen or so men in the bar as he pulled his thick, juicy cock out of the muscleman's mouth and held it up in front of his face.

Fritz, kneeling just outside the far end of the bar in boots, a leather cockring and a leather ballstretcher, tugged on his swollen nipples, his eyes glued to that big piece of cut cock.

"No, sir. Why?"

"It's fuckin' water-logged from all the cocksuckers who've worked on it."

"Ohhh…"

Butch might've been right about his cock. He tended bar at the Mineshaft every Saturday afternoon, shirtless in Levi 501s with the fly unbuttoned and his huge piece of meat and two big nuts hanging out. It was an impressive package on an impressive man and he loved showing it off. I'd say on average he probably talked a good half dozen men into deepthroating his dick every Saturday afternoon, usually first-timers, like Fritz, who'd flown over from Germany to visit the Shaft because he'd heard so much about it from his buddies back home.

"Ohhh" became "mmpphh!" when Butch shoved Fritz all the way down on his dick again. But the sound of Fritz momentarily gagging as his throat adjusted was then upstaged by "Oh! Oh! Ohh!" in a decidedly Latin accent.

Since I was leaning back against the bar about a yard away from Fritz and Butch, all I had to do was look straight ahead into the middle of the room to find its source, Ricardo, in his black boots and black leather vest, forced into a bending position over the pool table. He was clawing the green felt as a tall, powerfully-built stud with the front of his white tanktop pulled up behind his neck and his frayed denim cutoffs pulled down around his ankles fucked him hard and deep with his veiny monstercock.

Ricardo raised one knee up onto the table. I couldn't figure out if he was trying to give the man fucking him better access to his hole or if he was struggling to escape, discovering that as much as he craved big dick up his ass, this time he'd gotten more than he'd bargained for.

As interested as I was in Ricardo's pool table adventure, my attention was diverted to my right by Kurt, the muscleman/artist/bartender. Everyone in

Manhattan seemed to have what I call a "slash identity," making me, I guess, a writer/proofer/cashier—at least until yesterday.

Anyway, Kurt had just stepped out of the doorless men's room. He paused to readjust his post-piss meat in his black jockstrap, and then made his way over to his usual seat where the bar "L"s in for a yard, rejoining his sketch pad, his pencils and his beer. I saw him look down the length of the bar to where Butch was still facefucking Fritz, and I knew I was witnessing the birth of a drawing I'd see later at the Leslie-Lohmann Art Gallery in Soho, where his sketches of Mineshaft men in action were exhibited. He spent every Saturday afternoon here in boots and a jockstrap, sketching. He had short blond hair, blue eyes and pale skin. His muscled body looked more sculpted than pumped-up, as much a work of art as any of his drawings of the heavy-duty mansex that was the essence of the Mineshaft.

Beyond Kurt, in the men's room, I saw Philip, naked on his haunches between the urinal and the toilet. His face was the same height as the urinal and I knew he'd be spending the afternoon in there, as always, swallowing pissload after pissload from men like Kurt.

Then a scuffle to the right of the men's room redirected my attention yet again and I saw Cam the doorman throwing someone down the seventeen steps that led up to the Mineshaft entrance from the unmarked street door below. This happened a lot. Many men wanted to enter the Mineshaft, but not all were allowed. And sometimes the biggest sissies in the preppiest clothes put up the most fuss.

"You throw them down from left to right," I once overheard Cam say, "so they can catch the banister and break their fall."

If any one man epitomized the Mineshaft to me, it was Cam, in his square-toed boots, snug-fitting jeans, black leather vest and denim workshirt unbuttoned halfway down his chest. Of all the men of the Mineshaft, he was the hottest, not only because of his bulging basket, or his hairy, he-man pecs, or the day-or-so's growth of beard he always sported, but because of that burning look in his eyes and the sly way he had of seducing men into talking about their fantasies, drawing them out, so once he finally let them in, they were all hot and bothered, as if he had cast a spell on them.

Kurt lifted his beer can and gave it a shake in Butch's direction for another. Butch pulled his cock out of poor Fritz's mouth and walked away to serve Kurt, strutting behind the bar with his hard, spit-shiny dick bobbing before him, reaching into the beer bin for a cold Bud, snapping it open and setting it down in front of Kurt. Butch had worked Fritz up into a cockcrazy state and, needing dick much too much to wait for Butch to return, knee-stepped over to me to nose in on Danny, who'd been sucking me slow, steady and deep for the longest time.

Tall, lean Danny with the huge horsedick seated on the bar stool was a fixture Saturday afternoons. He'd turned worn-out into an esthetic, wearing an

126

old jockstrap that'd lost its elasticity, sagging sweat socks where he stashed his grass and poppers, and scuffed, dirty sneakers. Even the look on his face was worn, as if he were exhausted by his insatiable cockhunger. Men fed him their meat like leftover table scraps, pulling it out and shoving his face into their crotches for servicing while continuing to talk with their buddies, which was just the way he liked it, spending time alone with a man's meat, lost in a forest of men's legs while the guy was otherwise occupied.

Danny ceded my dick to Fritz to lick my balls while Fritz deepthroated me with no preliminaries and hardly any gagging. Now, I don't mean to brag, but you have to know this to fully appreciate Fritz's skill at cocksucking; I've got a thick, cut, veiny piece of meat I'm proud to say fits the stereotype of the Italian Stallion.

In no time I could feel the cum boiling over in my balls. I closed my eyes and leaned back against the bar. Oh yeah, just the way I liked it: buddy sex, hot and uncomplicated, with guys hanging out in a divey bar on a Saturday afternoon—men worshipping men, men servicing men, men taking care of each other's needs, helping out a mate or two.

I gave myself up to the moment, rode the feeling and thrust out my hips, moaning: "Ohhhh! Oh yeah! ...Yeah! ...Yeeaa..."

Just as I was about to pass the point of no return my right ear tickled with...

"You know what, Leo? You should get a job here!"

"...Ohhhh!!!!!!"

Tony's words mingled with the onrush of orgasm and I yelled out, shooting load after load of cum down the German cocksucker's throat. He swallowed it like a pro. One thing about Germans at the Mineshaft: they did everything well. Their English was precise and their sexual skills unparalleled, as if all German queerboys were forced into apprenticeships with expert masters before being set free in the world of man-to-man sex.

Oh yeah, he knows just how to milk me, how to bring me down from the flight of orgasm, when to stop sucking by letting my dick just rest in his mouth as I recuperate....

And then Tony. I've forgotten to tell you about him. He'd been next to me all this time with his own cocksucker. He tossed his head back and shot, upstaging my own orgasm with a roar. Whenever Tony came, he wanted everyone to stop, look and listen. Such a showoff, but with a body like his, he got away with it.

"Thanks a lot, asshole," I whispered into his ear. "You couldn't wait to tell me that until *after* I came?"

He might've been my best friend, but he wasn't too bright, and sometimes his sense of timing really sucked.

I pulled up my jeans and stuffed my meat back into them. I didn't even need to clean it off—like I said, the Germans do everything well. Bending over,

I whispered thanks into Fritz's ear. He was back to blowing Butch, and issued a guttural acknowledgement without breaking his cocksucking rhythm. I then crossed the room to sit on the bench that ran the length of it. The only illumination in the main bar, except for a few dim red bulbs here and there, came from four lamps suspended above the bar, shining down a quartet of overlapping circles, so I was in near darkness.

Tony joined me, cleaning off his cum-slimy dick en route with paper towels.

"Sorry. It just came to me. But it's a great idea isn't it?"

"Yeah, sure... Hey, I think I did a real stupid thing yesterday."

Here's the situation. Tony and I had moved down from Boston the year before, in 1976. No, we really were just best friends. In fact, we grew up together in the same neighborhood in Jamaica Plain, the working-class section of Boston. After earning my bachelor's degree I wanted to move to New York City to be a "real" writer, and Tony said, "wicked cool," which is what you say in Boston, and of course joined me. He figured he could wait tables anywhere, and said he was running out of men in Boston anyway, which might have been true considering the way he got around.

So after a year in New York, I had a sometimes on, sometimes off proofreading job at a law firm, and a part-time job nights working in a used record shop just down the street from our West Village apartment. I was miserable and, feeling that was no kind of life for a writer, had just quit both jobs the day before. It felt great doing it when I did it, but now I was... well, out of work.

"No, you did the right thing," Tony assured me. "I can cover us both until you find something. Like you say, you need to fucking *live* like a writer."

He was right about that. I needed to get a life before I could write about one. And a life wasn't being acquired proofing dull documents in a tense office, or selling used records under the suspicious eyes of a shop owner who thought everyone was out to rip him off.

"Just think about it, Leo," Tony continued, "working *here*.... You're hot, you like men, everyone says you're fantastic sex..."

"I think I need more than the qualifications of a fuckin' whore to work here. Besides, I can't just walk up to Wally and..." (Wally was the manager, an intimidating, heavyset leatherman who never seemed pleased with anything.) "...say, 'Hi, my name's Leo. I'm a writer. Got any openings?' And besides, men like me don't get jobs in places like this. I mean, *look* at the staff!"

"They're just other men, Leo. Hot as fucking hell, but just men, like you and me. Plus, I heard Butch say that Fitz..." (Fitz was Cam's bouncer on the busy nights, soloing as doorman on week nights and Saturday afternoons.) "...went off to Europe with Fassbinder, that weird leatherman who always looks like he's high on too many drugs...? Well, guess what? He's a famous film director, and said he's gonna make Fitz a star! ...Oh, look! There's Boots—the

128

one I told you fucked me on the roof last weekend...? Anyhow, think about it. Working *here*, Leo... The tales you could tell... Like Kurt with his drawings."

All at once Tony was off and running to greet the stud at coat check stripping down to tall boots and a metal cockring around the base of his dick, secured by black leather to several other rings along his thick dickshaft.

Sure, easy for Tony to say, I thought. Tony was outgoing. Besides, he looked like Michelangelo's David in boots, jeans and a leather vest. Everyone noticed the resemblance and whenever they told him, he'd say, "except my dick's bigger," which was very, very true. I had a damn good body myself, but Tony was the one who caught everyone's eye first, nudging their friends and pointing him out wherever we went.

And the thing about the Mineshaft staff being just other men? Not to my mind! No, they were *more* than men. They were demi-gods of the gay underworld. To me, the Mineshaft staff, the staffs of the other after-hours' establishments in the West Village and their friends inhabited a special world of their own. They all subscribed to a certain code of amplified masculinity—denim and leather, sweat and muscle, and rough, down-and-dirty, man-on-man sex. They all slept during the day and worked and played throughout the night. They had the sexiest men, the best drugs, and free entry to the hottest parties and places. They had all dropped out, living life on the fringes, like sexual outlaws.

But maybe Tony was right, that the only thing they had that I didn't was the courage to live out their dreams. They were the men I wanted to be, and hadn't I taken one step closer to their world just the day before when I mustered the guts to quit two jobs with no prospects?

I looked over at Butch tending bar with his dick hanging out, loud-mouthing men into sucking on it. Then over at Cam, who had a strange power over men, mesmerizing hot studs into taking off their clothes if they didn't conform to the dress code. I thought of David tending bar downstairs in the Den with Baby, his six-foot snake, wrapped around his arms and shoulders. And then I looked over at Kurt, who tended the second floor back bar during the weekends, in boots and a posing strap, soap-opera handsome with a flawless body as white as ivory. He'd won awards in several leathermen competitions, and there he was: off-duty, busy with his sketchpad, surrounded by unlimited sources of inspiration.

If Kurt could sketch, I could write! Imagine working at the Mineshaft and writing about it! Imagine writing hard-core erotica for men about events that actually *did* take place in a real live, after-hours, S&M, men-only sexclub!

I felt a surge of faith in myself—the same feeling that had come over me the day before when I quit my jobs—and before it could ebb away, I stood up, took in a deep breath and, recalling Cher saying "life is not a dress rehearsal," walked over to Cam to ask about a replacement for Fitz, though I had no idea what exactly I was going to say to him.

"You're going to have to talk to Wally," Cam was saying to the man standing in front of him as he leaned back against the wall on the barstool he always sat on, the two front legs an inch or two in the air, his thick arms crossed over his broad chest.

I'd seen the guy he was talking to twice before at the Shaft. In fact, he really turned me on, activating my Wild West fantasies. He looked like a desperado, with several days' growth of beard on his face, a blue bandanna knotted around his neck, and deep-set eyes darkly ringed, raccoon-like, as if he were wearing a black mask. He was lean and tight-muscled, with a big dick snaking down the left leg of his jeans. But both times I'd seen him were in the backrooms when he was close to punching out a man who didn't want to be punched out. There are men who come to the Mineshaft seeking other men to punch them out, but to choose men who *didn't* want to be punched out—well, that was a violation of the Mineshaft ethic. The staff broke up these scenes, but each time, it sort of threw off the activity that was going on around it.

The thing was, on both those occasions I really wanted to jump in and give him the fight he was looking for, but though I knew I had the muscle and the know-how for a good, knockdown brawl, I also had a bad case of stage fright.

Anyway, his face twisted up in anger and he stared at Cam with a murderous look on his face. Then things happened in a flash. He raised his left arm and aimed a punch at Cam. I jumped forward, blocking the blow with my right arm while my free fist hit him square in his left eye. He reeled back into the second-floor landing, bumping against the banister where it reversed direction up the flight of stairs leading to the roof.

"He *said* come back when Wally's here," I told him, aware that everyone at the bar had stopped whatever they were doing to watch.

Oh yes, this was *not* a dress rehearsal!

I liked the fit of the role. I liked the sound of threat in my voice. I liked the feel of my chest heaving, the clench of my fists, and the squirm of dick in my jeans.

The man looked at me in surprise, like no one had ever punched him before. A spark passed between us, binding us together, and I realized we were both getting off on the moment. But then he suddenly turned around, stomped down the stairs, kicked open the door and marched out.

"Thanks man. You're pretty good with your fists."

"My father was a professional boxer until my mother made him give it up. Taught me a lot."

"Well, you sure did a good job. I never thought I'd see the day Jake would turn tail."

As I thrilled to the sound of admiration in Cam's voice I watched his eyes scan me up and down. His gaze lingered at my crotch and I prayed it wasn't too noticeable I was getting a hard-on.

"Name's Leo," I said, extending my hand to him.

"Cam," he said, grasping it firmly. "I was just about to smoke a joint," he continued, reaching into his blue denim shirt pocket, producing one. "Care to join me?"

"Sure."

I felt like I'd just scaled Mount Olympus.

Cam lit up and the joint passed back and forth between us. It was potent stuff—didn't I mention Mineshaft men had the best drugs?—and after a few tokes I was flying high.

"I understand you're short a… sidekick."

"'A sidekick…' I like that. Yeah, Fitz's off to Europe to become a film star."

"It so happens I could use a job."

"And I could use a man like you, but there are two problems. One, Wally's the one who does all the hiring."

"But you'd put in a good word for me, wouldn't you? Tell him what I did to Jake?"

I couldn't believe I was asking this!

"Well, that's the other problem. He and Jake go way back. Fact is; Jake once saved his life. So, he might be a fucked-up son-of-bitch, but like always, Wally'll tell me to tell Jake to see him. Wally'll lecture him about punching out guys, and then he'll let him come and go as always.

"But Wally's no fool, so tell you what. Why don't you hang out with me this afternoon? I'll tell Wally you volunteered to fill in for Fitz until he can find a replacement. He'll like that."

And so that's what I did. Every time the downstairs door opened, Cam's eyes went up to the convex mirror at the top of the stairs, angled so he could sit just inside the doorway to the right and see who was coming in. By the time someone reached him, he'd sized the man up. The Shaft was a private club, but members could bring in guests, though even men with no sponsors could come in as temporary members if they looked like they'd fit in.

At the top of the stairs the strictly-enforced dress code was crudely scrawled on a large piece of poster paper showing bad signs of wear:

MINESHAFT DRESS CODE

THE DRESS CODE, as adopted by the membership on the first of October, 1976 will apply during 1978 & 1979

APPROVED ARE CYCLE & WESTERN GEAR, LEVIS, T-SHIRTS, UNIFORMS, JOCK STRAPS, PLAID & PLAIN SHIRTS, CUT OFFS, CLUB PATCHES, OVERLAYS & SWEAT

NO COLOGNE or PERFUME or DESIGNER SWEATERS
NO SUITS, TIES, DRESS PANTS or JACKETS
NO RUGBY STYLED SHIRTS or DISCO DRAG
NO COATS in the PLAYGROUNDS
NO LA COSTE ALLIGATOR SHIRTS!!

—The Management

Since it was a Saturday afternoon, most of the men who came in were members, and he greeted them with a smile and a "how ya doin'?"

But even then there were a few tourist types who just had to do the Mineshaft while visiting the Big Apple. None of them made it inside, with one exception. Three men in their early twenties had been refused admittance because they were wearing La Coste shirts. One of them had put up a fuss and the other two dragged him away, but he was back ten minutes later, shirtless and alone.

Cam let him in free of charge, but not until after he'd managed to get him to confess he was "addicted to cock—sometimes I need to suck off one man after another and swallow their loads, unless they want to shoot it all over my cocksucking face." Cam coaxed him into getting down on his knees in front of me, unbuttoning my fly and hoisting out my dick.

He was a real cock worshipper, staring at my meat as it responded to his rapt admiration of it. Respectfully addressing me as "sir," he asked for permission to lick my dick, then to take my dickhead in his mouth, and finally to go all the way down on it. It was while he was deepthroating me that the front door opened and I thrilled to the thought that, whoever it was stepping in, once he'd climbed those seventeen steps, the first thing he'd see was me getting my dick sucked. I looked into the mirror and saw Slater ascending the stairs.

Slater! I got damn close to cumming right then and there.

Slater was a regular at the Mineshaft. He was tall and lean, with a square jaw, handsome, clean-cut features and short hair. And he glowed with an obsessive interest in the clothing men wore. He especially liked men who sweat a lot, since they'd leave their scent on the clothes they'd discard over the course of the evening. He'd strut into the Mineshaft dressed not only as a policeman, a firefighter or a servicemen—as a "drill sergeant," his getting many a man to drop to the floor and give him twenty pushups was a favorite of mine—but also as a logger, a sanitation worker and a telephone linemen.

That day he was dressed as a UPS deliveryman. I was standing next to Cam when he reached us. Brad—that was the cock worshipper's name—didn't even bother to look up and see who'd just stepped up behind him. All he did was quicken his own jackoff strokes.

Well, Slater and Cam exchanged hiya's and Cam introduced me to Slater. After we shook hands, I said, "Oh, and that's Brad down there."

Slater got down on his haunches next to Brad.

"Hiya Brad."

Brad nodded hello through the obstruction of my cock in his mouth.

Slater took him by his hair and pulled him slowly off me. My dick leapt up in front of their faces, swollen and spit-shiny.

"He's got a nice one, doesn't he?" Slater whispered in his ear as the two of them stared at my meat, so close that their cheeks nearly touched.

"Yes sir, he does."

I was so excited my hard-on was holding their attention, that it continued to throb in their faces, oozing a steady stream of pre-cum.

"You'd better lick that off," Slater said to him. "Keep his dickhead clean. Only sloppy cocksuckers let it drip down."

"Oh, yes sir…! …Ohh!"

He'd worked himself close to the edge of orgasm and jackknifed his butt backwards to pull his dick out of his own hand.

"I think you'd better bring him inside," Cam said. "Show him around."

Slater stood up and gave Brad a light kick in the butt. "Clean off his dick and get up."

"Yes sir," he said, licking my pre-cummy dickhead clean and then rising to his feet. Slater threw an arm around his shoulder and led him inside.

More members than usual were coming in that afternoon because there'd been a party at the Loft. The Loft, I came to learn later, was a space that took up the entire fourth floor of the Triangle, a pie-slice of a building a block away on 14th and Hudson that also housed the Hellfire Club in the basement and Jay's backroom bar on the first floor. It was Wally's invitation-only clubhouse for hot men who needed more than even the Mineshaft had to offer. It had, among other facilities, a dentist's chair, an operating table, a prison with bars, a crucifix, and a freezer packed with "pissicles." Wally had scheduled a "School For Lower Education" party, with demonstrations in bondage and discipline given by some of Manhattan's most accomplished masters and slaves.

And not only that—at seven there was going to be a piss party in the basement, which was what the first floor of the Mineshaft was always called. What with all the walls and windows painted black, it did feel like a basement.

Around four, the front door opened and up came Craig and Little Ricky. Craig looked like a Swedish logger as he lumbered up the stairs. He was about six-foot-two, and packed with muscles stuffed into tight jeans and a flannel work shirt. You expected him to say things like "ja" and "by yimini." True to his Nordic heritage, he had blond hair and blue eyes, with a thick moustache drooping down on either side of his mouth. He had a broad smile and a bewitching gap between his two front teeth. Later, when I came to know him, I discovered he was an accomplished pianist. I recall one afternoon in his Chelsea apartment when he sat at his baby grand and played for me. He dwarfed the piano and subdued it with his overpowering technique until I expected it to fall to its knees and beg for mercy.

By contrast, Little Ricky, though just as blond-haired and blue-eyed, was short, and energetic—a shirtless, pint-sized muscleman. Though he was no taller than five-foot-six, he had an enormous dick rumored to be ten inches when hard. His chest was as hairless and shiny as the loose left nut that had popped out of his too-short cutoffs. Though he followed Craig into the stairway, he reached the top of the stairs ahead of him with, "Wally's on his way over in about ten or fifteen minutes."

"What's his mood like?" Cam asked after introducing us.

"He's okay," answered Craig.

"It was a hot party. I worked the bar and got fucked three times," Little Ricky added, pushing his ball back into his shorts.

As the conversation continued, I came to realize that the entire staff knew at all times every step Wally took and every change in his variable mood.

"He sent us over here early to move stock before the piss party," Craig said.

Now, in the basement of the Mineshaft there was a dark orgy room, the Tub Room, with a wide corridor running around three sides of it, housing a few creaky-door stalls riddled with glory holes, and, finally, the Den. The Tub Room was for men into water sports. It had a concrete floor, three unattached bathtubs, and a drain in the center of the room. During a watersports party you bought your drinks in the Den and played in the Tub Room. You entered the piss party from the storage room door next to the ground-floor stairway entrance, where you paid your admission and checked your clothes in black plastic bags before going through a second storage-room door leading directly into the Den. The piss party was a strictly private function. The doors separating the two floors of the Mineshaft were kept locked until eleven when the Mineshaft became the two-story, six room sexual playground that was its notoriety. And being June, it was warm enough to go up onto the roof and play around out there too.

"Everything seems to be under control here," Cam said, "so why don't you help them move stock, Leo?"

I followed them down the steps and into the storage room, as dimly lit as any other room at the Mineshaft, piled high with flats of beer and soft drinks.

Let me tell you, it's sweaty work lugging flats of beer two at a time up those seventeen steps, but I pulled off my tee shirt and got into showing off my straining muscles.

"Well, that's it," Craig finally said at a point when the three of us were in the storage room. He then nodded to Little Ricky, who shut the door.

"Hey!" I cried out more in surprise than protest when Craig locked my arms in his behind my back. As strong as I am, I knew it was useless to struggle against a man who could give Paul Bunyan a run for his money. But I made pretense of struggling for the sheer pleasure of it, trying to bump Little Ricky away as he got down on his knees in front of me and undid my jeans, pulling them down around my ankles.

"Wow!" he said, fondling my cock and balls. "Just *look* at what he's got, Craig!"

Craig looked over my left shoulder. "Nice. Get him hard and we'll see what it's really like."

So Little Ricky swallowed my dick and sucked me into a full-fledged hard-on in no time. He did something with his throat when my dickhead was lodged there that drove me wild, and so I was disappointed when he dismounted my dick and got up to undo his cutoffs, letting them fall to his ankles. He did indeed have a huge dick and he stood there for a second showing it off as if he were aware of the rumors and expected everyone to be curious about it. Truth be told, it looked several sizes too large for him. But when he then turned around, bent over hands-on-knees and backed onto my cock, I forget all about the size of his dick. His hole was already lubed and stretched from his three fucks earlier at the Loft.

Just imagine, I thought, *working in a place where you can wind up getting fucked four times the same afternoon while just going about your business.*

"Fuck him, Leo," Craig coaxed, driving me deep into Little Ricky's ass with a thrust of his crotch against my backside.

Craig relaxed his grip to allow me just enough freedom to fuck Little Ricky. The play of my muscles as I struggled against Craig merged with the sensations of my cock sliding in and out Little Ricky, and soon I was close to cumming.

"Ohh!" I cried out in warning. "Ohhh! Ohhhhh…"

And then the door swung open. In a shock of daylight, I made out Wally as he stepped in, followed by Jake, shutting the door behind them.

Little Ricky, buttpressed tight against me, looked up with a curt, "Hi Wally."

Wally might have been in a good mood before, but he was scowling now.

"That's the one" Jake said, pointing me out.

"You do this?" Wally asked, pointing at Jake's left eye, which sported a shiner.

"Yeah," I said, pushing Little Rick off me and pulling up my jeans. "He was about to…"

"Yeah, yeah, yeah. Cam told me all about it. Says you're good with your fists."

He then turned to Jake

135

"You got a real problem. You know that, Jake?"

Jake hawked up a wad of spit and shot it out on the floor in front of Wally.

Craig and Little Ricky froze.

Wally just stared down at the floor in front of him. After a pause, he turned his head slowly towards Jake and said, "You need to be taught a lesson," and walked out of the room.

"You heard him," Craig said to us, pinning Jake against him the same way he had done with me. "He needs to be taught a lesson. This is gonna be good! Hand me that rope there by the flats."

Little Ricky was quick to obey. They soon had Jake's hands tied behind his back, without his seeming to put up much of a fight.

Then Craig kicked open the door leading into the Den and with a shove sent Jake stumbling forward until he fell onto the floor halfway into the room.

The Den was the last room you reached once you entered the Mineshaft from the second-floor entrance—and the most extreme. It was dark and shadowy with ominous, electronic music fit for a modern-day torture chamber. Several lit candles on the bar gave the room a flickering, unreal quality. Positioned throughout the room was a variety of sexual equipment: the requisite sling, a whipping post, a small stage, a few leather-padded sawhorses, and several other instruments of "torture" I couldn't quite figure out. The bar extended into the room several yards in front of the opposite wall, with enough room on the right to step beyond the bar into an unlit open space for anonymous sex.

The Den was all set up for the approaching piss party. David stood behind the bar, lean, hard and sleek, dressed in a black biker's hat that shadowed his eyes, boots and leather chaps, his dick hanging heavily between his legs. He's a bit bowlegged, which I always fantasized was due to the weight of the meat they had to support.

Although the Den wasn't open yet, David was serving beer and passing around a joint to several of the men I always regarded as the superstars of the shaft. There was Slater standing by the bar with Brad on his knees before him, sucking on the thick log of a dick he'd eased out of Slater's work pants. There was Cam, who'd just been relieved of his post for a few hours before the evening crowd arrived. There were Little Joe and Baby-Face Bobby, two tall leathermen. Joe was "Little" because he was six-foot- three to Bobby's six-foot-four, and nine inches of cock to Bobby's ten. They spent a lot of time at the Shaft because their sexplay was so loud and violent their neighbors complained about the noise and the shaking walls and ceilings. They were leaning against the bar with their dicks out, and on his knees in front of them, sucking back and forth on their two enormous dicks, was Tony. *How does he manage those things?* I wondered, figuring that Joe and Bobby, usually unable to find a lot of men who could deepthroat them, must've discovered Tony's talent upstairs and then invited him down to continue pleasuring them. When Tony gets into one of his cockcrazy states, he can service men for hours on end.

Finally, the only "boy" among these men was Hey You, David's buddy who gave the illusion of being in his teens, being completely smooth-shaven except for a Mohawk, and completely naked. There was a dog collar around his neck, and a leash attached to it, the other end of it secured to the bar nearby David. When not assisting David, he waited compliantly on his knees for David's orders, which ran the gamut from fetching buckets of ice to rimming customers.

They all turned to see what the commotion was.

"I think I'd better light up another joint," David said in his unflappable way, which was part of his allure.

"Wally says Jake needs to be taught a lesson," Craig informed the group as David set not one, but three joints in motion among the dozen of us in the room.

"'Bout time," Bobby observed

"Yeah, I'm gonna enjoy this," from Hose, shoving Tony back onto his meat.

"Mmmpphh!!!" from Tony.

"So who does the honors this time?" David asked in his rumbling bass.

This time? Obviously there were secrets in the Shaft I wasn't privy to yet—rituals I had yet to discover that went on all the time.

"See that shiner? Leo gave it to him," Cam said.

Then he introduced me to David, Bobby and Hose. Tony looked up at me, smiled, and went back to sucking cock.

"It's your show, Leo," Cam announced.

Early that afternoon, I'd felt like a lower echelon member of the Mineshaft Club, jobless and down on my luck. Now some of the hottest men at the Shaft looked to me to call the shots.

"Untie him," I ordered.

It was good grass we'd smoked and I felt myself slipping effortlessly into a Wild West world. We were all in a frontier town barroom! This was the magic of the Mineshaft. You'd find yourself stepping deep into a fantasy, and somehow the fantasy worked.

"So, you want to fight?" I challenged Jake.

He responded by pulling off his shirt and raising his fists.

In the semi-darkness of the Den, with these... *men* looking on, Jake and I squared off. We bobbed and weaved and each threw a few exploratory jabs while sizing each other up. Then Jake got things going with a right hook that knocked me against the whipping post. I bounced back in the finest tradition of TV westerns and caught him with a left jab that sent him reeling backwards against the bar. But he came right back at me and soon we were going at it hot and heavy all over the Den, pretty evenly matched, until I got him with a volley of punches that knocked him back into the sling.

He aimed to kick me in the chest with his feet, but I jumped aside just in time and slugged him back into the sling, leapt on top of him, and pinned his arm up against the chains that supported the sling to its frame.

My body was pressed against his, our chests heaving as we struggled to catch our breath. He thrust his crotch up into mine. I ground back and felt a volley of sweet sensations that exploded like fireworks along the underside of my swollen shaft. Pressed together, dick and denim, we achieved a sort of union and I knew from there on in, we were in this for our mutual pleasure.

"You got this coming," I finally said, and then spat in his face.

His eyes blazed, he bucked to shove me off him, which proved unsuccessful, and then he allowed the fight to flow of out him.

The sling had arm and leg restraints. The other men tied his arms with the upper restraints and pulled off his boots and pants. He had a hairy chest, hairy legs, a huge dick embedded in a thick overgrowth of bush, and two large, hairy nuts hanging low in a loose ballsack, one a good inch lower than the other. Oh yeah, the body of a bad guy, the hot, hard body of a blackhat bandito who sweat like an outlaw, who smelled like an outlaw, who had the big, veiny dick of an outlaw resting on his belly. And I was going to fuck him up the ass in front of all these men.

"Please, let me keep my boots on," Jake begged.

With a nod from me, Craig and Little Ricky helped him on with his boots.

"Let me lube you guys up," Little Ricky offered. Without waiting for an answer he stepped over and scooped up a gob of Crisco from an open can on the bar.

Tony, meanwhile, paused from sucking cock to help me out of my own boots and jeans, and then back into my boots.

"Son of a bitch!" Little Ricky yelled out with three fingers up Jake's hole. "He's already greased up! See?" he added, demonstrating by giving Jake a rapid-fire, three-finger fuck.

I checked out his hole close up, and then put my face in front of his and burst out laughing. "You wanted cock up your ass all along, didn't you?"

"Please! No!"

"So why do you have a fucking hard-on, then?"

He did, and it was huge.

"I… ummm…" he stammered as his dick gave a huge throb, rearing up and then flopping down onto his abs again.

Cam grabbed him roughly by the hair on his head and pulled up so he could stare down the length of his naked body.

"See that?" he asked, indicating my hard, throbbing prick.

"It'll rip me in half," Jake replied weakly.

I stepped up to him and pressed my dickhead against his hairy butthole. The other men gathered around the sling, stroking their dicks. We were going to have a good ole circle jerk, with me and Jake providing the entertainment. I applied a little pressure, sliding the first few inches of my dickhead into his hole before stopping.

"Ohh!" he drawled out in his raspy voice, as I then proceeded to slowly slide my cock all the way up his hole.

Once my dick was buried inside him, I found the stance I needed to screw him. Withdrawing nearly all the way, I paused, and then fucked him hard and deep. I used his hole strictly for my own pleasure as these men looked on, each one busy with his meat.

"Ohh!! Stop! Stop! Ohhh!" Jake cried, his loud protestations bouncing off the walls.

I could feel the cum boiling in my nuts. I gasped for more air and quickened my pace, jackhammering his hole.

Jake picked up on my approaching orgasm and grabbed his own dick, stroking it furiously, his nuts bouncing in his loose sack.

And then, in that dim-lit room, surrounded by men with their dicks out, all close to their own orgasms, I closed my eyes, flung my head back in a mighty roar, and shot my load up Jake's ass as the others joined in—howling, grunting, moaning, each in his own style, as they shot their loads all over Jake.

We were one hot, sticky mess when we were done, and after a recuperative pause I slid my dick out of his hole while the other men rubbed their meat clean on whatever cum-free part of Jake's body they could find.

I ordered Jake unbound, adding, "And someone get Wally."

To which Little Ricky dashed out of the Den.

Jake fell out of the sling and onto his knees, his head bowed, his body covered with cum. He looked so hot, so defeated, so satisfied.

Wally walked in and stepped up to Jake, who stared down at his boots.

"I'm sorry, Wally," Jake mumbled with downcast eyes.

Wally just grunted in acknowledge and then turned his attention to me.

"Cam tells me you could use a job."

"Yes."

"Wanna work here?"

"Sure," I said evenly, buttoning up my fly. My god, if he only knew how I felt inside!

"Good. Be back at eleven to help Cam out."

In the course of that one afternoon, my life took a dramatic turn. I became the man I wanted to be. I worked at the Mineshaft for the next three years, living life on the fringes—sleeping days, staying up nights—living a life worth writing about.

I'M GOING TO LET
MY BALLS HANG OUT
Jeff Poniewaz

I'm going to let my balls
hang out in this poem
not the way some hang out
their dirty laundry
but like Rapunzel
let down her hair.
I'm going to walk naked
(at least for the length
of this poem) and let
my balls dangle as God
made them. I am who am
going to let my balls
hang out in this poem
not for shock effect
but for a bit of fresh air.
I'm going to let my balls
hang out in this poem
like a pair of Freedom Bells
tolling "Time for Freedom!"
Oh the balls, balls, balls,
what a rush of excitement
as above the phallus swells!
Watch out I'm letting my balls
swing like wrecking balls
toppling puritan steeples.
I'm letting 'em swing
like jazz, pure & prurient.
What did you think that saying
"Let it ALL hang out!" meant
all these years? I'm letting
my balls hang out in public
ready or not here they come!
I'm letting my balls
hang out in this song
but unlike Jim Morrison

Jeff Poniewaz

am not arrested. For
my balls are metaphorical
(or are they?) and are seen
with x-ray vision by
every audience I expose
this poem to. I've got
a lot of balls to read
this poem in public!

LEARNING THE FACTS OF LIFE
Antler

Had to wait half a century to learn
Only 3% of an ejaculation comes from the balls,
only 3% of come is sperm,
only 3%.
The rest of the fluid comes
from the prostate gland,
2 bulbourethral glands
and 2 seminal vesicles.
All those years worshipping semen,
All those blowjob ejaculations swallowed
in sublime and invincible ecstasy
overcome by romantic idyllic heroic visions
of balls in Eternity
Having no idea 97% of all the white come
came from somewhere else!
(How would you feel if you learned
when your mother suckled you
only 3% of her milk
came from her breasts
the rest from 5 other organs
you couldn't see
deep in her belly?)
Is semen as palatable delectable desirable
once you know only 3% of the come
that comes out a cock
comes from the testicles?
97% what you gulped
sucking off
all those years
came from the prostate,
came from 2 bulbourethrals,
came from 2 seminal vesicles.
Think of them as balls—
5 balls inside and hidden—
and you realize
you've got 7 balls rather than 2,

Antler

                7 balls rather than 2!
And most of the come
            comes from 5 balls
                    you can't even see!
So where do we go from here
Now that boys and men know
                they have 7 balls?
Now that girls and women know
            boys and men have 7 balls?
Now that human history from this point on
            continues with the knowledge
                boys and men have 7 balls?
And why did I have to wait
Till the Earth circled the Sun
            50 times since my birth
                    to learn
            the facts of life?

ANOTHER WAY
Peter Rice

The sun's warmth was melting the arthritic pain from his shoulders and drove the stiffness from his back. Resting his forehead on his arms, he listened to the gentle surge of the sea washing up the beach to lap at his toes.

His tactile senses inundated with long forgotten experiences, he sighed with pleasure. His cancer-riddled body seemed more whole for the release from inhibition. It was only an illusion; he knew that. His sixty years in the Order had prevented indulgence in any physical pleasure. While not considered sinful exactly, it was not considered a godly way of spending one's time. His youth and virility had been subjugated by determined repression, as had the love he felt towards an older Brother—all tainted with the heavy burden of sin.

When, one day, he had realized that he was old, he questioned what sort of god had condemned him to so sterile an existence and decided to leave the monastic life. True, he was dying, but unwilling to do so knowing nothing of the world beyond the imprisoning walls.

Why he felt as he did, when others of his brethren seemed so much at peace, he did not know. He was a rebellious spirit, the Abbot had told him, when he had announced his intention to leave. The Abbot had believed that it was the development of cancer that had made him resentful, but he was wrong. Perhaps that had unsettled him, but no more. He felt that his life, all of it, had been wasted, that he possessed a great capacity for love, which had been starved.

"No-one has ever done anything for me," he whispered, "and I have done nothing for anyone else."

The breeze caressed his skeletal form and raised the wisps of white hair from the back of his head. Although he was dying, slowly, unavoidably, he felt more alive than he had since childhood.

"If I could live again, I'd choose another road—another way."

The sea washed up further, to his hips. Because it was very cold, he sat up quickly and his eyes were drawn to a shining object left behind by the receding wave, which was gathering for another surge. The tide was coming in and, unable to stand quickly, this time the water advanced to where his head had been, depositing the shiny object at his feet. It was a bottle, like those he'd seen in the windows of chemist's shops, the lower half of the glass encased in a gilt metal mesh. It was an attractive thing. He picked it up and walked up to a point above the tide line, where he lay face down.

The soporific effect of the sun and the sounds of the sea soon made him drowsy again. Absentmindedly, his fingers massaged the glass of the bottle beneath his hand.

"Hi! You feel like a bit of company?"

He lifted his head, and when he opened his eyes he saw a shadow on the sand. A lifetime of humility and solitude formed his reply.

"Yes, of course, if you think I'll be good company."

"Good company, bad company; any sort of company would be welcome. I don't have many friends, get bottled up for years on end. I'm Malik. Do you have a name?"

Rolling over, he replied: "Brother Paul," then corrected himself. "Richard, I mean. I changed my name to Paul many years ago. I think it's time to be myself"

He looked up at the tall, athletic figure, silhouetted against the sun and holding a surfboard.

Malik laid his surfboard on the sand and sat down.

"The surf's no good today. I thought I'd have some fun now you've brought me out. You've got the best idea. Soak up the sun."

Richard found himself gazing at this beautiful young man's body and felt the meager stirrings of almost forgotten emotions.

"Is the surf any good for surfing in this country at all?"

"Recreational. Cornwall's not like California, of course."

"You get about the world a lot?"

Malik chuckled—a deep, disconcerting sound.

"You could say that," he said, "but still, not as often as I'd like."

"It must be wonderful to be able to just go anywhere."

"It has its points."

"I've never traveled, to speak of."

"I… guessed that."

Something in the young man's tone made Richard look into his face, and their eyes met. Malik's eyes seemed so deep, so inviting and warm. They were set in an incredibly handsome face, with something of the Arab about its clean-cut, regular features. He had sufficient body hair to appear very masculine, but not so much as to mask his amazing muscular definition.

"How did you mean, I 'brought you out'?"

"The bottle you've got in your hand. I popped out of there."

Richard laughed his most joyful laugh since childhood.

"The genie of the lamp, you mean? That's a good one."

"You don't believe me do you? Typical of the twenty-first century."

"Of course I don't believe you, but it's a good story."

"Suppose I tell you about yourself. I know you have been a monk, and that, for you, it was a far from fulfilling experience."

"How do you…? Oh, yes, I let that slip, didn't I?"

"You did, but I already knew. I also heard what else you said."

"Oh?"

Malik was smiling.

"About living again. Another way? I can help you with that. I can grant you three wishes. Used wisely, they could give you exactly what you desire."

Richard attempted to focus his rheumy old eyes clearly on Malik's face.

"I don't believe any of this for one moment. Three wishes? That's exactly as it goes in fairy tales!"

"Naturally. There's a lot of truth in such stories."

Richard thought for a few moments and realized how strange this young man's sudden appearance actually was, how very odd he'd heard the whispered sentences he had spoken to himself.

"I have no doubt about my first wish." he smiled. "I'd like to be young again."

"And how young would that be."

Richard decided there was no harm to this game.

"Shall we say, twenty? Not quite a mere boy. That was far too uncomfortable a time to have to go through again."

"No other wishes?"

Richard thought carefully, in spite of his disbelief

Why not play the game to the full?

"Well, yes, do you think my physique and looks could be a little more ideal?"

"And your third wish? It has to be for yourself, not for any other."

Richard remembered something that had occurred to him as a child, when he had been told the story of the Arabian Nights.

Why doesn't he ask for lots more wishes, Dad?

"At the risk of appearing just a bit greedy, is it permissible to make a wish for as many more wishes as I want, as long as I live."

Malik's eyes met his and a mischievous light played in them. Then he roared with laughter.

"Of course it is! You know, I have never been asked that. It would seem the most obvious request of all, but most people ask for gold or money, then a palace, and finally a beautiful wife or husband. Then my job for them is done and I have to return to the bottle. With your request, I can stay out of it as long as you live. Just one small thing, however: the physical transformation you request will take about twenty-four hours, once I have set it in motion. Are you sure you want to make these wishes? There will be no turning back once you have committed yourself."

"Those really are my wishes, and I would like it very much if you could stay around once they become effective."

"Oh, yes. I have to be around to fulfill all your wishes in the future. I can picture you, as you will be at this time tomorrow, and I shall want to be here then."

Malik placed his hand on Richard's ill-fitting swim briefs, on his wasted sex, and the warmth from the touch began to radiate through his body. The cancerous pain melted away, and Richard lay back. His body was at peace, and he slept. Quite unknown to him, Malik lifted him easily and carried him to the beach bungalow Richard had rented for a very limited future.

Richard woke to the sound of sea gulls above the bungalow. He had slept more soundly than he could recall. He felt hungry; that in itself was unusual. He lay on his back, looking at the ceiling. There were some hairline cracks in the white painted plaster. Odd—he hadn't noticed them before. Then the fact hit him like a thunderbolt. He could see clearly, without spectacles. He sat up and discovered he was naked. But it was not that which brought him up short again. It was his *body*, browned as though by the sun, and his long legs, powerfully muscled as they had never been. He stared at his erect cock. That, too, was much larger, tight against his belly. He gripped it firmly in his right hand while exploring every wonder of his body that he could reach—from the tightly muscled belly to his powerful, cushioned shoulders—with his left. He bounded from the bed and stood before the mirror that hung in the lounge. He could not see all of himself, but he gazed in rapt amazement at his face. Yes, it was *his* face, but... what he had always thought of as his less becoming features had been refined! His hair was blond and luxuriant again, though neatly trimmed in a manner he found he approved.

"I am a very beautiful young man," he said to himself, with satisfaction and admiration before feeling guilty at such vanity.

"Never feel guilty at the truth."

He turned sharply to see Malik standing in the doorway.

"I took the liberty of preparing some dinner," said Malik. "I hope it isn't too early for you."

Malik was wearing a pair of unfashionably brief shorts and a brightly colored beach shirt, unbuttoned. Richard was bemused by a sudden rush of conflicting thoughts and emotions. He remembered the previous day, how, as a sick and dying old man, he had left his religious order, to end his remaining days out in the world, away from monastic walls. It had to be some kind of delusion, he figured, but a very enjoyable, incredibly vivid one!

I could eat the proverbial horse, he thought.

He found it hard to accept that his body was in full working order. The habits he had acquired in walking and sitting, to avoid pain and preserve balance, still seemed fixed in his brain. At the same time his thoughts were better defined, keener.

In the small dining room the table was laid with great elaboration, the ostentation of which felt grossly self-indulgent.

Again, it seemed Malik had read his mind.

"The food was obtained to no one's loss, and the silverware and china is of my own fabrication. Pray be seated." With that he was gone, briefly, to the kitchen. He returned with soup.

There is no point in belaboring the richness of the meal, but one moment in particular is noteworthy. When Malik served the main course, Richard took hold of his hand.

"Malik. I don't want you to be my servant. I would like you to be my friend. Is that possible?"

"If that is truly what you wish, then I can be your servant *and* your friend. I must however always be enslaved to the magic bottle. Only you can release me from it."

"And how may that be?"

Malik stroked Richard's cheek with the palm and fingers of his free hand.

"It is too soon for that, but for now I will be your friend."

"Could you be more than that?"

Richard looked into Malik's eyes with the pent-up longing of a lifetime.

"If you wish it, I too would like that."

The moment passed, but a new understanding now grew between them.

"Let's swim!" exclaimed Richard. "I haven't had a swim since I was a boy." With that he was through the doorway, and down the beach.

"Richard," shouted Malik from the doorway, "your trunks. This isn't a nudist beach!"

"Who cares? Who's to see, and what does it matter anyway?"

"This has all gone to your head, my friend!" Malik shouted in reproach while chasing down to the water's edge.

Richard splashed into the water, its astringent chill invigorating and stimulating. He plunged into the waves, finding he could swim powerfully, as he never had before. The discovery impelled him further and he plunged through the waves, celebrating his newfound vitality.

For a short while, he was quite absorbed in himself, until, suddenly, an arm wrapped about his waist and abruptly halted him. It was Malik, who, swimming beneath him, had pulled him down, and beneath the waves they tussled and tumbled, slipping from one another's grasp until they broke the surface together, shaking the water from their eyes and hair. They stared intensely into each others' eyes until, charged with delight at their mutual freedom, they laughed aloud.

"Race you to the shore!" yelled Malik, above the water's roar.

"Okay, race you," Richard shouted back, and they set off, swimming the hundred-or-so meters they had drifted from the beach.

Richard was the faster, Malik having endowed him with an Olympian technique and speed that he could not match for himself, as his powers did not extend to gratifying his own wishes. Nonetheless, he was no mean swimmer and there was scarcely a second's difference between them.

Racing halfway up the golden sands, Richard flung himself down, and he opened his arms wide to welcome Malik. In a moment his friend was lying on top of him, hands cradling his head and his arms embracing Malik's body.

"I thought I would never know this," whispered Richard.

"I thought no one would ever set me free, to love, again."

Malik kissed his friend's lips, very gently, restraining the urgency he felt, just brushing his lips against Richard's. For Richard, that contact was like a miracle, a discovery denied for a lifetime, now to be savored, relished, and for which to thank Almighty God. This was not a sin, he realized without a doubt, could never be a sin. He returned the sweet contact, marveling at the wonder of Malik's lips.

Malik's hands began to stroke Richard's hair, and kissed his closed eyelids and forehead, and cheeks. For the moment Richard was happy just to absorb these new experiences, but Malik was a practiced young man whose actions were calculated to build his new master's confidence and reignite his lust. He knew as well that to be too aggressive with someone, who, like Richard, might harbor great inhibitions, would be unsatisfying, even disturbing. Richard was like a child, though not a child. He knew little of real intimacy, but possessed emotions that had only to be coaxed like a flame in the hearth, to blaze with fiery passion.

Richard felt Malik's hands smoothly massage his shoulders, Malik delighting in his power to have created such a fine physical specimen. Richard's frame had always been good, but his physique had never developed as an athlete's would. Malik's work had been well guided, and the form he had refigured was exactly as Richard, in his dreams, would have desired. Malik himself never understood how the gift worked, that it was not entirely his own, but Richard, in his wisdom, or perhaps momentary greed, had given him a creative freedom he had never dared hope for. With the pride of an artisan in accessing his creation, was the love he felt for Richard born of gratitude, he wondered, or was it true? For until that moment he had no knowledge of his creation's power to allure.

His hands moved further, appreciatively down to the prominent nipple buds, set in broad brown aureoles, tickling them, feeling Richard squirm beneath him. He manipulated them, twisted and ultimately squeezed them hard. Richard moaned but made no move to resist. Malik grazed first one, and then the other with his teeth and Richard pressed his chest upwards to encourage Malik to continue, to go further. Malik bit, closing his teeth slowly, but firmly, on the hardened buds, one after the other, and with his hands explored below, to the hardness that rose rigidly above the taut belly, and the range of prominently quilted muscles that landscaped its surface. One hand gripped the shaft tightly, making it pulse with pleasure, and the other ringed the circumference of the generous ballsac and gently pulled downwards. When Richard's unyielding cock began to throb, Malik hastily released it and pressed hard with his fingers on the perineum until the throbbing subsided. He moved his face down and lapped at the round globes in their protective skin, which was only lightly haired. He took first one and then the other into his mouth and suckled them.

Richard groaned and his hands moved down to his cock. Astonished by its size, he had not realized that a man's penis could ever be so large, but then again, the only one, before then, of which he had had any real experience had been his own in another life.

Richard felt Malik's mouth close over his cockhead, the moist warmth exciting the sensitive tissue of his glans. After plunging down on to the fierce erection, forcing Richard's hand out of the way, Malik buried his lips into the wiry blond bush. Richard floated and rocked on a violent sea of sensation. It was unbelievable, so amazing to him that his body was able to afford him such pleasure.

It was then that the final, massive wave engulfed Richard, gratifying Malik with a torrent of sperm, the majority of which he gulped down with great skill. Leaving Richard to subsiding emotions, the sides of his cock still liberally coated with translucent stickiness, Malik, unwilling that any should go to waste, clutched its base in both hands, and licked up the remarkably sweet-tasting semen until there was scarcely even a scent of it left on Richard's still erect, if no longer quite so wooden member.

Richard raised himself on his elbows to watch, and as he did so mindlessly tweaked his own tits, almost unaware that the sensation of doing so, combined with the luscious visual was restoking his libido. His cock regained its steel and by the time Malik was finished Richard was fully revived. He sat up and, cupping Malik's handsome face in his hands, drew him into a kiss. Different than before his orgasm, Richard tasted his own emission on Malik's lips and tongue as they made contact, and Malik's lithe tongue entered his mouth, probing and sparring with his own until he succeeded in penetrating Malik's smiling lips and sank his tongue deep within the capacious mouth that had enclosed the whole of his huge penis.

Noting that it did not feel any roomier than his own, Richard knew he had much to learn.

Breaking apart from Malik he said: "You are a stunning creature; do you realize that?"

"I know that…" Any pride that his words might have suggested was belied by Malik's embarrassed smile and downward cast of the eyes. "…But any beauty I might possess is only of value in what it may bring to others. Within, the ugliest man may well be the most beautiful."

Richard had not expected the homily, but although a cliché, it was certainly true. "In that case," he replied, "I hope that you will gain something from my new being."

"Haven't I shown you that already?"

"Of course, but I want to do for you what you just did for me."

"I hoped you might."

But at that moment Richard leaped to his feet and took off like a rabbit down the beach, shouting, "But you'll have to catch me first."

With the exuberance of their freedom they chased over the sands. They dodged, wrestled and played about the rocks and pools, like two young boys, until they both fell together, panting and out of breath. They lay in an alcove in the rocks—the evening sunlight shining directly into the space where, behind them, a tidal pool awaited the rising of the tide—quite sheltered from the prying eyes that, unbeknownst to them, had witnessed their revelry from the beginning.

Another of the beach houses was occupied, and its occupant, who worked nights and slept days, realizing that the entertainment was over for the moment, jerked his cock harder and faster until he shot his pearly blast of cum into two thicknesses of large Kleenex. Moving from his lounge window to the bedroom, he put on his uniform.

At that same moment Richard was experiencing the joy of a stiff cock in his mouth for the first time. He was unsure which was better, having his cock in Malik's mouth, or Malik's in his own, and was beginning to feel more than sheer lust for this olive-skinned young man. Oblivious to how his present situation had occurred, he had completely forgotten that he had only to express a wish and the thing would happen. All that he desired was here, in his presence, in his mouth, and he was, for the moment, content to let things take a natural course.

The head of Malik's cock was a streamlined form, aerodynamic, he thought. It was larger at the corona than the shaft, but not by a vast amount. Lower down, the shaft grew slightly wider again to a greater girth at the base. But it was truly a thing of beauty. Richard experimented with taking it further into his mouth, until it hit the back of his throat and he gagged a bit.

"Easy, my friend, easy," Malik gently reprimanded. "Little by little, until you can swallow it without trouble."

Richard had not been granted an automatic ability to do everything, so the learning process was important in itself. One word of Malik's—*swallow*—lodged in his mind and he did just that. Wonder of wonders, it worked! He pressed his head down on Malik's rod and, after swallowing a few times, found his face planted in Malik's shiny black bush. He withdrew again, breathing through his nostrils, before descending again. It became easier. He experimented, sucked harder on the upstroke, increasing Malik's pleasure.

"Oooh, *yes*, my baby, suck me... enjoy it. You are giving me soooo... much... *pleasure*. You're doing it just *right*... That is *sooooo* glorious."

Instinctively, Richard felt that what he was doing was right, but had he not, Malik's reaction would have been evidence enough to the contrary. Above all he *was* enjoying what he was doing. He stopped for a moment and admired the beautiful penis, so *right* for so fine a man. Gently he fondled Malik's heavy balls. Malik was quite hirsute in this area and his fur was raven black, with glistening sheen. He licked at the heavy scrotum in his hand, slicking the hair, and then experimentally sucked one of Malik's balls into his mouth. At the same time he slowly moved his hand up and down the circumcised cock, lightly skimming the glans as he did so. Malik's powerful shaft, engorged to a steely firmness, convulsed now and again, and his balls were rising on the shaft. He could feel the tug of resistance in his mouth as Malik softly moaned his appreciation.

Richard returned to minister to the dick in his hand. He lapped upward, along its underside, teasing the frenum and making Malik, who made no attempt to interfere with Richard's experimentation, beat his hands in the sand. Richard swirled his tongue around the glans and tasted the sweet precum that issued from the tip in profusion. He drew back, squeezed, watched the crystal liquid ooze down Malik's cockshaft in a slow, continuous stream, and then licked it up from the base of the superb erection to the slit atop the quivering dick. He then dipped the tip of his tongue into the shiny well while Malik groaned—his vent unleashing yet another rich stream of precum which flooded over Richard's tongue. He wrapped his lips about the head and began a rhythmic and deep sucking to which Malik responded with upthrusts of his hips, driving himself deeper into Richard's throat. It was not long before the expected flood of cum burst from the tightly raised testicles and literally overwhelmed Richard's ability to swallow. Forced to retract his head for breath, he attempted to catch what he could of Malik's spunk as it jetted into the air and spattered them both. Richard returned to the subsiding cock to savor the final throbs of sperm from Malik's manly repeater, after which he shifted positions to lick up the gobs that had escaped.

Malik reached under Richard's arms and eased him up his body in order to kiss him. The sun was setting and the tide rising up the beach. It was time to go home, but they would not sleep alone that night.

In bed later, Richard wondered what might happen next as Malik lay in front of him, apparently asleep. Nothing had happened between them since they had been on the beach, and Richard, still too new in his experience of physical relationships and hesitant to make the next move, was urgently feeling the need. Richard scooted up to him, making contact all along his body. He tentatively placed an arm over Malik's waist and was immediately aware that his fingers were resting in his profusion of pubic hair. Stealthily he searched down a little further and, finding the tips of his fingers in contact with the base of Malik's splendid prick, gently gripped the shaft.

Malik pressed back against him,

"Fuck me, Richard, please!" he grunted, half asleep. He reached back and placed Richard's cockhead against his hole.

"Don't I need a rubber, and lubrication?"

"We don't need protection, Richard; we never will."

"Are you sure?"

"We two have a far greater protection. Believe me, it's true. But we shall use protection with others, to ease their minds."

"There will be others?"

"As many as we want, for evermore."

The concept was too much to grasp at the moment so Richard dismissed it.

"And the lubricant?"

"Perhaps it would be better. Just a second."

In the darkened bedroom, Richard could not see where Malik went or what he did, but he returned quickly. He lay down again and spooned against Richard.

"It's fine now," Malik whispered. "Just push in."

Richard pushed as Malik speared himself in one gliding motion on Richard's aching tool. Smooth though the movement was, Malik tightened his muscles, in that action giving Richard the most intense moment of his entire sexual experience (which one has to own, was not great thus far). Although Richard had an idea of the right way to proceed, Malik took charge initially, but once Richard got the hang of things, Malik left him to his own devices.

Richard luxuriated in thrust after thrust of increasing excitement, absolutely loving the warmth engulfing his cock and the friction that was proving optimal for cause and effect to transport him. He never wanted this wonderful experience to end, but knew it would, all too quickly.

Malik was as profoundly grateful, as passionately affected by their lovemaking as Richard himself. When Richard reached up to pinch his nipples, Malik felt the charge zap from them straight to his balls, tightly drawn up in their hairy sac. It wouldn't be long for him either. They entered the final gathering of their climax and lightning flashed for them both, bathing them in the light of fulfillment.

The insistent rapping of the doorknocker woke them. Richard got up, looked out the curtained window and caught a glimpse of a dark blue uniform. He quickly flung on his robe and hastened to the door.

"Good morning, sir," his neighbor said.

Richard was surprised to see that it was a police constable—and a very nice-looking police constable he was! His mahogany-brown hair was unfashionably long, barely in keeping with police regulations. He was holding his cap under his arm and looking very formal. His eyes were dark, almost as dark as Malik's, but his skin was fair, which gave him a manly, freshly scrubbed look.

"Good morning," answered Richard, clutching the front of his robe together. Blessed with rapid response in his new life, this handsome constable elicited a quick stirring in Richard's groin. Malik came up behind Richard, not having bothered to cover himself. He put an arm round Richard's waist, totally unconcerned about appearances, figuring it was best to be direct. Richard felt slightly embarrassed, but only for a moment.

"Is something the matter, constable?" asked Malik.

"The first thing, sir..." the constable replied, "...is that the two of you have been noticed bathing nude on the beach. This is not a nudist beach. That is the first thing. The other is... that you've been seen indulging in sexual relations—in full public view—on the beach. Now really, sir, we can't have that. Unless, of course..." he added, his face breaking into a grin.

"Unless what, constable?" Malik had stepped forward, his erection preceding him.

"Unless I can join in!" The grin remained, and glancing down, he licked his lips.

"I'm sure that can be arranged," said Malik, laughing, and, seizing the uniform jacket, he pulled the sexy policeman inside.

Richard was still very inhibited, fifty years as a monk having molded his personality. By the same token, he was now a young man again, and the policeman was incredibly attractive. Malik was already kissing him—a deeply searching and explorative kiss—which was being enthusiastically reciprocated as Richard watched with rising excitement. Malik quickly unfastened the young man's coat and slid it back from his shoulders. Richard, deciding to toss caution to the wind, took the jacket and hung it on the hallstand. He then slipped off his robe and draped that over the top. All at once, Richard was as unencumbered (and hard) as Malik, and it would not be long before their caller would be the same.

Deciding that the bedroom would be more comfortable for the inevitable, he urged Malik and their guest into the room, as the uniform trousers came off, along with the boots, then the shirt, before they reached the side of the bed. Never to be anything less than a tidy man, Richard folded the trousers so they would remain uncreased, hung the shirt over the back of a chair and placed the boots under it. By then the hunky policeman was lying on the bed, legs spread wide apart with his arms above his head. The socks and briefs he still wore did nothing to hide the fact that he was a fine, athletic stud with a majestic cock that, fitted sideways, threatened to burst the seams of the cotton undergear.

"So, what are you going to *do* to me?" the policeman asked pointedly.

Richard looked at Malik questioningly, thrown off by this unexpected curve ball.

Malik winked at him then took control.

"You are going to get *fucked*, constable, by both of us—by both of us at once, maybe. You think you can just barge in here, with your uniform and authority, and take *advantage* of us? But first, we'll have your name; what is it?"

"Eddie, Eddie Townes."

Eddie looked first at Malik, and then at Richard.

"You'll use a condom won't you?" he asked.

"Of course," said Malik, "We don't want to catch any disease from your filthy ass."

Richard was out of his depth and knew it. He couldn't understand why Malik was being so unpleasant to Eddie. The man was gorgeous! Richard simply wanted to feast on his body and show him how much he liked him. Yet he also realized that this was an approach that was entirely unselfish on Malik's part.

"I believe constable Townes needs a little lesson in humility," Malik considered. "Yes... It's very clear he could use some discipline." Addressing Eddie directly he said, "Discipline for a very *bad* policeman."

He turned and opened a dressing table drawer, from which he took some padded cuffs with straps attached as Richard looked on in amazement. Where on earth had they come from, he wondered? First, Malik fastened the cuffs around Eddie's wrists and then secured the straps around the top of the casters at the head of the bed. He then withdrew two pairs of double cuffs from the drawer.

"Richard, please remove his socks and briefs before I fasten these."

Richard quickly did as he was asked. He was rather getting into the scene, seeing that Eddie was quite acquiescent—and almost bursting from the minute underbriefs he wore. Gripping the waistband, he quickly yanked them to Eddie's ankles—releasing the huge prick from its confines—took hold of the socks en route, and stripped the policeman naked. How perfect Eddie's body was, he thought. He was not a Mr. Universe type, exactly, but more like Greek statuary. Apollo, to be exact. Yes, the classical ideal of young manhood.

Malik, though just as admiring of Eddie's form, was not about to allow the impetus of the scene to be dispersed. Swiftly the cuffs were attached around Eddie's ankles and first one leg and then the other was lifted to its appropriate wrist and secured there, leaving Eddie totally vulnerable. His starry pucker would occasionally tense and then relax expectantly, as if inviting attention.

"We really do have a very, very bad policeman here, Richard. There is only one way to deal with this," he mused.

He went back to the drawer and brought out two broad leather belts, and handed one to Richard, who was not really sure what he should do with it.

Malik doubled his belt, and landed a neatly placed swat on Eddie's right ass cheek. Eddie drew breath sharply between his teeth.

"Who's the peeping Tom, constable?" Malik demanded angrily, applying the belt to the other cheek.

Eddie gasped. "I am; I am!"

"SIR!" Malik yelled, applying the belt again.

"*Yes* Sir! I'm... *sorry*, Sir."

"A peeping Tom, who bursts in on lovers early in the morning, it seems! Pretending to be on official business... You are reprehensible!" Malik delivered two more firm blows.

"Ah! Oooh... But I didn't..."

"Denial is useless, you swine. If it weren't true, you wouldn't be here."

He placed his hand on Eddie's fat balls and, squeezing just hard enough to provide incentive, said "Repeat after me: 'I am a sleazy, sex-crazed copper.'"

Eddie made no response.

Malik squeezed, hard.

Eddie squealed.

"I'm a sex-crazed, sleazy copper!"

"Mmm, not quite verbatim, but we'll let that go, for now. Richard, feel his prick See how hard he is?"

Richard gripped the splendid cock, pulled it forwards as far as he could and then let go, whereupon it sprang tautly back into place.

"See how the pig revels in this degrading situation. And he calls himself a guardian of the law. Punishment is absolutely mandatory. Are you ready, Richard?"

Richard was beginning to think that perhaps he was!

"Alternate strokes then, you to the left and me to the right. And *you*," he referred back to Eddie, "will receive your punishment in silence, or it will be doubled."

Richard wondered if Malik was counting because he immediately lost count himself. They beat on those finely shaped melons until they were a bright and shiny red, until Eddie finally cried out: "No more! Oh please, no more! I can't take any more!"

Malik paused for a second, looked at Richard and released one end of the belt. Holding the buckle, he then flailed the full length of it down over Eddie's winking anus. He nodded at Richard to do the same, who followed suit, accidentally catching Eddie's balls as well.

"Aaagh, no, not that!" he cried out as Malik and Richard alternated similar belt lashes.

"Count these aloud, you piece of crap," Malik sneered. "Make a mistake and we'll begin them again."

"Oh, no, oh, *please* God, no!"

Malik let loose with one mighty stroke across the buttocks. "Do NOT blaspheme!" he commanded. "And that one doesn't count!"

Malik gestured for Richard to plant his first in this new series of floggings. Richard did not believe his prick had ever been so hard. Seeing Eddie squirm in anticipation of the strike prompted him to lay it down the middle of his crack, right across his hole, as hard as he could.

Eddie stifled a howl and gasped, "One…"

Malik following Richard's example, aimed for exactly the same trajectory.

"Mmmmmmnnnng! Two," he sobbed.

The remaining strokes were delivered with varying severity and time-lapse between them, until the last from Malik—administered after a long delay—stung the tightly closed pucker with the tip of the belt. Eddie shuddered, no sound emerging from his lips for some moments, until finally a quiet sigh and an exhalation of breath was followed by a whispered, "Ten."

Malik took a small jar labeled "Soothing Fire" from the endlessly well-supplied drawer. Unscrewing the lid, he handed it to Richard who, noticing the substance looked like simple moisturizing cream, scooped some out with his fingers and massaged it into Eddie's bright red cheeks. Eddie moaned in appreciation. Richard took more and rubbed the entire assaulted area. He then he applied some to the policeman's cock and balls, making sure that the glans of his circumcised cock received its share of attention. Growing bolder, he applied a generous dose on the man's inviting anus and pressed, first one, and then two fingers inside. Eddie was no novice. He relaxed his sphincter muscles and eventually four fingers had slid easily inside.

Malik put his hand over Richard's and drew him back.

"Now watch," he whispered.

Malik put an arm round Richard's waist and held him close.

"Our guest is about to experience a new thrill this morning."

As they watched, Eddie began to writhe, extending his bonds as far as they would allow. His hole gaped open spasmodically, and then shut tight. He began to moan continually.

"Oooooh, *shiiiiit*… What is that stuff?" he demanded suddenly, tugging at his restraints more and more impossibly. His eyes flashed wide open and he began panting faster and faster, as though indulging in demanding exercise until… his creamy spunk lurched violently from his cock, his position being such that it shot over his massive chest and into his gaping mouth.

Richard was astonished, commenting with disbelief, "My God, he didn't even touch himself!"

"And now we will enjoy him," said Malik. "Don't worry, that's exactly what our policeman wants." He took, from the cornucopia of a drawer, two condoms. Deftly he rolled one down Richard's stiff penis. It didn't reach all the way to the base, but it would suffice. The condom's tightness only served to excite him further and Richard kissed Malik, long and deep, after which Malik put one on himself.

"We'll use plenty of lubricant, but there isn't going to be any problem getting in there. You first, my friend," Malik encouraged.

After liberally coating his cock with lube, Richard knelt in front of Eddie's truly luscious buns and aimed for glory. Perhaps he could be forgiven for a certain lack of finesse, but it was only his second time, and Malik had been very relaxed for his first. Thanking heaven he had certainly not received the treatment just meted out to poor Eddie, Richard plunged his hard cock into Eddie's tortured ass.

Poor Eddie? Perhaps not.

Although Richard's blundering entry was a battering annihilation of any resistance from Eddie's sphincter, and his dick's rocketing passage deep into Eddie's bowel would have been totally stupefying for a lesser man, Eddie, after an initial howl of agony, became a mean fuck machine. Within his capacity for movement, he rode every thrust and lunge Richard threw to him, his own prick remaining fully charged throughout, generously leaking precum.

Richard felt a kaleidoscope of emotions while he pounded away, his pelvis slapping hard against the creamy, smooth mounds of muscle. His hands felt along the cop's rounded thighs and up the powerful calves to the bound ankles. Eddie's darkly handsome features were possessed by a look of anguished abandon. His head rolled repeatedly from side to side on the pillow, eyes closed. Richard reached forward and seized Eddie's tits. He squeezed and pulled and pinched them, adding to the erotic sensation flooding Eddie's consciousness. Malik, sensing that the time was right to further Richard's education, knelt on the bed behind Richard, having applied plenty of lubricant on his own massive penis. Squeezing an additional amount from the tube, he liberally lubricated his fingers and placed one on his lover's virgin entrance. Moving in sync with Richard's rhythm he slowly insinuated his finger inside. Richard was so absorbed with his own fucking, so relaxed with the wonder of it, that the pain of entry was minimal. Malik pushed the whole finger inside, and Richard felt for the first time the exquisite thrill of deliberate pressure on his prostate. Malik did not prolong the moment, but he leaned over Richard's back and whispered, "Slow down, my love, I don't want you to come just yet."

Richard complied, and Eddie opened his eyes at the change of pace. When his gaze met Richard's, he flashed a lop-sided, pearly-white smile. Richard's heart melted at the sight and the smile that appeared on his own face was equally affectionate as he strove for deeper penetration, pressing down hard and churning his cock inside Eddie's guts. By this time Malik had three fingers fully inside Richard's anus. When he began spreading them, in an effort to ready the reluctant muscle for the entry of his cock, Richard gasped with the sudden pain and stopped fucking abruptly.

Eddie, who could see enough to realize what was happening, cried out: "That's it, man—give it to him! He gaggin' for it."

"Shut up, shitface," ordered Malik. "It's nothing to you what my lover and I do."

Eddie grinned again, loving every minute of his abuse. At long last he'd found a pair of quality guys who could fulfill his most secret longings. The strange, dark guy, he was sure, could be really cruel, and seemed to sense what he needed before he himself was aware of it. The fair one who had resumed fucking him with total abandon could be mean too, he thought—remembering Richard's forceful flogging—but for all his being a major hunk, Eddie realized that he was a novice. He was such a babe, though, thought Eddie. Each time their eyes met, he felt the electricity arc between them.

Malik's oversized cock moved inexorably up Richard's hungry but inexperienced chute. Richard loved the overwhelming sensation of fullness, but the pain was intense. It occurred to him that he could simply express a wish that the pain go away, and Malik would grant the wish, but he chose not to, intensely desiring the whole experience. Understanding that both were vital components in the making of joy, in the making of love, Richard began to find his rhythm with Malik, which in turn, gave Eddie his cue.

The trio's synchronization achieved a near-perfection that was sustained all too briefly before the white-hot passion rising in each of them surged from them in a unison that promised to be repeated time after time—for all time, it seemed…

((((◻))))

"Doctor Malik, I'm so glad you've come. Brother Paul is, I fear, drawing to the end, but he has been asking for you."

The middle-aged brother, showing real concern, ushered the doctor into the little cell that had been Brother Paul's for so many years. The old monk, emaciated from the ravages of his illness lay on his bed, his eyes wide open. The doctor felt for a pulse, but found no sign of life there.

"I'm afraid the dear man has gone, brother. We can do no more for him."

The good brother was obviously distressed. "Brother Paul… so often mentioned your name in these last hours."

Dr. Malik carefully placed his fingers on the eyelids and drew them shut. There was a moment's awkward silence.

"At least he is now in a better place," the brother concluded.

Malik looked at the brother, and then turned to exit. As he walked away, his eyes twinkled with devilment.

"I am sure of that, brother, absolutely sure," he replied.

He turned back to look at the bereaved man, and was sorry for him—for him and every man denied a second chance.

SERGIO SWIMMING
Henry Iblis

Sergio and I hitchhiked to the Costa Brava to visit Isabelle. She was my fiancée, and his sister, but everything had gone to hell when she found me giving Sergio a blowjob on the deck in the early morning. He and I had stayed up all night, confessing things the way a lot of red wine will make you do, and one thing had led to another. I'd always wanted to know what it felt like, how a man tasted, and whether I'd be any good at it. I must not have been too bad, because I managed to bring him right to the brink of bursting when Isabelle showed up behind the screen door, bug-eyed and sputtering, "What the fuck is going on!"

Sergio grabbed my head and wouldn't let me move. A second later he shot a load straight down my throat. I nearly choked, tears sprang to my eyes, and I swallowed the salty mess. "Man, you're in trouble," he panted, laying back on the chaise longue, chest heaving.

"Both of us," I said, Isabelle having stormed off somewhere. Sergio and I got out of the house, quick.

The day blazed. The sun was so intense you could almost *hear* it—I imagined a high-pitched ringing, like a fingernail flicked against a crystal cup. Sergio and I wandered down to the harbor in the afternoon and ended up downing espressos to inject some energy back into our hung-over bodies. We walked up the coast along a pathway that cut through rocky cliffs pounded by surf. At one point we could see Isabelle standing on the deck of the beach house, perched high above the cliff while we skirted its surf-blasted base. She was peering out over the town, probably looking for the two of us. We scurried along until she was out of sight.

We came to a shallow cove where the cliffs hid us from the houses built above. There was no one else on the crescent shore, and Sergio stripped to his boxers and ran into the surf. I would almost rather walk a tight-rope over the Grand Canyon than wade into the ocean—the slimy footing and opaque water terrifies me—but I stripped and followed, because it was all a part of my new attitude: *the only place to go is further than anywhere I've gone before.*

The water slapped at my legs, strong and cold. Sergio was already way ahead of me, just a dark head bobbing on the waves that rolled in from the horizon. I lunged, cast an arm forward and arrowed into the water. The feeling of having nothing beneath my feet, and not being able to see anything but sunshot murk below, curdled my guts. My hands tried to curl into fists and I had to concentrate to keep them straight, stroking against the tide and kicking up a storm that pounded in my ears. Fucking Sergio—I wanted to strangle him for leading me out here where two or three seconds of panic would be enough to make me sink like a stone, inhale salt water and die with a frozen heart and burning lungs on the seabed under six feet of ocean.

But anger cleared my head, injected my muscles with adrenaline, and focused my intent on reaching the clump of black volcanic rock where Sergio was pulling himself out of the water, standing dripping brown and lithe against the blue nothingness of the sky. He'd found a boulder the size of a king-size bed that poked half a meter above the waves. I climbed onto the jagged rock, shivering for half a minute until the sun began to bake me. We were only a stone's throw from the cliff face where the path cut along the shore, but the swim had felt like a marathon.

We sat on the crest of the boulder, facing out to sea, letting the waves lap at our feet and the sun sizzle on our backs. Sergio, with his long hair lying flat and glossy over his naked shoulders, looked like a scrawny girl from the corner of my eye. I watched the water bead on his skin, droplets sliding down his neck, rolling over his collarbones, plunging down the smooth and flat muscles of his chest, catching on the hard pebble of a nipple and then dripping into the wet fabric of his shorts. His stomach, hunched over, was a washboard of tight folds. He seemed to occupy so little space compared to Isabelle, who was round and full and abundant, seemingly bursting from within like a tightly wrapped sausage link. (Though she would be loath to hear me say that, it was precisely those qualities that made her sexy.). Sergio, on the other hand, looked like a study in the stretching of muscle over bone, a strong skeleton padded with just enough meat to be ambulatory. When he twitched his arm to flick at a fly, you could see a bundle of tendons slither over the ball of his shoulder. My appetite, somehow, called for both of them: Sergio and Isabelle, as different as woodwinds and brass.

He noticed my penis expanding through the opening of my shorts. He took me in hand, stroked me hard, then bent to flick his tongue over the purple head. I tried to recline on my elbows on the jagged boulder but ended up rolling off into the water to keep from slicing my back on the rough surface. Sergio splashed after me, and we slithered against one another in the cool tide, grasping at slick flesh, slipping together and apart. The waves lifted us and pulled us back down in a soothing rhythm. We kept to the seaward side of the boulder, out of sight of the beach and whoever might want to spy on a couple of frolicking boys. He pressed his ass against me, and pulled my hard-on between his legs. It took some gentle work, slowly entering him with the tide buffeting and pushing us against the rock, but we eventually made connection. I slid deep inside him, and scarcely made a move beyond flexing. Sergio gnashed his teeth and cried out like someone was gut-punching him, holding onto the boulder with his ropy arms straining and shaking. The current lent us its rhythm: slow and strong and unrelenting. I bit my lip, rolled my eyes back in my head. Isabelle was nothing like this. Not better, not worse, just completely different. A white light flashed through me and I lurched, thrusting, shooting streams inside of him while he howled. When I was spent, I pulled out and floated back on the waves. Sergio drifted off, hunched over in the water like a dead man, the brisk movement of his arms the only evidence that he was alive. He rolled onto his back in the water and I saw him working his cock, stroking it faster and harder until he groaned and gelatinous white globs spattered onto the water and washed about on its surface. We floated away from the boulder, carried into the deserted harbor by the gradual sweep of the tide. I lay back and let the water tap my ears and stared, squinting, into the blazing pale sky. I could be happy like this. It had felt like the real thing.

Sergio splashed me, drifting by. We touched fingers, having drifted together and then apart again. Both of us had lost our boxer shorts somewhere, and floated naked upon the surface, glistening from head to foot, savoring salt and breathing brine. Seagulls hung motionless high overhead, flapping into the wind but going nowhere.

Isabelle, on the deck, stood waiting for us to return, awaiting an explanation, but my mind had drawn a blank; I had gathered nothing as yet to say to her. All at once, I became aware that my terror of the murky, bottomless water had disappeared, as long as I floated on my back and kept my eyes on the sky.

Such a simple solution.

SNOWBOUND
Ken Anderson

Marble, Michigan, 1960

The temperature had dropped to freezing during the night, and light sleet and crisp snow had been falling all day. But Gun had cabin fever and decided that if he didn't go somewhere fast, namely the bar, he would wind up shooting himself. Even he saw the humor in the pun. Besides, he was horny, so horny in fact, that he was turned on by just about anything he touched: his feet against the soles of his hiking boots, his palms against the supple leather of the chair arms. Even the seat cushion felt like the spread crotch of a man.

The roads were icy, and since the bar was less than a mile away, he thought he'd walk instead of drive and hoisted himself from the chair. He slipped into a canvas field coat, wrapped a gray scarf around his neck, and, pushing back a big handful of hair, slipped a gray knit cap over his head. He stuck a stud through the hole in his left earlobe and fastened it in back. He then picked up his gloves and gave himself one last dubious look in the mirror.

The name of the bar—The Hot Spot—was spelled in pink neon lights, except that a couple of letters were broken so that the name actually read The Ho pot. The Ho pot, however, was the closest thing to social activity in a hundred miles, Stone Age as it was. The wind was up, and the letters glowed in a nimbus of mist, staining the snowflakes flying by the color of cherry petals. Beneath the lights, the silvery icicles hanging from the gutter looked like so many jagged, bloodstained teeth. Two ice-glazed pickup trucks—one black, one brown—huddled against the cold in the gravel lot.

The Hot Spot wasn't so hot for another reason, too. It was almost as chilly inside as out. Gun could even smell the chill.

"Jesus, Jacque," he groused, pulling off the cap. He shook the snowflakes off it, then stuffed it into a coat pocket. He pulled off the gloves, stuffing them into another. "You do have the heat on?"

The bartender drew a draft, staring at Gun deadpan, then escorted the mug down the counter. Just sitting on the barstool, though, struck a sensual match in Gun's groin. He felt as if a pair of big hands had clutched his buttocks.

"Where's Sylvia?" Gun asked, meaning the waitress.

"Car wouldn't start."

"Better off at home with this storm coming."

Gun loosened the scarf, then swigged beer. The jukebox had been playing Elvis Presley's "It's Now or Never," but when it switched to Paul Anka's "Put Your Head on My Shoulder," he noticed the group in the booth, two rough-looking men and, unfortunately, three equally rough-looking women. The dimly lit bar was basically a big rectangle with ragged maroon booths along the frosted windows in front, ragged maroon stools at the bar, a coat rack by the door, and a colorful jukebox at the end of the room. The blank space in the middle was the dance floor, and the bearish group densely wedged in the booth somehow seemed to counterbalance all the hefty emptiness.

"Hi, honey," one called. "Come on over."

The women's hair was a contrast in colors: fire red, oily black, and bleached blonde a la Marilyn Monroe.

"Have a seat," the redhead said, siren-like. "I'm Miriam." When he sat, she began the introductions. "This is Tie, short for Ty-rone."

When he reached across Miriam to shake Tie's hand, it was big, strong, and calloused. Tie's round, blowzy face tended toward a sour expression.

"The one who did not read the warning label on her pills," Miriam explained, "is Ruth."

Ruth was slumped, head back, mouth agape, against the booth's padding. As far as Gun could tell, she was dead. She certainly wasn't breathing. Her hair, all awry, looked like a nest of sleeping snakes.

"Stew's the other fella," Miriam added.

Stew flicked the tip of his nose a couple of times with his index finger as if sending Gun a secret message.

"And I'm Trudy," the blonde announced. "His date."

Trudy had a wad of green gum stuck to both a lower and an upper tooth so that as she chewed, it would stretch, but wouldn't break. And her coif was so sprayed in place that chewing jiggled it, like a chandelier in an earthquake, no single hair or pendant, the whole thing.

"But I ain't got a date," Miriam said, pinching the back of Gun's hand.

"Ow!" he blurted, yanking it away.

She whispered into his ear: "I kin take the chill outta the air fer ya."

When she bit him, he slid away, feeling his earlobe.

"If that's your idea of flirting," he informed her, "I'm not into S and M, especially the M." He showed everyone the red smear on his fingertip. "Imagine that."

He rose, clutched his beer, and strolled back to the bar. But before he even settled on the stool, Tie appeared at his side, startling him.

"Why didn't ya order the little lady a drink?" he asked. "You kin tell she wants ta wring your rag."

"Wring my rag?" Gun chuckled. "I'd rather fuck you." All he meant was that he was not interested, but it was, of course, a Freudian slip, though Gun didn't desire him. When Tie shot him a sharp look, Gun said, straight-faced, "Uh. Not that the little lady doesn't have her charms. It's just that—"

"Just what?"

"Well," Gun hesitated, trying to think of something. Finally, he confided, "Please don't tell 'er, but I'm suppose' ta wait ten days before havin' sex with anyone. You know, till I finish the medication." When Tie's eyes narrowed to a squint, Gun added, "Clap's a bitch." At that point, Paul Anka was finished, and a glacial hush fell on the room. "If you'll excuse me," Gun said, stepping off the stool, "I have ta piss." When he touched the restroom door, he turned and said, "Not lookin' forward to it."

In the restroom, he stood in front of the basin, looking at the small purple blood-blister where Miriam had nipped him. He tried to rub it out, then squirted a drop of liquid soap onto his fingertips and massaged his earlobe. After that, he stared at himself in the smudged mirror: pale skin, gray eyes, brown hair.

When he returned to the bar, the tension in the air was as palpable as the chill, colder. Tie and Stew were gone, but Miriam and Trudy were watching him as if waiting for the spell to take effect. When he dropped the dollar on the counter, he was not entirely surprised at Jacque's hostility, either.

"Why you so fuckin' rude to my customers?"

Jacque was leaning on the counter, hand on hip.

Gun thought he would try crossing the room without offending anyone, but as he did, Miriam and Trudy lunged across Ruth, whispering behind their wrists at such a furious pace they sounded like a crowd.

When he opened the door, a snow squall was blowing across the lot, and the two snow-encrusted men were posted by the pickups. Tie was holding a crowbar casually by his side, and Stew was hitting the gloved palm of his left hand with the wheel wrench in his right. Each was wearing his poker face, but even without the weapons, Gun could see what they were thinking. Gun was a big man with the meaty body of a boxer, but this time, when the fight-or-flight reflex kicked in, it was flight. He would simply rather run.

When he stepped back inside, Miriam was waiting for him, arms crossed, a cracked, red, patent leather shoe turned to the side.

"How come you don' wanna fuck me, big boy?" she snapped. "What's wrong with you anyway?" When he tried to jog past her, she stepped into his way, and he bumped her. "You don't like pussy?" she called after him. "What do you like, huh, cock?"

When he swung round the bar, he slammed into a doorjamb, bouncing into a back room stacked with boxes of liquor. He managed to get out the back door just as Tie was chugging around one corner of the building and Stew around the other. The bar was on the edge of town, and Gun was galloping as fast as he could through knee-deep drifts across a flat field he knew went on forever. But soon he couldn't see the men, or anything else for that matter, so he crouched in the snow, waiting for them. He was breathing hard and, at times, thought he saw them, light gray blurs focusing out of the white, then softening back in. He put on the cap, pulling it over his ears, and wound the scarf around his face, leaving a slit for his eyes. He put on the gloves, squinting into the whiteout, but when he decided that they were, in fact, not following him, he set off at a right angle to his tracks, paralleling the road, he thought, then cutting back toward town.

Till then, he had thought of himself as having a good sense of direction—some inner gyroscope keeping him on course—but after thirty minutes, he knew he was lost. If he was going to find his way back, he realized, he would've. He stopped, looked around, and tried backtracking, but soon his tracks played out. The wind had erased them like pencil marks, each fainter than the last, fading, at last, into a blank page of snow. He stopped and looked around again. Drifts sheared off, unraveling in long, sibilant, crystalline strings. A lull ensued, and the wind whispered over the field, gossiping about him, as he thought of it. When another gust hit, he could actually lean on it.

He set off on another tangent, his thighs tired from the high strides. Occasionally, he would step into a furrow or hole and fall, half swimming, half crawling back onto solid footing, and soon his boots and clothes were both miserably wet and ice stiff. His nose, ears, fingers, and toes began to ache, then went numb. His face felt like plastic, skin stunned with Novocain. The warmth in his body had retreated to his chest, he felt, had been turned down to a little blue flame, a wavering pilot light, and it was about an hour later, on the verge of collapse, head down, that he walked into something that gave a little but held, something that stopped him long enough for him to come back to himself: dark strings of icy barbed wire cutting across his chest. Then he saw the Buick Special, a red and white, four-door sedan half buried in snow. A drift sloped up and over the car on the roadside, but the fence side was up only to the handles.

Gun leaned over the wire until he flipped, landing on his back, then sat up and crawled to the car. The window was glazed with ice, and when he pounded it, it crackled, and a young man's face appeared behind it as if trapped under ice in a river. The young man was in the back, leaning over the passenger side. He studied Gun, then struggled to roll down the window. When there was enough room for his hands, Gun grabbed the top and pushed, and when there was enough room for him to climb through, he did, falling flat on the seat. He immediately noticed the warm male scent.

When the man tried to roll up the window, Gun's boots were in the way, so Gun swung them onto the floor and shoved himself up, sitting on a map. The man worked with the window, leaving a crack at the top, and when he plunked on the back seat, Gun pulled the map from under his hip and dropped it on the driver's side. Then he noticed the hush in the car. After the hiss of snow, the car was strangely quiet—quiet, that is, except for the ticking. A small, round clock in the dash. Then it clunked.

Gun faced the man: a moody, good-looking youth in a red sweat suit with the words Flash Point printed in black across the chest. He had a wide, angular face still tan from summer and framed by a thick mop of curly brown hair. His cheeks dipped in, and a two-day growth of stubble peppered his upper lip and chin. Hazel eyes glanced at him from lush lashes. Even at his coldest, Gun had had that little blue flame flickering in his chest, but at the mere sight of the man, a furnace ignited. He began warming up.

"What's your name?" Gun asked, shivering.

"Tommy," the man said in a soft voice. "Tommy March."

He was zipped to the thigh in an orange sleeping bag as if just hatched from a silk cocoon. Beside him on the seat were an open duffel bag, an open shaving kit, and a bright-yellow, goose-down ski jacket.

"Thanks," Gun said.

"You're welcome."

"I don't think—I would've—"

Gun's teeth began chattering so much he couldn't finish the sentence. He went from shivering to shaking, then from shaking to a kind of grand-mal seizure, wide-awake.

"Guess there's enough room in here for two," Tommy said, shoving everything aside. "Climb over."

Gun knelt on the seat, but Tommy had to grab Gun's coat by the shoulders and pull him over. Gun fell on top of him, then sat beside him, twitching. Tommy leaned over the front seat to slide it forward as far as he could, exposing a big, white flashlight under the driver's side.

When he sat, he glanced at Gun, then said, "You'd better get out of those wet clothes."

Gun managed to pull off his gloves and cap, but Tommy had to help him with the coat, scarf, and crewneck. He bent down to unlace and push off Gun's boots, setting them next to his athletic shoes on the floor, and when he skinned off the soaked socks, Gun's feet were red and swollen. Gun was shaking too badly to unbuckle his belt, so Tommy did it for him, drawing the wide leather through the brass buckle. He unzipped Gun's corduroys and, as Gun lifted off the seat, pulled them down his thighs. Though Gun's boxers and T-shirt were damp from sweat, they left them on.

"Scoot onto this," Tommy said, meaning the bottom fold of the sleeping bag. "Swing your feet in here."

When Gun was in the bag, Tommy zipped it, and there they were: side-by-side. Tommy hesitated, as if nonplussed by the awkwardness of the situation, then slipped his arm around Gun's neck. The position was the only way both could find room in the bag. Gun, too, hesitated, then laid his head on Tommy's shoulder.

"Jeez!" Tommy chuckled. "Your hands are like ice." Tommy held Gun's right hand, rubbing and blowing it. "Put your left under my butt," he said, lifting up. "I can even feel your feet through my socks."

When Tommy covered Gun's feet with his, Gun did not know what to think. Was Tommy gay or simply taking care of him, one man to another, as some men would in a storm? Whatever the case, Gun, of course, had no objections. He was cuddled with a man in a sleeping bag. Straight or gay didn't matter to him. He was cuddled with the man who had saved his life.

All at once, he felt weak and drowsy in a lightheaded, surreal sort of way, but the last thing he remembered before falling asleep was the comforting smell of Tommy's armpit.

Gun dreamed that he was lost in the storm again, but this time, instead of stumbling upon the stranded Buick, he could just make out, behind the billowing sheers of snow, the black snouts and eyes of two polar bears lumbering toward him. The dream frightened him so badly he woke.

The window was fogged and frosted on the inside, on the outside silvery gray with snow, and Gun could hear a subtle white noise in the background, the fizz of snow blowing over the car. But he was no longer cold, in fact, hot, embraced with Tommy. The smoldering animal heat of their bodies had warmed the bag so much they were sweating. Then he realized they had erections, Gun's pressed into Tommy's hip, Tommy's, like a stick of wood, cupped in Gun's hand.

Gun raised his head, and they stared at each other, but though they apparently knew at once what was about to happen, they simply hugged. On Tommy's part, the hug seemed a natural impulse to keep Gun warm. On Gun's, however, it was more like consolation.

Gun raised his head again, and they kissed tenderly, then hungrily, tonguing each other. Gun's hand slipped under the waistband of Tommy's sweatpants, then under his jockstrap, and five minutes later, Tommy was flat on his back with his feet on the roof, his hands, clasped in Gun's, pressed to the seat on either side of his shoulders. Gun kissed him, flicking his tongue into his mouth, but when he made as if to kiss him again, Tommy gaped, like a nestling, showing him his throat. Instead, Gun kissed his left nipple. Tommy's chest rose to meet his mouth, and when Gun realized that just his presence deep inside him was about to bring him off, he forget about himself for a moment, angling up vigorously.

"Oh, no," Tommy moaned, rolling his head from side to side. "No, Sir." He sounded as if he did not want to come, but when he cried, "Oh, man," his head tilted back and he did, squeezing his eyes shut as if he could hardly bear the intense pleasure. Then he laughed a nervous laugh, which immediately became a long-pent-up sob. When Tommy came—his body, like a fist, clenching Gun—Gun came too, grimacing, but his grimace burst into tears.

"Oh, man," Gun groaned, his forehead pressed to Tommy's shoulder. "Oh, Tommy, thank you."

Then the moment passed. Their breathing slowed. The car fell silent, and Gun could hear the clock ticking. They rested for a couple of minutes, but when Gun heard the clock clunk, he braced on his elbows, wiping his nose on the back of his hand. Tommy peered at the seat back, his face glum. Then he looked at Gun, who kissed him thoughtfully, brushing back his hair.

"Sorry," Gun said, adding as if to himself, "I don' know, I don' know. It's been quite a while."

Gun sat up, withdrawing from him, and grabbed Tommy's ankle, swinging his leg over. He lay down, his front to Tommy's back, pulled up the bag flap, and zipped it. He slipped his left arm under Tommy's neck and draped his right over his chest, cupping Tommy's biceps. Tommy laid his hand on top of Gun's. Despite the intimacy, however, Gun could feel him drifting away, wandering off someplace private, but thought he understood the feeling. Often after he came, he just wanted to get away from his trick, cute or not, as fast as he could. But not this time, not with Tommy.

"I can't believe I let you in my ass," Tommy said, squinting at the back of the front seat. "I'm not gay, you know."

Gun rose to gaze at him and smiled shrewdly.

"Tommy. Look," he began. "You came from just my cock in your ass. If you ain't gay, then I ain't goin' outta my mind with boredom in this god-forsaken place."

In some sense, Gun knew that he had opened him up, as in a Caesarean, had delivered the gayness that, otherwise, would have died, and Tommy certainly looked as if Gun had given him something to think about.

"You didn't happen to get a weather report?" Gun asked, lying down.

"I was afraid to leave the radio on," Tommy said. "You know, the battery. Mostly country music and Bible thumpers. The U.S. only got three gold medals at Squaw Valley. Won hockey, though. Beat the Russkies."

"Russkies, huh?"

"I was afraid to leave the motor on for the heater."

"Carbon monoxide," Gun commented.

"We going to die?"

"We're not gonna die," Gun assured him. "This'll blow over by morning."

Gun glanced at the window above their heads. The silvery snow was dulling to gray.

"I'm hungry," Tommy said.

"Well, you can eat me," Gun joked, "and I can eat you."

"Mine enough?"

173

"In spades, babe." Gun closed his eyes. "I could eat off yours for years."

"What's your name?" Tommy asked. "You know. Just in case I want to file a rape charge."

"Gun."

"What?"

"Gun. Short for Gunther, Gunther Rourke. I'm named after my German grandfather."

The car was growing dark, and after a couple of minutes, Gun could tell from Tommy's contented breathing that he had fallen asleep. Then Gun dozed off.

This time, Gun dreamed that he and Tommy, in jogging outfits, had ventured into a mine, but as they were leaving, it started to cave in. Gun jumped under a boulder, bearing it on his shoulders, like Atlas. The immense weight pushed him down to a squat, but he fought back, straining against the rock, until he had hoisted it high enough for Tommy to get by. At that point, Gun's strength began to fail, and he was slowly sinking back to a squat. Strangely enough, all he could think of was how beautiful Tommy's legs were—big, strong, shapely legs, the legs of an athlete. Tommy glanced at him helplessly, then ran.

Gun jerked awake.

"What?" Tommy asked.

The car was pitch black, dead quiet, except for the clock.

"Nothing," Gun said. "A dream."

"What about?"

"I, uh—" Gun paused, clenching a fist. His fingers were stiff. "I had this barbell on my shoulders, and I was trying to lift too much weight. Where's the flashlight?"

Tommy flicked it on, but left it on the carpet, pointed under the front seat.

"Why are you out here?" he asked.

Gun pressed his feet against Tommy's, could feel Tommy's toes wiggling.

"Hmpf," Gun chuckled. "You're not gonna believe this. I got lost walking home."

"No, I mean, why are you out here in the middle of nowhere? Where are we, anyway? "

"You don't even know you're in Marble, Michigan. Or someplace near it. That must be nice."

Gun ran his hand over Tommy's shoulder, then down his side to his waist, touching his navel, a waist so narrow that when Tommy breathed out, his stomach pinched to a tight little knot of pleats. Gun twiddled the line of hair on Tommy's groin.

"Why am I out here in the middle of nowhere?" Gun asked himself. "Because my father had a stroke, and I had to take care of him, that is, until he died a couple of months ago. Now I don't exactly know what to do with myself."

Gun's hand brushed past Tommy's cock to his scrotum, pulling free the sac tucked between his thighs. He rubbed the rubbery skin between his fingers, fingered the big, soft stones rolling around inside.

"Why are *you* out here in the middle of nowhere?"

"Thought I'd try this secondary road. Hoping to beat the storm. But the snow just got deeper and deeper. If it hadn't been for the fences, I wouldn't even have known where the road was."

Gun raised his knee and adjusted his own scrotum. He then lifted Tommy's cheek, sandwiching himself between the mounds. He draped his leg over Tommy's, rested his head on his, and began tweaking Tommy's right nipple with his left hand.

"Where you from?" he asked, fondling Tommy's cock with his right.

"Atlanta. On my way back from visiting Dewey."

"Dewey?"

"College roommate. Lives in Cheboygan."

"Old boyfriend?"

"Dewey's married to Norma. Or—'the frigid bitch,' as he calls her. They have two boys, Allan and Larry."

Gun could fill in the blanks, and all at once, he saw how defeated Tommy was, like himself, how emotionally damaged, as if Dewey had run a bayonet through him, then stripped him.

"You did 'im, didn't ya?" Gun smiled, flicking Tommy's cock. "Didn't ya? He reeled out some line 'bout the frigid bitch, and you bit."

"He has this cozy cabin on the lake."

"Still love 'im?" Gun asked, kissing the cool skin on Tommy's shoulder. When he failed to answer, Gun said, "You still love him."

When Gun squeezed Tommy's cock, a little tear of seminal fluid leaked from the slit.

"What do you do?" Tommy asked, changing subjects.

"I'm a stony," Gun said.

"A what?"

"A stony. What locals call a guy who works in the quarry." When Gun started humping him, Tommy was, in effect, thrusting Gun's hand. "An old quarry's a great place to swim in summer," Gun said. "Most people don't even know they're there. Daisies on the ledges." What had started out as a little front-to-back cuddling had gradually turned into a comfortable coupling. "What do you do?"

"I help my dad—" Tommy held his breath for a second. "—run a pool-supply center."

175

"So that's why you're so tan," Gun said, jostling him. "Must be a lot warmer in Atlanta. That would be nice."

"It can be—uh, just as cold," Tommy gasped.

"I doubt it," Gun said, picking up the pace. "It's cold here in all sorts of ways." As an afterthought, he asked, "What was your major?"

Tommy chuckled: "Psychology."

"Psychology, huh," Gun grunted. "Trying to figure yourself out."

Gun rolled partway on top of him, his face in his neck, and the foam seat puffed in rhythm. Gun's left hand was hanging over the seat, and Tommy laced his fingers through Gun's, squeezing them hard. Then he grabbed Gun's hair with his other hand and tried to pull him off his neck.

"Oh, no," Tommy whispered, coming. "Oh, man. No way…"

Tommy's climax, in turn, triggered Gun's, and Gun—sucking on Tommy's earlobe—wallowed in his hips. Gun's mouth must have tickled, though, for Tommy broke into what could only be described as a cross between ardent groans and giddy laughter.

"Don't cry," Gun joked, licking his neck. "Don't cry." He plunged his tongue into Tommy's ear. "You have nothing to cry about."

"You cried," Tommy laughed.

But his smile faded to a pensive look, a look of concern etched in the glow of the flashlight, and again Gun could feel him—though they were still connected, as physically connected as two men could be—leaving him again, drifting off, Gun presumed, to the cabin on the lake.

"I can't believe I let you fuck me twice," Tommy said.

Gun sighed, then lifted off him, sliding out of him slowly. He wiped Tommy's come off his fingers onto the edge of the seat.

"You act like I cut your fuckin' balls off," Gun said, pulling up the bag flap. "I didn't cut your balls off." He zipped the bag. "You still have a great pair of balls. Big ones."

Tommy turned off the flashlight, plunging the car into darkness. Gun embraced him again, front to back, and they snuggled like lovers in the warm lair of the bag. Gun breathed in the balmy scent of Tommy's hair, then fell into a deep sleep, a dreamless sleep as black and still as the night.

During the night, the temperature dropped to zero, but when Gun woke, Tommy was wrapped around him, his face in his neck, softly twining the tuft of hair on Gun's chest. The clock was ticking, and the windows on the fence side of the car glowed with a smooth, nebulous vermilion. At least, he knew where east was, Gun thought. Now where was town?

He clenched his hands a couple of times. His fingers were stiff.

"Well, if I dreamed anything last night," he said, "I don't remember it. That's the best I've—" He yawned, arching his back off the bag. When he flopped flat again, the bag breathed out a heady incense of sweaty crotch smells.

"I don't think I've ever slept that well. Sleep OK?" When Tommy kissed him gently behind the stud in his ear, his mouth touched off a pleasant flush. "I take that as a yes."

When Gun rose to unzip the bag, the west windows were dark blue, and when he lay back down, he raised his right knee, and Tommy laid his hand on Gun's pectoral.

"Great legs," Tommy whispered.

"Thanks," Gun replied. "You have a sweet pair yourself. In fact, you're pretty sweet all over." Gun's cock was lolling on his groin, but Tommy's hand stole past it to fondle Gun's scrotum. "Not exactly the biggest marbles in the game," Gun said, wiggling his toes. His balls, unlike Tommy's, were not in proportion to his cock.

"It's the aim that counts," Tommy said, "not the size of the marble."

"Well, I do have good aim." Gun chuckled too eagerly, Tommy, thoughtfully. "Speaking of which," Gun said. "I have to pee."

He propped on an elbow, kissing Tommy's lips. Then they dressed and climbed out the window. In the sharp, dry air, Gun realized how chafed his face was.

He slogged a yard off the back of the car, Tommy off the front, and as Gun stood there, peeing a yellow pocket in the snow, he glanced across the glittering field coloring in the sunrise. Small, comma-shaped clouds were fading from blood smears to pink fleece. The golden halo around the sun reminded him of those floating over saints in religious paintings.

"I know where we are," he said.

When he slogged back to the car, he scooped up a big handful of snow, which he ate, washing the gummy taste out of his mouth. He spit it out, then ate another handful, which he swallowed. He heard something and gazed down the road toward the tiny white feather inching along the fence. Then Tommy saw the snowplow, but when Gun glanced at him, he looked away.

When Gun said, "This is it," Tommy touched the brake with his shoe.

The car rolled to a stop by the mailbox, and they stared at the house: a brick, snowbound bungalow stark against the white plain and, in the sky to the east, big, muscle-bound clouds. Gun's blue Falcon, window-deep, sat in the drive.

"Come in," Gun said, glancing at him. "I'll fix you breakfast. You can take a hot bath while I'm fixing it. You must be starved. I am. You need to call home, anyway. Don't you? Let 'em know you're OK?" When Tommy just sat there with the motor running, his hands on the wheel, Gun said, "The highway's straight ahead."

He got out, slammed the door, and hulked off. But when the car crept forward, grinding on the ice, he turned, and when it picked up speed, he could not help himself. He ran after it. There was nothing else he could do. He needed him. Or he needed what only a young man like Tommy could give him.

The brake lights lit up, the car slowed, and a little white rag of vapor fluttered from the muffler, but when Gun caught up, he slipped on the ice, landing on his hip. The fall was cushioned by his buttock and clothes, but he hit the ice so hard the shock wave flashed through his body. When Tommy looked at him, Gun grabbed the door handle, pulled himself up, and opened the door.

"Officer Rourke here," he began, an arm on the roof. "I noticed you were going too fast for road conditions. May I see your license, please?"

"Gun," Tommy blushed, glancing up. "What are you doing?"

"May I see your license, please?" He stepped out of character and whispered, "Tommy, let me have a look at your license." Tommy looked at him askance, then fished out the license and handed it to him. Gun squinted at it in the glare, but his hand was shaky. "205 Pineland," he muttered to himself. "205 Pineland, 205 Pineland." Then he shook it in Tommy's face and said, "I'm not giving this back to you till you come inside. You're gonna give us at least one chance."

"I'll be back through here," Tommy said, staring ahead.

"Yeah, you and Halley's Comet. Oh," Gun laughed. "You mean Dewey." He tapped the license on his palm. "Think about it, Tommy. Married. Two kids." For some reason, he felt awkward looming over him, so he knelt on the ice, one knee, then both, the hand with the license on the seat back, the other on the window crank on the door. "Listen, Tommy. You can fuck me if you want. You can fuck me *all* you want. I don't care. I can think of only one thing I'd enjoy as much, and we did that."

"Twice," Tommy said, glancing at him with a neutral look.

Gun looked down, thinking, then up.

"Don't let this be the last time I see you," he said. "Please. Don't crawl back into that—that igloo of yours. OK? OK? I don't have anything to hold me here. See, I can move. We can see if things work out. I've saved money. My father left me money."

"What things?" Tommy asked, drumming his thumb on the steering wheel.

"What?"

"If what things work out?"

Gun grabbed the running board and slid closer, his face about level with Tommy's shoulder.

"You don't know how it is around here. Well, maybe you do. I don't know. But when you live in a cold world, you have to build your own fire. Right? The best I've been able to do is tricks at a rest stop a hundred miles to the north. Flint and steel, no spark. I can't get anything started." Tommy looked paralyzed, a test dummy in a crash vehicle. "I can be good to you," Gun swore. "I can be good to you for a long time."

When Tommy finally relaxed and looked at Gun, Gun offered him the license, but Gun's hand was shaking so badly he dropped it. When they reached down, the car rolled forward a couple of feet. Tommy stepped on the brake, pulled up the emergency brake, and leaned out the door.

"I'm sorry, Gun. I didn't mean to do that."

Then he faced forward and just sat there. Gun had slumped onto his hands, but he picked up the license, sat on his heels, and, hands on his thighs, evaluated his status in life. He realized what he'd come to. But he didn't care. There was nowhere to go but up.

"OK," Tommy said.

"OK?"

"Yeah." Tommy faced him, trying to smile. "Let me back up."

"OK," Gun whispered to himself.

He got up carefully, bracing on the road, one foot, then the other. When he walked around the back of the car, he could smell the exhaust, and when he reached the door, Tommy opened it for him. Gun got in, shut the door, and handed him the license.

"I'll stay tonight," Tommy said, tossing it onto the dash. "We'll talk."

Tommy shifted gears and backed in front of the house. When they went in, Gun immediately turned up the thermostat. And they were never cold again.

ELIJAH FOR REAL
Thom Nickels

Elijah cometh; Elijah raised on high; Elijah descending the mountain. Whether heard in Baptist sermons or in Old Testament lectures, the fearsome name used to make my blood boil. That is, until I met Elijah for real.

It began as an inconsequential day. I was working at my drafting table in front of the bay window in my apartment, examining photographs and measuring them for placement in a photo-illustrated history book. I'd finally reached the tail end of a long project that had both exhausted and exhilarated me. The bay window was a spectacular working space: I had a bird's eye view of everyone on the street—Penn students, dog walkers, mail carriers, you name it!

On the day in question I saw nothing at first but then noticed the movement of arms in the second floor apartment in the building across the street. I spotted a lanky, young blond man, perhaps in his mid-twenties, painting the inside of a window, his extended brush strokes showing the length of his arms. I watched as he dabbed his brush into a corner, then stroked downward in a long plunge, then upwards again so that his t-shirt clung to his chest. Thinking: *A perfect lanky specimen, so fine…* I put down the photograph I was holding and made a point of staring at him. I walked closer to the bay window and smiled, hoping to catch his glance.

He continued to paint, oblivious to everything except the brush, which needed replenishing with fresh paint now and then. When he disappeared into the interior of the room, I hurried over to my smaller kitchen window, which was situated at a different angle, where I hoped to discern his whereabouts. In a flash he was back where he was before, working those long strokes, his thick, mop-top hair a refreshing sight in a world filled with buzz cuts.

I did not feel desperation at the sight of such a beauty, but rather a strange tranquility—a feeling that enabled me to get back into my work, matching the historical era of each photo with the appropriate spot on the layout planner. I was working diligently when I thought I saw him look over at me. Was I dreaming? By this time I was feeling a definite erotic itch and drew close to the window. I tried to make out his face but the only thing I could see was his mop of hair.

When he disappeared again I forgot about him. Experiences like this in the city are not rare: You have a run-in with Beauty, your optic nerve is stimulated but then the screen goes blank.

When I'd first noticed him I was working on a particularly striking boxing photograph. The young boxer, maybe 16, had a chest of iron. He was Swedish, maybe German, possibly Irish or Austrian, his masculine beauty capturing the gaze of his ringside handlers. The photo was taken in 1920 so the boxer was currently either a very old man or a corpse withered down to nothing. In the photograph, however, he remained eternally young and his looks never failed to capture the imagination of people I showed it to.

"I wish I could meet the likes you during my travels," I'd often say aloud to myself while flipping the photo this way and that, looking at it close up to see if I could detect signs of his boxer's endowment.

I contacted the man who sold me the photo, old Kikel in Manayunk, who operated his postcard and photo factory in the back of an old warehouse. He knew everything about the photographs but nothing about the boxer himself except that the kid was supposed to have been a sensation in old Manayunk back in the 1920s. In the photo the kid was looking straight into the eye of the camera. He was in an outside ring, his arms raised above his head in a gesture of victory.

"If I find out something about this guy, I'll give you a call. Sometimes information comes up. I'll do some asking around," Kikel said.

Kikel called a couple weeks later.

"You know that photo you have with the man sitting in the bar near the train tracks? I found out he was living in some nursing home as recently as 1995. Let me do a little more investigating and I'll get back with you. Kikel knew everybody and he had connections.

"Thanks Kikel," I said. "It would be nice to identify the boxer, you know."

Days passed and, not having heard from Kikel had just about decided that the boxer would have to remain anonymous, when I received another phone call.

"Hey, I got some information on that guy," Kikel said, chomping gum. "Hard to believe, but he's still alive. He lives in a nursing home—Cathedral Village. He's ninety-nine and can barely walk. His name's Gallagher or something. Just call the Village and ask for him if you want to talk. I met his great-granddaughter. She said he still has his wits about him, and knows a lot of stuff."

"That's terrific, Kikel; thanks a lot. Maybe he'll tell me about his career," I said, hanging up.

I could not believe that the boxer was still alive. In a way the fact disappointed me. I felt overworked and getting information sometimes meant extensive interviews by phone or in person. Shortly after talking to Kikel I went to the bay window to check on the house painter. I could see him moving around inside the house but got no clear picture of him near the window.

An hour passed and I decided to go to the library across town. When I walked out my door, I saw the painter standing on the stoop across the street, having a smoke. My eyes were drawn to his sensitive and compelling eyes. As they proved eyes that seemed to take me in, by the time I'd crossed the street I felt he sensed my attraction. As I stepped on the curb and walked towards him our eyes locked. Our simultaneous hellos suggested that he was probably a free spirit. After that, I knew what I was going to do.

Elijah. Elijah. When I think back to that time now, the memory is even more captivating. Where did Elijah go?

"When Elijah comes your life will change." That's what I heard the crazy preacher say while channel surfing. He was dressed in ridiculous judicial robes with military shoulder stripes and the Baptist ladies were stomping their feet.

When Elijah comes your life will change.

The phrase stuck for some reason. I wrote it in my journal, even repeated it to a few friends, then forget about it. I did not remember it until Elijah was out of my life and the furor erupted over the Saint, but I'm getting ahead of myself.

When I came back from the library, Elijah was gone but I knew he'd be back the following day so went to my desk and composed a letter.

> *Dear ------,*
> *I don't know your name but we spotted one another when I crossed the street yesterday. You were having a smoke on the stoop. I was coming out of the house across the street. Excuse the strangeness of this, but I'm writing to ask if you'll call me someday when you get off work. Let's have coffee or a glass of wine. I'd like to talk to you so feel free to call me anytime.*
> *Dan*

'Dan' is the alias I use when I'm feeling wicked. The name brings me luck. Of course, there was no guarantee that someone else might not pick up the letter, despite the fact that I wrote "House Painter" in big block letters across the front of the envelope. Notes like this have gotten me into trouble before. One time, after I left a note on a car windshield, I was bombarded with calls from the guy's girlfriend who did everything in her power to try and find out who I was and where I lived. "You're too possessive," I finally screamed at her. "You deserve to lose him with an attitude like that." After that, the harassing phone calls stopped.

I slipped the letter into the appropriate slot and went about my day, finishing up the placement of photographs in the book and then reviewing the captions I'd written for them individually. Under the boxer's photograph, I wrote: "Young Manayunk amateur boxers often went to 'Rudolph's Row' in West Manayunk to test their skills. The fights became a magnet for young boys who did everything but swim the Schuykill River to watch famous pros like Benny Bass throw a swing or two." Fairly tame stuff, considering what was about to unfold.

I wasn't thinking of anything in particular when the phone rang. It was the painter, calling from a pay phone, saying he'd gotten my letter and would be glad to visit the following day. He dismissed my nervous view of the letter as "strange."

"Not at all, I've had letters written to me before, mostly by women. Women do it all the time," he said. He agreed that he'd be by the next day when he finished painting. Then he said: "My name is Elijah."

"Elijah? People name their kids Elijah?" I asked.

During our conversation he told me that he was from Denver, that he'd been in Philadelphia for just three months and didn't know a soul. He was visiting the city and met a girl one night in an Irish bar who'd gotten him drunk so she could take him home for a good fuck. *Girls do that?* I'd responded. *She sounds like a gay man!*

Of course she got pregnant. Frightened, Elijah fled to Denver but came back to work things out.

"I love my daughter. I came back for her, mostly" he said.

We agreed that he'd stop by my apartment the following day.

"Just come over and don't stand on ceremony," I insisted.

When Elijah comes, your life will change.

I started to remember the Bible stories I'd heard as a child: how Elijah ascended to heaven in a fire wheel and how, at least according to some, he was an earlier incarnation of Jesus Christ.

When Elijah visited I got plenty of close-up looks—of his long elegant fingers, his fine skin…. He wore painter's pants and a white t-shirt and stood for a long time in the middle of my living room, inspecting the paintings on the wall and asking questions about each. His pants were paint-spattered; around the zipper I thought I discerned a subtle swelling. He sat down for a few minutes but said he couldn't stay because his girlfriend, Megan, was expecting him home for dinner.

"She has a temper," he said.

The day had not been a success. Earlier, when I'd called Cathedral Village, they said that Gallagher was on a ventilator.

"I can come tomorrow night after work if you want," Elijah continued. "Then I can stay longer, but I have to get back tonight because Megan will be really pissed if I'm late," Elijah said. When he said "pissed" there was a snapping sound to his voice. I know he was aware that I liked him because he had his legs stretched out in front of him. "Megan has turned into a real bitch. We're not getting along. I sort of don't know what to do. I haven't fucked her in a while, at least not since Liz was born. So what did you want to talk about?"

The blunt question surprised me but I was not put off.

"I thought maybe you'd be up for a massage or something after I got to know you." Elijah didn't seem at all surprised. In the early evening twilight his skin took on a kind of glow. I asked questions about Megan and he told me how she had destroyed all his clothing in a fit of jealousy. I'd heard of women destroying their boyfriend's clothes, ripping them with scissors or steak knives or even throwing them out windows. From what I gathered, Megan enjoyed destroying things when life didn't go her way in an effort to get even. Obviously, she considered Elijah her property.

Elijah told me he was staying at the notorious Parker Hotel, Philadelphia's sleazeball version of New York's Chelsea Hotel. He was saving money but wasn't sure whether he was going back to Denver or whether he'd make a go of it here.

Elijah came today, I wrote in my journal. *Small indentation in his spotted painter's pants. He has beautiful hair, seductive eyes and an abusive girlfriend, but then again I don't think he's the commitment type. In many ways he must drive her crazy. He has a baby, little Liz. While he can't love Megan he's ready to die for little Liz. Said he'll be by tomorrow. I'll stock up on red wine and wait for the visit. I never knew painter's pants could have such an effect on me...*

In the evening the nursing home called. They said Gallagher was better and would put him on the line. I was placed on hold for a minute or two and then this old, throaty voice came on. I introduced myself and described the photo down to the last detail. He told me the photo in question was taken on his 21st birthday. He walked to the boxing match that day, then crossed the river and celebrated with his friends in an old ale house by the Manayunk canal. He told me that many of his friends were still alive and that three of them were in the home, all former boxing cronies: Wendell, Felix and Hans, by name. "All wild and still crazy in the head but if you want to meet us, come on up and I'll tell you about the boxing and the boys who hung around the canal."

I gladly accepted, thanked him, and said I'd come up that Friday, wondering what I was getting myself into. I didn't need this much information. I was only after a caption, a little bit of history. Gallagher, I felt, wanted me to write his biography.

When Elijah came over the following night he was in the same painter's pants. He drank one glass of wine and updated the Megan stories. I'd been studying his long legs and the way he kept crossing and uncrossing his feet. At one point he let his head rest on the back of the chair and he closed his eyes as if lost in thought. I wanted to go up and plant a kiss on his lips but held out in order to get the most out of the erotic moment. Finally he asked me what it was I wanted to do to him. I spelled it out. Massage this; probe that; rub here, yank that. His eyes widened.

"Okay," he said, smiling, "in other words, a total crank-up job."

"Yeah, let's… crank-up," I laughed, although I'd never heard it referred to that way. Then he laughed. I loved that. When he stood up the swelling in his crotch was no illusion. The tent was substantial and I noticed a flush on his cheeks. "Just tell me what to do," he said, throwing his arms out.

Just tell me what to do—imagine that!

I led him into the bedroom where he removed his clothes. His chest was long and angular. When his painter's pants came off he was all legs and erect cock. "So this is what makes Megan jealous and possessive; this is what drives her to cut up clothes!" I joked. When I pondered his erection I imagined him pumping Megan and impregnating her with little Liz.

Although I was more than twice his age, there he was, sitting on the edge of my bed, grabbing my body by the hips and guiding me towards his face. When he went down on me I placed my hands on the back of his head, caressed his painter's hair and pulled him snug against my loins. I rearranged the angle of my aim, straddling from a top position as I withdrew and plunged deeply into his Megan-kissing mouth. He turned his body according to my directions and took it all, that "straight" boy from Denver, as hungry and willing as they come.

I did not expect the kisses—wet, full-mouth kisses straight from the movies, authentic "in love" kisses that found me tasting what had hooked Megan. *Where does good fortune like this come from?* I wondered. *From a simple letter, a large bay window, a willingness to take a chance?* When he rolled over on his stomach there was no doubt what he wanted, but….

We settled on a vanilla climax with Elijah on his back as I held him from the side, after which I buried my lips in his Colorado, Rocky Mountain chest.

Gallagher was one of those tall, bony old men who retain an eternal youthfulness; I saw at once the "boy" beneath the layers of age. He had a full head of white hair and walked with a limp. He invited me to sit down. His room was full of family memorabilia and antique clocks. I sat across from him and took out my tape recorder when he began fumbling through a folder of old photographs. I watched as he withdrew several from the packet. There was a small table in front of us and he put the packet down. "Take a look," he said, nodding his head.

I noticed that the first photograph was a duplicate of the one I was using in the book. Each successive photograph after that showed Gallagher in another boxing posture with another contender. The contenders were short, dark haired handsome men, all Irish, German or Italian. In one photo Gallagher was lifting a petite young man off the ground. He had his arms around the boy and was squeezing him over his loins and chest, the contender clearly in a playful mood with his hairy legs positioned on either side of Gallagher's face. In another photo, Gallagher was stretched out prone over another youth. The youth had a stunned look on his face but there was satisfaction and awe in his eyes as if he enjoyed the seeming helplessness of his situation beneath the hold and the feel of Gallagher's body.

"These are remarkable," I said, not expecting what I saw next, a photograph of Gallagher and a fellow boxer, arms around one another, their faces almost cheek-to-cheek. "I didn't tell my wife about him, you know," he offered. "In those days you kept things like that secret. He meant the world to me. He wanted to leave America and take me back to his native Austria where nobody would know us, but I had a wife and children. I couldn't do it, so he stayed here. Suffice to say that life was difficult. I never hung around with the others on street corners, down by the canal. Those guys were outcasts; people knew what they were about. Mostly they befriended young men coming in from the boats or alehouses. If not for John, I might have lost myself down there too.

"You want to know a secret? I'll tell you a secret," he continued. "So many men in Manayunk were homosexual—from the Manayunk Businessmen's Association, to the Constable, to the fire fighters, the priests, the wagon boys, the canal workers... I don't know why there were so many of us—something in the water, maybe—but we kept it under wraps. More and more of us would come to the meetings in Nickels Hall on Green Lane and Baker Street. There used to be Saturday night dances there and we'd come with our wives and girlfriends and then find an opportunity to split up and meet while the women talked. It was a secret society, you might say, where nobody ever stated the obvious, nobody ever used a word like 'gay.' That way we felt safe. Hard to explain but it was a different time then, you know?

"Everything went up in smoke around the second world war. Men died, others moved out, and new ones stopped coming. The tradition was lost. We never kept records but I remember all the old tales..."

He stopped to open a glass candy dish filled with licorice. He passed me the dish and I took several. He stared at me for a long time while I chewed. I felt uncomfortable, thinking that he was either viewing me as an object of lust or sizing me up in comparison to the brave, bold men of earlier days. I wondered if he felt desire, if he resented me for being comparatively young and still in the game. I watched his eyes for quick angle thrusts near the area of my crotch. I thought how awful it would be to retain a young man's sexual desire trapped in the body of an ancient man. What possible recourse could there be except masturbation, celibacy or the depletion of funds in procuring escorts?

"When I was young John and I would hike up behind the canal along the old Indian path where the first settlers came. There are huge old trees there and in one spot a hollowed-out spot where a group of hermits used to live hundreds of years ago. We'd go out there with our fishing equipment, since we needed an excuse to be gone for the afternoon. John was considerably smaller than I. In fact, I could carry him on my back if need be and I often did that when his legs gave out. You see, John was beautiful but he was sickly, and he'd often lose his breath and have to sit down or lay flat on the grass to catch his breath. I'd look at him when he did that and sit down beside him and run my hand along his forehead. He wore his hair like a boy, a mop top with bangs, and his big blue eyes never failed to get me to do what he asked, whether it was to carry him or rub his legs because they hurt. In the hermit's hole we'd camp out and have long discussions. John would pontificate on the evils of society while I'd massage his legs, rubbing, then caressing, and then, feeling frisky, I'd take off his boots and rub his feet…

"'Don't you start,' he'd say, meaning sex, of course. John couldn't take much sex. It took the wind out of him, blew his sails apart. He'd push my hand away when I let it roam up near his thighs or when I'd insert it under his trousers and fish around for the 'other John…' Oh yes, that 'other John…' what a specimen it was! He called it 'Mr. Peepers.'

"Don't mind me," he said, suddenly embarrassed.

I told him I didn't mind and that he was giving me a personal glimpse into the gay history of Manayunk, an area I thought had little or no gay history. "Do go on," I said, reaching for another piece of licorice.

"You must have someone special," he said, reaching over to open a cabinet near his chair. He withdrew a bottle of sherry and two miniature glasses with tall stems.

"Yes, thank you," I said, accepting the glass. "I really don't have anyone special right now, although I just met a guy named Elijah, so we'll see."

"Elijah… a prophet! Now a boy named Elijah will probably do almost anything. It has to be. Think of what he went through with that name. I bet he's good looking."

"Oh, he's good looking all right. He's one of those tall, gangly types, but not freakishly tall you know, and his hair is the color of an October sunset. But, tell me about John."

"Sometimes, when John wanted me to massage him, he wouldn't care if I went whole hog. Now, I *always* wanted to go whole hog with him because… I desired him. I loved him. His body appealed to me, and his penis, if I may be so bold, was as memorable as his mind. I'd consume him right there in the hole. Once he got used to the idea he'd tell me what to do—you know, like, 'Make me feel pleasure *there*,' or 'Kiss me *here* and then plant your tongue and press *down*,' that sort of thing. John taught me to disconnect."

"Disconnect?"

"I'd been going crazy with some of the men in town, you know, bed hopping, playing one against the other, wasting time and neglecting my work, devoting my life to the pursuit of it, always fixated on the next thrill. John came along and forced me to look at my life. It worked. I became a respected Notary

Public, ran for public office and was elected. Became an elder in the church…
John didn't have a career because he was ill, you know, but he was always
thinking and going around doing things for people. The old ladies loved him
because he could fix anything. He'd paint their windows, replace their doors,
help them build stables and sheds. When he wasn't feeling good he'd go into
hiding and then you wouldn't see him for several weeks. These were the worst
times for me since he lived with his mother, which made visiting him very
difficult. I was engaged at the time, so had to temper my concern, but I'd visit
him whenever I could. John was a committed socialist from day one—but he
supported Teddy Roosevelt…"

"Do you have a photograph of John?" I asked, sensing that the old man
was becoming tired.

Without a word Gallagher got up and walked across the room. He went to
a set of bureau drawers, began to bend over at the waist and reach for the bottom
drawer when his body froze, leaving his right arm to dangle in mid-air.

"Let me help you," I said.

"Open that," Gallagher said, pointing to the drawer. I did as I was told
and saw a number of accounting ledgers, tablets and a lacquered Chinese box.
Gallagher said to take out the box. We went back to our chairs and I waited till
he opened the box and withdrew two photographs and a prayer card. The
photographs showed an earnest-looking boy of about twenty-one, petite and
rather impish, with brightly intelligent eyes and a swoop of dark hair over his
forehead. He was kneeling in a garden. The other photograph showed him as a
young man dressed in a cassock in the archway of a building. I immediately
recognized something familiar about his face. After that I looked at the card and
saw that it pictured Saint John Neuman of Philadelphia, the first American saint.

"I don't understand," I said, going back over the photographs, wondering
why the prayer card was there until I saw that John and John Neuman looked
like the same person.

"Why does John look like the saint? Were they… related in any way?"

"John's great uncle was Saint John Neuman. John was named after the
saint. He was looked after by his much older brother who knew the saint very
well and who was mentored by the saint and soothed."

Soothed…?

"The saint helped John's older brother and confided in him. The saint
confessed certain things to him that were passed down to John and that later
came to me through John. These secrets have remained with me for decades."

"So there's a secret here, something you know that nobody else knows,
something that most people would prefer to remain hidden, is that it?"

"Yes. The saint, you see…" The old man broke off. Something was
caught in his throat and he reached for the water pitcher on an end table. He
seemed to have a lot of phlegm, and it took several minutes before he was able
to speak again. "The saint, you see, was homosexual, had always been, but being

a priest, so honored his vows. But aside from that, he believed that homosexuality was part of God's plan and that homosexual acts within the context of..." At his point Gallagher cleared his throat again and reached for a handkerchief to wipe his mouth. "Excuse me—within the context of a relationship, where there's love, is also part of God's plan. He was direct when John's older brother, Frank, came to him with his problem, which in the saint's mind was not a problem at all. Over time he was able to make Frank Berger see this. Because of his counsel, Frank, and later John, did not feel the crush to marry and live a lie, which according to the saint was an even greater sin. There is a letter in the saint's handwriting that details his beliefs and in which he spells out in clear terms what young Frank should do."

I was fascinated by the prospect of a letter. "You have it, here? Signed?" Gallagher said that he did. He pointed to another part of the desk and urged me to open it. I pulled out the drawer and saw several folders. I flipped through them and saw one marked "The letter." I took it out and handed it to Gallagher but he waved his hand, a motion I took as a sign that I should open it. I opened the file in the middle and saw various pressed flowers, the remains of a Roman missal, old newspaper clippings, and finally a yellowed envelope written in elaborate script. It was addressed to Frank Prachatitz Berger. I hesitated opening it, but Gallagher urged me on with a wave of his hand.

I opened the yellowed parchment and saw the most exquisite handwriting arranged on the page in stanza form. It was addressed "My Dear Boy."

My Dear Boy,
When I was young, perhaps age 13 or 14, I fell in love with a schoolmate, an Austrian lad of exceptional athletic ability. He was equally gifted intellectually, so his mind had the same appeal for me. These tandem gifts made him seem the loveliest and best of God's creatures, but even more compelling was his positive and empathic spirit, his humanity and his willingness to serve God through serving others. I loved Hans from the first moment I laid eyes on him and we became inseparable. We studied, and took our meals together, hiked, went to museums, recited poetry, laughed, and made mischief together. Then one day we did what until then I had thought of as unthinkable. We slept together when his parents were on holiday, when his aunt, a rather strict spinster, watched the house.

It was in that bed that the fountain of love for my dear friend found a physical means of expression at last. It was as if the gates of Heaven had opened and I was being led into the most magnificent of chambers. When I held him, the all of my being flowed into him and I received his soul in return. For a long time we lay in each other's arms, floating, as if one person. I felt God's presence and I knew that my path would be different from that of my schoolmates. I would never marry, never raise a family, but would live in a different world where a special friend would be my conduit to the Almighty, my source of sharing by partaking in the life of another.

My constitution, however, being more complex than I had previously imagined, led me to take other roads. When Hans went away I did not know where to begin looking for another companion, nor did I have the stamina to do so. I prayed and soon discovered my calling to be a priest, that I was to take the love I had for Hans and diffuse it over many through Him, who is the source of all things. It is not from a sense of shame or rejection that I have chosen a solitary path but because God had placed me so squarely in His own.

You must face your own path, whether that be found in marriage, with a friend like my Hans, or as a solitary being in a different context than priestly life. Know that God sees beyond the thoughtless judgments of men, and that where there is true love, He dwells within.

Your loving Uncle,
John

I folded the letter, barely able to express my feelings. I made a motion to return the letter to the desk but Gallagher told me to keep it. "It's yours. Publish it in your book. The world needs it. Whoever examines it will see that it is legitimate. The signature is real. And even if the pious reject it most will sense that it is something authentic."

"Print it?" I said these words aloud, wondering what the reaction would be among the Catholic faithful and members of the hierarchy. I offered Gallagher a hundred thanks, then asked him if he was sure he wanted to give the letter up. He told me the letter was doing him no good lost in a file in his desk, that most likely after his death over-zealous types would destroy it, and that it was best I take it and make use of it in the world.

"I've never told anyone what I've told you—about my hikes with John and about our time in the hermit's hole. John, like his great uncle, became a priest when I married. We saw one another in a different context after that. We remained lovers but in a different way. As I am sure you know, if you reveal this story the Church will implode and dragons will seek to slay you. I haven't much time left, will soon be gone, but you have my permission to do what you want with the letter and photographs. Take good care of them."

When you meet Elijah, your life will change!

Thom Nickels

Ah, how the chant of the Baptist ladies danced in my head, once that I had living proof that a declared saint of the Catholic Church knew the joys of Greek love and even advocated those joys—in a monogamous way of course. In my possession, after all, was a third, smaller photograph of John and Gallagher crouching together in the hermit's hole, fishing rods cast aside, knees touching in boyish enthusiasm, *taken by whom*, I wondered. I hardly knew what to do or who to tell, though I made a call to my editor who was as astounded as I was and who said he saw no reason why I couldn't use Gallagher's claim.

Elijah, being Protestant, knew nothing of the Catholic saint. His mind was wrapped in meditation and learning other forms of spirituality, or so he said over another glass of wine when he came over a second time. That time Elijah sought me out, distraught because Megan had declared another battle: she was now threatening to take full custody of little Liz, the only thing Elijah loved in the world. "Everything is falling apart," Elijah said. Even people in the hotel were giving him grief—the neighboring crack addicts, an old man up the hall who sewed clothes for money, the prostitutes. "I lent one guy money and he skipped town. My boss threatened to lay me off. My life is going to hell," he said.

About an hour or so later, wrapped in Elijah's arms, I told him everything was going to be all right. My prick snug against his painter's behind, my lips glued to the nape of his neck, we were in "relax mode" after a frantic session— Elijah flat on his stomach with me kissing his back while holding his arms out in a bondage posture. There was no way I could refuse Elijah this time. I slipped in, let my body fall on his until our heads meshed together, and let loose an athletic, lust-driven in-and-out attack. Elijah's face, pressed into the mattress, was transfixed as I drilled him into the cosmos.

"Let's pray to St. John," I suggested, handing him a towel. "His shrine is at 5th and Girard Streets. Your life will change, I'm sure. You can focus on Megan, on getting your life together. Just tell him what you want. Don't question it. Just believe it."

Of course I knew by saying this I risked praying Elijah right out of my life. If his life was in torment because of Megan and the schism that this caused in his mind, then my being in his life was merely a result of that schism and ultimately not a healthy thing. Once the condition healed and he resolved his differences with Megan, would I still be needed or wanted?

Elijah put off going to the shrine, and eventually I knew he would never go. One time I thought I'd take him with me so I stopped at the Parker and asked for him at the desk. The clerk told me it would be five dollars to go up and visit. Instead, I called Elijah from the lobby phone and asked him to meet me downstairs. He came down ten minutes later and we ended up going back to my place. My original intention was to go to the shrine but I could see that Elijah was feeling lonely and needed release from Megan's dramas.

192

*

I called Gallahger and told him what my editor said about the photos then asked if he had ever gone to the shrine. "I went once after the canonization in 1977 but that was it. I sat for a long time in the front pew so I had a good view of him inside the glass coffin. I felt St. John's presence, remembering everything he wrote Frank Berger. I'm glad that people honor him even if they don't really know him."

I thanked Gallagher, knowing it was time to make a pilgrimage to the shrine and see for myself. I called Elijah at the Parker but the desk clerk told me there was nobody in Room 515. I decided to walk to the Parker again on my way to the shrine. Perhaps Elijah had gone out for lunch or a quick walk. I knew he often took walks around the block because his room was so small and confining.

Elijah was not there, so I headed for the subway, then hopped the #15 bus down Philadelphia's Girard Avenue to the big church where St. John's body lay encased in wax inside a glass coffin. The shrine is more or less a chapel in the basement of the cathedral with signs posted everywhere directing tourists to it. I'd never seen a body inside a glass coffin before, so was very curious about how it would look or whether it would even look human. When I entered the chapel the glass enclosure was the first thing I spotted. It was positioned near the main altar; people were kneeling or sitting in the pews surrounding it. I walked up the aisle with a certain amount of trepidation, unsure whether to stand or claim a pew when I was within viewing range. I decided I'd stand and view Frank and John's teacher, positioning myself at a discreet distance from the coffin so it wouldn't appear as if I was gawking. I looked at the saint's face; it was a flawless wax mold with every feature outlined to cosmetic perfection. The entire body was dressed in vestments.

All I could think of was young John in the hermit's hole, his fishing pole off to the side and Gallagher rubbing his feet and legs while the two talked about life. Beside me an elderly lady mumbled her prayers and I thought of all the people in need, all the little old ladies that the saint had advised Frank Berger to help when he was young and able. Now a different generation of old ladies and men were coming to him praying for miracles, this bishop who was once a boy who knew the joys of Greek love and who had once told Gallagher's boyhood lover's brother that the love they felt for one another was blessed in the eyes of God, even if that truth could never be uttered in church.

I did not pray, did not ask St. John for anything, but merely pondered his face and what his life must have been like. Then I thought of Elijah and unconsciously began directing thoughts to the saint to help him with his life. I don't know how long I stayed at the shrine. By the time I left it was rush hour; the bus was crowded and I had to stand on the subway but didn't care. I was filled with something buoyant and joyous, for here, in my hometown, was a gay saint I could call my own.

193

*

Later that night I got an urge to call Elijah and when I did was told that he had moved out. Moved out? I was stunned. He was nowhere in the hotel and I had no way of getting in touch with him. I felt betrayed and angry but when the shock of it passed, his decision somehow felt right. Whether or not my prayers had anything to do with this change, I cannot say, but suspected that somehow they did. For some time I was of two minds regarding the situation; I regretted having prayed to the saint and wished that I had just let things flow, because... when and how will I ever find another beautiful lover like Elijah? But then I realized I was being selfish, that if Elijah was truly unhappy then his exodus was perhaps a good thing.

Six months later, when my book was released, the Catholic Archdiocese pronounced me a sinner, saying that I had tarnished the name of a great saint. Gallagher had died by that time, so I am glad he was spared the media flurry. My name was tarnished, and I received threatening phone calls and emails. I refused to fight back or let the commotion upset me, even when they accused me of having invented the whole thing, that the letter was a forgery. Gallagher was gone so I wasn't able to use him as a witness, not that I would have requested he back the story had he lived. No, I was alone, although I still had the tape recording of Gallagher talking about the saint and his mentorship of Frank Berger.

Shortly after the controversy erupted the book jumped in sales and I became a notorious person, but there will always be questions about the story's authenticity. Publications that would normally have sided with me against the conservative Archdiocese became suspicious of my work, thinking I had done something unethical. Even the gay newspaper in the city refused to review the book and to a large degree I have been ignored since the initial controversy died down.

Had Gallagher been lying? Did he forge the letter? In my heart I don't believe this to be the case. In my push to prove the authenticity of Gallagher's claims I researched the life of John Neuman and discovered irrefutable proof that as a child he did indeed have a friend named Hans. For me this fact sealed the evidence, although one can never be 100% sure.

MAHIA'S TRUTH
M. Christian

Much has been said, and no doubt will continued to be said, about Subadar Mahia—yet much is not honestly known about him. If anyone, even today, were to ask Constable Sutia about him, he would have to shrug his old shoulders and admit to knowing little, save Mahia's title, that the Subadar had an older sister who lived in town, and that people said he was brilliant. Others, more in tune with Mahia's presence, could add a little more: that he was unmarried, that he was educated far beyond even his lofty title, that he moved in a way that, when at first beheld, seemed to make little—or *no*—sense, but when his actions (such as those involving a criminal investigation) had concluded you could see that how he had accomplished his goal was as straight and true as an arrow, albeit one launched from a completely unexpected direction.

It was best, these people said, to simply allow him his way and let him work his magic.

But when the Subadar said to Constable Sutia that day in the Surimia jail, "Please leave me alone with him for a time; an hour or two will suffice," the reason the elder constable did so wasn't so much from respect or a knowledge of Mahia's working practices as an eagerness to return to his midday nap.

Alone with him, the Subadar took the prisoner in with a few precise swipes of his incredibly focused eyes.

The man in question was young, probably near to twenty-six years of age. His hair was brown, but of a shade not common to the region. His body was strong and lean, neither overly muscular nor overly drawn to pot. His face, what the Subadar could see of it, was angled almost like a Yankee and not like any other ethnic type he could immediately perceive. The man's dress didn't bear out the Constable's initial assessment of a "man with little or no means"; while he was dressed simply, the clothes were only slightly worn in places. The man, obviously, had access to some funds—if only enough to keep food in his belly and clothes on his back.

"There was a reported theft in the marketplace. An item of jewelry was reported stolen from the establishment of Ling Po. While the Constables of the town questioned those in the area, you attempted to flee. When told to halt, you redoubled your stride. Innocence or guilt, I cannot determine instantly, sir, but I can say that your actions spoke of a man not wishing to be questioned, or inquired of. Will you, this instant, say why you attempted to flee Constable Sutia's deputies?"

Mahia's eloquent description of the incident in the marketplace that day did nothing but cause the prisoner to lift his head for a moment, as if to study the Subadar in the poor jail light.

What the prisoner saw was a tall, thin reed of a man. Skin the color of polished, aged coal. A regal, infinitely patient face, slow to move, revealing nothing of the soul beneath. Eyes that played and danced with a kind of laugh at the world they saw. His features were light and crisp, as if made of stone, polished to a near transparency. The Subadar was dressed in a simple suit, very formal for the small town, but it wasn't a pompous suit worn to impress the simple town people. Rather, it was part of the man. Looking at him, it was hard to imagine Mahia without his white suit; it was as much "him" as were the bones of his elegant face.

His voice, some of his less-eloquent police brethren said, was a blackjack dipped in honey.

"The truth, it seems, needs to be revealed. But that word—*truth*—has confounded some of the greatest minds throughout the history of mankind. It is a quick word, a word that can hide anywhere from anyone. So many kinds, as well—my truth, your truth. Everyone's different, you see, yet they describe the same world, at the same moment. But I am not here to discourse on philosophy. I am here as a Subadar of the Northern Provinces, and it is in that official capacity that I am inquiring about your attempt to escape, and your subsequent silence, that is compelling me to ask: did you take an item of jewelry from Ling Po's emporium?"

The accused looked up at being spoken to, his eyes locking with Mahia's. Once the Subadar had finished, the man spoke, "I did not, sir."

"Ah, at least we have established communication. Why then, if you are innocent of the crime the deputies were investigating, did you run?"

At this the man simply shook his head and again looked at the floor.

"Your refusal to answer puzzles me. You do not explain; you do not protest; you did not even offer to have your pockets turned out in order to prove that the item was not on your person."

"The deputies searched me."

"Ah. Further speech from you. Good! But you see, the mere volunteering of this information would signify your wish to be considered innocent. But this near-silence suggests that you are hiding something—and when one is accused of a crime, sir, that is most inadvisable."

The Subadar studied the man for a moment, scanning him from simple shoes to the black hair on his finely formed head. He watched his eyes and the lines of his mouth. The man had a pleasing face, one that Mahia could easily picture smiling or laughing despite his current dour mask. "I see I will be forced to take an angle with this interview that I would not normally take. I admit to you a fault, sir, in that I am pressed for time in this matter: my sister plans to be wed and since I am the eldest of the family it is my duty to inspect her choice in husbands. He is due to arrive tonight on the 6:15 train and I must not be made late and, thus, unavailable to accomplish my familial duties. Stand up, please, and remove your trousers."

The prisoner's face went blank for a second, as if his muscles had let go of their moorings with shock and confusion. So confused was he by this odd, if not normally rude request, that he actually started to stand.

"Yes, sir, you heard me correctly. The request for you to remove your trousers was a sincere and correct one. Please do so and then I will explain."

The man stood up and hesitated as the Subadar reached into the interior pocket of his simple suit and produced a black shoestring, saying, "There are indeed many, many forms of the truth. All faiths teach their own particular view, even those who claim that no divine powers have any sway over their lives. The government speaks one truth, families speak another. You speak yours, I speak mine. Oftentimes, however, the truth that wins in all these matters is the one that simply speaks the loudest. This is not a happy fact, but historically *is* one, none-the-less. I am here as Subadar of the Northern Province to ascertain if you should be formally arrested and charged with the crime of theft, or released back into the world. I am here to discover *my* truth in this matter."

The man, meanwhile, had kicked off his shoes and had as requested by the dark and elegant Mahia, removed his simple trousers. His legs were strong, long, and rippled with muscles from walking or running. The skin on his legs was as tan as that on his face, and hazy with a slight dusting of curly hair. The man's sex was uncut and large, lying in a denser field of that hair like a small, reddish urn, his testicles all but invisible behind it.

The Subadar of the Northern Province was silent for a moment before he spoke and instructed. "Excellent. Now sit down on the bunk and spread your legs apart."

As instructed, the accused did so, the bed creaking and groaning in protest.

Mahia took the black shoestring and performed some kind of quick sleight-of-hand magic, transforming its humble length into a baroque series of knots and loops. Then, with more deft handwork, he calmly and quickly—almost as if transformed into a doctor performing a routine examination—lifted the man's testicles and deftly inserted them and the man's penis into the loops and knots. When he was finished, in nothing more than a handful of seconds, he had the man's testicles and penis neatly bundled in the cord with a longer length trailing up and into the Subadar's hand.

"A technique," he explained, pulling once, sharply, on the cord, "taught to me by a fellow police officer a long time ago. The principle is almost too obvious to explain but I feel that I must at least allay your fears: there is no pain involved in what you could call 'Mahia's truth.' I will not harm you or cause you any immediate discomfort. I will, however, because it is my duty as a

Subadar, discover the truth of this situation, as I stated previously. Now, I ask you again: did you confiscate the jewelry?"

The man said, simply, shortly, "I did not."

"Why then did you run from the officers?"

When the man did not respond, Mahia jerked the cord, sharply, causing the man's penis to slap up hard against his shirt and belly, which, in the bare jail cell, sounded like a hand slap. The man responded with an eye-widening stare and a quick intake of breath. All but instantly, his penis began to stiffen and grow large, eventually straining against the cord binding it.

Again Mahia jerked the cord and again the man's eye widened, but this time a sharp hiss escaped his lips and he leaned back against the cracked and peeling plaster wall, his back arching in what appeared to be extreme pleasure.

"I'm quite sure if you took the ring you'd realize how lovely it is, or... so I've been informed: a gold setting, like three ropes coiled around one another, containing two pearls and one medium-sized sapphire. Does that sound familiar to you?"

When the man shook his head, Mahia once again jerked the cord. The man moaned in response, moving his hands towards the cords binding his testicles and penis. The reactions, however, were not ones of pain—rather, one could easily deduce from the great size of his penis that he was more than enjoying the binding, and reaching, not to remove the shoelace, but rather to stimulate himself further.

Subadar Mahia slapped him, once, across the face. In the tiny cell the sound was sharp and quick, more an explosion of sound rather than of violence. Shocked, the man fell back with a heavy thud against the wall and looked up at the calm and refined Mahia, the prisoner's eyes grown large with excitement and perhaps, with fear.

"I do apologize, but it is integral to this interrogation that your hands remain on the bed at all times. If you reach for yourself again, I will be forced to discontinue this line of questioning completely, thus jeopardizing your chances of acquittal."

The man thought for a moment, then nodded. "I understand," he said, making himself more comfortable on the cot by moving back from its edge and leaning his shoulders against the wall.

"Thank you," Mahia offered before resuming. "I ask you again: did you take the ring? It was not found on you when you were searched so, if you did, you either dropped it somewhere—a place it could be retrieved later—or passed it along to a confederate in the marketplace. Please speak the truth."

The accused man's penis looked, for all the world, as if it had a mind of its own and wished more than anything to leap from the prisoner's hairy lap in exalted pleasure at the Subadar's treatment. It was incredibly large and pulsed with a heartbeat rhythm, bobbing up and down, up and down from legs to shirt. At its tip, a crystalline dot of pre-seminal fluid slowly grew and began to run down the swollen head. With each jerk of the cord, the man grunted and moaned in near ecstasy, his groans almost as rhythmic as the bobbing of his penis, his hands digging into the cot's thin mattress and sheet to keep from crying out in pleasure.

"Why did you run from the officers, sir? Why did you flee?"

The man moved his hands from the mattress to his penis so quickly that the motion was almost a blur. Mahia instantly discontinued his jerking of the cord and made an effort to remove it before the man could assuage his throbbing torment. But choosing not to end the "line of questioning" the prisoner opted to grab the iron-like musculature of his knotted thighs instead, digging his fingers into his flesh with such pent-up strength, that Mahia was surprised that the man didn't draw blood.

"Why did you flee? Did you take the ring? Answer me, please, sir, or *I will stop this right now*!"

The man began whipping his head back and forth—a perpendicular metronome to the jerking and pulsing of his penis—shaking his head in order to convey that either he wouldn't answer or that he didn't want the questioning to stop, the Subadar wasn't sure which. In the throws of his mounting pleasure, the prisoner had begun to bite and chew his lip. His eyes were closed at certain points but when they were open Mahia could see how they had dilated into two brown pools of vibrating pleasure, like dark tea set on a long, low boil.

Mahia changed the tune of his torture, utilizing slower but firmer jerks on the cord, as opposed to his previous, more fluttering twitches of it. The man actually screamed a lion's roar of frustration and sexual pleasure and dug even harder into his own thighs to keep himself from touching his—at that point—practically purple and bursting manhood.

All at once, the Subadar desisted his movement of the man's penis altogether. A heavy, painful silence filled the room. "Answer me, now," Mahia commanded, repeating with greater emphasis: "You must *answer* me, NOW!"

The man started to mutter something, but his words were too softly uttered for Mahia to hear. "Whisper whatever it is you have to say," he urged the man in gentle tones, "in my ear."

With tears of pain, frustration and pleasure, the man whispered something into the Subadar's ear. But whatever it was that he said had little if any effect on the polished ebony of Mahia's face. He simply listened to the man's words, calmly tugging the cord tied around the man's penis and testicles every now and again in order to encourage the flow of confession to continue.

When the man had finished, he leaned back, his chest heaving with deep sobs, his hands still gripping his bruised thighs like a vice.

Without a word, the Subadar of the Northern Province placed his hand on the man's penis and stroked him slowly—once, twice, a third time—utilizing the man's copious overflow as lubrication.

A fourth stroke, a fifth… Mahia's hands were as gentle as his soul, as smooth as his demeanor.

Faster, and faster, he stroked, until… the man let loose a feral scream of pure animal joy, and jetted his seed into the cool air of the cell, spattering to the rough boards between his feet.

Mahia removed a plain white handkerchief from his pocket and dotted the perspiration from the panting, emotionally spent man's forehead, before then wiping the seed from his lap and his own hand.

"You are free to go," Mahia pronounced, leaving the door to the cell open after he'd stepped out.

Mahia found Constable Sutia basking in the fading late-afternoon light, calmly working his way through a giant bowl of ripe figs. Surprised, Sutia sprang comically to his feet and wiped his sticky fingers on his wrinkled, ill-fitting uniform. "Subadar!" he exclaimed, "did you get the man to confess?"

"I am sorry for your deputies, Constable," Mahia said, folding his handkerchief neatly and returning it to his pocket, "for it seems they will need to continue their investigations: it is very clear to me that the man—beyond a doubt—is innocent."

"But Subadar, he took flight when questioned!"

"He ran from nothing but a moment of guilt over his reason for being in the marketplace, Constable. He is a simple man who only sought intimate companionship, believing that to be the crime he was being sought for."

"You are convinced of this?"

"I am, Constable."

"Then that is assurance enough for me, Subadar, more than enough."

Sutia extended hearty thanks to Mahia, and, with Sutia's assurance that the prisoner would be given a free meal by way of compensation for his detainment, the two parted company.

Before leaving, however, Mahia handed Sutia the address of his sister's house, with the instructions to pass it along to the very man they had suspected of the theft. "Tell him that it would be my honor, should he desire a warm bed for the night, to put him up at my sister's home, to amend any discomfort I might have caused him."

Sutia did so and Subadar Mahia, walking into the gathering dusk, headed off towards town.

THE SAME WORDS
Jerome Szymczak

It was as if Yianni were waiting for me. I was jet-lag jagged and still seasick, tripping toe-to-heel down a meshed-iron gangplank slick with rain, weaving top-heavy with my overstuffed enemy of a backpack, and being pushed nearly over the edge by the animated crush of fifty or so suddenly very rude, very noisy Greeks. They seemed to know something I didn't about how little time we had to disembark, and all that sweet slumber on the overnight ferry had made them as cold and merciless as the September whitecaps that threatened to christen me. Sturdy, rubber-sandaled *Zorbas* and younger, barefoot *Christos* and *Michalis* grunted and shoved me aside as they battled with bulging bags of fresh milk, canned goods, and blue jeans from the city. Sure bare toes gripped metal treads and snowy white teeth bit tough lower lips as they struggled stubborn rope-tied cases of Coca-Cola, beer, toilet paper, and damp cigarettes to the quay. A handful of black-clad, leather-faced and widowed *yia-yias* orchestrated the ruckus, barking commands from the shore to no one, anyone, in particular, their voices defiantly more shrill than the sirens of wind and waves that had mocked my 10-hour journey from Athens.

It was a full five minutes of mythical Greek chaos, complete with a half-dozen donkeys standing by on shore braying the chorus, their minders lazily eyeing the commotion as they waited for a 'fare' to carry uphill to the village. Yianni was among them, trying to stay dry under a flapping, ripped and faded-blue awning. He was leaning heavily against his chest-high charge, right arm slung lazily over the saddle, head slightly cocked—exactly like the donkey's—cheek resting on his bare, rain-slicked shoulder. Both were tight-lipped but grinning—stifling laughter it seemed—with two sets of big, black-licorice eyes looking right at me.

I elbowed my way to the center of the exiting crowd, and was carried upright down the sloping runway like a woozy, cut-loose buoy riding an incoming tide. The moment I felt solid earth beneath me, my sea-legs buckled and I fell back onto my pack. I exhaled with the nervous relief of a deserting rat and watched a few intrepid young men bravely, lithely, jump the widening gap from ship to shore like dancers. The boat ramp was quickly cranked up, metal against metal screeching triumphantly, and the tired old tub slowly groaned away. As I would learn later, these frenetic natives would break the sweaty, melodious cadence of island life for this rusty tether to Athens only twice a month.

"The Gods could've lived anywhere," the brochure had said. "And they chose Greece!" No doubt they'd had an easier time getting here. Never had Lord Byron, Shirley Valentine, even Edmund White talked about *this* part of the voyage! I sat up halfheartedly and looked for someplace to get out of the rain.

A welcoming, smooth-stoned path curled around a crescent-shaped port to my right. Stalwart, two-story storefronts shuttered against the weather wore rough-cut wooden signs hand-painted in Greek and broken English. "We serve olive-oily foods," one creaked in the wind. "Rent rooms in the sea," proclaimed another. They do it on purpose, I thought.

Higher up, on craggy hillsides, resolute rows of blue-sashed, sugar-cube houses were proud, brilliant sentinels against the black-and-blue sky. Ancient, gnarled olive trees bent low by too much time and wind—too much witnessing—desperately hugged steep ravines. Grape terraces criss-crossed by centuries of winding trails and low, rock walls bore witness to the back-bending work of clearing the land. Goat bells teased hoarse, barking dogs over the gale, competing with the clamor of bells atop the masts of a dozen fishing boats rock-and-rolling inside the seawall. The rain seemed to be moving on with the ferry, but the same stinging wind and waves that had fought our low, engine-grinding push from the city remained, evidently as anxious to pound a shore—*any* shore—with its fists as I was! I breathed another sour-mouthed sigh of relief just in time to see Yianni lead his snorting beast right for me.

I had spent too many hours braced and martyred in a bathroom-stall doorway on that boat, hands and feet approximating an upright St. Peter on his X-shaped cross. Foolishly I'd tried to fight the bucking and rolling—tried to take my mind off the teasing lift, and then sudden drop, of the floor from under me—by chanting the names of twentieth-century Greek celebrities. Callas, Onassis, Stephanopolous, Savales… Oh Melina, Melina, Melina, I *really* didn't want to see that lousy airplane food again! I was *never* going to leave this island. It would mean getting on another boat.

By the time I slipped off my soggy pack and struggled to my feet, Yianni was at my side, gripping my arm and shoulder and helping me up. Though he was still grinning, his warm hands betrayed some earthier compassion. He had seen it all before. Bruised pride would heal, his sure grasp seemed to say. I would dry. The wind would die down. Life was still for the living—or at least for those still able to stand.

Or maybe he just knew too well what I had yet to realize. His was now the last 'taxi' left to take me up the steep, winding, slick-with-wet-donkey-shit trail to the village. His steady lead—his comical 'steed'—were my only alternatives to hoofing it on my own for at least an hour, balancing my soaked belongings on top of the nausea. There were no real roads here, I had read, no cars or even motorbikes. Just the considerable, determined charms of the donkeys and their equally able donkey-boys. Or was it the other way around?

"Oh these Greeks!" Yianni bellowed in throaty, broken English. "Like Turks dipped in honey, no?" As I struggled to rise, his arms now lifting me under both shoulders from behind, I fell against him and unwittingly blushed as I turned and smiled back at him. I was embarrassed by my temporary lack of sure-footedness, and he laughed out loud as I stood and tried to find my land-legs again. He seemed anxious to make light of the weather, the chaos—anything that had contributed to my slapstick abuse. But above all, he seemed eager to help, was my first kind, if bemused, face in a foreign land. Before I even braved a glance into his breezy, black-olive eyes—already 'nibbling away' at me I fancied—before I fixated on the smile that betrayed a randy recklessness, I noticed the heady aroma of fresh hay and anise, cigarettes and sweat that defined him—a welcome odor that would linger with me on those long afternoons after he had left my room.

Yianni was about my age, perhaps a few years younger—it was hard to tell. At first glance, his taller upper body didn't seem to quite fit his stockier legs, as if he'd been put together with the wrong spare parts. On closer inspection, this was merely the 'flaw' that, for me, accentuated other physical perfections. His thick, auburn hair was streaked blond by long, languid, sunny, summer afternoons. Solid arms and sculpted shoulders spoke of simple hard labor. A torn, white, too-small, sleeveless t-shirt stuck wet and tantalizingly to his skin where sinewy muscles strained to pop free. As he stood in front of me and lifted my sodden pack to the saddle, his shirt rode-up for a glimpse of flat, tanned stomach and those maddening 'front-pocket' muscles pointing downward where the hips meet the abdomen. His well-worn and now sopping, rolled-up khakis were barely held up with a length of the same rope that harnessed the donkey. They clung tight to his thighs as if for warmth—like fresh *filo* dough over honey-soaked *baklava,* I thought—and threatened to reveal even more: Yianni's summer-long disdain for underwear.

I suppose my heart was cinched then and there, along with the donkey's riggings. As he secured the saddle with a sharp, practiced yank on the shiny, well-worn strap, I watched his hands. The graceful fingers, the weathered, resilient palms, the sure thumbs: all moved as concertedly, as certainly, as the rest of him. Even in my 'altered state', I was starting to have fantasies of standing thigh to thigh with him, drenched with cool rain but steaming with passion as our slick, hard cocks stood just touching, attentive, pressed together and pumped by gently alternating fists, perhaps with a bit more of that rope coming into play. The donkey just staring—not jealous, not disapproving, just watchful. When we came, together, explosively, like the thunder now in the distance, we'd still be challenging each other to see whose knees would buckle first. Then Yianni would gingerly bite my ear, and the donkey would hee-haw.

I snapped out of it and felt myself blushing again. Christ, I'd just arrived! I stole a glance at Yianni, afraid he might've somehow read my filthy, feverish mind. Not a clue. He was all the more seductive because he seemed so guileless—didn't realize he was so beautiful—didn't know how he would come to haunt my urgent dreams.

He motioned for me to walk with him alongside the beast, who provided a windbreak from the receding gale as we trudged, head-and-shoulders bent low and dodging waves, along the port path. The loud crack of his hand on the animal's haunch was unexpected, and he howled again with laughter when he saw how he'd startled me. The donkey protested, but only perfunctorily. "Welcome to my island," Yianni turned and bellowed as we stopped to let the waves wash the path just ahead of us. One eye was on me, the other out to sea. "You need a room," he added, his boyish-cohort grin teasing irony.

"You're doing WHAT!" Maureen shrieked into the phone. "I *hate* you!" she quickly added, in that sisterly tone that meant 'not really.' "Why Greece?"

"If you have to ask, you've never been there," I said, paraphrasing the brochure with mock snobbery.

"Aw, fuck off, Joe," she said. "What are you going to *do*?" A fair question, even if it was accompanied by her usual mix of incredulity and envy. I should have never told her that I only had a one-way ticket.

"Not much," I replied, trying to sound benign in my search for 'nothingness'. Then, because she was my sister, I confessed.

"I really don't know."

I would write, certainly, catch up on my reading, perhaps even paint a bit. I wasn't planning on packing the frayed Puritan whip both of us had grown up with, the one from which we'd never been weaned. Abandoning work-ethic guilt was a primary runaway goal for me. An open-ended break from a ten-year string of heartaches, a going-nowhere-fast writing 'career', and a growing list of dead and dying friends and lovers was, I rationalized, well-deserved, and... long overdue.

If I could kill time without injuring eternity, all the better. I had squirreled-away enough money to last about six more months in Chicago before I'd have to beg and cajole my editors to assign me more puffy magazine pieces or ghostwriting work, my psychic knee-pads firmly in place for each demeaning query. In Greece I might be able to stretch that money to float me for a year, if I was frugal. Besides, that biting autumn wind off Lake Michigan was reminding me of the imminent, soul-numbing hibernation to come. The winter litany against loneliness there was all too practiced by now: too many shots knocked-back at the bar, too many needy strangers sharing my bed, too many pale, empty afternoons spent reflecting green-gray in front of a blank computer screen. Maybe in Greece I could finally figure out if I really *had* been Genghis Khan in another life.

The hardest part was going to be leaving Maureen behind. We were the only family we had—"frightfully close" she was fond of saying. Both our parents had died blind-drunk in a car wreck twenty years before, when Maureen was seven and I was nine. The grandmother who raised us—my father's mother—made no attempt to hide the anger she felt toward our 'wild' mother for leading her son astray.

A murky well of bitterness dug by her grief soon replaced any loving feelings Grandma may have once had for us. As Maureen and I grew older and more rebellious, more like our mother in Grandma's eyes, she became more unhinged. Perhaps she was afraid of dying with all that anger locked inside her, I don't know, but just as natural as poison she unleashed all her frustration on us kids. "They were running away from you two as well," she told us often and with cruel dispassion. "They would've kept goin' too."

Even now, when I hear people reminisce about a dear, sweet grandparent who showered them with kindness, cookies, money and hugs, I pout with the martyred covetousness of a child who never experienced such affection. To this day, when I look at my sister, the forced focus in her green-gray eyes reflects the pain and tears we shared all those years. It would've been better if we'd been true orphans, left to drown in the melancholic and sure undertow we all call 'existence'. As it was, we were both baptized and remain barely afloat in a stormy sea of self-doubt. We know instinctively that, in this life, we can only ever be buoyed by each other, no matter who else we might find to temporarily fill our emotional and physical chasms.

Years of therapy has washed us both up on the quicksandy shores of forgiveness for our granny, but Maureen has fared no better in life than I, neither in love nor as a nurse. Her insensibility toward illness—especially among older people—and her three estranged husbands are as visible and damning a proof of her emotional scars as are my cultured string of loser-lover 'pearls'. My being queer is at least some respite from our emotional incestuousness, though even Freud might've gone rosy over the way she and I sometimes gigglingly, nervously point out prospective partners for each other. "We all use the same words in the dark, eh, Joe?" Maureen is fond of slurring after a couple drinks.

"I'll miss you, you bastard!" It was one of her throaty whispers, struggling to crawl out over its own lump of emotion, and I felt an accompanying tear tickle my ear as Maureen hugged me good-bye at the airport. "But you're doing the right thing," she quickly added, rubbing a clenched fist under her nose and pulling away to contemplate some garish, elliptical pattern in the rug. "You deserve a break, Joe," she said, looking back at me now, trying to hide those pained eyes with a veil of tough-little-sisterhood. "Find yourself some sexy Greek fisherman, someone I'd *never* approve of, and then—call me!" This last command tripped out over her self-conscious laugh at the same time her familiar flat-palmed pat to my chest percussively reiterated our bond—thumpingly suggested that she was maybe half-serious.

"Come join me at Christmas," I called after her as she turned to walk away. It was too loud, too pleading. "We'll see," was all she managed, loping away and not bothering to turn around. She knew well my tendency to want to share my life with her before I had thought it through myself.

On the plane I laughed so loud the patronizing Nordic stewardess strode down the aisle like an annoyed gazelle to chide me for waking the other passengers. Maureen had slipped a book into my carry-on at the airport that I had just that moment discovered. ***HOW TO RETIRE WITHOUT BLOWING YOUR BRAINS OUT!*** the bold-faced title screamed. She *did* care about me after all!

Yianni doesn't look Greek, actually. But then, so few Greek men really 'look' Greek, not like Zorba anyway. Bushy salt-and-pepper mustaches, thick dark corkscrews of unruly hair, skin the slick-mahogany color of Kalamata olives—none of these features are as prominent as one expects.

In fact, many younger Greek men look like Brad Pitt: reddish-blond hair, more ruddy than olive-skinned, almond-tree brawny and dolphin-quick, with playful, mischievous smiles ever ready. Like Sicilians, Albanians, even the Irish, they sport unaffectedly the sure, muscle-toned manliness of a life spent mainly working out-of-doors. Jumping in and out of the sea on a regular basis helps too.

As they warmed to me over the next few weeks, Yianni and his friends displayed an unpretentious, boyish bravado that made me flush when one of them would suddenly put an arm around my shoulder, or brush-up too close. At first, my overdeveloped gay-male pride saw it all as a come-on, a closing-in on some sexual scent. However baffling it was for my libido, a playful stroke of the hair, a holding of hands while maneuvering donkey-shit lane late at night, even a sloppy, drunken kiss had to be construed as completely innocent. Greek men are just naturally demonstrative, I reasoned, not 'macho-ly' adverse to a comforting caress, however public. I reluctantly down-periscoped my American 'gaydar', chiding myself for reading the simple humanity of Yianni's touch as more than what it was. It didn't help either that I was completely out of my element, thousands of miles removed from my desperately cruisy Westernized world, in Yianni's orbit now, and unable to read any signs on his part that he was interested in anything beyond 'innocent' wrestling and playfulness.

All of this did not, of course, stop me from fantasizing that Yianni was stuck somewhere between portside philosophy and 'behind the stables' bisexuality. Sometimes a cigar is just a cigar—except when it isn't. I replayed fantasies of going beyond mere camaraderie with him many times, usually during the daily requisite siesta, when no one was missed. In my tossing and turning, we'd stand, smiling, in the sun, face-to-face again, maybe chest-deep in a blue and sleepy afternoon sea, trunks removed and dutifully strung around our necks as we took forever to get each other off—yes, that was it—always coming together, with no witnesses but grinning, puzzled fish. Or we rocked in sweat-drenched *frottage* on hay bales in the stable as he pumped his spit-primed cock between my legs and came while groaning in my ear, maybe this time while the donkey slept nearby.

If Yianni was just another closet-case, it was a moot point. Over the next few months, my rapid acclimation to the island and its social mores muffled what little politically 'out' sensibility I had brought with me. My feverish fantasies about him were driving me mad, and there was still no sure sign of any sexual interest on his part.

I don't know when Yianni suspected I was gay, but I did feel he sensed my outsider dilemma quickly, because it was also his. At least that was clear. He never mentioned a girlfriend, and what women we did see out and about were either sisters, cousins, or severely serious, serenely religious and judgmental, black-clad widowed aunts and shrill *yia-yias.* Grandmothers too much like my own had been.

If he had any desire to be with me, he simply couldn't follow through because the village was so small (or so I wanted to believe). Homosexuality is, at best, frowned upon in Greece—even though the rest of the world likes to believe that the Greeks 'invented' it. (That historical observation is usually met with the stone face of Medusa, or a drunken, unwelcome invitation by some fat, former Greek communist to "sure, bend over!"). Besides, what are two lovers of any persuasion to do in a town so small that everyone knows your business? That's a universal jam.

The older, mostly-idle fishermen on the island held a daily silent court in the port, eyes endlessly massaging the sea, thumb and forefinger expertly, seductively, polishing well-worn wooden worry beads, their weary smiles waxing philosophic, pondering the horizon between sips of *ouzo* (Greek 'milk'). One morning when Yianni and I joined them, he broke the long contemplation of the horizon to tell me that, in ancient poetic Greek, the words for 'time' and 'weather' were interchangeable—in fact, they were the same word—*keros.* There were other words that had multiple meanings too, but he could not recall them.

This may have been just another Greek 'fable', but if it was I didn't want to know. As my stay on the island became more infinite—the spread of time and scenery more surreal, more unaccountable—something deep in me relished the heavy, philosophical weight and possibility of such a notion—one word or words with multiple meanings. Over the next few weeks, I massaged this fantasy too, hoping to at least amend, to counterbalance, my bottomless sexual wet-dreams.

If, for instance, you depended on the sea for your livelihood—indeed, were surrounded by it—then both subsistence and escape would be dictated by the whims of weather. That was *keros*—waiting for the weather, and weathering the waiting, like I was doing with my love for my donkey-boy/philosopher. In a more limited, insular, ancient vocabulary, maybe fewer words defined abstract and corporeal concepts at once: time and weather, love and compromise, paradise and prison. The short, fleeting, abstract time of one's life on these islands was shaped by storms and calm, rain and wind, the blinding sun and prying family disapproval that illuminated every bedroom corner. It made sense, then, that both external influences and internal feelings might be summed-up with the same words.

By mid-October, I was still swimming in the afternoon sea, though it was turning a chillier sapphire day by day. The island was small, only ten miles long and a few miles across at its widest point. Most mornings I explored it on foot, greeting locals who were still suspiciously laconic but polite. It seemed every gleeful child was a nephew or niece of Yianni's, every black-clad matriarch a widowed sister or aunt or, at the very least, a nosy neighbor. We were too surrounded, too imprisoned, by Yianni's *ikoyenia*—his extended family—for me to ever profess my budding love, for me to ever consider bedding-down my donkey-boy. For these monocultural, island Greeks, lovemaking was still a church-sanctified duty for husband and wife.

Nearly every sunset I would sit in the port on the world's most uncomfortable chairs and ponder the ethereal gifts of sea, sky, and waiting for Yianni to walk by. Most evenings, I hung out with him and his friends outside our little taverna till well past midnight—laughing, drinking, singing and chatting in fractured Greek and broken English—quenching the dramatic winter light with unrestrained glee and cheap, chilled *retsina.* Falling in love with this place mixed in my mind with falling for Yianni, which was like painting a long-forgotten closet a bright, new blue by way of disguise. So I *was* painting after all!

Irony was not lost on me. After all, it had unraveled Socrates too, hadn't it? I'd traveled all these thousands of miles, resolved to 'run away' and rediscover my life's pace, determined to catch up with myself after years of false starts and heartaches—yes, to finally 'find myself'—only to find myself… right back in love *and*, of necessity, back in the closet! I had regressed to my tortured teens, hot under the volcano of repressed sexual yearning. My life, like some giddy Gilligan's, was becoming a rerun in paradise. Not bad as closets go, mind you—the endless blue Aegean expanse of sea and sky its 'confines'—but a closet of the mind nonetheless. The weight of my predicament pressed unrelentingly against my swelling, lovesick heart almost daily. I could leave, and go back to my vacuous life, my likewise empty bed, in Chicago. Or I could stay, and let *keros* set the course.

By late October I had my answer—more a stay of execution than a solution, perhaps—but a much-needed resolution nonetheless. The winter sparkle of luminescent plankton in the water mirrored a cobalt sky. Countless stars seemed stunned by their own beauty. The nightly wail of bluesy *bazoukia* either begged me to stay or screamed for me to go, depending on my mood and state of drunkenness. In the end I held fast. I would neither profess my love nor hide it. I'd take my cue from Yianni. I would cultivate the patience of one of his dumb donkeys.

In a few short weeks I'd learned that Yianni did indeed have talents beyond the stables. He helped his uncle keep the books at the bakery, he played the guitar, wrote lyrics and, of course, fished and loved rock 'n' roll. We conversed, very elementarily, in a mis-spoken English that meandered willy-nilly between funny, frustrating, and enlightening. A lot of nodding, charading, and a laughing arcade of "ohs!" and "ahs!" accompanied our conversations. The drinking helped too.

"The Greeks are never Greek in summer," he slurred one raucous Saturday night. We were sitting safely off to one side of a name-day celebration. A dozen *Michalis* were dancing, breaking plates, knocking-back bottles of Metaxa brandy, and belting out both Greek and Tina Turner vocals loud enough to actually summon St. Michael. "But in winter," Yianni yelled above the clamor, "they throw out all the cat-calendars, pull out their *komboloi* (to spin against worry), and drink and dance with the plumber.

"And drink and dance with the plumber," he repeated with that mischievous, enigmatic grin.

As if on cue with poured courage, he then winked at me, scrambled up on one of the flimsy metal tables, and swayed his eye-level, blue-jeaned hips to the bittersweet whine of the *rembetika.* It was pure drunken seduction. He was trying to impress me with his passion, at least for the dance, and the other revelers bellowed "*Opahs*" of encouragement, flinging arms, spilling wine, and snapping fingers heavenward. In the next instant, he jumped to the floor and was leading me on rubbery limbs in snaking semi-circles to the steps of the *horos.* As Yianni's hand vice-gripped my shoulder and his glassy, pleading eyes searched mine for fellowship, I suddenly remembered what a Greek sailor in New York had told me years before, following our brief encounter. He had laughed outright at my notion of a 'gay sensibility', saying he preferred to think of himself as just "mildly amused. Every bar in Greece is a 'gay' bar," he'd added, quite solemnly. "We are not looking for 'sisters'."

By early November, Yianni and I were spending more time with each other but less time in the sea. As the wind and cold challenged his outdoor chores, he was able to sneak away more often and we would scramble down to the rocks for some provocations of our own, mainly the testing of our manly stamina for cold water. Neither of us wanted to be the first to admit the swimming season was over.

One afternoon we dove in together, yelped in unison, and immediately rocketed out. Hopping up and down, we choked on laughter as we shivered and flapped our arms like noisy, mocking gulls. Yianni was still deeply tanned but quickly going blue-lipped in his sun-bleached and tattered, dripping-wet cut-offs. Together we fell flat-bellied against the black, smooth rocks, pressing gooseflesh to stone in a vain attempt to soak up whatever warmth they retained.

Yianni slid so close to me that my heart beat like a fidgety squid hiding from determined fishermen. He was still breathing hard and chuckling, but then suddenly stopped, caught his breath on the wind, and just smiled at me. We had been this undressed together before, but never while this close and horizontal. The salty smell of the sea on the breeze was so heady, the sound of the waves so urgent, my imminent confession of love so near the surface, that I was suddenly afraid of scaring him off—of losing him as a friend. I pressed my swelling cock harder against the unforgiving stone. How long could we lie there on our stomachs?

"They say the sea and human blood are almost identical," I blurted nervously. "Chemically, of course."

Poseidon's shadow veiled Yianni's smile with confusion. He squinted and cocked his head—not unlike he had on that first day in the rain at the dock—and tried to sort-out my disarming earnestness. I shut my eyes against the awkwardness and reached clumsily for my towel, my jeans, anything to hide the bulge in my trunks that was betraying my affection. With the towel barely covering my middle, I rolled over on my side and clumsily lifted my head and shoulders, resting on one elbow. As if challenged, he did the same. Our heads were now level, our eyes fixed, our concentration focused on each other. A lone, shrieking gull glided overhead.

Spurred by the yearning he must've seen on my face, Yianni rolled over onto his back and closed his eyes tight to, what... hide? I was certain he knew I was watching him. He worked his hands deliberately up his wet, brown body—a nonchalant, yet not guileless glide that had me mesmerized. Now I was certain, almost gleeful. This was seduction. He dabbed the salt-water tickling his navel with those long, slender fingers, rubbed his silken, freckled chest with a flat-handed, self-conscious sexiness, soft-stroked his stubbly cheeks as if they were not really his, and then lightly touched each salty fingertip to his tongue.

I followed his hands' journey with a briny, wet hunger of my own, no longer gripping my towel, no longer self-conscious of my own desire. As he licked his slightly quivering lips, my own urgency began to throb like a fasting appetite whetted for an Easter feast. He rolled his head sideways to look at me, one eye still half-shut against the milky autumn sun, and smiled wide with an eager innocence that said "now." My eyes flashed the same wanting back into his and, as a maverick cloud covered what little sun we had, he bolted upright, looked around anxiously, turned, and covered my mouth with the brackish palm of his hand. It tasted of need, and fear.

Laughing again, he quickly removed his hand and grabbed my arm. "Come," he said, pulling me up with him while reaching for his clothes. The swelling excitement through his cut-offs gave him away too as he struggled to yank a tattered sweater over his head. He had a wild-goat gleam in his eyes and a determined smirk that I had seen only once before when he'd been 'teaching' me how to drink *ouzo*. My heart hee-hawed.

I stood and tried to pull on my pants in a frantic balancing act of one-legged slapstick. We both laughed with riotous release when I fell flat back on my ass. He grabbed his flip-flops and scrambled up the rocks to the trail, his own solid ass now voluptuously leading the way. When he turned to make sure I was keeping up with him, he stopped, grabbed me firmly by the shoulders, looked in my eyes, and whispered: "No one can know Joe, ok?" He flashed a quick, anticipatory grin, no doubt surprised by his own brazenness, and touched a rigid index finger to his tightened lips. "Ok Yianni," I answered, my hand squeezing his. "No one will know." We walked quickly, conspiratorially, side-by-side back to town, not touching, purposeful, smiling politely at passers-by, two men on a secret mission.

We'd barely entered my room and closed the door behind us before I had him stripped and swooning. I bit and licked, kissed and sucked his still-salty neck, cheeks and shoulders like a thirsty animal. He held me fast and moved me toward the bed where we fell heavily, laughingly, and then 'shushed' each other for fear that we would awaken my sleeping landlady just below us. When I had him pinned on his back, and moved down to take his far-from-timid cock in my mouth, he at first tried to stop me, but then gave in with an inquisitiveness that seemed to want to mimic my verve. He pulled me up and spun around on that polished ass and, still on his back, ankles high and spread atop the headboard, buried his face between my legs, squeezing my balls and matching my every up and down motion. If Yianni had not done this with a man before, his strong, adept hands and eager adaptation betrayed a natural enthusiasm, just as his searching tongue spoke a new truth. He smelled, he tasted, of hay and cigarettes, of anise, and the sea—and finally, of his love for me.

We missed that evening's sunset, but shuddered and glowed in one of our own in the refuge of my room, through time and weather marked only by an overhead fan moaning on low. We made love again, less urgently this time, and yes, came together while cupping each other's mouths against any noisy giveaway. Instead, donkeys raucously brayed on a distant hillside. We laughed uncontrollably. It was time I fully lost track of—which is to say time I also lost control of—perhaps for the first time in my life.

Jerome Szymczak

We lingered afterward long and silent, breathing low and sweating heavy in the darkened room, until wrenched back to reality by shrill, familiar voices and plodding hooves passing by on the path below my window. When I did finally sleep, supine and peaceful, it was because I felt his breathing had also found measure and contentment in my arms. I awoke to a cool, blue moon beckoning through the shutters, the sound of distant laughter and clinking glasses, and the dark, familiar croon of Greek singer *Delarus* coming from the taverna. Yianni had gone, leaving his flip-flops behind in mid-step—as if they were glued to the floor between the bed and the door. I took this for more than a sign of forgetfulness—longed for it to represent some inadvertent promise of commitment, however impossible that might be.

Maureen was coming for a visit in a few weeks, too. *She'll certainly have something to say about all this*, I mused. *She'll be so happy for me*. I leaned out the window and beamed back at the moon.

Five years have passed since that first soul-stirring afternoon and I still can't decide which is worse. Do we 'come out' to Yianni's *ikoyenia* and risk alienation or even banishment from the island? Or do we continue to pretend our love for each other is invisible, act as though we are 'just good friends' amongst friends and family who, by now, certainly suspect much more? Even after all this time, the arrangement we've all come to, the adjustments we've all made, sometimes rubs rough against my need to sing and dance my love for Yianni to someone other than an uninterested donkey and the unforgiving wind.

Yianni is content to maintain our affair in secret forever—in "private from my family," as he says. To him, this is the most practical course, the most face-saving and least tumultuous of lines in the sand, in spite of the fact that he loves me—indeed *proof* of that fact, according to him. I suppose what keeps me here in this prison/paradise is that, for the first time in my life, I am certain that someone besides Maureen really does love me.

It helps that the Greeks *can* be discreet when they disapprove of something strongly enough. Those who suspect our relationship seem to appreciate our keeping it to ourselves, especially now that Yianni has a wife and kids. I'm very protective of his family as well. Hell, one of the kids even looks like me!

The arrangement works for Maureen too. Like me, she came for a visit, fell in love with Yianni, and decided to stay. After some awkward weeks of feigned outrage, we three calmly weighed all of our options. In the end, she married him and had children, knowing full-well about us, and with my eventual approval. It was our way of planting our own *ikoyenia,* our way of nurturing

212

some order to our lives. However unconventional, she and I have finally found a family-dynamic that works. We share a husband who is also getting the best of all possible worlds: progeny, societal approval, and all the 'dalliance' he can handle.

The 'closet' we all now occupy is as complex, beautiful, undemanding, and as philosophically wide as that Aegean sky and sea just outside the window. It holds a fine wardrobe of intimacies and disguises that may be unusual—even taboo to some—but have never been stained by jealousy or competitiveness. Blankets of love. And from this finery, we all fully expect—perhaps naively, but hopefully—that the children will grow to be more open, more free, more accepting of out-of-the-ordinary life-arrangements.

Some Sunday mornings all five of us share the bed with milk, coffee, yogurt and honey, and (now) television while the church bells ring unheeded right down the lane. "And what were my philandering *philandros* up to last night," Maureen sometimes queries in a teasing whisper. We all three smile, but know better than to ever divulge details.

Whether to rock the boat or not depends on the journey, I've learned. If we are lucky, we all get, if not what we expect, then at least what we need. Sometimes we don't know just what puzzle we are piecing together until it is complete. Here in Greece, where psychology was born and tragi-comedy is key, blinding whites and moody blues give little hint as to the final image. I have conceded an 'out' relationship for an arrangement that works in our own little piece of paradise, far from the urban heartaches and the uncaring pace of the Western world, albeit with its own concessions to a judgmental, Levantine sense of propriety.

Over time, real love—like real family—creates its own rules, bending like a sage olive tree to sometimes-stormy, but never uprooting, tenets of togetherness. And here, time and weather—like love and family and paradise and prison—are maybe, sometimes, in the dark or in the light, the same words.

WHITE-HOT SMOKY NIGHT
Christopher Pierce

The night is hot.

Very, very hot.

The scent of incense fills my nostrils. A light breeze blows in through the window, wafting gently down to where I lie on the floor.

My apartment is just big enough for one. I am alone and horny, the summer evening having made me anxious and sweaty.

It would be simple to find another person. The phone, the computer, the street outside—sex isn't hard to find around here. Men are everywhere, prowling the bars, the streets, the alleys, desperate for someone, another man, to connect with—if only for a night.

But I don't want anyone else here.

Not tonight.

Tonight is for me.

My life is just fine right now without the clutter of other thoughts, other feelings, other lives. I like my solitude.

Lying on my back, I am holding a porn mag up in the air with one hand. I hadn't begun reading it with the intention of jerking off, but now…

My cock is warm and hardening, packed tightly in my underwear. Rolling onto my stomach, I start grinding it against the floor. *Mmmm, that feels good.* As I get harder I grind harder. *Yeah…*

No turning back now.

I get to my feet and begin my ritual.

Stripping off my underwear, I then close the blinds on the window, close them against the night so I can be truly alone. The phone and answering machine are silenced. A pillow from the bed is tossed to the floor and fresh incense lit. Low chanting begins, tribal music on the CD player casting a hypnotic spell.

I pull off my shirt, enjoying the rough scratch of fabric against my nipples.

Catching sight of myself naked in the mirror leaning against the wall, I am pleased. My dietary program and new lifting routine are working. After years of concentrating on them, my pecs and abs are finally coming into their own, are now rivaling my arms and legs and ass, which are usually singled out by others as my best features—after my face, of course.

I see sharp, dark eyes behind thick lashes, great cheekbones, a strong nose, and two rows of flawless white teeth behind thick, pouting lips.

I pull a few things out of my closet and place them next to the pillow. Turning off the lights, I drop to the floor and settle onto my back with my head on the pillow. I then blindfold my eyes with the handkerchief I've brought out from the closet. The night becomes even blacker now, as darkness settles over me and pushes into my mind.

I feel on the floor and find the pair of dirty underwear I took off. It smells rank and intoxicating as I stuff it in my mouth. An old gym sock retrieved from my laundry sack is stretched around my mouth and tied behind my head, holding the shorts in my mouth and gagging me tight.

My knees rise to my chest and I loop the torn T-shirt between my ankles and around my feet. Expertly, I cinch the knots, binding my feet together. Forcing my left arm behind my back, I settle onto it with the full weight, the sheer mass of my muscular torso, and struggle to move it, but cannot.

My cock has gotten harder with each body part that is restricted, the sensation of being tied up awakening deep memories of pleasure from previous lifetimes. My nostrils flare as I inhale the scent of incense and feel its mystical, moody power enter my brain. I have already begun to leave this specific place and time.

I am lying on the floor of my home, bound and gagged, and begin to imagine how... I need no one else. *No one.* For no one can follow where I am going.

The dark recess of my erotic imagination is a magical place I only go to when pumped with the courage to face my deepest fantasies.

My free hand finds my crotch. Caressing my throbbing cock, I am free at last to pierce the heated air as the summer breeze slips between the lowered slats of the blinds to envelop my dripping dick, to take it gently into its whispering grip.

Squeezing the down-turned bottle that I found with searching fingers, I feel the exquisite coolness of lube settle into my palm. Replacing the breeze's grasp with my own, I wrap my fist around my quivering hardness. The cum inside me burns and boils, becomes a living presence within my body that is both a part of and separate from me. It is demanding release from the bondage of my body and so... I have placed myself in bondage in order to give it that release.

My fingers clench around my cock's girth and I feel the shattering wonder of lubricated skin against sex—a feeling that can drive all of mankind to the brink of madness and beyond. There is nothing I would not do to experience it, and isolation from it is the deepest damnation I could imagine suffering at this particular moment.

My transportation is complete; there is truly no turning back now. I have entered a state of ecstatic transcendence comparable to indigenous natives in their tribal ceremonies. I am here to throw myself at the mercy of my own body, to worship forces within me that are both easily understood and totally beyond my comprehension.

I imagine that the thin, wispy trail of incense smoke is filling my vision, is rising, as is my hand, caressing my cock within its grip. *Bliss.* Tiny sparks of electricity have appeared around my hand as it moves through the crystalline prism of my mind's eye, through which I can see the incense smoke. But now it wafts more substantively, whirling like the timeless patterns of fingerprints. Circles within circles within circles of pleasure.

The whorls of smoke are changing. Or am I just seeing them more clearly? They are no longer merely circular shapings, but have become images, portraits in smoke.

A gallery of men.

Men of beauty and men of power, men of light and darkness, men of muscle, mind, and spirit, men bonding together, making love—touching, holding, hugging, kissing, competing for dominance, sucking, rimming, and fucking: they are worshipping one another.

My vision shifts downwards, and I see that the smoke is not coming from the incense at all, but from an enormous fire that is blazing on a beach at the edge of an ocean.

The inferno is enormous, sending fireworks of sparks into the sky and the cascading volumes of smoke I have become absorbed in.

The men who surround the fire are chanting and calling to each other. Are they worshipping spirits contained within the smoke, calling them forth? No matter, for whatever the reality of the situation, both the men and the spirits are beautiful beyond comprehension in their savage nudity.

My eyes drink in every sculpted torso, every muscular arm and leg, every inch of skin adorned with body art and brutal, exotic piercings, every exquisite phallus swaying and dancing. Their faces are stunning and harsh, with no trace of civilization to flaw them. These men are feral, their eyes as steely-bright as wolves'.

The firelight dances on and around them, blazing its hue into their already bright and burnished bodies as they move away from the fire toward something I've yet to see—a raised platform, constructed of rock and roughly-hewn tree limbs, with torches ablaze surrounding it.

Shadows twist and contort around the platform—or perhaps it is an altar—as the men fall into position surrounding it. In the strange light it is difficult to see what has been laid atop it. Between the dancing bodies I can just make out a shape. Human. It is moving, alive.

It is me.

I am lying on the platform: naked, bound and gagged, writhing in fear—or is it pleasure? The blindfold is gone; I can see quite freely now as the men chant and howl above me.

My hand strokes my erection faster. The fire within me rises higher, almost matching the flashing intensity of the natives' blaze.

What do they mean to do with me? I am their captive, their prisoner; that much is clear. Am I their enemy? Do they mean to kill me in a ritual ceremony as a warning to others who might dare to offend their tribe? Am I to be sacrificed to appease their gods, the man-spirits dancing in the smoke of the fire, all for the good of the tribe in this ceremony by the ocean? Are they cannibals? Am I to be consumed by these men, cooked alive and devoured like any other wild animal hunted down? Or am I one of them—a fellow tribesman who has failed his initiation trials? Am I a disgrace to them? About to be castrated?

I jerk myself faster and faster, my mind reeling in excitement and terror. In my bliss I welcome my fate, heedless of whether it will mean redemption or death, for now they are one and the same to me.

I am a prisoner, bound and gagged, a piece of meat to be used however they see fit. My will has been taken and I have no recourse other than acceptance of whatever the next moment will bring as the fire in my cock burns ever hotter and hotter, as I rise to a higher plateau.

My neck strains to raise my head and what I glimpse sends me further into ecstasy. Standing straight and tall in tribute to the night and the man-spirits, every native man present is fully erect, their powerful forearms flexing, sinews of movement confirming that the tribesmen are jerking off, standing around me in a gigantic circle. Beyond them I can see more men, and beyond them still more. There are thousands present, in ever-widening spirals of self-stimulation. And I am the focal point of their energy.

Understanding ignites and flares in my brain; I am one of them! I have passed through trials by fire unscathed and am about to be marked with the seed of the tribe, to have my manhood bestowed upon me! I stroke my dick faster, the slickness of my hand causing more sparks of current to arc around me. The energy that has been building for so long is about to be released…

…*Now.*

All the stars flare as if going nova simultaneously and the chanting becomes a crescendo of animal passion. I close my eyes and untold gallons of hot man-come shoots at me from all sides, covering me, filling my world. I am swept away by a convection of sperm, am swimming in a sea of it, into a roar of oblivion, every cell of my body a part of the come-electric.

I am a man.

Amplified.

Where am I?

I am still bound and gagged as before, incapable of moving, but where?

I am lost and alone.

I am inside a building; there is a roof above me, containing billows of smoke, but now...

I force my line of vision down from the wooden planks of the ceiling to a large room with row after row of bunk beds extending into infinity, each covered with a dark green bedspread.

And men.

Soldiers. Hundreds of them, of all sorts and ranks. All the armed forces are here: Army, Navy, Air Force, Marines... recruits, lieutenants, grunts, pilots, sergeants, admirals, commanders, captains, privates, corporals... a cross-section of military men so complex and convoluted that my mind must stretch in order to wrap itself around so vast a concept.

My eyes widen to pick out random details from the crowd—round muscles beneath camouflage T-shirts, big cocks bulging beneath khaki pants, the glittering brass of medals pinned to the coats of high ranking officials, row after row of shiny black boots, piercing, lustful eyes and short buzz cuts hidden beneath caps and green berets, guns in holsters, bulging green duffel bags slung over shoulders, dog tags hanging around necks—as the smoke from their cigars rises to collect at the ceiling of the barracks.

They are all looking at me.

I am naked, bound and gagged, sprawled on my back on a footlocker with my cock standing at attention beneath the killing heat of their collective gaze.

Why am I here?

Am I a recruit who tried to go AWOL—caught and about to be disciplined by all these men? Am I an enemy operative, a prisoner of war soon to be tortured, interrogated until valuable information has been pumped out of me? Am I a spy who has been working undercover as a grunt, found and exposed at last, ready to accept my punishment at the hands of the entire U.S. Armed Forces?

My hand pumps my dick faster and faster.

The man closest to me, a hulking drill sergeant with biceps like cantaloupes walks over to me and halts just behind my head, his protruding crotch hanging directly above my face. He looks down at me and breaks into a lascivious smile.

What is happening here?

Sucking deeply on his cigar before setting it down, utilizing both hands to loosen his belt and unbutton his fly, he unleashes his cock. Monstrously long and thick, it hangs nearly to my face.

Now I know.

A second later, my not responding immediately provokes the man to hit me, smacking the side of my head while grunting gutturally.

My mouth stretches open, ready to receive.

His cock descends, enters my mouth and fills my throat entirely; how am I to breathe? Inhaling deeply through my nostrils, taking in the clouds of tobacco smoke choking the room, I figure it out quickly enough.

The drill sergeant begins fucking my face. There is nothing at all sensual, nothing subtle or romantic about his thrusting. He has no regard for my pleasure whatsoever. This is all about him. I am a toy to be used and thrown away like a gum wrapper. My life amounts to nothing more than keeping my mouth open to receive his immense penis.

My own dick has become more achingly solid with his every brutal downstroke. When his assault has grown so forceful that I begin to slide off the footlocker, the man anchors my shoulders with his hands to keep me in place. My peripheral vision is completely eclipsed by the drill sergeant's massive form but I can feel the presence of the other men in the room. They are watching the spectacle, and this knowledge intoxicates me.

All at once his cock distends like a steel rod and the man explodes down my throat. I swallow and gulp the dense, warm liquid shooting down my gullet greedily.

With a satisfied groan of release, the drill sergeant pulls his slimy dick out of my mouth and steps out of my field of vision. Squinting through the billowing smoke, what I see staggers my already overloaded mind.

All the men in the room, all the soldiers and grunts and captains and sailors have formed a single-file line that leads to me. The wave of self-knowledge that overtook me on the beach returns to crash down upon me again and I realize exactly what I am.

I am a whore.

I am an unpaid hustler, a sperm receptacle—nothing more, captured for the use of all these men. I will never, for the rest of my life, leave this place. From this point forward my sole function will be to service this ever-lengthening queue of hard cock multiplying before my very eyes.

But no time for sight-seeing; the next man in line—a young black recruit with skin as smooth as a statue's and a body as hard as cement—is getting into position above me as the men behind him impatiently puff on their cigars, anxious for their own turns. Their smoke has filled the entire barracks with a cloud so vast I can see nothing through it, can only feel the rough, brutal thrusting of dick in my mouth as I jerk myself harder.

Coming violently, I am spinning through space like a leaf in a hurricane of smoke.

Am I alone once more? Yes…

The white of smoke is darkening, being invaded by other colors. A surface is solidifying beneath me.

I am lying on my back as before, but definitely somewhere else.

What was the sky above the ocean that became the roof of an army barracks has become something else again: the ceiling of an apartment. But not mine.

Where am I?

The huge cloud of smoke has dissipated, dissolving down to a thin wisp, trailing into the air like a tiny smoke signal. I glance down to see that the wisp is coming from a solitary candle that burns near me on the floor, where I remain bound and gagged, shackled and chained to large metal rings that are imbedded in the hardwood. A smooth leather collar encircles my neck.

The room is small, well hung with various abstract paintings, a single doorway opening onto a vast darkness that suddenly fills white! Is it the smoke again? No…

It is a man.

He is tall, well over six feet. His eyes are the blue of the native's ocean; his massive frame embodies the power of every man in the barracks combined. He is dressed entirely in white, as if the smoke had solidified into fabric around him. A white T-shirt barely contains the expanse of his chest. White jeans grip his ass and legs in a way that sets my erotic imagination ablaze—his cock, as formidable as a fire hose, showing through them.

He is my Master.

I am worshipping him with eyes that beg and plead and love and adore. All I want is to serve him, to please him in any way wants, to do anything for him.

I am a slave—an owned piece of property that belongs to him as surely as his car, his apartment and all his other possessions do.

I live to serve him.

I reach out to touch him but am held fast by the chains. Straining against them, attempting in vain to grasp this vision in the doorway is such exquisite torture.

My Master steps into the room and looks down at me with an unreadable expression. Surely a creature as basic as I cannot begin to fathom the complexity of the mind behind those eyes. But I can hope against hope that he will allow me to debase myself for his delight, to perform every indignity imaginable for his amusement—for this god-like presence standing before me.

My Master drops to one knee between my legs and unlocks the shackles binding my feet. Bliss and power flow into me as his strong hands close around my ankles and lift my legs high into the air, his touch causing my heart to flutter and skip a beat. Having hooked my ankles over his shoulders, the man in white loosens the buttons of his jeans, releasing the cock within, its piss-slit dripping with excitement. My Master slicks his fingers with pre-come and slides them into my asshole. The feel of him inside me is electrifying. The cool slickness fills my passage, preparing it for the assault to come.

I catch my breath and moan into my sopping gag, drooling like a dog and whimpering with desperation. My Master touches his hand to my spit-covered chin, utilizing the saliva to get his dick wet and shiny. Positioning himself, he thrusts his cock into me with a single motion, my silent scream heard by bats and dogs worldwide.

Pain fills my world as surely does the ecstasy that cannot be separated from it. Beyond anything I have experienced before in dream, fantasy or reality, our fucking is beyond incredible or mind-blowing, beyond cosmic or explosive. It is symbiosis of the highest and most sacred order. I feel as if a universe were being created within me, filled with pleasure and pain, fire and water, storm and calm.

With his every thrust I become more and more his property, his slave. The utter mastery with which he uses my body is like the almighty power of gravity as it directs and guides all movement of matter in the universe.

I belong to him.

I *belong*.

I hear his sweet groan stiffen and feel his holy seed shooting within me, igniting my every cell with his might and glory. My assaulted channel is soothed by its spurting white warmth. I am his vessel, the object for his release.

And just as quickly as he entered me, he leaves.

I am left barren and empty by his retreat.

He rises to his feet, towering above me, tucking his spent passion back into his pants. I am suddenly gripped by a fear that he is about to leave the room, and me, never to return.

My every muscle flexes as I twist wildly against my bondage, crying out for him to please not leave me, that I cannot be away from his presence, not now, or ever again.

Without a sound my Master reaches down towards me. Fearing being hit for my insolence, I duck my head and clamp my eyes shut. The sound of metal against metal surprises me and I open my eyes to see my Master unlocking all my bonds.

The chains fall to the floor and I am free!

Noting my questioning gaze, he lies down beside me, holds my body in one powerful arm against his, and takes me into hand. Slick with my constant stream of pre-come, the lubricated friction of his fist is so sublime that I cannot hold back much longer. I have become a manned space probe that has entered its final countdown before blast off. I am a balloon, being blown up so quickly I will burst at any second.

There is no turning back now.

Within seconds, arching bolts of white-hot sperm jet out of me, the sparks of electricity becoming lightning bolts that flash as bright as the sun. The gag

I'm still wearing is the only thing preventing my gasps and cries of rapture from being fully expressed as galaxies crash together deep within me, setting off repercussions of cosmic proportion, destroying themselves in order to bring new life into the cosmos. My final self-realization is at hand, *his* hand, and the absolute knowledge that accompanies it has incinerated all awareness but the ecstasy in coming.

Indifferent to the fact that I am spattered with semen from chest to head, my Master pulls me to my feet and, leaning forward, slings me over his shoulder. He walks from the room into a perfectly white hallway. I feel as if we are ascending into heaven as, hanging over his back, I see the floor fall away from below us. Not to be abandoned after all, I am filled with satisfaction. It doesn't matter where we are going, as long as I am with him.

My Master has brought me to his private chamber. Everything within is white and one wall is entirely mirrored. White candles burn on every surface, their smoke gently wafting into the air. A white bed, a white floor, white ceiling… But in the mirror I can see the opposite white wall and… what is hanging on it from a large steel hook.

It is a black leather sleeping bag, big enough for a man.

Big enough for me.

It hangs entirely off the floor—a single teardrop stolen from a giant, obsidian statue's eye, suspended and frozen in a world blasted white.

I am filled with such desire and hope as my Master carries me over to it that my vision blurs with tears. His exquisite touch is replaced by the cool kiss of leather as he slides me into the sleep-sack, which fits my body perfectly, as if molded specifically for me.

My Master is the Alpha and the Omega, the truth and the light, the beginning and the end, and I am his slave. I will serve him, and when not serving him, I will be stored in this sack until he wants me again. Such will be the extent of my experience.

I cannot imagine a more desirable life on heaven or earth.

When all but my head is inside, my Master takes a long, last look at me and smiles for the first time. He has transformed me into a new being. Shedding tears of gratitude and joy, I die from sheer happiness only to be reborn into my true self—an utter slave with no other thought, no other life—as he gently pushes me down into the sack and closes the top, cinching it tight.

Surrounded by darkness once again, I snuggle into the warmth of the leather surrounding me and feel myself beginning to doze, confidant that I will never again be alone. For I know that less than five feet away from me, the man I adore above all other, the man I have given my life to, is in his bed, settling down for a good night's sleep.

The last thing I recall imagining is the many white candles that will burn slowly down through the course of the night… until nothing is left of them… but thin wisps of smoke.

223

Darkness.
And sleep.

I stir awake and pull off the blindfold. The first thing I see is a thin wisp of smoke; my incense has burned down to the stick. I pull my arm out from under me and slowly untie my bonds. Dried come flakes and falls from my torso as I sit up and remove the spit-soaked gag from my mouth.

My jaw and joints are sore. Stretching, having freed myself, I settle back down onto the floor and rest my head on the pillow.

Wondering if I really can feel the grittiness of white sand on my skin as I shift my body on the floor, wondering if the odor I exude is really the stink of lingering cigar smoke, wondering if the sensation of just having been fucked is imaginary or not, wondering if these things are real or imagined and then wondering if it matters at all, the delineation between fantasy and reality remains blurry.

About to descend into dreamless slumber, I wonder if I should climb into bed, slip between the sheets.

No, I decide at the gate of sleep.

It *doesn't* matter.

Because…

The night is hot.

Very, very hot.

White-hot.

JOHNNY WAS
Greg Wharton

Not a day has gone by when I haven't thought about him.

He was some image of beauty, Johnny was. A smile that could kill. That funny space between his front teeth. Every time he flashed that smile at me, I melted. I couldn't stay mad; I could forgive him anything.

Johnny had a perfect body. Trim, strong, compact. Lovely large pierced nipples that were so sensitive he could come from just a few minutes of either soft sweet caressing or my heavy-duty tugging. He had a beautiful long cock and a perfect ass—round and firm with skin as smooth as a baby—that I both gratefully worshipped and tortured for hours on end.

But I never understood what was going on in his head. He never allowed me to know his thoughts, his past, or what he wanted from his… or our future. Never shared emotions other than his sexual desire and a random "I love you" during orgasm. It's almost like he used me, like I was set up. Like he was just waiting. Like he knew all along how it would end.

I loved him. I could forgive him almost anything. But I will never be able to forgive him for leaving me like he did.

David never really understood me. I loved him, which he never seemed to believe, but he was chosen right from the start to be The One. We weren't destined for a lifetime together, to set up a home or share banking accounts. We were destined for exactly what happened. And I love him more than I have ever loved another for what he gave me. The only thing anyone ever gave me that truly mattered.

We met in a most bizarre way, Johnny and I.

I was leaving work late and heading down the block by my office, thinking of a stiff drink to wash away the memory of a long day, when I saw him leaning up against my little Honda's front hood. As I neared, I felt a bristle of both fear and excitement stir through my body. It was dark, but there was enough light from the streetlight. It illuminated him. And he was gorgeous. God, he was gorgeous. Black hair framed his pretty face. His two- or maybe three-day-old beard added even more depth to his already high cheekbones. And his pale blue eyes stared right through me.

And my cock hardened with thoughts of tasting him, of working off the day's frustrations.

I couldn't tell what he was doing. It almost looked like he'd been waiting for me. When I was but ten feet from the car, he stood up and I saw that smile for the first time. He flashed me that smile, and that funny space between his front teeth. I smiled back; how could I resist?

And then he kicked out my front left headlight.

"Fucker!" I yelled and started running towards him.

He bolted quickly down the block and I did my best to keep up, all the while yelling obscenities at him. I'm not sure what I thought I was going to do if I caught him, but I ran anyway.

Only a chance car turning from a cross street gave me the opportunity I needed. He dodged the car, tripped over the curb and fell hard. And I pounced.

"What the hell was that?" I screamed as I grabbed his shoulders and roughly twisted his body onto his back.

"I… "

I held him down with my body and wrapped both hands firmly around his neck. Something had snapped and I was going to get a reasonable answer or hurt him real bad. I might hurt him anyway, the stupid fucker.

"Who the fuck do you think you are, doing that to my car?"

"I… "

"Tell me why you did that or I'm going to beat the shit out of you!"

My spit flew out in a shower across his beautiful face as I screamed and pressed my hands tighter around his neck and squeezed. I really wanted to hurt him. That's when I saw his smile the second time and felt his hard cock pressing up against my body.

"I wanted to get your attention."

It worked.

I kissed him firmly on the lips, all anger giving way to desire, white-hot lust, and when he returned my kiss, grabbing me by my hair and holding me tight to him, I knew I was in trouble. I fell from lust into love. God help me, I fell in love.

He thought I did it because I was hurt by what he said. Not true. He thought it was his fault. It wasn't. The time was right and the doorway was finally open: I had him upset enough that I could take advantage of the moment and finally escape. Poor sweet David. I didn't want to hurt him, but I needed to do it. He just never understood me; I needed to do it. And I needed him to do it for me.

The fight was dumb. About nothing really, but it ended up getting out of hand. I said some stupid, mean things about him being an emotional cripple and that he didn't deserve me. He did what he'd always done during the six months we had been fucking when confronted by my anger, or any emotion for that matter: he just smiled. But that night it pissed me off and I slapped him hard across the face and told him it was over.

"It's over, asshole! No more. I can't play these games any more!"

He started crying and his tears burned deep into my heart. I should have known better than to try and make up. Should have known better than to engage in the play we so often did. It was foolish to play when I was mad.

"Baby, are you okay? Does it feel good?"

I had found that talk was important in the play I enjoyed so much. The play I needed so much. Sex was where I let it all out: all the loss of control I felt in my life every single day was overcome by taking that control back. I sometimes pushed too much, losing touch with reality in the moment. Communication was key so that I knew when it was enough and when it had become too much, because sometimes I couldn't stop unless told to. This was especially true with Johnny. Our sex had become more and more dangerous with time.

He encouraged me, it. Said he needed it. And he told me he knew I needed it, which was true.

I trained him well for the purpose he was meant to serve. Death had always escaped me—or rather—I had always escaped it. I wasn't afraid of it, just unable to follow through with crossing over. But... when I saw David—at a sex-play party where he totally beat the shit out of some boy—but looked so guilty afterwards—I knew he would be the one to help me. I knew he would help me as no other had.

He didn't see me that night. I tracked him down. I watched him and learned his schedule. I arranged our first meeting and I made him fall in love with me. And I trained him to be my assassin. He was perfect.

Johnny was on his back and his arms were roped to the corner posts of my bed. His beautiful strong legs were over my shoulders and my cock was buried deep within his ass, his sweet hairless ass that willingly took so much abuse from me. Both of my hands were firmly circling his delicate neck and I was beginning to cut off his air supply by pressing my thumbs down firmly across his windpipe.

"Baby, are you okay? Does it feel good?"

"Yes. Come on! Do it! Fuck me... Damn it, fuck me hard!"

"Let me know... "

"Shhhh... just fuck me, David. Shut the fuck up and do it."

And I did. Sweat dripped down my body and pooled on his chest and stomach as I continued pounding even more deeply into his gut with all my energy. Grinding my length into his tight ass, letting my passion take over. He would never look me in the eyes while I fucked him. Never give me any indication of either pain or pleasure with his face when I applied pressure to his windpipe. It was so risky. I had to watch his coloring and try to tell from his body's tenseness when I needed to stop.

But then he would surface from death's haze, breathing deep, and I would feel his ass clamp down around my cock, then he would look deep into my eyes. And I would mistake it for love. I would mistake his body's natural reactions for the emotions I so wanted and needed. And I would come hard as I looked into those eyes, so hard, then melt into his arms and hold him tight.

We had a rhythm after doing it for months; I knew just how far I could push him. He wanted to get right to the edge, taunting death, as he liked to say. *To taunt death...* Should I have known it would end as it did?

Yes, baby. Tonight is it. I feel it. Come on. I need you now more than ever. Don't disappoint me, David. You'll forgive me in time. Fuck me. Fuck me hard. Hurt me. Kill me. Kill me, lover. I want to feel death as you come. Kill me now.

I knew just how long I could deprive him of air to give him the rush he so desired. Then I would let go with both hands to allow him to resurface from death's embrace. His eyes would meet mine and my hard cock would pound once more with such fierceness I would scream and then erupt as his ass clenched tight around me.

I thought I knew just how long, how hard to strangle to prolong his desire, my passion, his death, my orgasm. My control. I thought I was in control.

But, something wasn't right. He didn't resurface. He didn't come back. I had gone too far. My Johnny left me. He left me as I emptied myself and I knew it was too late to stop either of us.

I couldn't stop.

Thank you, David, my love. Don't be angry with me. My last sensation was of your cum pulsing into my ass and I feel it still. I love you so much. I know you don't understand, but I do love you. Thank you. It was perfect.

Johnny died. He died with that damn smile on his face and my cock deep in his ass. But I won't forgive him. That time the smile didn't work. He died from my hands. And to my death it's going to haunt me.

I watch the liquid flow through the IV tubes the State Medical Technician has put into each of my restrained arms. First he will feed me the Pentothal to put me to sleep, then the Pavulon will follow in a dose large enough to paralyze my diaphragm and lungs. Then the final drug will be administered. The Potassium chloride will induce cardiac arrest, and I will die.

Not a day has gone by when I haven't thought about him.

And that funny space between his teeth.

DRIVING HOME
Stephen Albrow

I'm okay for gas, aren't I? Good. Then let's get the fuck out of here—*fast*. Thank God *that's* finally all done with. I mean, I really loved the son-of-a-bitch-bastard, but you can only let someone treat you like shit for so long. So now it's over. Totally over.

OVERCOME HOMOSEXUAL TEMPTATION!
Lamar Beverly Davis, Senior Pastor
Word Is God Worship Center

It has been said that the average male thinks about sex every six seconds. With "beefcake" being used to sell everything from toothpaste to cars it's no wonder that today's Christian man feels bombarded and under assault. Learn how you can overcome homosexual temptation and flee from this abomination before it's too late.

"No Regrets" Seminar, schedule of events to be posted,
03 / 03 / 03
ALL ARE WELCOME!

What the fuck did that billboard say? *Overcome homosexual temptation? Worship Center?* Some homophobic, Christian bullshit?

…God, I loved him, though. He was so strong and muscular. I loved the way he held me in bed, after we'd made love—his massive arms wrapped around me, so warm, so real. But then, so did lots of *other* guys enjoy that experience, so I was right to end it. No doubt about that. *Bye bye Max. Thanks, but no thanks.*

I love the roads this time of night. Not too much traffic. Cruising time. Cruising for a *good* time. *Hey, fella, fancy a ride?*

Whoa, did you fucking see that? What is it with cyclists these days? They don't seem happy unless their tight, little Spandex shorts aren't digging at least three-inches deep between their buns. *Hey, I got something in my pants that'll plug the gap, if that's what you really want. Shit man, I'll stick it in, poke it around. You'll be saddle-sore for a fuckin' month.*

Jeez, I'm glad it's over and done with. I'll miss the early morning showers together and I'll miss his smell. I used to love those dirty overalls he wore to work, really hated it when he washed them. There was just something about him turning up on my doorstep covered in oil and grease and God only knows what other fluids. Mmmmmm. *Hi, Max...* Big kiss. Big dick. Whoop-tee-doo. Suddenly, I'm naked, bent over. Down on all fours. In, out, in, out... *Yeah, fill me up with that big cock, baby...*

Must phone Mom and Dad tomorrow. Nearly time for the big party. I can't believe they've been together for forty years. And then there's me: incapable of holding down a relationship for more than six months. I mean, it's great they still love each other, but... I wonder what that *billboard* said?

...Can't wait for the party, though. Gotta phone and tell them what time I'm going over.

You don't call home enough, young man. Your papa and I just sit here, waiting...

Just look at your buns, baby... I need a date for the party; and that guy would definitely do. I really do dig these cyclists nowadays. Spandex shorts over peachy buttocks. *I'll pull 'em down and part those buns for ya, sweetcheeks. Yeah, Johnny's comin' to* get *ya!*

God, I'm glad it's over. What was that chick at work saying today? Getting married to someone she's known for two weeks? Met him in a bar, too. I give them four months, max. You can't *know* someone after two fucking weeks! Certainly not well enough to...

"SON OF A BITCH BASTARD! YEAH, *YOU*, MISTER..."

Jesus *Christ*, the people they let loose on the *roads* nowadays! That was a fucking *red* light. Couldn't the moron see it was fucking *red*? That it was *my* fucking right of way! The bastard could have killed me.

He was cute, though. Cute little fucker, but he still could've killed me stone fucking dead.

That's his car, isn't it? Fuck it, I'm gonna pull up alongside him at the next light. Fucker... No way he heard me shouting. Is that his car or not? Yep, that's it. Is he looking at me? Don't make it too obvious, Johnny.

Damn, he *is* cute. For *sure*. The T-shirt's a little on the tight side, but then again, if I had pecs that size, I'd probably not be wearing a shirt at all! Jesus *Christ*... Any bigger and he'd need a fuckin' bra! Just imagine *that* huffin' and puffin' on top of you. Imagine *that* mounting your body and slipping it to you. Yes, *please...*

Hey, baby, look over here. I'm a single guy, again. Wanna help me forget that bastard, Max?

Obviously not. Off and away he goes. And with a hell of a lot more acceleration than this piece of shit's got. I gotta trade it in soon. Get something big, something *flashy*. Hey, I'm single again. The old reliable VW was fine when I was cozy with Max, but now I need something that's going to get me noticed. I need a motorized *cock* extension. *Hey there, Mr. Mechanic, how'd ya like to polish my* hood?

Jesus Christ, it's late. Is that *really* the time, or has that clock stopped working? Let's see... I left work at seven, must've gotten to Max's apartment 'round eight thirty. How the fuck long was I *there*? It's not like we messed around or anything. Just a quick chat, collecting up the last of my shit and then I was *outta* there. There's no way it can be past eleven. What, have I crossed over into the fucking *Twilight* Zone or something? Maybe that's what the billboard said?

"MOTHERFUCKING SHIT!"
What's going on up there? Why aren't we moving?
"FUCKING SHIT!"
That's all I need. Some huge delay. Let's ask the stud in the uniform...
"HEY! OFFICER! WHAT'S THE HOLD-UP?"
"SORRY, SIR, BUT A VEHICLE'S COLLIDED WITH A FIRE HYDRANT AND WE'RE GONNA HAVE TO SHUT THE ROAD DOWN."
Ah, this is totally *fucked*... "SO, HOW AM I SUPPOSED TO GET TO THIRTY-FIFTH?"
"YOU'LL HAVE TO TAKE A LEFT AND HEAD FOR THIRTY-THIRD, THEN CROSS BACK, SIR. OR YOU CAN WAIT, ALTHOUGH WE'RE LOOKING AT AN HOUR, AT LEAST."
Jesus, this is *truly* all I need. "OKAY. THANKS, BUDDY."
This is the goddamned mother*fuckin'* answer to all my prayers. Thirty-third's a fucking thirty-minute detour, meaning I won't get home until...
He was a babe, though. Nice smile. Nice *uniform*. I'll take bad news from a guy like that *any* day. Or good news. Yeah. I could sure take some *good* news from someone like him. *"I'm sorry, sir, but someone has hit a fire hydrant, the direct consequence of which means I'm going to have to fuck your ass ragged. I'm terribly sorry about this inconvenience, sir, but... in it goes. It's no good screaming, sir, the matter is entirely out of my hands. Yes, I know it's big. Nine-inches, hard, to be exact. ...Why,* thank you, sir! It's nice of you to say so."

Shit, shit, *shit*—I forgot to do the goddamned Willows Report. That makes it five days late now, although it's not *my* fault I didn't get the data till Friday, but even so, I should have handed it in yesterday, but what with Max fucking the pool guy... I mean... *fuck.*

Calm down, Johnny. No real panic. Keep your mind on the road ahead of you. We don't want you banging into a fire hydrant, now do we? I'll do it first thing in the morning. If I ever *get* home, that is—which doesn't seem likely.

It's all Max's fault, damn it. God, I'll miss him; I already miss his arms around me. And his lips... Like they'd been pumped with silicone, but of course they hadn't. God, I used to love the way they felt, squirming all over my face. All over my dick... *Especially* my dick! Slipping my helmet between them, feeling them push back my foreskin, sucking on my glans, flicking his tongue in my slit, the way he swallowed my cum after sucking—sucking—sucking: *God,* I'm going to miss that!

Shit, now I'm getting hard. *Concentrate,* dickbrain. Focus. You're driving a potential death trap. Keep focused on...

Hmmm, who's the babe in the outside lane? Stylish. One hand on the wheel, one hand on the gearshift... Jerking it off, like a great big prick. *You wanna pop over here and grind my gearshift, baby? Spank my monkey? Beat my meeeeet? Oooo, you're so sweeeeet, so hunky You got me all unky, bunky, clunky, dunky, e-funky, gunky, hunky* (Ooops, used that one), .i... i... aw, fuck it. *...Junkie, kunky, lunky, monkey, nunky,* forget o, *punky, qunky, runky, sunky, tunky,* u: I already used unky. Let's see: *vunky, wunky, yunky, zunky*—done! No, wait! How about this: *You're so hunky. You're so sweet. Flip me 'round and fill my seat... with lots and lots of tasty meat. It can't be beat. Tweedily deedily deet!* Cockin' Robin! Ha!

Jesus Christ, shut the fuck up, Johnny. You ought to put your foot down a little. Gotta get the Willows Report in tomorrow morning and at this rate you're not gonna get to bed till after midnight.

Doubt I'll sleep much, either. It's just not the same in an empty bed. I think that's where I'll miss Max the most. I've always slept better right after a good fuck. Always does knock me out, a good hard screw. In and out... in and out... for an hour, yeah, and... out I go, like a light. *Yeah,* after a good, hot *orgasm,* with my butt still tinglin', sweat all over on my body... *yeah,* that's it.

Could always hire someone for the night, I guess. Unless I'm very much mistaken, this little detour is gonna take me right through where the rent boys hang out...

Hmm, there's that tobacco shop where Max and I got those dumb-ass Cuban cigars that time. Jesus Christ, the size, and the *price* of those fuckers! We only had one puff each; they were so fucking strong. Wound up coughing for like a *year.* Must have been around last Christmas... Why the fuck did we buy them, I wonder? Neither of us smoke.

And there's the place we had coffee that day. And that's the store where I tried on those god-awful green and orange shirts. What a freak I looked in them. Jesus, we laughed about that...

Here's my turn—which means there should be a little love for sale right around the corner, just before I cut back towards Thirty Fifth...

And what do you know; there's the first of them! Cute, but far too young. And there's another, and *another*. Jesus Christ, there's *zillions* of them and the cops are just sitting there, watching them. Good Lord, I better not slow down, or they'll nail me for something. I mean... that kid can't be more than sixteen. And look! He's getting in a car and the cops just don't seem to give a shit!

Now *that* guy looks a little more age-appropriate. Legal age of consent, for sure, but those kids down there... No way, Jose!

Now *he's* nice. He really shouldn't be out in those shorts, though. I mean, it's cold out there tonight. Good God, I'm starting to sound like my mother. Here we have a hot, twenty-something-year-old stud out there on the streets, selling his body, and all I care about is whether or not he's *warm* enough? Jesus! *Well, I'll keep ya warm, you fuckin' stud. Drop a load of white-hot cum on those naked thighs of yours. Start a little fire in your cornhole with my tongue, then stoke it with my big, fat dick...*

Better keep moving. Rent boys, rent boys... all around me, and, Jesus Christ, I've gotta keep moving. I'd love to stop and buy one for my very own, but I really must keep moving. I mean, will you just look at that? He's practically *naked*. Was that his *dick* poking out of... *whatever* they were—split-crotch boxer shorts or something? It's fashion news to me, but good news, at least. Especially on a taut, slim blond, with just the right amount of muscle on his upper body. *Flip me over and fill me up, baby. Drown me in a big spurt of liquid man.*

This fucking road goes on forever. Unlike Max and me... But that's over. All in the past. *Fuck* it. I'm a single guy again, for Christ's sake—a single guy with money in his wallet. So what d'ya reckon, huh? The blond guy, maybe, or some other stud? Take him home, show him a good time, get him to show *me* a good time: what d'ya reckon, huh? I've got nothing to lose.

Gotta do the Willows Report. First thing in the morning. Rise and shine. Crack of dawn. No time for jollies. Not tonight. I'll check out that billboard on the way back home...

God, that stud was cute, though. And there's a turning lane ahead. Quick U-turn, head back down the road, ask him what's on the menu, sample the local goods. Hell, I'd be doing the guy a favor. He has to eat, doesn't he? If he *don't* get a little bit of meat inside him each day, then he *don't* get a little bit of meat inside him each day, if ya know what I mean.

Right, then. Shall I? Come on, Johnny. Come on now...

Jesus, I'm heading back. I can't believe I'm doing this. I feel like a whole new man tonight. I'm not half of Max & Johnny any more. I'm Johnny, period.

God, this is fun. It's like one of those restaurants where they have all the lobsters in a tank of water and you get to pick which one you want to eat. And there's so much to choose from—a little bit of black, a little blond. Maybe some thick black body hair for the evening. Someone a little like Max—only younger, like the younger version of me he ran off with, the prick.

Must call Mom and Dad tomorrow. Let them know what time I'll be heading over for the party. Gotta get a present for them, too. Maybe something for the kitchen or those chocolates that...

Now *that's* nice. That, I like a *lot*. Slow down, Johnny. Let's see what's cookin' for the evening. That I like a *hell* of a lot. Man, I could *live* with that. I could *marry* the fuckin' guy.

"HOW MUCH FOR ANAL?"

"FORTY FOR A SUCK, NINETY FOR A FUCK."

Flirt, Johnny.

"WELL THEN, NINETY SOUNDS LIKE A BARGAIN TO..."

Jesus Christ, what's the motherfucker...

"HEY, COME BACK."

Oh Christ, man... Shit. What the fuck have I done? Just keep driving, Johnny. Concentrate on the road. *Shit*. He's definitely coming after me. Left, go left. *Shit*. Go a little faster, Johnny, but not too much. Why the fuck did I have to go and do that? I'm a handsome guy. I can get laid without the help of my wallet.

Shit. He's still following. What the fuck do I do now? Pull over or just keep going?

Keep going, Johnny. Keep going. They'll fucking crucify me if they catch me. I'll be fucking front-page news. Everyone will fucking know. Mom. Dad. Max. Everyone. All those numbskull chicks at work. They'll all fucking know.

Take a right, then another right. It's dark up there. Stay calm, Johnny. We don't want a crash. That's the last thing I need right now. Shit. He's still on my tail. That fucking blue light in the rear-view mirror...

Oh *great*, now the fucking siren's blaring. This is for *shit*. Fucking motorcycle cops!

Go down the alleyway, Johnny. It's dark, but...

Shit. He's still on me. He's gaining. That fucking blue light scares the piss out of me. Fuck it. Just mother*fuck* it, man; I gotta pull over. Hey, you've done nothing wrong, Johnny. You just asked the kid for directions. He never got in the car. You never agreed to a price.

Okay. Okay. Let's take a few deep breaths. He's stopping. He's tall. Jesus Christ, just look at those leather pants. He's cuter than the fucking rent stud.

"STEP OUT OF THE CAR, SIR—*NOW*!!"

"SURE, OFFICER, WHAT'S THE PROBLEM?"

"*YOU'RE* THE FUCKING PROBLEM, YOU FREAK. BEND OVER THE FUCKING HOOD, FAGGOT!"

"WHAT THE FUCK ARE YOU DOING?"

God, he's... Jesus, he's...

"YOU WANT YOUR BUTT FUCKED, THEN YOU'RE GONNA GET YOUR BUTT FUCKED."

Jesus Christ, what the fuck is he doing? Is he gonna *rape* me? I think the fucker's gonna *rape* me! Hallefuckin'*lujah*! Wait, he's letting go of me, putting on a...

"WHAT ARE YOU DOING TO ME?"

"I'M GIVING YOU WHAT YOU FUCKING WANT, FAG-MAN, AND WHAT I WANT, TOO."

He's gonna fuck me. Oh, baby! The fuckin' cop's gonna *fuck* me. Jesus Christ, my pants are down around my fucking ankles. I'm in the middle of a fucking alleyway and my pants are down and everyone can see my ass.

Only there's no one else around. Cool. Gotta stay cool. It's just the two of us. Don't move. Just let him do what he wants. You're a single guy. Let him do what he wants. Make him do what *you* want, too, though. Oh, that's good. ...*Yeah, tongue me, baby.* Tongue *me. Kiss my sweet ring. Lick me; stick it in. God, it's so wet, so warm. Make me wet, baby. Get me ready for that big, fat prick of yours. Come on. Give it to me. Oh, God... You didn't shave this morning, did you, officer? You're scratchin' my buns, baby, but don't stop, 'cause I dig it sooooo much.*

God, he's really sticking it up there. Come on, baby, snake that tongue into me; make me good and wet. It's just that... he's so *tall* and... those leather *pants* he's wearing and...it feels so fucking good, and...

"FUCK ME, OFFICER. FUCK ME NOW!"

Oh, yeah. That's...

"OH, *GOD*... OH, *YEAH*..."

What the fuck *is* this? He's fucking *massive*. God, it's... *No, not so fast, man. It's...* Oh, grip *tight*, Johnny; make it tighter for him. Jesus Christ, it's burning. I can feel my butthole burning with...

More! There's *more*. Jesus *Christ*, how much meat has this fucker got? It's burning and it's... beautiful and... *yeah*... and it's... *yeah*... Oh, my *God*. It's almost too much and it's... almost too much and it's... almost too much and I... want *more* and I want it... *harder*, and I want it...

"*HARDER*, MAN. COME ON. *HARDER*."

...And in and out, and... in and out, and... Keep it coming. That's so fuckin' *good*. So big. So strong. So hot. Big, good-lookin' cop. Massive, solid thighs. Huge prick. *I want more of you inside me, man. Keep it comin'. Good and hard. Yeah*...

Jesus Christ, my prick is gonna burst. That *feeling*... so deep... inside me. It's just too...

"JERK ME OFF, OFFICER. PLEASE JERK ME OFF."

And... *yeah*. That's *good*. That's *fine*. And *harder*, and... *faster*, and... *harder*, and... *faster*. Oh, *fuck* me and *jerk* me and *suck* me and *kiss* me and *love* me and *fuck* me and *jerk* me and *want* me and...

It's gonna happen. Hold back, Johnny. No! I *can't* hold back, I… Hold back, Johnny. It's gonna happen. And… Jesus Christ, his *prick* up my *ass*. It's *burning* and it's… *awesome* and… *Yeah*… And… here it *comes*…!

"OH, *YEAH*…. OH, *YEAH*…. OH, *YEAH*… NOW LET ME TASTE IT! LET ME TASTE IT!"

Sticky spunk on sticky fingers. Lick it up, Johnny. That's *you* on those fingers. And feel that stab of meat still pumping in and out of you. Feel those throbs, Johnny. You're making it happen for him, too. Feel that prickhead throbbing, Johnny.

"FUCK *YEAH*, FAGGOT! *YEAH*…"

You've made it happen for him, too, Johnny. Feel it spurting inside you. Grip those muscles tight. Can you feel him spurting? Shape your hole around that pulsating prick.

And suddenly it's out. And now it's over, but we still have our lips. Kiss. Kiss. Tongues. Scratchy stubble. *Oh, rip my skin, baby, rip my flesh*. Kiss. Kiss. *Cup my buns*. Oh, Johnny boy, you've found the real thing this time. Hold him, Johnny. Hold him tight. Don't let this one get away. More tongue. More kisses. More passion. More heat.

And, Jesus *Christ*, what the fuck does the rest of it matter? *Screw* Max. *Screw* what the billboard said. *Screw* the Willows Report. *Screw* calling Mom and Dad, God love 'em. *Screw* the whole fucking lot of it. *Screw* getting home late home tonight. I'm *already* home. I've *made* it home. Screw it *all*! Screw the whole fucking *world*.

"SCREW ME ONE MORE TIME, OFFICER."

THE SPELL OF GEORVAL
Mel Smith

Fearghal felt the pain before he was conscious. It seeped into every pore in his body and flowed through his veins with his blood. When consciousness arrived like a blow, his eyes quickly sought his lover.

Droost was watching him from across the dungeon, his arms chained above his head. Droost's face was drawn and tears streaked his cheeks.

Fearghal met Droost's eyes and they exchanged relieved smiles.

"How long was I out?"

"Half the night."

Fearghal tried to relax his shoulders but his arms were stretched and bound too far above his head to make comfort possible.

"Did you miss me?"

Droost smiled. "With every beat of my heart."

"Did he come?"

Droost's smile faded and his face tightened. He looked away from Fearghal.

It was all the answer Fearghal needed. "Are you all right?"

Droost nodded.

They were silent and Droost would not return Fearghal's gaze.

"Do you know what I would do, my love, if I were free now?"

Droost kept his eyes down, but a smile tugged at his lips.

"I would place my tongue at the space between your eyes and I would blaze a wet trail down your nose, across your lips, along your luscious throat and stop at the spot between your nipples."

Fearghal smiled as he watched his lover's flaccid organ begin to stir.

"I would lick and suckle those tiny, tender erections on your chest so gently and for so long that you would feel your testicles being pulled up through your body."

Droost's cock began to point towards Fearghal. His eyes rolled up and watched his lover as he spun his tale of their seduction.

"Your balls would suck into your body and travel up to your chest, drawn by the power of my lust for you. They would beat against your heart, then your sacs would be torn from one another, one to go to your left nipple and one to go to your right. I would suck each through your chest and into my mouth where I would caress their silken flesh with my tongue, until they were hard and swollen with your seed. And then, my love, I would burst them and your essence would fill me until, just before my death from drowning, I would achieve orgasm. My own semen would drench you and, suffocating, we would die together, free from this Earth and all of its tortures."

Droost's cock was now fully erect, bleeding its pearls of arousal.

"Fuck me," Droost whispered.

"Never the romantic, were you, my love?"

"I am romantic, but nothing in this life compares to being fucked by you. Fuck me, Fearghal. I need you deep within me."

"If set free, I would slam you to the wall and I would penetrate you with such force that you would feel the tearing of your anus in your hair. I would fuck you with a cock left untouched for too long and a love so great it will survive throughout the ages. I would plunge my sex deep within your bowels, over and over, each thrust harder and harder, until my balls rise into my throat and we explode together in a rapture of cum."

Droost threw his head back against the wall and he ejaculated into the air, a fountain of semen raining down onto the dungeon floor.

Fearghal smiled as he watched Droost slowly recover his senses. Before he did, though, Droost suffered an attack of emotion, which he was prone to do this last year of captivity.

Tears flowed down his cheeks and he seemed unable to catch his breath.

Fearghal soothed Droost with his voice, just as he had aroused him moments before. "We will be free someday, my love, I swear it. We will be free."

It took some time, but Fearghal was able to lull Droost to sleep. He tried to adjust his own pained body but sleep was a thing of the past for Fearghal. Consciousness and unconsciousness. Those were all that were left for him.

Droost did not get to sleep long, for Georval and his men arrived to take Droost to the Dragonfield. Fearghal had fought the day before and today was Droost's turn.

Georval stood before Fearghal. Fearghal looked down, away from the only man he had ever hated.

"I can smell the sex." Georval grabbed Fearghal's face in his hand and dug his nails into Fearghal's cheeks. "I've warned you about continuing with your perversions."

Georval's foul breath and the piercing of his nails made Fearghal's eyes water.

"Say goodbye to your lover. He's been weakening with every battle. I don't expect him to survive much longer."

Fearghal's stomach tightened. He tried to look at Droost, but Georval's grip was too strong.

Georval snapped his fingers. "Prepare him for battle. I'll be up shortly."

Fearghal heard Droost's chains being removed, then he heard Droost calling for him under his breath. "Fearghal."

It carried everything with it, that whisper from Droost; his love, his goodbye, his desire. Fearghal closed his eyes and heard it echo in his mind a thousand times in a span of a second.

The dungeon door shut as Droost was taken away.

Georval squeezed Fearghal's face harder. "Your suffering can end so easily. You know how to make it stop." Georval pressed his lips to Fearghal's ear. "Kill him. Denounce your vile relationship and kill him. You will be set free."

Fearghal did not answer. He had stopped answering ages ago, because Georval knew what his answer was.

Georval released Fearghal's face and stepped back. Pinpricks of blood marked Fearghal's cheeks.

"You'd be doing him a favor. He's not as strong as you. He'll die in battle very soon and it will not be a pleasant death. You could make it swift for him."

Fearghal stared at the ground, fighting back tears.

Georval's hand glowed as red as an ember. He grabbed Fearghal's cock and Fearghal screamed. Georval squeezed hard and smoke rose up between his fingers as flesh burned into flesh.

"This perversion you call love will be eliminated and it will be by your own hand, I promise you that. I will defeat you both. Your unnatural obsession with each other will cause you to suffer for the rest of your lives."

Georval released Fearghal's organ and left the dungeon. Fearghal hung at the end of his chains, sweat and tears dripping from his face. His cock was unmarred, lingering pain the only sign of Georval's torture.

Fearghal hovered on the edge of consciousness. Visions of Droost dying in battle brought him more pain than the fire from Georval. Fearghal knew what Georval said was true. Droost was weakening. Physically and mentally, he was losing the ability to endure. Only his love for Fearghal kept him alive.

Fearghal's head snapped up at the sound of the dungeon door opening, but it was only Brenjo, the dungeon keeper.

Fearghal hung his head again. The day-long wait for Droost to return was the greatest torture Georval had ever devised.

"You battled well yesterday. You get stronger every time."

Fearghal did not answer.

Brenjo set a pail of water on the floor at Fearghal's feet. He pulled a rag from the water and began to cleanse Fearghal's wounds. Fearghal closed his eyes. Brenjo's touch was the only pleasant physical contact left to Fearghal and Droost. He often dreamed it was Droost touching him. He kept his eyes closed to help the illusion.

"How was your awareness during the battle?"

It was impossible for Fearghal to maintain the fantasy with Brenjo talking.

"Worse. I blacked out for most of it."

"And the offering?"

Bile rose in Fearghal's throat. He did not want to remember. He had not told Droost about it.

"You wanted it, didn't you?"

Fearghal nodded. He opened his eyes and met Brenjo's gaze. "The desire to devour it it was so powerful, it took everything I had not to take it."

Brenjo shook his head. "It won't be long now."

"Isn't there anything we can do to stop it?"

"No."

Brenjo filled a cup with water from the bucket and let Fearghal drink.

"I need to tell you some things. The time is right."

Fearghal watched Brenjo as he overturned the bucket and seated himself on it.

Brenjo was ancient and tiny. He weighed but seventy five pounds and his face was nothing more than a dried piece of fruit. His eyes, though, were pinpoints of life; intense and brimming with a mystery that Fearghal had never been able to decipher.

"I know you've heard the stories about life before Georval began his reign. Droost and you were caught on the sea, so I know you've heard the legends of the ancestors who escaped to another land."

Fearghal nodded. "We did not really believe them, but dying together on the sea was better than the life we were living here. We couldn't touch for fear of discovery. There were some who suspected us and they followed us everywhere. More and more, Droost and I couldn't even be together. So we took the chance, but were caught while we pushed our boat from shore."

Brenjo nodded. "The stories are true. In the early days of Georval's rule, a large group fled to a land across the sea. I have faith that they flourished and still exist."

"How do you know this?"

Those intense eyes of Brenjo's fixed on Fearghal's. "I know."

Brenjo shifted his weight on the bucket. With the still wet cloth, he began to wash Fearghal's feet. "How much do you know about wizards?"

Fearghal shrugged. "I know they are immortal; only another wizard can kill them. I know that Georval is the most powerful wizard ever and he killed all the others. There has been no one but Georval for one hundred years now."

Brenjo scrubbed between Fearghal's toes. "Wizards do live a long, long time, but they are not immortal. Georval killed many other wizards and the rest fled to that land across the sea. There is only one other wizard left here, besides Georval."

Brenjo stopped his washing and looked up at Fearghal.

"When a wizard gets older and feels his powers diminishing, he takes on an apprentice. When the apprentice is ready to, he begins to take his mentor's powers. Eventually, the older wizard dies, but his powers live on in the younger one."

Brenjo stood on the bucket and loosened Fearghal's chains. Fearghal's wrists were still manacled but he was able to relax his shoulders.

Fearghal looked into Brenjo's eyes and waited.

"Georval was my apprentice."

Fearghal's mouth hung open as the tiny man climbed down from the bucket.

"When Georval was a child, he already had immense power but he could not control it. My powers were once great but had just begun to weaken. After our first year together, others warned me that Georval was becoming dangerous."

The life in Brenjo's eyes deadened and he took a deep breath. "I refused to listen. I loved the boy like I had loved no other. By the time I realized the others were right, it was too late. Georval had drained most of my powers and he was unstoppable. He killed every wizard who tried to. The others fled."

"Why were you spared?"

"He needed the rest of my powers. He wanted everything he could take. Now…I think he keeps me around because it amuses him."

Brenjo sat down on his bucket. Fearghal felt pain for him. The great sadness in his eyes could only come from love. Brenjo, Fearghal saw, still loved Georval.

"Why are you telling me all of this now?"

"Because a wizard can only be destroyed by a power greater than his own. Georval's power can be taken from him by a greater power and, I believe, when that happens his power or, at least my old power, will return to me."

Fearghal waited for more explanation but Brenjo offered none.

"Again, why are you telling me this?"

"Because Georval fears you."

Fearghal laughed. "Fears me?"

"You and Droost."

"The greatest wizard ever fears two men he has imprisoned and tortured for two years." Fearghal felt anger building in himself. "You're mad, old man."

"His hatred for you is so passionate, it must come from fear. One hundred and fifty years ago, when Georval began his rule, he slaughtered hundreds of people—parents and their children, lovers, husbands and wives. The result was that he made heroes of the dead. He raised love to an even nobler height. Georval realized he needed to turn people against each other; make them destroy their own love. That is when the tortures, games and battles began."

Brenjo paced. He seemed to relive those days as he described them to Fearghal.

"I saw mothers kill their own babies to stop the torture. Violence was rewarded. Ransoms were paid to those who turned in lovers. The games and battles became a kind of sex, and true sex became nothing more than breeding. That is when a love like Droost's and yours became the most reviled of all, because your love serves no other purpose. It exists purely because it is love."

Brenjo stopped pacing and looked through Fearghal. He was silent for a long time.

Fearghal spoke softly to bring Brenjo out of his reverie. "Why do you think Georval fears us?"

Brenjo blinked, then sighed. "You are the only ones, in all these years, he has been unable to divide. He can not conquer your devotion to each other. He can not even keep you from making love. When Georval comes in here and finds the evidence of your pleasure, despite the fact that he has you bound and separated, it enrages him. Even when he kept you in separate dungeons, you would call to each other and dream of each other and would continue to spill your seed for each other."

Brenjo laid his hand on Fearghal's chest.

"The spell is his only chance to defeat you. He will succeed if the transformation becomes complete. You will kill Droost."

Fearghal exploded in anger. "I will never. How can you say such words? I will not kill him. I will not."

Brenjo pressed harder on Fearghal's chest. "You won't have a choice. You know how strong the urges have become. You told me you have little awareness during the battle. You will have no control over what you do. And you will kill Droost."

Fearghal cried as his anger dissolved. Denying Brenjo's words was pointless. If Fearghal battled Droost, Fearghal would be the survivor. Fearghal had known it for months.

Brenjo wiped at Fearghal's tears then brought the bucket closer. He stepped onto it, tightened Fearghal's chains, and looked into his eyes.

"If you are the answer to Georval's destruction, we must discover how very soon. Time is running out."

Brenjo got down from the bucket and left the dungeon.

Fearghal wiped his face on his arms. Droost would be back soon and, although he would probably be unconscious, Fearghal did not want him to see his tears. Brenjo was probably insane and Fearghal felt it was best not to tell Droost of their conversation.

Droost was dragged into the dungeon moments later. The guards hung him by his chains and left.

Droost was unconscious. Flesh was torn in strips from his chest and stomach. A piece of his right thigh was missing and still oozed blood. Fearghal knew it had bled heavily by the dried stains streaking Droost's leg. His face was scratched on both sides and a large puncture in Droost's chest barely missed his heart.

Fearghal took a deep breath. He knew he had come very close to losing Droost this time.

"Can you hear me, my love?"

Droost did not stir.

"I love you."

Fearghal closed his eyes and tried to rest, now that he knew Droost had survived, but rest was impossible with Brenjo's strange words swirling in his mind. It was not possible that they could destroy Georval. Brenjo had to be mad.

Fearghal could not keep himself from thinking of that land across the sea, though. What if it did exist? To share his love for Droost openly would be an almost unimaginable joy.

Fearghal smiled as he saw them kissing in public, sharing a bed without constant fear, and making love with no thoughts other than the ecstasy they brought one another.

Droost's screams tore Fearghal from his fantasy. He opened his eyes, his heart pounding painfully.

Droost's eyes were huge with horror and he seemed incapable of stopping the scream.

Fearghal yelled over the frightening sound. "Droost. Droost. Look at me."

The screaming stopped, but he continued with a moaning whine. His eyes were unseeing and his body shook.

"Look at me, Droost. Look at me."

Droost's eyes shifted to Fearghal. Tears ran down his cheeks. The sounds softened to whimpers, but the horror had not subsided.

"What is it, Love? What's wrong?"

Droost could barely speak. "The offering." His eyes unfocused again. Fearghal knew Droost was back on the battlefield. "I took the offering."

Fearghal's stomach lurched and he tasted bile in his mouth.

Droost looked into Fearghal's eyes. "It was a baby. A girl baby. And I devoured her."

Droost suddenly vomited. He retched and sobbed until his stomach was empty. Fearghal fought his own urge to vomit.

"It's happened, Fearghal. It's complete. I had no awareness during any of it. There was nothing until now." Droost squeezed his eyes shut and cried harder. His voice was a whisper. "Oh, Lord, Fearghal. I can't go on. I can't do this anymore."

Droost's eyes flew open and he pleaded with Fearghal. "Please, Fearghal. Do what Georval asks. Denounce our love and kill me." He spoke faster as he saw the fury rising in his lover. "Please, Fearghal. We will battle soon and you will kill me, anyways. If you do it now, he'll set you free."

Fearghal's rage echoed in the small dungeon. "And what kind of freedom would that be? How free do you think I would feel without you, knowing I had killed you? Knowing I had denied my love for you. I won't do it. I won't."

Droost's eyes were so full of pain, Fearghal had to look away. Droost pleaded again. "Please, my love. I can't do this anymore."

Fearghal looked back into Droost's eyes. "Then you do it. Tell Georval you no longer love me and then slit my throat."

Droost's horror grew as Fearghal's words sank in, then he closed his mouth and looked away.

"Don't speak of it again, Droost."

Droost nodded, still looking away.

They were silent as Fearghal tried to calm himself. He watched his lover and felt joy and pain and love and sadness. Droost was, for Fearghal, all emotions. He was everything. He knew there could be no life for him without Droost.

"I need to hold you, Love. I need you in my arms."

Droost gave the tiniest shrug.

"My arms are tight around you. I am holding you close to me." Fearghal's eyes traveled slowly over his lover's body. He felt his cock stirring. "May I kiss you, Droost?"

Droost nodded. Fearghal saw the jewel-green eyes looking up through his lashes. Fearghal pushed his hips forward as his cock lengthened.

"Mmm. Your lips are so sweet. Like fresh raindrops on my tongue. That is how you always taste."

Droost's eyes dropped again. "I must taste putrid."

"You know you don't. Your taste has always aroused me."

Droost's voice was harsh. "I taste putrid. The evidence lies there in the dirt at my feet. I am foul."

"No!" Fearghal took a deep breath to keep the anger down. "That is not you, Droost. That is not us. Listen to me. We are not what Georval makes us."

Droost cried quietly, but nodded.

"Do you love me?"

Droost nodded violently.

"Tell me."

He raised his eyes and the tears in them made the green shimmer. Fearghal caught his breath. Droost was so beautiful.

"I love you."

"How much?"

"There is no way to measure it. My love for you beats in my heart. It is in every thought, every breath." Droost wiped his tears onto his shoulder. "I love you, Fearghal. I'm sorry for what I asked."

"I forgive you. Can I kiss you again?"

Droost smiled shyly. "Please."

"My tongue pushes through your lips and explores your sweet mouth. Your saliva is like honey to me. My hand holds your head and pulls you deeper. I will never get enough of you, my love. I can never get enough."

Droost's tongue ran along his lips. "Take me into your mouth, Fearghal. I want to feel myself swelling in your throat."

Fearghal smiled. "I am on my knees at your feet. My tongue leads the way down your body. It finds your cock, soft and beautiful. You know how much I love it like this. I hold your thighs and I simply look. The tip of your cock is peeking from your skin. I can't resist and I lick it as it emerges."

Droost squirmed and giggled.

"Ahh, I have found the source of your nectar. This is why you taste so wonderful. It oozes from your every pore."

Droost closed his eyes and sighed.

"I push your skin back as your cock grows. It is the color of seashells; so pink and lustrous. I can't stop...you are in my mouth and I am drooling, desperate for you. You fill me. You grow inside me. I can't breathe, but it does not matter because you give me life."

Droost rolled his head against the wall. His cock, erect and hard, glistened at the tip.

Fearghal's voice became desperate and breathless. "I am sucking you. Your balls are in my hands. They fill as I hold them. They feel like a heart, beating strong in my grasp. I let go of your cock and swallow your balls. I must have you, Droost. I must have you."

Fearghal closed his eyes. His breathing increased as his cock reached his belly.

"Your balls fill my cheeks and my tongue caresses them. I love you so, Droost. Sweet heaven, I love you so."

"Fuck me, Fearghal. Penetrate me. Fill me while I fill you."

"My mouth holds your cock and your balls. Your fluid drips down my throat with the rhythm of my heartbeat. I am so hard for you, it hurts. Your opening is so tight but it quivers for me. You want me to fuck you."

"Yes."

"You want me to enter you and pump my fluids into you. You want me to fuck you and fill your body with my seed while you fill me with yours."

"Yes. Fuck me. Lord, Fearghal, I love you. I need you. Fuck me."

Fearghal's cock thrust forward in rhythms he could not control. He felt the penetration. He felt Droost's body tight and hot on his cock. He smelled his sweet freshness and his intoxicating cum. His body lost control and he fucked the space between him and his love.

Droost's cry was agonized. "I love you, Fearghal!"

Fearghal's cock jumped and spurts of cream poured out and down his balls and thighs.

"I love you, Fearghal."

The dungeon door slammed open and Georval seemed to suddenly fill the room. His anger reverberated from the walls as Droost and Fearghal cringed.

"This vile perversion is forbidden. I have warned you and punished you and still you persist in your disgusting exchanges. No more."

Georval moved to Droost, blocking him from Fearghal's sight. Droost screamed and Fearghal's skin crawled. His heart tried to escape his chest, it beat so wildly. He fought against his chains, trying to reach Droost, but it was useless.

Droost's scream ended abruptly in a choking gurgle. Georval stepped aside and Droost's head dropped toward his chest. Blood flowed from his mouth and down his body.

Fearghal couldn't breathe. He tore his eyes from his unconscious lover and looked at Georval. A bloody piece of flesh hung from his fingers.

"Perhaps without a tongue, he'll find it more difficult to participate in these revolting acts of yours."

Georval walked slowly to Fearghal. He held the tongue in front of Fearghal's face and Fearghal vomited.

"This is what your depravity has brought you. This will always be the result of your unnatural acts. You caused this yourself."

Georval turned and left, Droost's flesh gripped in his hand.

Fearghal threw up again. He was unable to speak as his tears and bile choked him. He closed his eyes and listened to the moans of his lover.

"Can you hear me?"

Droost did not move. A puddle of blood formed at his feet.

"Droost?"

His head moved but the moans and gurgling were his only sounds.

Fearghal knew that Georval had the power to keep them from speaking simply by waving his hand, but he wanted the lesson to be as painful and horrifying as possible.

Fearghal's hatred for Georval made him shake. He threw his head back against the wall and he screamed. He screamed until no sound would come. He hung from his chains, exhausted, and watched Droost.

It was hours before Droost moved. Fearghal's eyes never left him.

"I love you."

Droost lifted his head. Dried blood caked his lips and chin. His eyelids were heavy; the jewels no longer sparkled. With effort, he focused on Fearghal.

"You are in my arms and we are free." Tears ran into Fearghal's mouth. "We sail like birds across the sea and we find our new home."

Tears cut stripes into the blood on Droost's face.

"We will spend eternity together, my love, free and unafraid. I promise you."

Droost leaned forward as far as his chains would allow. He closed his eyes, and his lips parted slightly.

Fearghal leaned forward and mirrored Droost. He pressed his lips together and kissed.

"I promise you."

Droost settled back against the wall. Fearghal watched until his lover's breathing told him that he slept, then he whispered, "I promise you we will be free."

In the morning, Brenjo came with food and water. Droost could not eat and Brenjo had to give him water very slowly. The inside of Droost's mouth was so swollen that merely swallowing his saliva was difficult.

Brenjo shed tears as he washed Droost. Fearghal had never seen the little man cry before.

"I heard he took the offering."

Droost pulled away from Brenjo and turned his head to the wall.

"He's lost his tongue, Brenjo, not his ears. Don't speak as if he were not here." Fearghal felt dead except for the pain that crushed his chest. Nothing mattered now but Droost.

"I'm sorry." Brenjo continued to bathe Droost. "Have you thought of how you might defeat Georval?"

Droost looked at Fearghal, puzzled.

"Pay no mind, Love. He's gone mad. He thinks we frighten Georval and hold the key to his destruction."

Droost smiled and made a sound like a laugh. Fearghal smiled back and the pain in his chest grew, then Droost's laugh became a violent cough. Brenjo hit him in the chest several times until Droost spit up blood.

Tears came to Fearghal again, as they had throughout the night. He spit out his words as he spoke between sobs. "Kill us, Brenjo. Kill us now. Maybe in death we can find the peace and dignity we have been denied in life."

Droost nodded repeatedly and made an odd humming noise.

Brenjo shook his head slowly. "I can't. Not if there's a chance you can defeat Georval."

"How can you let us suffer? Your idea is ridiculous. We have no power that could possibly harm Georval. Do the humane thing, Brenjo. Kill us."

Brenjo looked at them both, then shook his head again. "I can't."

Fearghal looked away with disgust. "Then leave."

Brenjo sighed. "As soon as you are fed."

Fearghal looked back at the old man in disbelief. "Do you think I would eat while Droost chokes on his own spit? You are even more mad than I thought. Leave."

Brenjo watched Fearghal for a long time before gathering his things to go.

"If you are the cause of Georval's destruction, I swear I will send you both to that land across the sea and you will be together for eternity."

Fearghal did not respond and Brenjo left.

247

Every day Brenjo brought food, but Droost could not eat and Fearghal would not. He refused to even talk to Brenjo.

On the third day Droost was able to take a small amount of food. Brenjo tore bread into tiny pieces and fed them to him, following every bite with a sip of water. Only after Droost was done would Fearghal take some food for himself.

Georval and his guards arrived as Brenjo was feeding Fearghal the last of the bread. Fearghal felt nausea at the sight of Droost's tongue worn round Georval's neck like an amulet.

Georval smiled and held it up. "Do you like it?"

Fearghal looked at Droost, whose eyes swam behind tears.

"You fight in two days. The guards will exercise you." Georval crossed the dungeon and stood by Droost. He ran his hand down Droost's throat, then his chest and down to his belly. He held Droost's cock and stroked it. "I'll stay here and exercise this one."

"Please, Sire. Please." Fearghal struggled against tears and nausea. "Please leave him alone."

Georval's free hand reached into his own britches. "Don't worry. We've exercised before together. I know what he needs."

Georval gripped Droost's organ harder and Droost whimpered. Georval looked at Fearghal and said, "Do as the guards order or he will lose more body parts."

Fearghal nodded and his tears broke free.

Droost tried to smile as Fearghal was led away, but Fearghal saw the terror in his lover's eyes.

Fearghal's exercise consisted of being forced to run until he collapsed. Without food for days and without real sleep for months, Fearghal quickly became exhausted and disoriented. He saw things that were not there and his mind was crowded with thoughts of Droost and the things Georval was doing to him.

Georval had always preyed more on Droost. Fearghal never understood it, for most of Georval's hate was focused on Fearghal. Then one day, as Droost screamed in pain at Georval's hand, Fearghal had cried out, "Why must you always punish him? Punish me instead," and Georval had smiled and replied, "That's precisely what I'm doing."

Now, Fearghal was given full buckets and told to hold them out from his sides. The guards ate while Fearghal's body quaked from the strain. When Fearghal let part of a bucket spill, one of the guards spit on him. "There goes one of your lover's body parts."

All of the guards laughed while Fearghal held his breath and ignored his pain, trying to keep the buckets aloft.

Fearghal did not understand how he could be weakening every day, yet get stronger with every battle. Droost simply got weaker, on and off the battlefield. He wondered if it was part of Georval's spell; if he wanted to ensure that when they battled each other, Fearghal would defeat Droost. Punish Droost so that Fearghal suffered; that was Georval's pattern.

When the guards finished their meal, they allowed Fearghal some water, then ran him back to the dungeon.

Fearghal was pushed through the door as Georval stood up from Droost's prone and unconscious body. Georval closed his pants and smiled at Fearghal.

"Hang them both back up. Tell Brenjo to feed and water them later."

Georval stopped in front of Fearghal and held his face close. "Even without a tongue, your woman screams well."

Fearghal tried to reach Droost, but the guards held him back.

"He spilled some of his bucket, Sire, while we were eating. I told him that would cost a body part."

"He spilt, did he?"

Fearghal sank to his knees and laid his head on Georval's boots. "I'm begging you, Sire. Please don't hurt him anymore."

"His suffering will end with his death. Confess your perversion. Tell me you have never loved him; that you despise yourself for ever having touched him. Tell me he is evil, then purge yourself with his death."

Fearghal buried his face in the dirt. It would be better to end Droost's suffering now, in this way, but Fearghal could not say the words. He was incapable of denying his love for Droost.

Georval kicked Fearghal away, then snapped his fingers. The guards dragged Fearghal to his chains and hung him by his arms.

"Hang that one back up, too. I'll remove a part when he is conscious. What would be the point of doing it now when he can not feel the pain?"

The guards chained Droost, then followed Georval out of the dungeon.

Blood trickled between Droost's thighs. His face was swollen, bruised and bloody. Burn marks, in the shape of a hand, covered much of his body. He made the same moaning, gurgling sound he made when Georval first took his tongue.

Fearghal hung his head, unable to look at Droost, and whispered over and over, "I'm sorry. I'm sorry."

Brenjo came later to feed them and give them water, but Droost could not be awakened. Brenjo cared for his wounds, then stared at Fearghal. He seemed to want to speak, but did not. Brenjo finally gathered his things and left.

Droost was unconscious for longer than ever before. When he did come around, Fearghal knew something was different.

Droost's jewel-green eyes were lifeless and empty. He was unresponsive to anything Fearghal said. When Brenjo came, Droost would not eat.

For hours Fearghal cried and pleaded, but Droost only stared at the ground, his eyes focused on nothing.

Finally, Fearghal took a deep breath and whispered, "Do you know what I would do, my love, if I were free now?"

Droost did not move.

"I would make love to you—glorious, joyous, soaring love—then I would find the sharpest knife and I would plunge it into your heart. As your suffering ended, I would kiss you farewell, then bury the blade through my own breaking heart." Fearghal caught his breath, the pain in his chest unbearable. "We would be free, my love, just as I promised you."

Slowly, Droost raised his eyes and focused on Fearghal's face. As Fearghal wept, Droost smiled and his crystal eyes smiled, too. He made a noise that sounded like a growl, but Fearghal sobbed, for he knew the sound was, "Thank you".

The next day, Fearghal was taken to do battle.

The Dragonfield was immense, with seats for spectators on either side. At both ends were the chains that kept the opponents from escaping. The chains were long and heavy but allowed freedom of movement during the battle.

Fearghal was led to the chains at one end of the field. There was only one, enormous manacle and Fearghal was placed in the center of it. He closed his eyes and pictured Droost—smiling and clean, his green eyes sparkling and the smell of raindrops surrounding him.

Fearghal took a deep breath and felt the transformation begin. He opened his eyes and the world before him shimmered. His lungs burned as if they would ignite. Fearghal's shoulder blades ached and swelled, then they ripped through his flesh and spread up and out. Fearghal threw his head back and screamed, sending flames into the sky from his mouth.

He breathed rapidly, trying to cool the burning and ease the pain, but he felt his arms bloating and he looked down at them. They expanded like bladders, the skin stretching tighter and tighter until the strain was too much. His arms split in two, the skin tearing from his hands to his shoulders. Fearghal's skin fell away, leaving behind scales as black as night.

His fingers began to lengthen and great, curving claws burst from the tips.

Fearghal's neck pounded and stretched. He had difficulty breathing as it grew and grew until the manacle was tight around his throat.

His vision became distorted. Colors changed, shapes were distinct but not recognizable. He felt as if he were spinning. Fearghal closed his eyes to stop the dizziness.

His spine began to throb, then a dagger of pain tore at his tailbone. His skin split open and a speared tail emerged, growing longer and longer until it equaled the length of his new body.

Fearghal raised his head and screamed again, but this time a roar came out. Flames shot even higher as Fearghal's wings began to beat. Instinctively, he tried to fly away but the chains, as usual, prevented his escape.

He closed his eyes tightly and concentrated on the image of Droost. He repeated to himself a chant, "I am Fearghal. I am human," but the blackness began to settle over his mind.

When the blackness lifted, Fearghal had his claws in the stomach of another dragon and his teeth were tearing at his opponent's throat. The sudden awareness made Fearghal release his grip. His opponent swung his head and hit Fearghal in the face.

Fearghal roared in pain. He did not want to fight; the urge to give up and allow himself to be killed was great. Droost's image loomed in his mind, though, and Fearghal whipped his tail against the other dragon and bit into his throat, just below the head. Blood flowed down his throat, arousing him and making him sick at the same time. The shrieks of his opponent hurt his ears and Fearghal felt the heat from the other's flame. The other dragon dug his claws into Fearghal's back, but all Fearghal could see was Droost unconscious on the dungeon floor, Georval's blood-covered cock dripping onto him. Fearghal felt his own blood pouring down his back, but the pain he felt was Droost's as Georval tore his tongue from his mouth.

Fearghal shook his head like a mad dog, his opponent's neck still in his mouth. He felt the other dragon loosen his grip. He felt the dead weight of the lifeless body in his grasp but still he continued tearing at and shaking his opponent. He swallowed chunks of meat and the taste of blood made his sex harden. Retracted inside his body for battle, the organ began to emerge.

Fearghal's mind hovered on the edge of darkness, between human awareness and bestial instinct. The more blood and flesh he consumed, the more aroused he became, yet he was sickened by what he was doing. He could not stop though, and he drifted to Earth, dropping his opponent on the ground and devouring him.

Fearghal heard cheering and saw shapes in the distance. He raised his head as high as he could, spread his wings wide, and cried out his agony. Flames filled the sky and blood covered Fearghal's face and body, soaking into the Earth as it dripped from him.

Fearghal heard a closer sound and his eyes focused on movement on the field. Less than twenty feet away, within easy reach of his serpentine neck, was a crying child of about six. He was chained at the ankle and tethered to the ground.

He was the offering; Georval's test to see if the transformation was complete.

Smoke puffed from Fearghal's nostrils. Spit hung in threads from his mouth, some reaching to the ground. His cock ached with his desire for more flesh.

Fearghal stretched his head towards the child. He could smell the fear and Fearghal's cock emerged completely. The child screamed as smoke swirled around his tiny body and Fearghal's saliva pooled at his feet.

The spectators were screaming and chanting. "Take it! Take it! Take the offering."

Fearghal's body trembled as he opened his mouth. The taste of blood, the smell of fear, the chaos of the screaming crowd excited Fearghal beyond thought. Semen, as molten and searing as the fire in Fearghal's lungs, oozed out of his organ and burned into the ground.

The child collapsed in the dirt and curled into a ball.

Fearghal tore the spike from the ground, but the child was too frightened to flee, so Fearghal turned away and laid in the blood-muddied dirt. He closed his eyes as he felt his transformation back to human begin.

As a dragon, the pain from his wounds was severe, but as a human, it was intolerable. Fearghal covered his head and drew his knees up to his chest but it was soon too much and Fearghal passed out.

When he regained consciousness, he was back in the dungeon. Droost was watching him, wide-eyed and anxious. Fearghal smiled and Droost relaxed.

Fearghal saw the fresh burns on Droost's body, including one on his cock. There was dried blood around his mouth and between his legs.

Fearghal shivered and lowered his head.

Droost made a noise and Fearghal looked back up at him. They smiled at each other and the familiar ache tore at Fearghal's heart.

"Was I out long?"

Droost nodded.

"I can see that Georval was here."

Droost looked down and nodded again.

"I didn't take the offering. I should have. Maybe that would end all of this sooner, but I couldn't do it. The child—he was about our age when we found each other."

Droost smiled, his eyes sparkling.

Fearghal laughed. "You remember that day? I snuck into that root cellar and was digging around for something to eat when I saw green eyes glowing in the corner. I thought I had gotten lucky and cornered a cat. I was drooling at the thought of catching it and having a real meal."

Fearghal's eyes flowed over Droost. He remembered precisely the delicious feelings Droost had awakened in him that day years ago.

"I crept closer and there you were, huddled in the dark. You were the most beautiful creature I had ever seen. I wasn't even sure you were human, you were so breathtaking."

Droost tried to look embarrassed but he was too pleased.

"We found snails and roots that we shared. I kept sneaking extra portions to you because you were so tiny, it frightened me. You were in my life for mere moments and already I was terrified of losing you. You were the first thing I ever loved. Before you, I didn't even know such a thing existed."

They looked at each other for a long time, so filled with their memories of each other that they were unaware of their growing erections.

"The moment I saw you and was drawn into those startling eyes of yours, my chest ached as if you had reached inside and were squeezing my heart. We've been together for fifteen years now and I still feel that pain every time I look at you."

Fearghal stopped to catch his breath. The memories were so vivid. "We spent that first night together under an abandoned wagon. I held you so tightly, you kept pushing me away because you couldn't breathe."

Droost smiled.

Fearghal's eyes and nose burned with approaching tears. "Did you know I did not sleep that night? I barely allowed myself to breathe. I was afraid you were a dream and in the morning you would be gone, so I kept my eyes open the entire night. How did you do that, my love? How did you capture me so completely with one look?"

Droost shrugged, then with a coy look up through his lashes, he ground his hips in a circular motion.

Fearghal laughed. "No, you weren't quite so whorish then. It was a while before we discovered those particular joys." Fearghal shook his head, still smiling. "If you had been a girl, life would have been so much easier. We could have fucked in the street and simply told everyone we were trying to make babies. But my heart was destined to belong to another boy. A boy with eyes like jewels, who tasted like new rain."

Fearghal's eyes again swept over Droost. Somehow, after all they had been through, he still looked like that beautiful, wide-eyed child to Fearghal. Then his gaze settled on Droost's full erection. Thick and dark and oozing pre-cum, it looked anything but innocent.

"A boy who had the sexual drive of a rabbit."

Droost laughed his raspy sound.

"We probably would have escaped detection if you hadn't required sucking or fucking every hour on the hour."

Droost's smile was huge. He pushed his hips, with their swollen, dripping appendage, towards Fearghal.

Fearghal laughed. "It has to be a quick one. We don't want to get caught."

Droost's head bobbed up and down.

"If I were free, I would bend you over the nearest object and fuck you so hard you couldn't breathe. I would squeeze your sac in my hand and hold back your seed until you said…"

Fearghal stopped. Tears blurred his vision as his heart was crushed. "You can't say it. You can't say anything. You were my precious gift and look what I have allowed to happen."

Droost squeaked and shook his chains, trying to stop Fearghal.

"I'm so sorry, Droost. I should have killed you when Georval first told me to. I should have spared you all of this." Fearghal sobbed. He felt suddenly unable to continue and he wanted life to simply cease. "I should have never loved you. I should have walked away from you so you could live a normal life, but I couldn't. Forgive me, Droost. I couldn't." Fearghal's voice dropped to a whisper. "I needed you too much."

Droost's cock softened as he watched his lover's body shake with tears and guilt he could no longer control. When Fearghal quieted, Droost made three short hums.

Fearghal whispered back, "I love you, too."

In the morning, Droost was taken away to do battle. Fearghal was more frightened than ever. The only thing that kept Droost fighting before was his love for Fearghal. Without that awareness, he would be fighting on instinct and, as weak as he was, Fearghal feared it would not be enough.

A small grate in the dungeon ceiling let Fearghal know if it was day or night. Darkness came and Droost had not returned. Neither of them had been kept past nightfall after a battle before.

Fearghal called for Brenjo, hoping the old man could tell him what had happened, but Brenjo did not come.

When the light from the grate began to pinken, Fearghal screamed Droost's name. By the time the dungeon door finally did open, the midday sun shone down through the opening and Fearghal's voice was nothing but a rasp.

Two guards dragged Droost into the cell. Brenjo followed them in. Droost was hung by his left arm; his right hung twisted and limp at his side. A large chunk of flesh was missing from his right side and Fearghal could see bone. Droost's right eye was so severely disfigured, Fearghal was not sure the eyeball was still there. Fearghal tried to call Droost's name, but no real sound came out.

The guards left and Brenjo sat on the ground at Droost's feet, his back against the wall. Occasional spasms shook Droost's body but he was otherwise lifeless.

Brenjo fell asleep. Unable to even speak to his lover, Fearghal waited.

The sun was rising again when Droost moaned and laid his head back against the wall. Fearghal tested his voice and he was able to say Droost's name.

Droost moaned again, but did not open his unswollen eye.

Brenjo awoke and examined Droost. He wet a cloth and cooled Droost's face.

Fearghal tried again. "Droost. Please look at me."

Droost's left eye fluttered, but a spasm shook him and he did not open it.

"I need to see your eyes, my love. Please open them."

Droost moaned and his eye fluttered again, then he slowly opened it. Fearghal sighed when Droost's one good eye focused on him.

"I missed you."

Droost tried to smile, but his head fell forward and he seemed to be unconscious again.

It was days before Droost was fully conscious. Brenjo visited several times daily, caring for Droost's wounds and feeding and watering them both. He tried to talk of the future, but Fearghal would not respond. He wanted only to be alone with Droost.

When they were alone, Fearghal talked for hours. He tried not to speak of sex, but it was impossible for the two of them not to arouse each other. They avoided detection but one of them usually ended in tears. They could not hide from the truth; their time together would end soon

The day of Fearghal's next battle, he stood on the Dragonfield and chanted his chants, the vision of Droost filling his mind. The blackness settled in, though, and it did not lift until he awoke in his cell.

Fearghal's first awareness was a flash of images from the battlefield. The strongest image was of him accepting the offering.

Like Droost, Fearghal vomited until his stomach was dry. When he was finished and he looked up, Droost's eyes told him that he understood.

The next day, Droost did not battle. Georval did not want him killed before his battle with Fearghal.

Their last days together were an endless series of tortures. Georval abused Droost in every imaginable way as Fearghal was helpless to do anything but watch.

The day before their battle, they were exercised separately. Georval left them alone. Brenjo fed them extra rations and did not try to talk.

When they were finally alone, and the light in the dungeon was softening, Fearghal said, "After tomorrow, my love, he can no longer hurt us. The one who survives will be dead without the other, so there is nothing he can do to harm us."

Droost nodded. His left eye sparkled still, the green so clear and brilliant Fearghal, as always, could not breathe.

"If I were free, do you know what I would do?"

Droost smiled and closed his eye.

They made love throughout the night. Fearghal caressed every part of Droost's body with his voice. He fucked him with bone-crushing power, and with a tenderness so divine it moved them both to tears. They filled each other's mouths with their hardened flesh, and their throats, stomachs and bowels overflowed with each other's semen. They kissed with such passion that they cried out from the ecstasy, and their lips explored one another so softly, they felt almost afraid.

They relived memories from their years together and they performed acts that were impossible outside of their minds. They said goodbye without words and expressed their love with touches that did not exist except within their hearts.

When the sun came through the grate, Georval and his men entered the dungeon. The lovers' seed muddied the dirt that lay between them and the smell of their lovemaking overpowered the stench of the cell.

Georval's anger was immense. He ordered the guards to take Droost to the Dragonfield immediately, then he stood in front of Fearghal. "You will kill him today. You will consume his dead body. When you awaken, you will remember every blow you struck and every pain you caused him. The flavor of every bite of his flesh and every drop of his blood will linger in your mouth forever. I will keep you alive, here in this dungeon, and I will make you suffer every moment you live." Georval pressed his mouth to Fearghal's ear and whispered, "You are mine now."

His tongue flicked into Fearghal's ear and bile filled Fearghal's mouth. Georval held Fearghal's cock and squeezed with all his strength. "I have won. You have paid for your sickness."

Georval released Fearghal and snapped his fingers. The guards unchained him and led him to the field.

Fearghal was held in the center of the manacle and he saw Droost at the far end of the field. He felt panic because he could not see Droost's eyes. He shouted "I love you" as loudly as he could but, of course, there was no response.

The transformation began and Fearghal flooded his mind with visions of Droost. He held his breath and chanted a new chant. "Let us die together. Let us die as one."

His human skin began to split and, as always, the pain was great. Fearghal did not feel it, though, because the pain in his heart was far greater.

His vision distorted and he could no longer see Droost. Fearghal called out again, but his voice was now a roar, with flames that could destroy his love.

Fearghal screamed the chant in his head, but soon the blackness swallowed his mind.

When Fearghal awakened, he was confused by what he saw. He was still on the battlefield and in front of him was a dragon; a dragon so beautiful, Fearghal could not breathe. Its scales were purple and iridescent; the stomach green and shimmering, like jewels in the sun.

Fearghal looked into its eyes and they were smiling at him, clear and sparkling and undamaged.

Fearghal threw back his head and roared, sending his flames to the heavens. The crowd cheered with excitement and Georval smiled, his long-awaited battle about to begin.

Fearghal looked back at Droost, then they flew at each other. They collided in mid-air and the crowd rose to their feet. With their limbs and tails entangled, Droost wrapped his neck around Fearghal's. His head came to rest under his lover's chin.

Fearghal's cock emerged and, shielded from the crowd by Droost's body, it penetrated Droost's anus, sinking deep into his bowels.

Droost's neck snaked away from Fearghal's and he flung his head back. He screamed and writhed and the crowd went wild, believing Droost was in agony. Only the lover's knew it was pleasure Droost felt; a pleasure so divine and so long-denied that it did, indeed, resemble agony.

Fearghal and Droost beat their powerful wings against each other. Fearghal's teeth bit softly into Droost's throat and he held him as he began to stroke in and out of his body. He tasted Droost's flesh and his organ grew still larger as he was flooded to the core with the freshness of raindrops—that wondrous flavor of Droost he had dreamed of for so long.

Fearghal's passion became frenzied and he bit deeper into his lover's throat. He fucked faster and faster, matching the rhythm of their beating hearts and wings.

The crowd's applause was thunderous as they watched blood drip from Fearghal's mouth.

Droost screamed and wailed, his body thrusting against Fearghal in violent rapture. He tried to keep his organ withdrawn, but it began to emerge and it dripped its molten pre-cum onto Fearghal's tender belly.

Fearghal let go of Droost's neck and roared. Flames shot into the stands and spectators scattered, all but two escaping death.

Georval gripped the sides of his dais. His cock was rigid as he watched the former lovers twist and claw, convinced they were fighting to the death.

Fearghal and Droost grew delirious as they fucked in front of Georval, flaunting their love for each other before their enemy and his people. The sounds of their lovemaking filled the sky, inciting the crowd to an even greater frenzy. Fearghal's hind legs crushed Droost to him and plunged his organ deeper into his lover with every penetration. With a final blow that shook the stands, Fearghal's cock exploded into Droost. His seed, as searing as the heat in his lungs, filled Droost's bowels. Droost's own cock emerged fully and his semen sprayed Fearghal, burning a trail down his body and seeping into his anus.

The lovers screamed as one and, still tangled together, they soared heavenward, their joy making them forget. They flew higher and higher, their necks entwined, their faces pressed together and their bodies still coupled. Semen ran down their tails and rained onto the field below, sending up plumes of smoke as it burned into the ground.

The sounds of the crowd were far below and Fearghal and Droost believed they were free. Droost pulled his head back and the happiness in his eyes made Fearghal sing.

Then they hit the ends of their chains and were jerked back down toward Earth. Fearghal's cock began to slip from Droost's body and Droost clawed desperately at Fearghal. Fearghal bucked and thrust, but he could not maintain their union. As Fearghal's organ slipped from Droost's grasp, Droost pressed his head against Fearghal's chest. His tears, as cold as ice, ran down Fearghal's body and washed away the smoldering evidence of their lovemaking.

Droost looked up at Fearghal and he made three short hums. Fearghal made four back and licked Droost's tears away.

Fearghal raised his right front leg and, with his claws fully extended, he buried them deep into Droost's heart. Droost sighed and his moist eyes smiled at Fearghal, then he slid from his lover's embrace.

The spectators were ecstatic, applauding as Droost fell to the ground. They chanted Fearghal's name as he drifted back to Earth, following his dying lover.

Georval's face was frozen in a look of rapture as he rubbed his crotch against the dais and watched Fearghal land next to Droost. Georval's victory would soon be complete. Fearghal would tear Droost to pieces and consume him, then Fearghal would be Georval's. Georval rubbed harder as he thought of the years he would have amusing himself with Fearghal.

Fearghal's feet touched the ground next to Droost. Droost began to sparkle and shimmer. Fearghal shed tears as his lover returned to his human form. Fearghal spread his wings and raised his face to the sky. The sound of his broken heart pierced the air and could be heard throughout the countryside, stunning the crowd to silence.

Georval neared orgasm as Fearghal raised his right front leg, the claws dripping Droost's blood. Georval's cum soaked his britches as Fearghal's claws slashed downward. Then, too late, Georval shouted with realization.

Fearghal's claws plunged deep into his own chest, piercing his heart in five places. He laid his head across Droost and he covered him with his wings. He looked into Droost's smiling eyes and Fearghal felt himself transforming.

Georval swept his arm through the air, trying to transport himself to the lovers and prevent their deaths, but Georval's powers would not respond. He screamed at his men to retrieve the bodies and he jumped from the dais, running with them.

Human again, Fearghal pressed his lips to Droost's. Their tears mingled as he whispered, "We're free now, my love. We're free."

With Georval and his men nearly upon them, Fearghal and Droost kissed. As their blood flowed together, the lovers shared their final breath.

Georval stood over the dead bodies and screamed with fury at being defeated. Powerless to do anything else, he ordered his men to mutilate the lovers. The guards raised their weapons but the bodies began to rise.

Georval's men looked at him but he was as stunned as they were.

The bodies began to swirl, like leaves in the wind, faster and faster until, in an explosion of dust, they became birds.

The birds flew round each other, beating their wings together and filling the air with their joyous song. They flew straight up, higher and higher, dancing and twirling until they were almost out of sight, then they turned and flew together towards the sea.

Georval flung a spear after them, but it was useless. Only their song lingered.

Enraged and powerless, Georval began striking at his men. As the guards swarmed over their former leader, a wizened old man floated down from the stands and, smiling, headed toward the sea.

COLLAR OF STRANGE NON-EXCHANGE
Michael Huxley

While musing stereotypes that evoke
flashes of the non-filters you smoke,
joints you toke, brew you suck,
and cheerleaders you'd
so love to… *stoke*
in the bed of your truck,
you emerge as if by invocation,
spattered with tar and dirt,
your T-shirt stripped off
while paving the road,
compelling my I-beam to goad
the bronzed dream of your gritty skin,
slaving hotter than sin
beneath a sweaty sky ablaze.

The rub, oh blue-collar guy,
is that though we both
are men of strong desire,
my glance alone will raise your ire,
but you needn't deal me
such a scathing dagger
by looking so askance;
it's the proletarian swagger
of your jeans and boots
the tool belt slung so low,
the long, disheveled hair,
the scowling face and beard,
the tattooed arms, the furry chest
—and not you per se—
I like the very best.
So be advised, blue-collar dude,
not to misconstrue my response
as anything more than that,
and save your precious attitude
for the much bigger scrimmage

Michael Huxley

of living up to
so intensely wrought an image.

When just a child
it was much the same:
I thought you admirably wild,
myself longingly tame,
for even then I knew,
when you dunked me
in the phys-ed pool at school,
you wanted to be rid of me
'cause even wet
the teacher's pet
represented a threat
to you who realized,
if only subconsciously,
that your budding caricature
of masculinity alone
would never set you free.
Perhaps it's the cruelty
of days like that gone by
that make you now
so easy to objectify.

Clearly the high-minded strife
of my fantasy life is rife
with brief encounters with you,
oh blue-collar tease,
but put your little mind at ease,
for it's just a harmless game I play
called *Blow Me Away*
that's all of you I'll ever need:
a conjured passion reduced
abruptly to seed procured by hand,
then returned to the land
where, sown amongst your crew,
you'll earn your simple wage or two,
while I tend the squalling issue
conceived of ink and page,
—both borne back by uncanny knack
to each his separate box:
you, the unsuspecting fox

and me, the supposed brain
—neither ever hoping to gain
a mutual trust in doing
what we feel we must
to insure that the tradition
of lust and longing to be held
in each other's desirous disdain
will forever remain

the weld of strange non-exchange.

Bigger than Life

A novella by
Don Luis de la Cosa

BIGGER THAN LIFE
Don Luis de la Cosa

Johnny

"I had a similar experience, once."

Johnny paused, staring through the flames that leapt between him and his camping mates, and smiled at the flood of memories that washed over him. Although he thoroughly enjoyed recalling this part of his past, Johnny wouldn't have normally revealed this story to a group of strangers, but given that everyone else was spilling their guts while passing around a jug of home brew, he figured who the hell cared? No one would remember it in the morning anyway.

"He burned me."

"Yeah, I've been burned before!" came from somewhere in the large circle that had gathered around the open pit.

"Right, but I mean he *literally* burned me," Johnny clarified. "Like with brands and such. The man was a fetishist. Why did I stay with him? It's not that he was the sexiest man alive, or all that great in bed, or had an incredibly huge cock. It was more that… I couldn't help but love him."

"So, why did you finally break up?"

"'Cause he broke his own rules," Johnny sighed with resignation, his response having drawn more than a few confused looks from the many men in attendance. As if meant to add emphasis, a late night zephyr breezed through the site and lifted the scent of roasting beast to everyone's nostrils. The man in charge of the roasting looked Johnny's way and grinned through his beard. An immense specimen of manhood, his leather vest and matted body hair was redolent of a torture master in a medieval castle. The man in question, a certain Carlo, slathered more herb paste on the roasting beast, smiling with unspoken intent as he carefully absorbed every word of Johnny's discourse.

"We didn't meet at a point when I was weak, or following an extremely messy break up," Johnny continued. "Nor was it my first relationship ever or a morbid fascination with the dark underbelly of the sexual arena. No, I actually met Fernando under surprisingly normal circumstances."

"Well *that* doesn't sound like any fucking fun," spat a particularly noisome listener.

"Wait! That's not the end of the story," Johnny shot back. Undeterred, rising from amongst the circle, the disgruntled man harrumphed and headed back to his tent for… only the *gods* knew what, but, given the way the last couple of days had unfurled, it could have been most anything.

Johnny resumed his story. "All *righty* then, where was I? Oh yes, how we met…

"Fernando's a relative of my mother's best friend from South America who brought him to a dinner party at my mom's place when he was staying in Chicago for a time—I can hardly believe it's over five years ago now—and somewhere between cherries flambé and dessert wine, we really started to click. After dessert, he and I took off together on our bikes for a nice long ride up Lakeshore Drive in the warm moonlight of summer, choosing the longest possible route back to…"

"Hey," shouted the man who had left the circle, reemerging from his tent. "I thought you said this was gonna be interesting!"

"I'm… just about to *get* to that bit," replied Johnny, more than a bit disconcerted. "*Jesus*, man, don't get your panties in a bunch! What I was *going* to say was… the longest possible route back to *his* place where, in no time flat, we ended up naked in his pool."

"*Now* you're heading in the right direction!" said the heckler, reclaiming his seat in the circle. Johnny shot him a dirty glance and the jerk finally quieted down, a stupid grin plastered on his face. To everyone's relief, Johnny continued.

"Seeing that we were both already naked, I decided to skip the pleasantries and got straight to the point the second we'd finished rinsing the road dust off our bodies in the pool, and… Fernando certainly didn't offer any resistance.

"Well, needless to say we were enjoying the hell out of one another: the two of us kissing uncontrollably, the water churning as our bodies collided, weightless and slippery as seals, our cocks pounding with desire just below the water's surface. My god, it was *heaven*," Johnny sighed passionately. "Anyway… we eventually retired to the bedroom, where we continued what we'd begun in the pool. He took everything I had to give, seeming, in his frenzy of pleasure, completely nonplussed, yet at the same time, entirely *focused—on me*. I don't know how else to put this, but… I felt almost as if I were being *auditioned*. In any event, I collapsed with exhaustion after experiencing perhaps the most violent orgasm of my life up 'til that point, only to wake the next morning and find him missing."

"*Missing*, from his own house?" someone from the circle asked, adding: "I've heard of the coyote syndrome, but that's pretty bad."

"Well, turns out he wasn't *really* missing, but in the kitchen, assembling an impressive breakfast, and I mean *impressive*. Various fruits, fresh croissants, a three-foot-long baguette, a huge mound of creamery butter, an assortment of jams and compotes, filet mignon served with poached eggs: all of this and more was awaiting my arrival at the table.

"Handing me a mug of good strong coffee, Fernando said, 'I see you found the robe I laid out for you. Cream, sugar...?'

"'Huh? Oh, uh... no—black is fine,' I replied. 'I'm really not sure what to make of all this. I mean... *wow*, I just woke up! This is a completely new experience for me.'"

"'*Well*, then! Sounds like you might need a little stimulation, a bit of *coercing* to make all of this a little less surreal. Come over here, you beautiful man, and lay across my lap.' Figuring his game would prove a prelude to something fun, I complied, but after lifting the bottom half of my robe like I was a naughty child, he gave me three sharp whacks with his bare hand before I had the presence of mind to jump off his lap and out of harm's way.

"'*Whoa*, dude,' I yelled. 'What the fuck are you doing?'

"'Still sleepy?' he smirked, his one cocked eyebrow registering amusement at my predicament.

"'Jesus *Christ*!' I wailed, rubbing the sting out of my cheeks. 'Not anymore!'

"'Good,' he replied cheerily, as if nothing whatsoever out of the ordinary had occurred. '*So*... Have a seat before your breakfast gets cold.'"

Carlo, lovingly marinating the roasting beast, and several others in the crowd chuckled lasciviously at the idea of Johnny being turned over *their* knees, but the handsome storyteller was too caught up in verbally recreating that fateful morning to pay them much mind.

"My indomitable sense of pride would normally have compelled me to leave the house immediately after being treated like that, but for some reason, I couldn't tear myself away from him. Besides, I was suddenly famished, so much so in fact that I wasn't sure I'd be able to make it home! And so, wincing a bit, I sat down and ate. And ate and *ate*...

"Sipping our coffee luxuriantly on the living room sofa after breakfast, we slowly rolled together and began to cuddle. Well, next thing you know, we were getting it on again *big*-time. Taking control of the situation before I had a chance to instigate a repeat performance of the night before, Fernando took full possession of my body, and as it all seemed so natural, I gladly allowed him to.

"After our morning aerobics were magnificently concluded, a maid entered and began clearing plates and picking up in the kitchen. Overly made up and dressed stereotypically in a frilly white apron over a black dress that was far shorter than one might have expected, she uttered not one word the entire time she was in our presence. As she had walked in at precisely the same moment we'd finally caught our breath, wiped up a bit and pulled our robes back on, I couldn't help but wonder how long she might have been watching us, not to mention what a fine visual that would have made. Sure enough, she smiled and winked at me as she stooped over to gather the empty cups and saucers from the coffee table. Discreetly glancing up her skirt, it became immediately apparent that 'she' was in fact a he.

Don Luis de la Cosa

"I might mention here that Fernando and I were most definitely not alone on the property. In fact, as we crossed through his house on our way to the courtyard, I noticed workers—landscapers and pool maintenance guys—many of whom were suspiciously good-looking, in every corner of the yard. Naturally, I thought it odd, how they all looked up and acknowledged our presence in passing with overly-familiar gestures and smiles, but dismissed the thought as I hurriedly followed Fernando to the shower station by the side of the pool, where we washed away the evidence of our passion in comfortable silence.

"Afterwards, I put my dirty clothes on, kissed what I assumed would be my fabulous one-night-stand farewell, hopped on my Harley, and sped home, far from completely in sync with my surroundings—a definite hazard when riding a bike.

"The following day, I went to work. I'd inherited a position as journeyman electrician from my father, and had to finish rewiring the bottom two floors of an office building, but every molecule of my ass was aching, and I was unable to focus the entire day until later that evening, when I went to the gym; but even there, it wasn't until after a half-baked workout, until I entered the steam room, until I found *him* again, did the fog begin to lift.

"I had no idea he was in there until he dragged a feathery finger across one of my shoulders after creeping up silently behind me. I wheeled around in place, only to see his tattoos disappearing into the mist, and recognizing them, my heart beating wildly, I followed, only one step behind him. All at once Fernando turned, caught me in a great bear hug and, shoving me toward the wall, started kissing me deeply. I'm still trying to figure out if he knew the hot steam jet was right behind me or not. Fernando never *impressed* me as being particularly unobservant, but…"

No one listening needed any additional information to know what was coming next.

"…Needless to say, I ended up with my ass getting mildly scalded, but something strange happened in the exchange: It seems I *liked* it, and Fernando *saw* that I liked it. After that I was his completely. Over dessert and coffee following the gym, he told me he'd been observing me from a distance for quite some time, but hadn't figured a good-enough angle for approach until miraculously discovering the connection between his third cousin-or-whatever and my mother. His arranging the fateful dinner invitation was easy enough, and… the rest is history."

The jug came around, and Johnny took a long swig of the potent brew in an effort to further loosen his tongue—an effort that proved successful.

"I spent the next year with him, during which time he demonstrated, in no uncertain terms, what it meant to be sexually dominant. Up until my involvement with Fernando, I figured I'd pretty much worked all that out of my system, taking my flagrant sexual conquest of the entire club scene into account, but I soon found out… differently.

"First, he trained me to serve him, to satiate his desires, to read his moods. I learned how to approach him, how to conduct myself by his side in social situations, precisely how quick to respond when summoned, how he liked to have his dick sucked. Each infraction of a rule that had been clearly established was met, first with a blaze of icy blueness that only his eyes are capable of, followed by... an appropriate number of whacks, either in public, or when we got home, depending on the situation.

"I had free reign of most of the house, but certain parts were off limits. Naturally, I thought that a bit strange and quickly grew dissatisfied with his not allowing me to view what was behind the proverbial curtain. So one morning fairly early on, I ventured into the hallway that led to the forbidden wing of the house. Thanks to the impeccable soundproofing, insulation, and solid-core doors lining the hallway, ghosts tap-dancing on cotton would have made more noise than what I heard coming from behind the forbidden door. Surprisingly, I found it unlocked! Upon entering, my first glance found the room normal enough, conforming perfectly to the rest of the complex with its antique furniture and artwork and crystal service pieces. But then I noticed that one the bookcases was turned at an odd angle, and upon further investigation discovered a passageway behind it that led to the first evidence of sound I'd heard all morning."

"Oh, *wow*... Secret passageways! The plot thins!" the same heckler spewed as sarcastically as before. Johnny, resolving to do something nasty to him later, put forth his best effort to ignore the prick.

"*Anyway*... I'd found his private dungeon, which he used as a means of supplementing his trust fund payments with American money, but I'm getting ahead of myself here. As I was soon to discover, all of the men who worked on his estate, served him in his parlor and catered to his machinations, were paying *him* for 'training services,' to become precisely the servants that they were. Several of them were permanent fixtures who lived in 'the stables' I'd stumbled onto. Those amongst them who held jobs outside the compound willingly allowed their incomes to be absorbed into Fernando's estate. I found all of this out much later, however, as I was stopped by one of the slaves before I could even set foot inside the chamber.

"That's when I received my first brand. The guard was twice my size, easily, and wore a hood to obscure his identity. He had no distinguishing marks, not even a scar that was visible. He was totally prepared, as if he new I would be arriving. He blindfolded and cuffed me roughly, forced me to my knees, then stepped on my neck, forcing my head to the floor. All at once I heard the screams of someone I'd noticed who was tied or chained to a nearby wall, but I was rendered completely unable to move and terrified beyond any rational consideration of escape. I heard a whip falling on the captive's body time and again, although I could see nothing but the floor at that moment, as I awaited my fate. Before I was released from off the floor, I recognized a pair of Fernando's boots striding towards me slowly, and all-too-familiar whiptails began dragging

271

gently across my body. I had innocently neglected to dress before curiosity compelled me to wander away from where I'd been sunbathing, and it soon became clear how grave an error that had been. Since I could only hear with one ear, I had to strain to listen to the monster's voice.

"'I was wondering how long I'd have to leave the door unlocked and the bookcase ajar before you moseyed in here."

"What's this all about?" I screamed, "What have I done?"

"'Nothing,' he said, 'but it was the appropriate time for something more to happen.' I had never heard Fernando's voice sound quite like that: slow, deep, measured. I was positive something drastic was about to happen, and I must admit that, despite my fear, the suspense was killing me. He continued to drag the tails across my back and thighs, letting them swing between my legs and tease my scrotum, occasionally sweeping them past my ass in a feint promise of a whipping. I finally became truly frightened. Not because Fernando hadn't whipped me before, but because I was almost positive at that point that I *wasn't going to be* this time."

Carlo, tending the roasting beast was on the edge of his makeshift seat. Some of the juices from the meat dripped onto the coals and hissed as they vaporized. Everyone listening had the same thought sizzling in their minds: heated steel singeing flesh.

"Who likes it rare?" Carlo called out with a knowing chuckle, indicating—despite the fact that the climax of Johnny's story still lay ahead— that dinner was officially being served. People began queuing up for their helping of roast beast, but there was none of the usual chatter as everyone kept their attention focused on Johnny, whose voice became nostalgic as beers were passed around to wash down the main course.

"He did whip me after all, for you see, skin that has been pre-warmed is much more pliant and accepting of what mine would soon be experiencing. The whipping certainly wasn't the worst I'd ever received; Fernando seemed to know exactly how much preparation was required as, lying prone on the dungeon floor and quivering over the prospect of what was to follow, I heard a bellows whooshing and coals crackling in the fireplace. Whatever I was in store for, it was guaranteed to be very, very *hot*.

"'It is time that you bear my symbol, Johnny,'" Fernando stated simply. "'All of my properties wear them with a tremendous sense of pride as it is an internationally recognized emblem that identifies one as intrinsically linked to a network of the best-trained submissives on the planet. Seeing that you've demonstrated several months of exemplary service, I feel I can trust you to represent me." That stated, a blanket of silence fell over the dungeon, as the bellows continued to stoke Fernando's dastardly purpose. Not even the man bound to the wall was making any noise at that point. After several minutes, I felt some sort of cream being applied to my lower back and then… the approach of heated metal.

"'This may feel a little—How shall I say it?—*warm*.'"

"With that, Fernando slammed the red-hot steel against my flesh and held it there. I screamed in agony and bucked as authentically as any thoroughbred horse would have, although the far-larger guard assisting Fernando was able to keep my lower back surprisingly still. As soon as he was sure that the mark would be permanent, Fernando pulled the iron away and his guard released me at last. I guess I wasn't the stallion I'd supposed, because I collapsed. I'd never experienced such pain, am not positive I was even fully conscious; yet lying there, I couldn't help but think about how much I reveled in Fernando's attention, how loving and (in his own way) *gentle* he'd always been with me, and about how long I'd waited to feel that I was truly "his." Fully aware that this barbaric branding was symbolic of his finally claiming me as such, that he'd imparted an indelible mark that would, for all time, communicate to whoever saw it that I was his property, I smiled with satisfaction.

"How long I remained in the dungeon that day is beyond me, but I do remember that when I was finally returned to the main house, it was dark outside.

"For the remainder of our relationship, whenever we were out, he made sure to show off his mark on my body to everyone in the room. At every single club he took me to, people seemed to have an innate fear of Fernando, even though they might have drooled over me when we entered, the moment anyone saw the mark they backed off."

Johnny pulled his pants down to display the brand, whereupon jaws dropped and plates clattered to the floor. Apparently, there were more than a few people in the crowd familiar with the mark as well.

"That's... that's..." stammered several of the attendees.

"Yeah, that's it," Johnny confirmed. "And it's important to mention here that I'm possibly the only man to have escaped Fernando's service free and clear. I'm still unsure whether or not that's something to be proud of."

"That's... impossible!" blurted Carlo, hacking a slice of rare roast beast with a knife the length of his forearm. "I know this... '*Fernando*' and no one has EVER left his service without paying a price. You'd better provide us with a very good explanation by the end of your story, my friend," Carlo sneered, edging toward Johnny menacingly while licking the knife's blade clean of dripping-red *au jus*.

"He loved me too much," Johnny stated emphatically. The sudden declaration stopped everyone listening dead in their tracks. No one dared to move. Even the fire seemed to quiet down until it popped, loudly, and anyone who'd ever heard a whip snap close to their flesh jumped out of their seat.

"My relationship with Fernando had had always been one of strict service, 'til one day, he called me at work—something he'd never done before— inviting me to dinner that night. Now, our history had thus far proven that by accepting such an invitation, I could expect the rest of the night to be spent

273

getting clamped, tied, suspended, and whipped, not to mention sucked, rimmed, fucked, and whatever else his devious mind had concocted in the hours we were apart. As appealing as the proposition was, I begged to decline knowing full well I had to be at work hours earlier than usual the following day and explained as much to him. He told me not to worry, that his plans only included eating, and our sleeping next to one another. Taken aback by such a foreign request, I reluctantly agreed to his plan, wary of severe repercussions should I persist in declining.

"When I arrived at his place later that evening, he was in the midst of cooking of course. It's funny; Fernando never did trust anyone else in his kitchen. Who knows? Perhaps he was afraid someone might try to poison him! But I digress. After a delicious meal, we sipped cognac by the pool, and chatted about this and that for quite some time, after which we retired to his bedroom, where we made love—slowly, lovingly, and passionately before falling asleep in one another's arms. I couldn't have been more shocked... or more elated."

Silence continued to reign supreme amongst the tribal gathering of men present. Johnny, unaccustomed to so many ears hanging on his every word, found it almost more difficult to forge ahead with his tale without a continuous din of background noise, but he forged ahead nonetheless.

"Our usual regimen of service and torture play was suddenly interrupted by these strange, and wonderful, new encounters, each more amorous than the one before. I can't say I didn't want it either. I had developed a new respect for him; he suddenly appeared more human, more appealing, move vulnerable. I felt myself slipping, falling... deeply in love with Fernando. I absolutely craved his touch, his tenderness. He had also begun to neglect the others in his stables, and they made clear their discontent."

Johnny threw his head back and laughed the free, heartfelt laughter of a soul unchained, and with it, all the pain previously apparent in his voice suddenly took flight. He took several minutes to calm down, during which time his fellow attendees were wondering if perhaps he'd taken leave of his senses.

"Ah, it was all so terribly melodramatic: the day of the big confrontation, the day we all turned into bitchy queens. 'Keep away from our man!' being the essence of the general complaint I had to endure from Fernando's stable. All united, I'd never heard such vitriol escape from their lips before. Come to think of it, there wasn't very much that I'd *ever* heard escape from their lips, but they made up for it that day. I stood my ground, telling them to either back down or fuck off, and yes, I used the name 'Mary' more than once, I'm ashamed to admit. After the henhouse scene had dispersed, upon deeper reflection I realized that I'd allowed Fernando to undermine an entire family structure, one that had grown from years of dedicated service by a group of men who cared deeply for their master. He was their daddy, their teddy bear, their director, *their anchor*, and I was rocking the boat, as it were. Intruding on sacred ground.

"Needless to say, that last discussion was a definitive end for my relationship with him. We both realized the implications of what had happened, and one evening, swimming naked in the pool together as the sun set, we realized we had to say goodbye. Tears spilled out of my eyes as I kissed him one last time and fell into the water surrounding us. I pulled my jeans on which I'd left at the edge of the pool, leaving a trail of tears and chlorinated water between them, stuffed my feet in my boots and straddled my bike, thumbing the starter as I slid down the driveway. I pointed myself west, into the sun, and headed home."

Carlo, remaining uncharacteristically silent, his face unreadable, settled into serving his tribe for the time being.

Mikel

After Johnny's story, everyone found themselves starved, his captivating account having left the collected audience as drained as if they'd been through the same experience. The meat on their plates scarcely satisfied their greater hunger, and many listeners hurriedly finished their plates to head off to their tents and what comforts might await them there.

Hours later, much more sober and hungry for a midnight snack, the multitude had reassembled. One step ahead of the crowd, Carlo had already begun to prepare his famous after-dinner, full-moon sugar overload—s'mores, toasted marshmallows over the fire, a variety of sweet cornbreads to be served with honey, and more hot chocolate (made with real melted chocolate, using whole milk of course, because anything else would be criminal, *plus*… a secret ingredient known only to Carlo and his mother, who had passed along the recipe to her son)—more than anyone could possibly hope to metabolize in a month.

Mikel stepped into the line right behind Johnny, announcing himself by squeezing one of Johnny's cheeks slightly.

"Wow! Your story really got me going!"

"Thanks, but that was kinda—not the point," replied Johnny, gently removing the stranger's hand from his ass. "What was your name again?"

"Mikel," he returned as they shook hands. "I have a story too, although I don't have any visible marks to show for it."

"A story doesn't have to leave you permanently scarred to be good."

"Thanks. Mine started innocently enough. We were both on the wrestling team in college…"

"Now, everyone knows there's nothing innocent about huge, sweaty men wearing spandex, groping all over each other." Johnny and Mikel turned around to see the same heckler as before and both men made it known that his interruptions would not be tolerated, after which Mikel continued:

"We were a weight class apart, and since I was the smaller, our coach used to pit us together during practice sessions so I'd learn to rely upon

275

technique instead of strength. It usually worked, but he was still stronger and bigger than I, and his stamina was amazing! He could keep a match going for hours."

The line for Carlo's desserts was growing, bodies extending in single file farther than the lights from the campsite stretched.

"We'd only really interacted on the mat until training for the regional meet had begun. We were matched up one day, and as I was trying to pitch him forward off my right shoulder, he hooked his leg around my upper thigh, got his arms under my armpits and completely wrapped me up on his way over. We hit the mat hard on our right sides, when I suddenly realized I was immobilized as I struggled to escape him. My ass pressed against his cock and I felt it flex inside his suit. His face appeared on my cheek, his hot breath on my skin, his stubble grinding into my ear, all of which had me well on my way to being completely hard. I knew if I didn't get out of that hold soon, it would become problematic."

"Had you been with many larger men before?"

"Hell, I hadn't been with *men* before! I was still only a few months out of my parents' house, and had no idea, really, what my dick was capable of. And, coming from white-bread America, I'd been brought up well 'versed' about the evils of homosexuality. Suddenly, I was faced with this monster erection, and didn't know how to deal with it. It's not like it's all that easy to hide an erection in a wrestling singlet!"

"Not much space for that, I imagine," Johnny agreed.

"Right. So... I wrenched myself free and wriggled around until I was facing him, but with my knees tucked up in front of me, and forced my arms down through the hold. I kicked out, and quickly got up on one knee in an attempt to keep my coach from seeing what was happening in my singlet. I later learned that he'd been on the other side of the mat the entire time, watching my erection grow as I struggled."

"So you were a college boy, huh?" commented Johnny. "Whad'ja do with yourself once you grew up?"

"Teacher, high school. I realized after getting my philosophy degree that I was completely prepared to run a McDonald's for the rest of my life. So, I took the necessary certification exams and aimed for the only real money to be made with an undergraduate degree in my field: High School English—yeah, I know, feel sorry for the kids...

"Anyway, we went to the meet and as soon as we stepped off the bus, we were taken to the arena straightaway, with no time to rest or get ready, so, we hit the showers in order to wake up a little bit. At that point, Lucas had been competing for several years already, so was used to that sort of routine. Well, as I was bent over my bag, unloading everything into a locker, he strode past me and whipped my ass with his towel. Of course, there was too much foot traffic for me to pursue him, but I resolved to take care of him later.

"In the showers, we finally got a glimpse of each other, even though we were on opposite sides of the room. By the time I got around to rinsing myself clean, my mind was fixated upon anything but the upcoming matches. After hearing Lucas laughing and carrying on with the other, more experienced wrestlers, I knew I had to do something, so… got myself off in a toilet stall before I got suited up, covered my face in antifungal gel, and ran upstairs without tying my shoes.

"Lucas helped me stretch while everyone else cleared the mats. It had worked out that I would be the first wrestler on the mat that day, the usual progression through weight classes having been reorganized into heats according to regional location—something about one of the other teams having to get back home for 'religious reasons' …I dunno. Anyway, there I was at the side of the mat, the lights, screaming supporters, the announcer, and my coach all demanding my attention as Lucas worked my aching muscles, trying to get the blood flowing. Right before I went in, Lucas cautioned me to watch for my opponent to try and work a headlock sweep combo, and to go heavy on his right foot—that he'd broken it the previous summer at the tri-county meet. Being so well advised, I easily won that match, and every other one I participated in that day.

"Totally exhausted, all I wanted to do afterwards was go back to the hotel and die, but when I got there, it seemed that Lucas had somehow managed to be my roommate. He walked out of the bathroom in a towel that left one of his tree-trunk-like legs exposed. I put my bags down and heaved a sigh of relief. He came over and without a word began to work the kinks out of my muscles. I stretched out on the bed and just let him go for it, shedding clothes as necessary. When he turned me over to work on my front side, it was impossible to hide my raging hard-on. I tried to relax into the experience, but the anticipation was too great. He massaged me from head to toe, seemingly ignoring the fact that I was bursting at the seams, until he was finished and started inching his way slowly up my legs.

"'Now, this is a muscle that no amount of massaging is going to loosen up,' he said, his hot breath indicating that his mouth was scant inches from my erection. With that, he began kissing my dick through my shorts, eventually pulling it through the fly and into his mouth. I almost exploded right then and there. I had never before considered being with a man an option for me, and my excitement on the practice mats back at home had totally thrown me for a loop. Sure, there'd been a few girls in the picture since I'd been at school, but they were all fairly peripheral company. As I allowed Lucas to have his way with me, my excitement grew. He continued working my cock, stroking me with his hand while he sucked. Before long, I was out of control, clutching the bed sheets as my toes tingled in a prelude to what I knew would be an explosive orgasm, but just as the cum had begun seriously gathering for its breakneck race up my elation superhighway, he withdrew his mouth and, although I felt my erection stiffen even more, the prospect of coming was suddenly stalled indefinitely."

Mikel's discourse had lasted long enough for the men to have gotten within 'commitment distance' of Carlo's makeshift kitchen, which was Carlo's term for being too close to the goodies to resist being able to turn away from them. Yep, the men were in for a sugar rush, and there was nothing at all they could do about it, save for calling the emergency room and suggesting they stock plenty of extra insulin. Mouths watering, stomachs rumbling, sweat glistening on heated flesh: if you weren't diabetic before you got there, it might well prove a turning point in your life. Dessert was always Carlo's favorite part of the evening, a ritual that, to his mind, separated the sheep from the hogs. It was obviously going to get sticky

Johnny had attended several of these events before, and knew that the secret of surviving an extended weekend bash with Carlo was to take everything in moderation. There would be more than enough to go around, and Carlo never allowed anyone to sleep until all dishes were licked clean. As Johnny's stomach grumbled in anticipation upon his arrival at the "service station," Mikel launched back into his narrative:

"'Slow down, cowboy,' Lucas told me. 'We're not quite through yet.' If I hadn't been so damn exhausted right then I might have hit him. From out of nowhere appeared a condom, and suddenly, he was riding me, swaying back and forth on my cock, his balls up on my stomach, his right hand on my chest, clawing and massaging it as his other hand worked his own erection. I felt like I was under him on the mat again, pinned with no way out. God, I was *loving* it, hoping to hold out for a while, anxious to see if I could get him to give up his load first.

"I'd gotten used to his rhythm, but there was a point where he lost his balance and so I rolled him sideways off of me. He managed to hook a leg under my back before I knew what was happening and he pulled me along with him. Already headed straight for the prize, I slammed into his ass to the hilt, into his stomach it felt like. Well, I went to work on him like it was a match I'd been told I was going to lose and finally came in powerful, soul-draining spurts, positive that I wouldn't be able to support myself vertically ever again. I collapsed on top of him and fell immediately to sleep on top of his enormous pecs.

"We woke up the next morning with barely enough time to pull on the same sweaty clothes we'd worn the day before, grab our gym bags and head for the arena. But every kink that Lucas had worked out of my muscles the night before had crept back into my body, and I was in serious pain. Hoping against hope that there'd be time enough for him to work on me a bit, I was forced to accept the fact that fate had made different arrangements for us.

"We hadn't been there five minutes when the coach approached Lucas and sent him on an errand for the team, whereupon I found myself casting about, looking for anyone with hands strong enough to work on me the way Lucas had. My eyes settled on a guy named Willy who was in my same weight class, and I approached him.

"'Hey man, I've got some terrible kinks in my shoulders and legs; can you help a brother out?' He agreed to do me the favor and no sooner had I stretched out on a towel beneath him, than he bent down and began whispering in my ear.

"'I heard you two last night. I'm in the room right next door and it really got me going. I didn't get to sleep until waaaayyyy late, wishing I could've been there, in the same bed with you guys…'

"Even though I was still half-asleep and fighting for lucidity while he worked lotion into my knotted muscles, his implication was obvious.

"'Hmmm, I'm not sure how to respond to that one,' I finally said. 'I'll… have to check it out with Lucas. If he doesn't have a problem with it, I'm certainly game,' I added, figuring that if I was going into this headlong, I might as well go all the way, no holds barred.

"'Just knock on my door after bed check,' he urged. 'I sure hope he says yes.'

"Although I didn't have the time to devote to his flattering request, having to concentrate on the matches that lay ahead of me that day, I wasted no time bringing the subject up to Lucas afterwards, when we spoke at great length about it. Agreeing that we liked the idea very much indeed, we resolved to carry through with the scandalous plan that very evening.

"We went home and showered together; the hot water in the hotel was somehow vastly different from that in the locker room, and once we both felt 'clean…'"—at that point, Mikel winked at his audience—"…we fell into discussing how best to take advantage of the offer we'd received.

"As suggested, right after bed-check we tapped on the door that connected the two rooms. We spent very little time on preliminaries, opting to dive right into the main course. Who started where and ended up in which position, I'm still trying to figure out. All I know is… that we spent hours trading places, taking turns and shifting locations. In the end, I don't think there was a piece of furniture in that room that wasn't somehow utilized until the three of us fell into an exhausted heap with barely enough time left for sleep before we had to be back at the arena next morning.

"Lucas, whose matches were that day, was definitely showing the effects of having been up late two nights in a row. You wouldn't know it to watch him perform though, as he tossed his opponents around with little effort, scarcely breaking a sweat in any of the three matches he participated in, his athletic prowess and experience effectively saving the day. All told, we all managed to walk away from the weekend's competition winners, in *one* way or another." Innuendo confirmed, Mikel winked at Johnny.

"Once back at the university, we fell quickly into a lively routine of bouncing back and forth between each other's apartments, and sometime in August, we began searching for a three-bedroom place to share. Eventually finding the perfect space, we moved in together. Lucas would be graduating that semester, but as Willy and I still had two more years left, we continued to train with the team. Once we'd all graduated, we continued to live in the same apartment, converted one bedroom into a wrestling room, another into office space, and retained the third as a communal sleeping barracks. The rest is history. When the apartment went condo several years later, we pooled our resources, bought it, and to this day, Lucas, Willy and I continue to work, train and love together."

"So, where'd you leave your partners?" someone from the tribe called out.

"They're right here. I brought 'em with me, of course!" Mikel shot back, chucking a thumb over his shoulder, indicating two immense slabs of manhood, both intense objects of desire, both considerably larger than Mikel himself. One of them—Lucas, it turned out—stood well over six feet tall and easily weighed a solid 300 pounds. Leaning against him, his massive, beautifully sculpted and tattooed arm draped over Lucas's shoulder, his tattered blue jeans clinging to rippling masses of calf, thigh, hamstring and glute muscles, Willy was star-caliber gorgeous, in a WWF sort of way. Both men smiled and nodded to Mikel's appreciative audience, both looking, for all their apparent friendliness, as if they could easily frighten away the angriest of grizzly bears lurking in the shadows.

Mikel's storytelling had lasted long enough for them to reach the head of the line, right in front of Carlo's service station. The fragrance of chocolate and other decadent ingredients that comprised Carlo's dessert course was truly overpowering, but then again, that was half of why anyone would come to these tribal gatherings—to throw one's self on Carlo's mercy. Knowing that, Johnny had brought his own cup with the objective of attempting to regulate the dosages of diabetic shock-inducing contents he ingested, knowing that it was semi-futile, of course. Thrusting his cup forward, Johnny prepared to face his destiny.

Carlo

Carlo was an enormous man. When shopping at the local leather outfitters, his size necessitated that his clothing be custom made and therefore extremely costly, or was told by shop personnel that they simply couldn't accommodate him. His curly black hair and perfectly trimmed beard accentuated a strong jaw line and amazing, blazing blue eyes. His formative years, spent tending to the daily chores at his family's ranch in Argentina, had colored his speech with an unflinching accent and lent an indelible hardness to his body, though the latter had subsumed a magnificent, rounded belly. Johnny, knowing better than to trust a skinny chef, all of these details flooding his mind, acquiesced as the intimidating iron tongs that Carlo used for moving logs, hot pans (and apparently catching young men unaware) snapped shut around his neck with a mighty clang.

"I've got you now, boy!" Carlo laughed into the night. Securing the tong's handgrips, he pulled the younger man towards him, around the edge of the serving station. Johnny struggled valiantly against the inches-thick collar, but to no avail. Carlo was simply the bigger man.

"Boys!" commanded the chef-in-chief, "no one goes to sleep until they're 'glazed'"

"Yes *sir*!" Carlo's two "boys" (in reality, beefy young men in their mid-to-late-twenties), replied enthusiastically. It was the most Johnny had heard the chef's current slaves-in-waiting speak thus far that weekend. Both, having been down similar roads before, obviously knowing better than to arouse their master's temper, were quick to obey the enigmatic command and dashed off.

Refocusing his attention on Johnny, the huge man gave a yank on the tongs and dragged him into the blackness towards his truck, where, behind the rear bumper, the sadistic chef secured the grips of his tongs around a tree and stared deeply into Johnny's eyes. With his head pressed against the tree trunk, Johnny suddenly became aware that there was a knife pointed at his throat, that a drop of burning liquid trailed down the side of his neck where the knife was poised—whether sweat or blood, Johnny wasn't sure, but prayed it wasn't the latter. His captor's eyes blazed as if the last shred of humanity had left them, as if his only thought was centered upon his being the much larger predator who'd just secured his dinner. As a lion might, before pouncing on its defenseless prey, Carlo licked his lips slowly, as his victim's heart raced.

"You are an incomparable idiot!" raved an impassioned Carlo. "Did you really think that you could come here, show that brand off and expect no one to take exception? That symbol comes from my family's ranch in Córdoba. My grandfather traveled from Spain to start that ranch, having heard of the vast *terrenos* available and the fortunes to be made in Argentina. My father still speaks of him reverentially, as if he were in the next room." The proud chef's eyes misted over at the mention of his family—proof enough for Johnny that, for all his ferocity, Carlo had a heart that his enormous chest could scarcely contain. Johnny's eyes fixed on the twin emblems on Carlo's leather vest and saw the undeniable resemblance between the scar on his own flank and the tooled cowhide as Carlo continued:

"I come from a family long involved in Argentinean politics, and my half brother, your former master, was the result of my father's predilections for Creole women. Once it was discovered that the woman was pregnant, Vicente was brought to the ranch to avoid embarrassment, as his mother's family's *rancho* was much smaller than ours and only provided enough sustenance for their survival. Naturally, Vicente's fortunate position was a godsend for his maternal family. I remember, growing up together as brothers, that there was always something extra for them. Even when hoof and mouth disease decimated our herds, they wanted for nothing.

"We also bred horses, and had several stallions to which many of the local ranchers brought their mares. Only one of our horses ever escaped us. A week later, we saw one of the neighboring *rancheros'* sons riding her, their attempt to rebrand her proving unsuccessful. A fight ensued between our two families, and when all was said and done, we had successfully taken over their land and their horses."

Carlo, upon concluding this remembrance, laughed heartily. By that time, the tongs had disappeared from around Johnny's neck. Between Carlo's truck and the tree to which Johnny had been pinned sat two enormous boulders. Once *el Chef* had released Johnny, the two men eased onto the rocks as they would into leather-covered easy chairs and made themselves comfortable. Carlo kept the blade out and toyed with it as he spoke, indicating to Johnny that he was not necessarily in any less danger than he had been earlier.

"What did you say his name was?" ventured Johnny, feeling only slightly more adventurous. "Vi-*cente*…?"

"Yes, Vicente," repeated Carlo. "Vicente *Fernando* Jaín de Santa Rosalia… Santa Rosalia is the Creole family name."

Totally shocked by the revelation, Johnny could scarcely even mutter, "Oh, my *god*…" before Carlo, momentarily lost in reflection, continued:

"Of course, we shared our first sexual experiences together, although we were barely old enough to know what sex was. True, we had observed horses during mating season, but neither of us had any idea that human beings engaged in the same activity, much less that such peculiar activity was pleasurable. I'll never forget it: After a long ride one day, we came back stinking of sweat, the horses, and saddle leather, odors we would soon find enticing until this very day. As I slid from my saddle, his riding crop fell playfully across my ass, and I struck back with my own. What had begun innocently enough soon turned into a lively swatting chase to the corral, where we took shots at one another until we were exhausted. Stinging with welts, but laughing, we walked arm-in-arm back to the stables. That night, settling into bed beneath the covers, I soon found myself with a magnificent hard-on. Even though I'd bathed, faint wisps of saddle leather tickled my nostril's fancy, reminding me of our afternoon whipping match, making it impossible to fall asleep. I massaged my erection until I exploded all over myself, after which I found sleep, totally unaware of the implications of that experience."

Carlo fell silent, staring through the blackness into his history, back to his childhood home, perhaps the only place that really made sense to him. From out of the blackness, however, the taller of Carlo's omnipresent boys materialized, the one Johnny had noticed earlier. With some trepidation the boy approached Carlo.

"Uhhh, Carlo? We, uhh… It's just that…"

"Speak, goddamit! Can't you see you're interrupting us?"

"Well, it looks like we're running out of hot chocolate, Sir. I never thought I'd see the day, but it's true."

"¡*COÑO!*" spat Carlo, ordering, "You guys wait here!" He disappeared around the front of the truck and a few minutes later he returned, pushing an enormous drum full of liquid splish-splashing as it rolled.

"This is why I always carry a spare, *por si acaso*," he said, passing the dolly over to his underling. "Mix this with the batch that's already over the fire, and if that starts to get low, continue to dole out half cups until everyone's too hyperactive to speak. Be careful, though; one can never tell what will happen when people drink too much of my mother's special recipe." Nodding in silent obedience, the polite intruder took the dolly in hand and, with a bit more difficulty than his master had displayed, wheeled the container out to the service station, the weight of its load inspiring the wheels to squeal their discontent.

"Now, where was I?"

"Stables, rope…" Johnny offered.

"Ah, yes! Now I remember!" exclaimed the big man, resuming his tale. "…The night our father was debating for the Leader of the Senate position was the same week of our graduation; Vicente and I were almost exactly the same age. It was an incredibly exciting time. Of course, there were the requisite family dinners where far-removed cousins we hadn't seen for more than a decade found their way to our table, and the wine kept especially for certain occasions deep in our cellars was brought out. We cultivated our own grapes and bottled our own wine at the time. Half of my family's fortune stems from the wine business, still productive today.

"Because everyone in attendance that evening was busy engaging in political talk, catching up, and telling stories, Vicente and I, who had become bored with so many relatives, weren't even missed when we decided to steal away.

"We headed for the stables, intent on taking the horses out for a trot into the vineyards…" (At this point in Carlo's story, Johnny, aware that the mad chef was approaching the "good part," felt his tight jeans becoming even tighter as his erection rose to the occasion in anticipation.) "…and when we got there, casually noticed that someone had hung a *lazo* on his saddle. Paying it no mind, I began preparing my horse, my back to Vicente, who dropped the loop around my waist from five meters away! Completely taken off guard, I couldn't escape as he pulled me towards him. Seems the little fuck had looped the other end of the rope around one of the roof supports, thrown it over the crossbeam, and tied it off before lassoing me with the other end!" Carlo paused in reflection, chuckling to himself. "Ah… he might have been better with the rope, but I was always better with the knife… Anyway, in no time I found myself wrapped in the rope, unable to move my arms, and being hoisted off the ground. Exerting a tremendous effort, he pulled me up until my belt was almost even with the top of his head.

"Once he'd raised me to the correct height, he resecured the rope around the support, took a knife, and damn if he didn't cut the pants clean off of me! Throwing the shredded breeches aside, he began making very different use of his riding crop from the way he had when we'd chased each other around the corral, flicking the head of my dick tauntingly as a sort of wicked appetizer while I hung there. Then, moving around behind me, Vicente applied several firm lashes to my legs, hips, and ass before pressing the rounded ball at the end of the crop's handle against my anal opening and began twirling it in circles, the ropes groaning as I relaxed against them. Just as I began groaning, he moved around my other side, swatting me here and there with the whip end of the riding crop. Finally arriving back in front of me, he faced my by-then very stiff erection, which, after a longing glance, he took in his mouth.

"Well, he must have been practicing with bananas or something, because he swallowed my entire length at once. He worked his mouth back and forth several times and that alone was too much for me; I let loose with all that I'd stored since my previous orgasm, screaming almost loud enough to alert the collection of family members inside the house. Had anyone heard it and come running, we would have caused an unbelievable scandal, but as luck would have it, we were spared that embarrassment.

"Vicente lowered me to the dusty floor as soon as I'd recovered from the shock of orgasm, and untied me. We hung up the rope, picked up my shredded pants and headed for one of the empty stables, where, on top of fresh hay, he stretched himself out and I performed the same service for him that he had for me. He also came quickly, as might be expected for a first time, after which I lay down next to him, eager to share my reaction to what had just happened.

"'What are you thinking about?' I inquired cautiously.

"'I… wanted you to keep doing that forever, Carlo; I didn't want it to end.'

"'*Boy*, neither did I!' I exhaled with relief. 'You know, I've heard that… the more you do it, the longer it lasts…' Vicente smiled at me and we reached for one another, anxious to whip ourselves into a second round. Of course, at that age, there is always a second round—and a third, and a fourth… From that day forward, we found ourselves frequently in each other's beds, both of us having remained on the ranch after graduation from University. With our father by then totally immersed in the Senate, Vicente and I had no choice but to take over the daily operations of the family property as well. However, despite our hectic schedules, we kept up with our riding, which remained one of our greatest shared pleasures."

The enveloping nighttime quietude was suddenly rent as an enormous crash, announcing the collapse of the makeshift kitchen's pots and pans shot up from the clearing. The cacophony continued for several minutes as someone was obviously attempting to extricate himself from an uncomfortable situation. Carlo discontinued his story and stormed off to check on his precious kitchen. Much to our collective surprise, he returned shortly thereafter, with the heckler who had annoyed us earlier slung like a sack of potatoes over one of his ample shoulders. The Argentinean made quick use of his rope skills to lash the troublesome offender to the same tree trunk that Johnny had been pinned against not half an hour before. First immobilizing the heckler's arms and legs, Carlo grabbed the man's jaw and, stuffing a thick dishtowel into his mouth for good measure, resolved to "take care" of the "*lame huevos*" after he finished his story. Hurling an abundance of additional invective while taking his leave of the cowering figure gagged and bound to a tree, the imposing chef settled his bulk down upon the rock opposite Johnny and resumed his story.

"*Hijo de la... De qué hablaba? Ah, jesss...* So, our last experience together occurred at the end of a long day when we were busy massaging saddle soap into the custom-tooled saddles we had received for graduating from high school—ah... we rode like princes, Vicente and I, both of us shirtless in the heat of summer—when it occurred to me that it was high time I take revenge on my gorgeous half-brother. Ha...! I reached for the very same *lazo* which had hung, unused since that infamous day, on a nail in the support beam and accosted him in exactly the same way he had me—but with one exception: he'd suspended me horizontally, whereas I had decided to utilize more of a harness-type configuration in order that he hang more vertically. Knife still in hand, I had removed his pants in similar fashion, so there were no impediments to my diabolical plan-in-progress.

"Once he was floating in mid-air, I took the riding crop hanging from my belt and put it to good use, covering him with welts. And then... Perhaps you've heard that gauchos can eat and shave at the same time? Well, I did just that. As I blew him, I scraped the hairs of his pubic bush until they were very short indeed! Let me assure you that between the razor-sharp blade being *that* close to him, and the restraints I had used, he scarcely moved, barely even breathed, but my God how he sweated! Because we had both gained incredible stamina in the time we'd been sexually involved, that session lasted much longer than the first one had; a fact that pleased us both immensely.

"Having successfully trimmed Vicente's pubes to the nice and clean look I'd set out to achieve, I stood back and took several minutes to admire my work, not to mention his compelling erection, before I resumed fellating him until he exploded violently down my throat. I finally let him down, but not until after expending several more minutes torturing his body with my crop. To make a long story a bit shorter, we spent that entire night in the stables, taking turns, utilizing different modes and positions of dominance and submission. Noting the rising sun, upon realizing we'd been preoccupied all night, we resaddled the horses and rode out to the edge of the *jungla* that bordered our property, wearing nothing more than the simple peasant shirts we'd donned the day before.

285

"By that time, a military junta had taken control of the country, and, unaccustomed to being under the boot of any authority, we did what many Argentineans felt they had to do: we left our beautiful homeland. I, as you know, headed for culinary school in New York, and Vicente... Well, after storming about the globe seeking an adventurer's life, he ultimately returned to Argentina, where he continues to maintain the wine business as it has been run for the past two generations on the *rancho*. Of course, we visit frequently, and speak on the phone but... we're both very busy now, and have our own interests, so..." Carlo's voice trailed off plaintively—yet another indication of the abundant emotion he kept so stoically hidden.

"You really miss him, don't you, Carlo?" Johnny enquired quietly.

"Well, what would you expect after essentially being with the same person for more than twenty years? After hearing your account of how you came to be with my beloved half brother, surely you can understand why I cannot allow you to escape. You might have gotten away from him, but you will NOT get away from me. And regardless of how you might manage to escape, or where you might go, you will always be recognized as one of ours."

Carlo indicated that the end of story time had arrived with a hand gesture. He and Johnny arose from the boulders they'd been sitting on and headed back for the clearing. Despite his vociferous protests, the heckler remained tied to the tree. Either Carlo-and-crew would be back for him later, or the wolves would have their way with him in their absence. Perhaps he would be the next roast beast: spitted over a low fire, his limbs secured with twine, Carlo's boys taking turns slowly cranking the rotisserie in shifts, the hot juices sputtering... Whatever the man's punishment would be, Johnny was sure it would be severe and well justified.

The second they were in sight of the service station, Johnny's jaw first went slack and then worked uselessly in an attempt to express his amazement at the scene he beheld. Carlo, having instructed his kitchen assistant to be careful in doling out his mother's potent cocoa mix just shook his head.

"WHAT THE HELL IS GOING ON HERE?" Carlo's voice boomed through the forest. Piles of four and five men lay naked and writhing in heaps, more entangled than flies in a web, but infinitely sweatier. Perhaps prescient of tomorrow night's main course, one unfortunate man had been wrapped in a pup-tent and suspended just above the fire pit, attached by ropes to trees at five points while revelers whipped him with their leather belts. Worse, Carlo's two boys lay hogtied, belly-down on the enormous grills, apples jammed in their mouths while someone else was busy stuffing tinder into the ashen space beneath! At the sound of the big man's booming tone, all activity in the clearing immediately ceased. And none too soon, as one reveler actually stood with a lighted match, ready to drop it into the flammable material. Racing to the "scene," Carlo blew out the match and lifted his boys, one in each arm, off the grills after slicing their bonds with the arm-long steel blade he forever kept strapped to his side.

"*No one* touches my boys without my permission," he swore viciously between his teeth. "NO ONE!" As if to punctuate his displeasure, Carlo grabbed the knives housed in his butcher's block and sent them flying towards the ropes holding the suspended man in place. The gray pupa shape of pup tent fell as gracefully as a pregnant hippopotamus into the soft dirt to one side of the fire pit. Those holding the leather belts dropped them on cue, thinking their expressions of contrite submission would save them from the behemoth's ire, but no. Fixing them with his incensed glare, Carlo continued his rant, which surprisingly also conveyed more than a little hurt and disappointment.

"I pull together these magnificent feasts, and *this* is how I'm rewarded? Where do you suppose your breakfast tomorrow morning will miraculously emerge from—the middle of nowhere, like manna from heaven? And do you propose to pick your midnight snacks from the trees?" Receiving no response from the humbled assemblage, he continued. "No. I didn't think so. Now… GET this place cleaned up so I can begin food preparations again!" bellowed the enormous epicurean. Nobody stirred; they stood, awestruck by the powerful figure before them. Realizing that he must exert further dominance before anyone dared to challenge him, Carlo removed the gaucho's knife from its sheath and with one fluid movement sent it hurtling towards one of the stilled orgy piles, where it landed, plunging full to its hilt into the dirt, squarely between the legs of a participant on the bottom.

The crowd immediately snapped to attention, realizing the seriousness of the situation and scurried to carry out orders. Several men began to reassemble the stones around the fire pit, overturned chairs and tables were righted, and Carlo collected his blades. Walking back towards his truck, he spotted the overturned, emptied drum of hot chocolate and glared at the taller of his boys, the one who had taken it in the first place.

"I told you to be careful doling that out," Carlo said with forced calmness, shaking his head. The boys knew they would be punished severely for such a flagrant transgression, a mistake on their part that all too correctly spelled out the reality that there'd be no more hot chocolate for anyone's remaining time there.

Sasha and Danny

"That's probably not the best place to put that."

Johnny had been put to work while Carlo was busy with the heckler. Before departing, Carlo had ordered them to serve fruits, bread with butter and honey, and peanut butter balls, but nothing remotely related to chocolate or coffee. Johnny had been lugging huge plastic vats of water, and had left them next to the grill Carlo would begin heating up for breakfast the minute he returned.

"Oh, right. Hadn't thought of that," Johnny replied, appraising the dark and statuesque figure standing before him, deciding at once he'd better get acquainted with his "brothers," and so extended his hand.

"I'm Johnny, by the way."

"Sasha," responded the Adonis, his voice dripping like honey out of his mouth. Sasha appeared to be of Mediterranean extraction, stood just under six feet and exhibited the practiced grace of someone accustomed to being in the public eye. He wore beaded braids on either side of his face, indicating the length of his hair, which was tied back just then. Once again the hypnotic melody of his voice cut a hole through the surrounding clatter:

"Don't forget to bring the peaches, and remember; we're out of cups. The fucking wild men broke all the wooden utensils during the orgy, so you'll have to lug the steel ones."

"Right. You, uh... want fries with that? Johnny chuckled, fully aware of the lameness of his joke. Undaunted by receiving no reply from the shorter of Carlo's acolytes, he continued: "Y'know..." he pried, "...I'd sure like to hear the story of how you two came to serve Carlo."

"I'd be delighted, but not until you get back with the stuff I asked for." So taunted, Johnny returned in a big-ass hurry with an entire bushel of peaches and probably 1,000 cups loaded on the same hand truck utilized for transporting the notorious drum of hot chocolate just a few hours earlier.

"Mission accomplished, bro," Johnny stated expectantly, parking the dolly. "So... *tell* me, already!"

"Fine," returned Sasha. "You can get started cutting up those peaches if you like."

"Quartered, halved, sliced, cubed, or finely chopped?" ventured Johnny.

"Hm, you know your stuff. That'll please the big man," smiled the "big man's" boy, adding, "sliced, please."

"How *lovely* for me," Johnny replied sarcastically, setting up a cutting board and picking up a knife. "Lord knows I aim to please. Now, your story...?"

"Sure, let's see... we were in Barcelona. After finishing his stint at the culinary institute in New York, Carlo went in search of an internship and secured a position at one of the larger restaurants *en las Ramblas*, where it just so happened I was employed. As one of the sous chefs responsible for monitoring everyone's job and expediting orders, we shared the closest contact with the chefs.

"At *El Caballo Castrado*, we were accustomed to new chefs coming and going, as it was, and still is, a kitchen famous for training some of the world's finest chefs. So needless to say, we had experienced a whole gamut of prima donnas, including more than a few of the most unbearable perfectionists you can imagine, so when Carlo stormed into the kitchen for the first time, naturally we were curious, not knowing what to expect. I'll never forget that day. As is his normal fashion, he took control of everything immediately, but in such a way that inspired camaraderie and cooperation. No one could help being drawn to him. There wasn't a day that every one of us didn't leave that kitchen at workday's end without having laughed until our stomachs hurt.

"One morning, we were alone in the meat locker, taking note of the inventory. As I bent over to pick up a box, Carlo's hand towel snapped against the seat of my pants, which was not entirely out of the ordinary. Since his arrival, most of us carried towels around the kitchen if for no other reason than self-defense! I quickly stood up with a yelp, but he was on me before I could retaliate, much less speak, kissing me, pinning my hands against the wall and binding them together with the heavier twine used for sewing the large birds served at banquets.

"Once my hands were well-fastened, he lifted me onto a meat hook, and let me hang there a second. He then spun me until my ass faced him, took my pants down, and proceeded to punish me with the towel until I could feel the heat rising through the chill of the meat locker. My cheeks finally reddened to his liking, Carlo then attached his mouth to my asshole, deftly working of his tongue, utilizing ample amounts of saliva to make sure it was more than ready for penetration.

"The pleasure his fucking me provided was so intense, it was all I could do to keep from screaming, not that doing so would have mattered, as no one could have heard me through the closed locker door had there been anyone else in the restaurant to begin with. How he knew I would enjoy this type of ride, I'll never know, but… it lasted just long enough for both of us to be pleased. All at once he started growling like a bear, dug his fingers into my abdomen, and I felt him explode inside me.

"After getting his head together, he let me down and informed me that he wanted us to meet after work at a club he frequented. Well, I spent the entire workday in anticipation of what else might be awaiting me at the end of the tunnel. Seems I had good reason to wonder, because I certainly wasn't expecting the series of events that occurred later that evening…"

Johnny took a moment to contemplate just how similar this man's experience had been to his own, that it was obvious Vicente and his half-brother were cut from the same cloth.

"…I arrived at the club shortly after work, having only taken enough time to change out of my food-stained clothing into a clean pair of jeans and T-shirt. Even so, he was there, waiting for me, wearing the same vest he's wearing tonight, smiling up at me from the bottom of the staircase. We spent the requisite amount of time taking in our surroundings, talking to acquaintances, being introduced to new people, things like that. After about an hour of socializing we headed deeper into the club where Carlo escorted me to a 'play station.' He instructed me to strip and, laying my clothes to the side, I sat down on the device, fit my legs into the designated slots, and quickly found myself immobilized as wide leather straps were wrapped around my limbs and head then pulled tight and fastened. Opening his toy bag, which appeared from nowhere, Carlo produced more implements of torture than there appeared space to hide them. I still have no idea how he fits everything into that little case.

"On a pedestal located near the play station, Carlo set out a riding crop, a spiked wheel, a flogger that seemed somewhat worse for the wear, nipple clamps, and a device I had never seen before, nor could possibly describe to you right now, save to mention that it had an electrical cord. He then lowered his mouth to my nipples and proceeded to suck them until first one, and then the other, were almost bursting—'perfect,' he said, 'for placing the clamps properly.' That executed (*whoa…*), he moved on to demonstrate why he refers to his beard as his 'inner thigh sander.' Carlo chewing and licking his way up my legs toward my crotch made it incredibly difficult to sit still, but then, what option did I have, secured as I was? In response to his being occupied in this manner, my dick wasted no time in standing straight up from my lap, pulsing in a most pleasant rhythm. Seeing my excitement, he took the spike wheel and ran it down the length of my body, each little prick of the wheel sparking my erection to jump even more. Once confident that I was as hard as I could possibly get, he brought out the flogger and treated my legs and belly to a rough going-over. Every time I jumped or strained, the weighted chain on the tit clamps would swing back and forth, reminding me of their attachment. My skin was flushed and sweaty. I was unbelievably hot, but not as hot as I was going to get, let me assure you.

"Carlo grabbed the strange device I mentioned before, plugged it into an outlet attached to the pedestal, flicked a switch, and a bulb at the end began to glow. He touched it to my leg. I wanted to yell, but my voice seemed not to work. He passed the bulb over the inside of my leg, brought it dangerously close to my scrotum, but at the last second arched it up and over my erection, and reconnected the current to my belly, whereupon he proceeded to drag the hot bulb—perhaps not as hot as the tip of a wood burning device, but almost—slowly down my other leg. By the time he was finished, I'm almost positive I would have been cooler sizzling in a frying pan placed over a gas jet set on high, but it's difficult to say for certain," Sasha chuckled.

"Sensing that I'd had enough of the 'magic wand', that his prep work had been completed to his satisfaction, Carlo clicked it off and placed it back on the table. Drawing close to my face, he gazed longingly into my eyes for quite some time before he began kissing me—gently at first, but with gathering passion—at the same time working my painfully hard erection with a smooth and steady hand-stroking that nearly drove me to distraction. I was swooning, sweating profusely from the searing heat that lingered on my flesh, not to mention the heat his lips and tongue were generating in our kissing, which only served to ignite fires ever deeper in my manhood, which he relentlessly stoked with his gliding hand, as I writhed and strained against the bonds that held me. After— God knows how long a period of this sweet torture, in a fit of indescribable ecstasy, I released every spurt of pent-up excitement that had built up during the course of the entire day all over the play station, while Carlo sat there laughing softly to himself.

"While I was busy descending from the clouds, Carlo disappeared for a few moments, only to return with a shorter, darker figure who was carrying a bowl of ice and a container of fresh, steaming towels. Having been instructed to do so, this new addition to the party rubbed the ice over my abdomen, legs and nipples, cooling off the heated flesh, after which he wrapped me with the warm towels. Once I had been cleaned off and gotten dressed again, we spent an hour or two at the bar. Carlo had a plate of caldo brought to me, I quickly recovered my strength, and at closing, all three of us returned to Carlo's apartment." Sasha concluded this last sentence with a long wistful sigh.

"Gaaaahhhh…!" exclaimed Johnny, at precisely that moment. Unfortunately, his doing so had been precipitated by not paying attention to what he was doing with the knife for just long enough to slice a finger practically in half. The bloodgate had been severed. As if by instinct, Johnny grabbed his wound with his other hand, squeezed it shut and raised both hands above his head.

"Danny!" screamed Sasha. "Bring the medical kit—NOW!"

Danny…? Mused Johnny, his dripping hands stretched tightly overhead, clamping the detached skinflap ever tighter as it throbbed with every bloody beat of his heart.

In a matter of moments the shorter, darker Danny came jogging up with a metal box in hand. Not even taking time to catch his breath, Danny opened the box and, quickly donning a pair of sanitary gloves, took hold of Johnny's finger, making sure to approximate the pressure on the digit in the transfer.

On top of his game, Danny sprayed the area with topical anesthetic before examining the extent of damage.

"Let's take a look," encouraged the shorter, darker man, gently getting down to work, sterilizing the wound in preparation for its being sutured, his first observation being that, luckily for the stunned Johnny, Carlo never allowed his cutlery to dull, so the cut was clean. All the better for the patient.

"Hmmm, it's a fairly deep cut—around two centimeters—but you missed severing any muscle tissue, thank god. Can you wiggle your finger back and forth?" Much to everyone's relief, Johnny was able to. "Good," the paramedic continued. "At least we'll be able to take care of you here. What were you two doing that you sliced yourself so deeply?"

"Well," Johnny began, "I was slicing peaches and Sasha was telling me how the two of you managed to come into Carlo's service…"

"Akh, not *that* story again!" smiled the hunky paramedic.

"We were just talking about what happened at the play station that first night in the club," the Adonis-like Sasha informed his "brother."

"Oh, that's one of the best parts!" gushed Danny.

"Right, and since it's 'enter, Danny' time in the story anyway, I'll return to getting the service station ready. Make sure Johnny's at least functional so that Carlo doesn't *echarnos una bronca*," Sasha reminded him.

"*Dja...*" Danny replied dismissively, at the same time extracting the necessary works to close his new partner's wound. Eager to return to tending his most attractive patient, he queried, "So, how far did Sasha get in the story?"

"Something about ice and hot, moist towels being brought to the play station... afterwards..." Johnny returned, with a hint of a grin.

"Oh! Well... there is a bit of history that perhaps you might not be privy to yet, that it's important you know in order to continue. You see, when Carlo came to Barcelona, he already had a friend there from his town in Argentina who was also a chef and making his way very well. Carlo had been offered a room in his friend's apartment, close to the beach, and on one of his days off, found me sitting on a towel, scribbling in my sketchbook." Danny spritzed the area to be sewn with another shot of topical anesthetic, and then began his work with the needle and thread as if he were fixing a rip in his favorite jeans.

"Anyway, he approached me, said he admired my tattoos. I said something like, yeah, I was a walking portfolio, that the designs were my own work, blah blah blah... He then asked if I would consider helping him design a piece for himself, that he'd been wanting to get tattooed since arriving in Barcelona, but, given the fact that he had a design in his head, yet lacked the ability to express it on paper, Carlo still hadn't managed to work it out. We spent the entire day discussing it, sketching broad lines, refining details, and at the end of the day, in a café on the boardwalk, we finished the design at last. After coffee, we found our way back to Carlo's apartment, and shortly thereafter, I began laying down paint in his skin. He was naked from the waist down, and the light cotton shirt he wore unbuttoned was a scarcely noticeable prop. The whole fucking scene was charged with eroticism.

"The design was an extended, heavy black line piece that he originally wanted to reach from his lower back around to the top of his right front leg, but I convinced him that he would ultimately regret the imbalance of only doing one side. We were in for quite a long session, so I launched right in, beginning on Carlo's impressive lower back—from center to right side, then back to center and left—he silently gritting his teeth, and I, just as silently, focused on creating perfection.

"Since I had worked completely from behind him up until that point, there was no way I could have appreciated the gorgeous cock his nakedness had first revealed upon removing his jeans, even if I *hadn't* been so hard pressed to focus on my work. But... once I'd made it around to his front, it became increasingly more difficult to concentrate. As I worked, trying to lay as straight a line as possible with my needle, my face getting closer and closer to the head of his dick, he became more and more excited. By the time I was finished with the right side, Carlo's erection was pounding in my face and he wasn't saying 'no.'

"I set my tools aside and took him in my mouth, where, in no time flat, I sucked the hot, white pigment out of that man like ecstasy blasting through a living valve. But wait; I'm getting ahead of myself." Danny snipped the thread and knotted the loose ends a couple of extra times before clipping the suture close to the skin. The tuck points had been executed seamlessly, Danny noted with satisfaction, proud of his hands-on expertise. "Here," Danny offered, handing his patient a couple of pills while putting away the tools of his emergency trade, "these are for pain..." But, before he could recommend a suggested dosage, Johnny swallowed the pills with some orange juice Sasha had squeezed for him earlier. Danny swung around to look frantically at his patient.

"Oh no! You didn't take them both at once, did you?" Danny begged against hope.

"Well, yeah... Why? You mean, they weren't like, Tylenol?"

"*No, idiota*, they were Vicodin! Ten milligrams apiece!" responded the terrified nurse.

"Yikes, Vikes! Sweet Vicky, vitamin V! Ahahhaaa... Eat your hearts out, fellows," laughed Johnny. "No *telling* how much more fun this night might have to offer!" Getting semi-serious for a moment, Johnny assured his caretaker that he'd had some measure of experience with Mistress V, that twenty milligrams shouldn't prove more than he could handle. So mollified, Danny continued his narration:

"So, back to Carlo and me: ...There I was, blowing this half-naked stud in the middle of his living room, in the middle of his tattoo, and he's like, *totally* into it. Well, the feeling was mutual, because I'm fucking *gone,* working his dick, when all at once, he picks me up and slowly begins to turn me upside down. I swear to God, I never lost my liplock on that fucking *luscious* hard-on, man, when—oh my God—he began blowing me simultaneously. My mentioning that I felt totally relaxed in that position is meant as a testimonial to the power of Carlo's strength. Fucking A, man—he moved us into the bedroom, pronto.

"We sat down on the bed, gingerly, then arched backwards until he was lying down with me on top of him. We stayed in 69 position for quite some time, but his technique was too good. I mean, between his tongue and that... hum, or moan he uses sometimes—that subtle *vibrato*—proved more than I could handle, and so allowed myself to come like a beast gone berserk. My orgasm was intense beyond description, an entire day's anticipation, an entire day's fantasy, suddenly blasted, in exquisite frenzy... into *Carlo*. The thought consumed me. Nothing could have thrilled me more at that moment, or so I thought.

Don Luis de la Cosa

"In my return to Earth, Carlo had withdrawn from my mouth and, turning around, quickly sheathed and lubed himself before mounting me in missionary position. Instinctively, I raised my legs and he glided in smoothly. For just a moment, he stayed there, rotating his hips a bit, barely wriggling his dick inside me, but Carlo became accustomed to being inside me right away and began moving gently back and forth, thrusting in and out, beginning with short, smooth movements that ever-so-gradually progressed to longer harder strokes. God knows I had a hand on myself the whole time he fucked me and I got off again big-time while he was pounding me. Well, I guess the sight of me coming must have pushed Carlo over the edge, because damn if I didn't feel his cock shoot off round after round of sperm up my ass—as if his crying aloud in pleasure and suddenly altered thrusting pattern weren't evidence enough of satisfaction.

"As might be expected, we both were sweating from the exertion, but no sooner had he emptied himself inside me then he jumped from the bed and headed straight for the kitchen. Yes, it turns out that Carlo is *energized* by sexual activity! Not the next day… but immediately afterward. Instead of afterglow, Carlo experiences turbo-boost."

Johnny sat back and considered all the details: *a very large man with an enormous cock, brute strength and stamina, plus a sadistic mind. A man who is very good with knives…* Either he was going to have a blast, or he was in terrible trouble.

"Okay, this is great and all, but, how did you come to be working in the S/M club, and what happened after the three of you went back to Carlo's?" Danny grinned the patient grin of a father figure who'd been down this path several times before.

"*Juuuuu* Americans… *juuu* are all the same—very little patience. I was just getting there." Johnny harrumphed at his comment, but by then the sedatives were kicking in and all he felt was lovely!

"Juuu see," Danny droned melodramatically, "I am a trained paramedic, and several times I had visited the same club, with the intent of finding amusement. Because I saved someone from being permanently damaged by one of the machines in the dungeon, they asked me to come back and be the monitor/staff nurse. Since I was taking a hiatus from work after an affair with a married doctor ended badly, I accepted, thinking it would be just the thing to divert my attention. Carlo knew my story, and he suspected I would be amenable to a situation with two men and a power exchange relationship besides. I liked the idea, and figured I had very little to lose since I had been suffering a complete absence of sexual stimulation with another man in my life just then. It was fantastic! Over the next several months, we spent many nights together as a threesome, and many nights together at the club. Carlo would work one of us, while the unoccupied one stood by at attention, ready to hand over instruments, towels, ice cubes, whatever… Sometimes he'd work us both, simultaneously, like the night of his birthday. *Jesus*, what an ordeal!"

"Let's be stickin' to de *point*..." Johnny emphasized, raising his foxy eyebrows slightly

"*Bueno. Si...* very cool, okay. Well, we got to the apartment where Carlo was staying and began searching for food in the refrigerator because Carlo and I were starving. We were pleased to find some cheeses and pepperoni, bread, leftover paella, membrillo, and we quickly threw a salad together using the peppers, spinach, tomatoes and onions just waiting to be consumed. Even Sasha dredged up an appetite after his ordeal, and sat down to eat with us. We reclined on the sofas, all wearing as little clothing as possible. When for instance, some of the membrillo would drop off the bread it was spread on, Sasha would lick it off my chest, and I from his, and so on until we'd found a completely different purpose for the food spread before us.

"Sasha grabbed a handful of membrillo and smeared it all over my chest, working his tongue while I sat there. Since Sasha was stretched out anyway, Carlo yanked his pants down, covered the small of his back with the paella, and buried his face in the mess. Carlo had set some of the cheese on the stove to melt for a fondue, and once he'd finished with the membrillo, he went to the kitchen and brought out the fondue mixture, which he poured over my stomach, whereupon both he and Sasha took turns dipping cubes of pepperoni and bread into it, alternately feeding me and themselves. Some of the cheese ran down into my trimmed pubic hair, and we found out just how difficult it is to suck melted Gouda out of hair. It took Sasha a good half an hour to finish his portion, after which he decided never again to eat Gouda any other way!

"Dessert took just as long, if not longer, and it was soon clear that no one would be getting any sleep that night. Sasha lay stretched out on one sofa, holding up handfuls of salad for me to finish. Carlo returned from the kitchen, flipped Sasha over, and nestled a whole peeled banana between his ass cheeks. He then took slices of peach and arranged them in circles, one on top of the other, on either side of his back. Finally, he placed a bunch of grapes at the base of Sasha's neck, making it completely impossible for him to move without disrupting the presentation that *el Chef* had just constructed. He placed whipped cream in the center of the peaches and drizzled trails of chocolate across the banana, ensuring that both of Sasha's ripe cheeks were well covered. Of course, a plate of fruits was put aside for Sasha, but that was for his refreshment... later. I finished my salad, like a good boy, and started nibbling a few grapes, since they were so close... Carlo began with the banana, which caused Sasha great difficulty in staying still because Carlo's beard is so ticklish.

"After we had finished dessert, we decided that Sasha probably needed his rest so we handed him a bottle of Rioja, and Carlo brought down a length of rope that was sitting on top of the bookshelf in the living room, saying that it was a *lazo* he'd brought all the way from Argentina." Johnny blinked at the memory of the story Carlo had told him about the *lazo*. He might've interrupted Danny's storytelling to let him in on the big man's secret, but by that time, of course he was too sedated to speak. The most he could do at the moment was to smile stupidly and lift a finger in recognition of his new master's origins.

"This is where and when we found out just how much of a master of the rope Carlo is. Before I knew what was happening, he had my hands tied together in such a way that, when he bent me backwards over the sturdy coffee table, he could simply slide the knot under one of the legs, and do the same to my feet. I found myself very soon thereafter stretched across the table from corner to corner, unsure of what to expect given the night's preceding events. When Carlo's toy bag reemerged, I knew I was definitely going to get a workout.

"I was still excited from the preliminaries with our mutual partner when Carlo attached the nipple clamps. That done, out came the riding crop with a sharp *snap*. Carlo wasted very little time unleashing repeated blows to my stomach and chest, making sure to leave no area unscathed. Between thrashings, he used the whip's knob to massage the length of my shaft, and once I was unequivocally hard, he bit and chewed on my abdomen while stroking my penis lovingly. The heat of his mouth and the scratching of his beard against my abused and sensitized flesh—stinging fresh from the flagellation—set me aflame.

"Apparently, Carlo wasn't completely satisfied by the previous meal, and after making sure my front side was appropriately 'heated' he spread me thick with what was left of the membrillo and instructed Sasha to clean me off. While Sasha was doing that, and since we were no longer in the club, Carlo moved around to my head so that his cock and balls were within easy reach of my mouth, and he ordered me to suck him. I had never been in this sort of situation before, and was finding myself more sexually excited than I'd ever been.

"Of course, we had all forgotten one minor detail: Carlo was not the only resident in that apartment. And, while we might have left the club at closing, the chef had to close up the kitchen before he left, and so was another hour or so behind us in getting home. Arturo burst into the apartment at just that moment, carrying a bottle of Manzanilla he had expected to drink slowly by himself, or perhaps share with his roommate as they were both winding down from an eventful evening. But alas, fate had a different plan for him that morning. Arturo was taller and thinner than Carlo, but similarly muscled, yet lacking the characteristic rounded belly that chefs often display. His long, straight hair was raven-black, which he always wore loose when not in the kitchen. So... walking in on our little party like that, he decided to watch the entertainment for a while. He bade us to please continue, saying that after drinking a little more of the wine he'd brought with him, he would be participating in the display he'd so happily stumbled upon.

"This seemed to please Carlo even more than it did me, and we were all in a very open mood, so... once Sasha had succeeded in licking me perfectly clean of dessert, he wrapped his tongue around my burning erection... and I mean *burning*. Once he'd set that in motion, Arturo joined in, and set to work licking or sucking whatever Sasha didn't have his mouth attached to. Meanwhile, I was busy working on Carlo's dick."

Even to Johnny's addled brain, the graphic details Danny added to his story were proving more than titillating. Through his narcotic haze he'd managed to retain complete motor function, though any recognition of social inhibition had flown out the window. Johnny openly stroked his rigid cock with his unbound hand, and leered lasciviously at his orator, who began to wonder if taking advantage of the situation might not be in order. Danny decided that yes, perhaps later, as soon as the patient had managed to regain some finer motor skills, that would be most definitely advisable, but that for the moment, his luscious patient still remained far too heavily under the influence…

Danny had talked long enough that Sasha, having put the finishing touches on the fruit salad, had come looking for the two he'd left behind. When he happened upon the scene, he wasn't quite sure how to react. Danny was checking Johnny's reaction to directing a light beam into his eyes, and measuring his pulse. The paramedic didn't see any reaction from Johnny's pupils and just as Sasha reached the two, Danny began vomiting. As if the situation couldn't have gotten any worse, "*el Chef*" was sure to have a fit. Just then, the trio heard a stream of curses being hurled in Spanish against a backdrop of muffled screams and the measured cracking of a heavy whip undoubtedly against some poor soul's naked backside. Everyone, including the intoxicated Johnny knew exactly what was going on at that moment: Carlo had finally gotten around to exacting the heckler's punishment. None of them envied his position; they knew what was at risk for anyone who even joked about damaging Carlo's precious cooking utensils.

The two veterans of Carlo's service looked at the new addition and asked in unison, as if thinking together aloud: "Can you walk?" In response, Johnny, slowly emulating a fawn that has just discovered the significance of his limbs, wobbled to his feet and… promptly fell back into his chair. Sasha and Danny shook their heads and lifted their new *confrere* from his perch, one vet beneath each arm, half-dragging, half-shuffling the walking wounded along towards the service station. As they walked, Danny continued with his account:

"So, dere I was, stretched across the coffee table…"

"Good God, you're not *done* yet?" intoned an incredulous Sasha.

But Danny wasn't about to be bested by his gorgeous companion. "You had every opportunity to take as long as you wanted when you told the story."

"Whatever, then. Fine," grumbled Sasha with a dismissive hand gesture. "Just… make yourself useful while telling it, hotshot." Arriving at the service station, they sat the woozy novice against a tree and instructed him to stay put as Sasha and Danny returned to preparing the late night snack—Danny having positioned himself closer to Johnny for story continuation purposes.

"So, dere I was, stretched out across the coffee table, and… Arturo gets this idea in his head. 'Let's turn him over,' he says to the group. Well, they all thought whatever was going to happen sounded like great fun, but let me tell you: I wound up thanking the fates that night for having led me to yoga studies some years earlier, because my practiced flexibility was the only reason I was able to achieve the position they desired. Arturo slid the binding up the leg of the table so that when they flipped me over, my legs stayed crossed, though I was able to balance myself on my knees. Carlo followed suit with my arms, and I unexpectedly found myself balanced on all fours. Wasting no time, Arturo entered me from behind, Carlo, standing in my face, presented his oozing rigidity, and Sasha, who has a firm grip on himself, slid under my belly and began sucking my cock, seemingly quite content to jerk off while doing so. All told, it was an excellent tableau we'd created, and all were being well taken care of." Danny glanced over at Johnny who, at the moment was rubbing his cheeks against the tree and otherwise didn't look like he was going anywhere very quickly.

"What are you doing, man?" laughed the paramedic.

"My… face is itchy and… my arms don't work," explained the wounded novice simply. It was all the two veterans could do to keep from slicing their own fingers off, given their spontaneous burst of laughter. Sasha had discontinued his preparations and glanced over as soon as he heard the mirth in his brother's voice. It was the first time Johnny realized that the taller man actually knew how to laugh.

"Are you, uh… *laughing* with me—I mean, like, *at* me, or *what*?" Poor Johnny stumbled over his words much like he'd stumbled over the ground on his way to the service station. His awkwardness only served to instigate his new partners further, who convulsed into a second round of hysterics.

"Jusss… finish the story!" Johnny pleaded.

"Dja…" Danny replied between lingering chuckles. "So, um—hahahaa, ahem—Sasha was the first to come."

"I was not!"

"Djess, you *were*."

After a moment's careful consideration, Sasha conceded. "Fine, but you didn't last too much longer."

"That's true of course, but… you *did* come first." Truth revealed, Danny turned back to Johnny. "Anyway, after Sasha got himself off, I filled his mouth with the evidence of the damn fine time his oral expertise was providing me, and immediately after that, Arturo followed our lead and, cursing like a sailor, came like a motherfucker up my ass. Carlo, never to be outdone, held on a few seconds longer, obviously in the throes of unutterable pleasure, and finished last, spurting a huge load, which I savored on my palate for a moment before swallowing. The four of us remained frozen in position for a minute, and then, one by one, we slowly disengaged. After Carlo untied me, we all collapsed on the sofa. Arturo began passing around the bottle of Manzanilla, and we took advantage of the moment to relax and talk about what had just occurred.

"It was at that point that we decided on the particulars of our new situation. It was first understood that responsibilities pertaining to being in service could not interfere with general life responsibilities such as jobs, family, or anything related. The two masters each chose one of us—I was to serve Arturo, and Sasha was to serve Carlo—and decided between themselves that neither one could put into action any plan that involved the other's servant without first securing the consent of both the other master, and that master's servant. On top of which, any swapping scene orchestrated required the presence of both masters at the same place and time once permission had been granted.

"It was then agreed upon that weekends would be spent mostly at the club, a convenient solution that further ensured the presence of both masters and servants at the same location. Once that had been settled, we went on to discuss the specific duties the masters would expect us to perform."

"Whoa, whoa, whoa, whoa, *whoa*..." Johnny, whose ambulatory skills had seemingly returned from nowhere, interrupted with a vengeance. His legs successfully supporting him again, Johnny was able to extricate himself from his seated, slouched position against the tree, and so he stood, liberated from its support, his hands held high in protest. "Hang on just a minute. You said a little while ago that *Carlo* was working both of you, or one of you at a time, or..."

"Right, because you hadn't *heard* this part yet," Danny was quick to point out.

Johnny sighed his frustration at still not being able to express himself correctly. "Okay, then... I'll shut up. So, uh... what happened on his birthday?"

"Ah. Carlo's birthday just happened to be on a weekend that year, and, as planned, we were all at the club, dressed in new gear, strictly *de rigueur*, to celebrate the occasion. Carlo had brought the day's unsold desserts from the restaurant, along with more fudge sauce and whipped cream than should be legal to transport. Anyway, he and Arturo stowed the whipped cream in the club's refrigerator until the end of the show, and set the fudge sauce in a slow double boiler—which of course, he'd *also* dragged to the club—to make sure it would be ready, but not scorched, when called for.

"The entertainment for the evening was a suspension routine, and once Carlo had hoisted us high enough off the floor, out came the 'magic wand,' just to heat things up a little. Sasha and I then received a hearty round of *his* birthday spankings with the brand-new paddle that one of his cohorts from the club had given him as a gift. The paddle was not made of wood, however, but of leather, *two* pieces of leather in fact—an interesting design feature that greatly amplifies the sound effect of each blow when the second paddle snaps down upon the first. Very dramatic, you see... At any rate, I believe it's safe to say—and I'm sure that Sasha will corroborate this sentiment—that thirty-five whacks in a row with that baby is more than most people would be able to handle, especially with Carlo wielding the weapon." At that point, Johnny instinctually reached for his butt, thought he felt a slight burning sensation there, Danny's description, and Sasha's silent nod of agreement reminding him of a different time.

"Well, we somehow managed to last until the final blows, and just when we were beginning to think that the torture was over, Carlo lugs over this… oversized sawhorse contraption with a leather-encased foam pad wrapping the cross beam, which he places between the suspension bars that were holding us in mid-air. Carlo lowered Sasha just enough so that his poor stinging ass could rest on the pad, then repositioned me in such a way that I found myself sitting on Sasha's lap, facing him. Carlo bound our legs to the respective sides of the sawhorse with leather straps, then lowered the bars enough so that we lay suspended flat as a table to either side of the sawhorse, both our legs and arms bound, rendered completely incapable of extricating ourselves from the position.

"So suspended, *el Chef* began decorating us with desserts, whipped cream, and hot fudge sauce. As soon as he had 'set the table' he invited all his friends in the room to help him 'lick his plate clean,' as it were. Of course, the second we thought we were clean, more fudge sauce would magically appear in a crucial area, or extra whipped cream dolloped elsewhere. At one point Arturo emerged from the kitchen to rejoin in the fun, and brought with him a jar full of cherries, some sliced oranges, mangoes, and several bowls of pears stewed in brandy that he'd been saving especially for the occasion. What happened next was the most unbridled scene I'd ever witnessed until earlier tonight. But, of course, few things in the world are more intoxicating than Carlo's mother's cocoa mixture.

"Later that evening, once the scene at the club had begun to unravel, we headed through the kitchen, up the stairs that led to the street level, through the supply doors in the sidewalk, and out onto the street. Luckily, Arturo had left this convenient escape hatch open because he was expecting a delivery or whatever. Anyway, on the way out, he barred the door to the kitchen, shut down the grill and turned out the lights. We escaped into the street in fits of laughter, knowing we had just left the owners, who were still at the party, with a horrendous mess to clean up!

"We headed for the closest bar, half-naked and covered with remnants of whipped cream and chocolate sauce, looking like we had just been spit out of the depths of culinary Hell, but not caring one iota. Getting comfortable at the bar, we sat down and slowly imbibed our drinks, all four of us laughing intermittently during the entire time about being on both sides of the 'ultimate dessert experience.'

"Once we got home, off came every last shred of leather any of us still had on, and we headed straight for the shower, *en masse*. The fun thing about Arturo's apartment was that the shower was more like one in a locker room that we could all fit into. Oh, it was lovely; we washed ourselves of the sticky residue and watched the brown water swirl down the drain…Well, in the midst of all this good, clean fun, I dropped the soap."

"You did that on purpose!" barked Sasha, who was ready for a good argument.

Johnny, eager for the story to continue and sensing that this digression could easily get out of hand if allowed to progress any further, cut in immediately. "Okay! All right, already! Just let him finish!" beseeched the patient with newfound flexibility of his facial muscles.

Successfully put in his place, Sasha offered a contrite, "Sorry…"

"*Thank you*, Johnny," Danny gloated, shooting a quick side-glance to his humbled friend before continuing. "So *anyway…* I dropped the soap, whereupon Carlo mounted the back of my neck, lowered his torso over my back, which completely prevented me from standing up, and began smacking my ass! Sure enough, Arturo joined in the revelry and, the two masters instructing him to follow suit, so did Sasha.

"After everyone had taken their turn spanking me, Carlo, still lying over my back, grabbed my ass cheeks and spread them wide. Arturo found the soap and after lubricating me with it, entered me from behind. Sasha somehow managed to wriggle his way between everybody's legs, got beneath me, and began sucking my cock—his talented lips and tongue making it exceedingly difficult to hold myself back. God knows I was loving the experience, perhaps even more than being tied to the table, and I was praying that the hot water wouldn't run out. After one hell of an extended fucking, Arturo finally released the fruit of his labor, and fell with a violent groan against the wall in the heat of his passion.

"Carlo finally let me up and, bar of soap in hand, approached his roommate. The big man then lifted one of Arturo's slightly smaller legs with one of his massive arms and, pressing him against the wall with his magnificent chest, began soaping his asshole with his hand. Sasha and I simply watched as the drenched behemoths, risking slipping on the wet tiles, fucked like wild beasts. Further tantalized by the vision, Sasha began jerking off like a madman, as Arturo urged Carlo to fuck him harder and faster. *El Chef*, happy to comply, took forever to finish, as is his fashion, and right around the time the hot water started to run out, began roaring like a lion. After pounding Arturo two or three more times, he arched his back at a dangerous angle and quickly withdrawing from the smaller giant, Carlo *and* Sasha (who'd lurched suddenly forward) spattered Arturo's chest and belly with blast after blast of cum. Thoroughly cleansed and purged, we turned off the shower and wrapped ourselves in the luxuriant bath towels that only men of that size would make sure were always available in their bathroom.

"After our shower, we all repaired to the living room, where we sat down to coffee and pastries, watching out the window as dawn broke over the city. I had seen that event hundreds of times, and always cursed the sun's rising when I'd been up all night, but… at that moment, I felt honored to witness the cycle of another day beginning with the people I love surrounding me. It was slowly dawning that I was beginning to derive a great deal of... not only pleasure, but *satisfaction* from serving Carlo and Arturo, that I was learning all sorts of new things about myself: about the amazing potential for expanding my physical and emotional limitations, about how to experience the sense of empowerment that being one who is consistently directed can instill, about the rewards of selflessness." All at once, Danny turned to Sasha and asked: "Do you mind if I speak for both of us?" By way of answering, Sasha simply nodded his assent, after which Danny resumed his monologue:

"The four of us quickly learned respect for one another. We learned how to satisfy and support each other. In serving Carlo and Arturo, Sasha and I have learned to serve ourselves, and thus our passions have been allowed to flourish. Very subtly, our services have evolved from strictly following orders, to knowing most assuredly that we are pleasing people who deserve to be pleased—the people that we most care about. We have come to realize that the objective of all the training, the discipline, the rigor, was to ensure that in knowing how to properly take care of the people we were involved with, we, in turn, would be taken care of by them. Of course you can you see the difference, Johnny, but many people cannot understand the dichotomy. Anyone can play-act following orders for a single night's kinky passion, wallowing in strictly physical sensations, and that's all fine and good. What the four of us have come to share, however, has set the stage for a longer lasting relationship.

"Carlo's internship at the restaurant lasted for the better part of a year, and soon thereafter, the owners asked if he would stay on permanently. That pleased everyone concerned and so it was that our tenure in each of our respective positions was fully secured, until two years later, when Arturo was called away on an emergency."

"What happened?" interrupted the increasingly less intoxicated Johnny.

"Sadly, a family crisis necessitated his return to Argentina. By that time, none of us had any reason to suspect that we wouldn't continue together as a unit indefinitely, that anything would split us apart. While Arturo was making arrangements to leave, we were all having a very difficult time of things, as might be expected. For who knew when we'd be reunited, if ever.

"By the end of his crisis, Arturo had lost his mother and became the sole scion of his family's estate. He adopted his nephew who had been abandoned by his profligate brother more than a decade before, and eventually started his own restaurant in his native town, which had grown substantially in size. Arturo has become very successful, and continues to live in the family home in which he was born.

"Last August the three of us decided to make a group trip, and spent four weeks in the region of Argentina that both he and Carlo are from. We traveled around the province and spent several days at Carlo's family ranch. The difference between the two family homes was amazing! Whereas much of Arturo's land has been parceled for development, Carlo's ranch is far more extensive and still retains space for the horses and vineyards, which stretch into infinity. Herds of cattle and sheep have seemingly unlimited pastureland on which to graze. His *rancho* is indescribably beautiful. Naturally, Carlo's first stop upon arriving home was the stables, where he looked in on the workers and confirmed which animals were still in service. That was the first time we met Vicente…" Danny added pointedly.

Johnny was fairly certain where this new tangent was headed. Any second now, Danny would launch into details about *lazos* and whips and branding irons, followed by a segue into all kinds of hell breaking loose in the living room, or kitchen, or any one of the nine bedroom suites in Carlo's family's house. Attempting to redirect the story back on track, even though it was still somewhat difficult to focus his own thoughts, Johnny innocently inquired: "Wasn't the three of them being in the same place at the same time sort of a conflict of interest? I mean… three masters and two servants, one of whom was a kitchen manager—sounds like too many cooks in the kitchen to me!"

Looking at one another, the toothsome Spaniards chortled at Johnny's almost assuredly unintentional joke. "No, not at all! Arturo even accompanied us the day we went to the *Rancho Negados Piedad*. We were treated with the greatest affection and care. As a matter of fact, all the ranch hands and family members that were in the vicinity that day magically arrived at the ranch, as the news of Carlo's arrival had traveled swiftly throughout the region. The rancho was stuffed to the gills with visitors, all of whom I might add, ate very well. Yes, as you might imagine, there was a great deal of revelry that evening. That was also the occasion when I was introduced to Carlo's mother's cocoa mixture. Of course, Carlo and Vicente had grown up drinking the stuff, so were capable of keeping themselves in check while everyone else completely lost their senses. Humph, if you think there was an amazing scene when we handed it out here— my god! Half the town was there, many of whom are related to Carlo, crammed inside the rancho, and I can't even begin to describe the type of bacchanal that unfolded. It took the staff the better part of a week to put everything back into some semblance of order. I kid you not; floor tiles, *roof* tiles, furniture, window casings, walls—all had to be repaired or replaced. Naturally, we all pitched in. Between restoring the place and eating *very* well, we spent our free time out on the horses, exploring the forested mountains near the property. In fact, our last four days on the rancho were spent touring the family property on horseback, Carlo and Vicente leading us over trails that only regional natives could have possibly known about. What a fabulous time we had!

"At the end of our stay, we had to make decisions. Obviously, Arturo wouldn't be returning to Barcelona with us, and although we had a wonderful experience, we knew in our hearts that a provincial life was definitely not in our plans for the future. The three of us returned to Barcelona, Vicente returned to Chicago for a time, and Arturo stayed in Córdoba. His restaurant is now enormously successful, and he and Vicente, who is in Argentina far more frequently than Carlo, have become very close. Shortly after returning to Barcelona, Carlo received an excellent opportunity in New York City, and so found himself packing the entire apartment and heading back to America. We, of course, followed him. In the process of negotiating for his new post, Carlo insisted that Sasha be hired at the same restaurant as his personal sous chef and, although it took some time to transfer my qualifications in order to acquire a work permit in this country, I eventually secured a well-paying position as a paramedic for the city. Having pooled our resources, we bought a house in the Bronx, where we enjoy throwing lavish dinner parties, after which we encourage our guests to retire with us to our extensively furnished playroom in the basement."

By the conclusion of Danny's story, Johnny was exhibiting major signs of restored mental and physical acuity after his hours-long ride on his sedative of choice. His posture was much improved, his movements more deliberate, and his speech pattern tremendously less garbled when he asked the following question: "So, if Carlo is so satisfied with his life with the two of you, why does he work so hard pulling together these astoundingly enormous gatherings, which I'm sure take months of preparations and contingency planning?"

"Ah, but don't you see? That's icing on the cake!" cut in Sasha. "And you're right; he doesn't *have* to do this. But, Carlo likes his vacation time, and to him these tribal celebrations are just that. When away from home Carlo loves to be surrounded by people he can relate to, or who share many of his ideas. Trust me; it's much easier than flying to some untried hotel situation where it's not out of the question that he could end up having a major altercation over some off-hand remark or insinuating glance from someone—implying, I don't know what—about three men traveling and sleeping together, for as you might have noticed, Carlo is an extremely volatile personality. He figures if he's taking vacation time, and prefers to be surrounded by like-minded people, why not make some money in the process? So, to answer your question: yes, it does take months to organize these extravaganzas, but it keeps the big man happy."

The three new comrades, having resolved all the questions that were meant to be resolved, spent the rest of the night talking about their favorite predilections as they served the midnight snack, wondering aloud what the big man had in store for them once they all got back home.

Dessert

Breakfast, by comparison with the plethora of edibles they had been party to during the previous evening, was an austere experience. Given the time Carlo had spent "rectifying" the situation with the heckler and Johnny's own slow recovery from his chemical roller coaster ride the night before, as well as the very real terror that Sasha and Danny had experienced with apples in their mouths, the kitchen staff was in no shape to perform miracles the following morning. Nobody seemed to complain, however, and they were perfectly fine with downing cereal, served with milk, fresh fruit, toast, and coffee made with the cleanest-tasting water, which *el Chef* himself had drawn from the mountain stream just outside of camp. People were eager to get home, not because they hadn't had the best time ever, but in order to begin anticipating Carlo's next performance, the next over-the-top celebration of manhood, and the kitchen staff, busy as they were with packing up, seemed to corroborate the sentiment.

As always, Carlo was generous with the oversized bear hugs he gave to his enthusiastic supporters, equally so with the barbed threats and invective hurled at those who'd misbehaved during the event. To Johnny, it was plain to see that a great majority of the attendees were men who lived for the opportunity to pay the exorbitant price of admission to Carlo's world in order that they might escape the banality of their everyday routines and live, for a few short days, within the illusory fantasy that this hulking, beautiful heathen had—yes— *lovingly* created for them.

While riding in comfortable silence back to the Bronx surrounded by his new family, Johnny could not help but ponder his new living arrangement, deciding ultimately that it was something far bigger than anything he'd ever chosen or been involved with before—and he was not alone in that sentiment. For truth be known: to Sasha and Danny, to the big man himself and all parties concerned, their commitment had come to represent something bigger than life itself.

(AMPLIFIED BY) ANTICIPATION
Jamie Joy Gatto

Michael has left me a package. One of the clerks at my office brought it to me: a plain, manila envelope of normal size and dimension, perfectly average—except for the smudge. A tiny bloodstain, so small, virtually unnoticeable, marked by his garnet-brown fingerprint in the lower left hand corner. I know the smudge belongs to the man whom I need, that it was created by a part of his lifeblood. A single drop of blood, a tiny smear of semen, just one man's thumb print. The return address is always different; the return sender, hand printed or typed, is never in his name. I only know it's from him by the smudge.

I've been awaiting this package for weeks, and yes, I have slacked off a bit in my anticipation. Some days it drives me through the maddening boredom of my job. Every letter that appears on my desk is a challenge, a new proposition. Sometimes I wait. I look at the mail after lunch, or if I can stand it, will save the mail, drag it out sweetly, painfully until closing. Usually by noon, if I've waited that long to check all my letters, I'm in the john, cock in hand, wanking to the sound and smell in my mind of tearing, opening up a manila envelope, shuffling through paper—finding instructions? Photos, maybe? Commands, possibly?—until I can no longer stand the anticipation. In my head I rarely get to the contents inside the package. I come thinking about getting Michael's mail.

Other days, I barely think of him, but then it hits me: I'm alone and Michael is out there, out there in the world, the wide, wide world. I am here in my office, tie around my neck like a noose on a hot summer's day, opening regular letters from old clients, taking calls, scheduling meetings, phone on chin, hand in Rolodex. I have no way to reach him. He always finds me, calls me, beckons me to him. This is our agreement.

There are days when anticipating the arrival of his package is my only focus, never knowing *if* it will arrive. I don't even know his last name. I am never sure what will be inside. Today I tremble as I hold it gingerly between two strong hands bearing white, hairy knuckles, as I try not to open it right away, try not to dash off into the john, try not to fumble in my drawer, looking for a letter opener. Last time I tore his letter. I'll never do it again. Last time he told me if I ever tore his letter again, that would be the last one.

The last letter. The last smudge. No more Michael. I am certain, by the panic that hits me hard in the chest and falls into my belly like a duck full of buckshot hitting swamp water, I am absolutely certain that I would lay down and die if this were to be the last time.

I check the clock. It's three forty-two. I feel flushed, am aware I'm visibly shaking. The phone rings and I nearly jump out of my chair. The office is busy and my paranoia is at an all-time high. More clerks rush past me with more letters. For the first time in ages, I no longer care, no longer lust for those bundles of promise. I feel weak; I might faint; instead, I answer the phone. Milhaus places a huge order for which I'm certain I'll get a bonus. Instead of celebrating, I panic. Michael's letter has no return address. This is new. This is different. What could it mean? I sharpen every pencil on my desk in the electric sharpener until the last one is as keen as a lead needle. I wait until four o'clock.

In the john, a fluorescent light sputters a melancholy wash of vague orange and hums a cyclic song of repair. "Replace me," it says, intermittently flashing a sigh. Michael's letter is thick, I think, and I want to make sure I keep it all intact—no tears, no rips, not even a smudge. I sit on the john, trousers round my ankles, and hope for a sign that we can meet.

The envelope is filled with page after page of blank, printer-quality paper. I count each page one by one, searching for clues. I almost think I am counting out loud, but no, it is just the echoes in my head. The seventeenth page has a note. "Stay," it says. That is all. I go through every last page. All blank. I carefully place the papers, exactly as they were originally found, back into the envelope. I do as Michael says, of course; I stay.

I wait. And wait. I wait in the john in office suite 332 on the twelfth floor of the Starnes building for Michael the clerk to show up in the john. My cock is hard; my mouth is watering. I'll never know when it is he'll call on me again, but I'll always, always wait.

THE CONTRIBUTORS

Stephen Albrow: *Driving Home*

Stephen Albrow is a freelance writer who lives in England. He has contributed to a number of adult publications, including *Forum, Torso, Coming Out* and *Cherry Boys*. "Driving Home" is Mr. Albrow's follow-up to his STARbooks debut in *Saints and Sinners*. His first novella, a transvestite romance entitled *Adam or Eve* has been published by *Mags Inc.* Stephen Albrow's work may also be found in the upcoming anthology, *Love Under Foot* (Hayworth Press).

Barry Alexander: *Indulge Yourself*

Romance! Humor! Big Dicks!
!!*1-800-BARRY*!!

*I WRITE THE PORN THAT MAKES
THE WHOLE WORLD CUM...*
INDULGE YOUR FANTASIES!

Barry Alexander's stories have appeared in **SCADS OF GAY MAGS!!** In anthologies like ***Best Gay Erotica '03 *** Friction 1, 2, 3, 5 *** Best of Friction *** Casting Couch Confessions *** Divine Meat*** and... **NUMEROUS STARBOOKS' ANTHOLOGIES!!!** u can email Barry at barryalskander@aol.com

Ken Anderson: *Snowbound*

Professor Emeritus of English, Ken Anderson's fiction and poetry have appeared in over a hundred journals and anthologies, such as *Bay Windows, The Gay Review*, and *The James White Review. Permanent Gardens*, his first book of poems, was published by Seabolt Press. His second book, *The Intense Lover: A Suite of Poems*, is available from STARbooks Press, and his play, *Mattie Cushman: A Psychodrama* has been produced twice and aired on cable. His novel, *Someone Bought the House on the Island: A Dream Journal* was a finalist in the Independent Publisher Book Awards. His most recent book, a best-selling collection of ten short stories entitled *Hasty Hearts*, was published by STARbooks Press.

Antler: *Learning the Facts of Life*

Allen Ginsberg wrote of Antler in 1976: "More fineness than I thought probable to see again in my lifetime from younger solitary unknown self-inspirer US poet... one of Whitman's 'poets and orators to come'." A 1985 Whitman Award winner, Antler recently received the Major Achievement Award from the Council of Wisconsin Writers. Despite the boldness of his work, Antler was chosen to be Milwaukee's poet laureate during 2002-03. When not wildernessing or traveling to teach and perform poetry, he lives near the Milwaukee River in Milwaukee, Wisconsin.

Blaise Bulot: *The Power*

Blaise Bulot's voluminous and diverse writings include articles on the history and philosophy of science and architecture, as well as scientific papers, contributions to textbooks, novels, short stories, poetry, and book reviews of non-fiction. He has published two gay novels set in New Orleans: *Dark Waters* (1993) and *Starr Lyte* (1996). His homoerotic short stories have appeared in the STARbooks' anthologies *Heatwave* and *Huge 2*, and in *Bar Stories* from Alyson Publications.

Leo Cardini: *Mineshaft Men*

Leo Cardini is the author of *Mineshaft Nights*, inspired by his experiences as doorman at the legendary Village sexclub. His short stories have appeared in a variety of publications, including *Freshman, Advocate Men, FirstHand* and numerous STARbooks editions. Further information about Mr. Cardini can be found on the walls of better men's rooms everywhere.

Dale Chase: *The Great Man*

Dale Chase has published over sixty stories in *Men, Freshmen, In Touch* and *Indulge* magazines. His work has also been featured in numerous anthologies from Alyson Books—most of their *Friction* series, including *Best of Friction, Twink, Bearerotica,* and the upcoming *Full Body Contact*. One of his early stories has been acquired by an independent gay filmmaker and should reach the big screen in the near future. Prior to turning to erotica, his fiction had been published in motorcycle magazines, including *Cycle World, Cycle,* and *Motorcyclist.*

M. Christian: *Mahia's Truth*

M. Christian's stories have appeared in *Best American Erotica, Best Gay Erotica, Best Lesbian Erotica, Best Transgendered Erotica, Best Fetish Erotica, Best Bondage Erotica, Friction,* and over 150 other anthologies, magazines and websites. He's the editor of over 18 anthologies, including *The Mammoth Book of Tales of the Road* and *The Mammoth Book of Future Cops* (with Maxim Jakubowski) the *Best S/M Erotica* series, *Love Under Foot* (with Greg Wharton), *The Burning Pen, Guilty Pleasures,* and many others. He's the author of three available collections, the Lambda-nominated *Dirty Words* (gay erotica), *Speaking Parts* (lesbian erotica), *The Bachelor Machine* (science fiction erotica), and the upcoming new collection, *Filthy,* from STARbooks Press. For more information, check out www.mchristian.com.

Don Luis de la Cosa: *Bigger Than Life*

Don Luis is a long-time leather lifestyle person of Latino heritage. Part of his family hails from Argentina and related themes frequently find their way into his work. His current projects include advanced graduate studies and writing as much erotica as his hectic schedule will allow. When not sitting in front of the computer screen, Señor de la Cosa enjoys tearing around scenic roads on his motorcycle.

Jamie Joy Gatto: *Amplified by Anticipation*

Jamie Joy Gatto is a New Orleans sex activist, author/editor whose work has been included in dozens of projects such as *Best Bisexual Erotica 1 & 2, Best SM Erotica, Of The Flesh, Guilty Pleasures* and more. She is the founder and editor-in-chief of www.MindCaviar.com and its sister sites, www.OpheliasMuse.com and A Bi-Friendly Place. She has authored three collections: *Unveiling Venus,* a poetry chapbook, *Suddenly Sexy* an eBook available at www.renebooks.com and *Sex Noir* (Circlet 2002). Look for Jamie Joy Gatto's forthcoming *Villains and Vixens,* edited with M.Christian.

Henry Iblis: *Sergio Swimming*

Henry Iblis lives in Mexico City where he works in a bank and lurks around the Zócolo taking candid photographs of strangers in an effort to compile an exhaustive catalogue of human expressions. You can write him at henry_iblis@hotmail.com.

Rick Jackson: *Working Things Out*

A popular author of gay erotica, often with a military flavor, Rick Jackson is the *nom de guerre* of a frequent contributor to STARbooks Press. His book *Shipmates* was published by Prowler Press in London. Because he spends most of his time sailing about with the Navy in these Don't-Ask-Don't-Tell times, security demands that his true identity be kept classified—from all but the very juiciest sailors and Marines. Before beginning his very satisfying career afloat, Rick earned BAs in History and German, an MA in English, played hard in the Peace Corps, and plumbed the depths of hot, hard men across the globe. Although his frequent deployments keep him very, very busy with his fellow warriors, he sometimes is able to receive email at [RickJacksn@aol.com]. Mr. Jackson lives in Hawaii.

Ron Jackson: *Ishta Devataa*

Ron Jackson is co-editor with PJ Willis of the STARbooks Press anthology, *Kink: Stories of the Sexual Adventurer*. Using his surname Suresha, he authored the groundbreaking GLBTQ studies book, *Bears on Bears: Interviews & Discussions* (2002) and edited the anthologies *Bearotica: Hot, Hairy, Heavy Fiction* (2002), and *Bearotica vol. 2* (forthcoming 2004), His own erotica has appeared in the magazines *American Bear, 100% Beef,* and *Holy Titclamps* and the anthologies *Quickies 2, Bar Stories, Tales from the Bear Cult,* and *Sex Buddies.* He resides in Providence, RI; his online presence lives at www.suresha.com.

S. M. Jeffrey: *Athletic Performance*

Mid-Westerner, S.M. Jeffrey is a former Air Force officer who no longer has to write generals' speeches or publish military history. His erotic fiction has appeared on several websites, including *www.ShackleAlley.com* and *www.assgm.com*. Mr. Jeffrey prefers the S&M genre, as the controversial "Athletic Performance" clearly demonstrates that men can be amplified—painfully!

Jim McDonough: *The Other Half of Me*

Over the past several years, McDonough's erotic fiction has been published in over a dozen magazines such as *In Touch, Men,* and *Freshmen,* as well as several anthologies published in the U.S., Canada and the Netherlands. Mr. McDonough made his STARbooks Press debut in *Saints and Sinners.* Look for his work in the forthcoming *Friction 7* (Alyson Publications) in 2004.

Jesse Monteagudo: *One Out of Ten is Magic*

Jesse Monteagudo is a freelance writer and gay activist who lives in South Florida with his life-partner. His bi-weekly columns, "Jesse's Journal" and "The Book Nook", appear in gay publications from Miami to San Diego and in the online magazine *Gay Today.* His short fiction has been published in over twenty anthologies, many published by STARbooks Press. Jesse Monteagudo is currently in the process of collecting his stories and essays for publication in book form.

Thom Nickels: *Elijah For Real*

Thom Nickels is a Philadelphia-based author/journalist/poet with five published books to his credit. STARbooks Press has featured Nickels in many of its erotic anthologies. His *Two Novellas: Walking Water & After All This* was nominated for a Lambda Literary Award and a Hugo Award. *The Boy on the Bicycle* was a cult best seller. Mr. Nickels writes for the *Lambda Book Report* and is a weekly columnist for Pridevision TV in Toronto. His latest book, *Tropic of Libra*, was recently published by STARbooks Press.

Christopher Pierce: *White-hot Smoky Night*

The erotic fiction of Christopher Pierce has been published in *Advocate Classifieds, Bound & Gagged, Care and Training of the Male Slave, Cuir, Daddy, Eagle, Firsthand, Honcho, Inches, In Touch, Indulge, International Leatherman, Mandate, Manifest Reader, Manscape, Mantalk, Powerplay, Super Mr., Torso, Urge* and in the Alyson Books Anthology *Friction 6.* You may write to him at *chris@christopherpierceerotica.com* and visit his website at www.ChristopherPierceErotica.com.

Ian Phillips: *Man Overboard!*

Ian Philips is one amplified fey bear of a man. His first collection of erotic fiction, *See Dick Deconstruct: Literotica for the Satirically Bent* (AttaGirl Press), won the first-ever Lambda Literary Award in the category of Erotica. His second collection, *Satyriasis: Literotica²* (Suspect Thoughts Press) should curl the pubic hair of the most straight-laced reader. He resides in modest infamy in San Francisco—where else?—with author Greg Wharton. To read his fiction, surf on over to www.ianphilips.com.

Jeff Poniewaz: *I'm Going To Let My Balls Hang Out*

Jeff Poniewaz teaches "Literature of Ecological Vision" and "Whitman & Ginsberg: Liberating American Bards" via UW-Milwaukee. His book of eco-poems, *Dolphin Leaping in the Milky Way*, was praised for its "impassioned prescient ecological Whitmanesque/Thoreauvian verve and wit" by Ginsberg. Jeff has been Antler's camerado since they met in a poetry class at UW-Milwaukee in 1966 and discovered Whitman was each other's favorite poet. Together, they have taught and performed poetry at the Kerouac Poetics School in Boulder, Colorado. Jeff's last name is pronounced Poe-nYEAH-vAHsh and is Polish for "because."

Peter Rice: *Another Way*

Peter Rice was born in Birmingham, England. After National Service in the Navy, he began his college career, graduating from the University of Liverpool and Trinity College of Music, London, after which he became a music teacher at various British Schools. His chief joy in life has always been music, his appreciation of male beauty, running a close second! Since his retirement, Rice has published his stories in a British weekly magazine, but his chief delight has been the extensive publication of his erotic short stories at STARbooks Press. Peter Rice would like to take this opportunity to express both his gratitude to late STARbooks editor and founder, John Patrick for having taken the work of a novice storyteller seriously and his regret that he and his mentor never had the opportunity to meet.

Simon Sheppard: *Geezers*

Simon Sheppard is the author of *Hotter than Hell and Other Stories,* co-editor with M. Christian of *Rough Stuff* and the forthcoming *Roughed Up: More Tales of Gay Men, Sex and Power.* He's also finishing up a nonfiction book,

Kinkorama. His work has appeared in over seventy anthologies, including *Best American Gay Erotica 2002* and *Best Gay Erotica 2002.* You can visit him at *www.simonsheppard.com.*

Mel Smith: *The Spell of Georval*

Mel Smith's stories have appeared in magazines such as *In Touch* and *Indulge,* online at *Velvet Mafia* and *Suspect Thoughts* and numerous anthologies including *Best Gay Erotica, Best American Erotica, Latin Boys, Sacred Exchange,* and *Buttmen 3.* She is a single mom with one extraordinary daughter. Mel is currently working on a collection of her short stories and her first novel.

Horehound Stillpoint: *The Genitals of God*

For more of Horehound Stillpoint's funky-ass poetry and seedy short stories, check out anthologies such as *Poetry Nation, beyond definition, Sex Spoken Here, Poetry Slam, Out in the Castro, Tough Guys, Roughed Up, Quickies, Of the Flesh,* and *Pills, Thrills, Chills, and Heartache.* His one-act plays were produced in the San Francisco Fringe Festivals of 2000 and 2001 and at the Jon Sims Center. He represented San Francisco at the National Poetry Slam in 1995 and 1996. A little Kapow! book of his poetry, with illustrations by KRK Ryden, is called *Reincarnation Woes.*

Jerome Szymczak: *The Same Words*

Jerome Szymczak is a freelance writer and photographer whose travel and academic non-fiction has appeared in *National Geographic Traveler,* New York's *Metrosource Magazine,* and St. James' Press' *Gay and Lesbian Biography.* He is based in Alameda, CA, but likes to think of the world as his 'home' too, including a tiny Greek island he will never name. He subscribes to the Jan Morris philosophy of travel: "If you lived in a mansion with sixteen rooms, why would you spend all your time in only two of them?" His fiction is derived from true experiences, overheard conversations, and imaginings that can't always be fit into neat, narrative packages... fiction as "real life—and vice-versa," to quote the talented Mr. Szymczak himself.

Meander Weeks: *The Game*

Meander Weeks was born in a small town in Western Massachusetts. He attended the University of Massachusetts at Amherst, majoring in both anthropology and the theatrical arts. He now resides in Copperas Cove, Texas. "The Game" is Mr. Weeks' follow-up to his STARbooks Press debut in *Saints and Sinners*.

Greg Wharton: *Johnny Was*

Greg Wharton is the author of the collection *Johnny Was and Other Tall Tales*. He is the publisher of Suspect Thoughts Press, and an editor for two web magazines, *SuspectThoughts.com* and *VelvetMafia.com*. He is also the editor of numerous smutty anthologies including *The Best of the Best Meat Erotica*, *The Big Book of Erotic Ghost Stories*, *Law of Desire* (with Ian Philips), *The Love That Dare Not Speak Its Name*, *Love Under Foot* (with M. Christian), and *Of the Flesh*. He lives in San Francisco with his honey, Ian, a cat named Chloe, and a lot of books.

Mark Wildyr: *Mythas*

Born an Okie, prolific author Mark Wilder presently lives in New Mexico, the setting of much of his fiction, which explores sexual development and multicultural intercourse. Besides being a regular contributor to STARbooks Press (*Wild and Willing, Fantasies Made Flesh, Saints and Sinners, A View to a Thrill, Lovers Who Stay With You, Kink,* and the forthcoming *The Wildest Ones*), his work has been published by Companion Press (twelve stories), Alyson Publications' *Full Body Contact 2* and the upcoming *Bearotica 2*, and Arsenal Pulp Press, in its upcoming *Quickies 3*.

Huxley, sweaty in his banana patch, amplified by Florida's heat and humidity, August, 2002. ...Photo by Ori Dassberg

ABOUT THE EDITOR

Since his STARbooks' publishing debut in 2000, Michael Huxley has contributed to many STARbooks anthologies. He has compiled four anthologies of literotica thus far: *Fantasies Made Flesh*, *Saints and Sinners*, *Men, Amplified*, and the forthcoming *Wet Nightmares, Wet Dreams*. A poet, playwright, and former contributor to Denver Colorado's groundbreaking *Out Front*, his most recent work appears in *A View to a Thrill*, edited by Paul Willis, the poetry collections, *Van Gogh's Ear, vols 2 & 3* (French Connection Press, Paris/New York), and *Friction 7* (Alyson Publications). Having accepted the position of Editorial Director at STARbooks Press in April 2002, Huxley now finds himself amplified by author's concerns and deadlines on a full-time basis. Michael Huxley resides in Sarasota, Florida with his long-time spouse, Paul Marquis.

Feel free to contact The Editor at mikeh@starbookspress.com.